FROZEN TRUST

FROZEN TRUST

A WWII HISTORICAL SPY THRILLER

RAE RICHEN

Frozen Trust

Published in the United States of America by
Back Beat Publications, an imprint of Lloyd Court Press 3034 N.E. 32nd
Avenue, Portland, Oregon, 97212 www.lloydcourtpress.org

Cover design by Diana Kolsky
Book Design by Amit Dey

ISBN 978-1-943640-02-7
E-book ISBN: 978-1-943640-04-1

Publisher's Cataloging-In-Publication Data
(Prepared by The Donohue Group, Inc.)
Names: Richen, Rae, author.
Title: Frozen Trust : [a historical thriller] / Rae Richen.
Description: Portland, Oregon: Back Beat Publications, an imprint of Lloyd
                 Court Press, [2024] | Subtitle from copyright page.
Identifiers: ISBN 9781943640027 |
                 ISBN 9781943640041 (ebook)
Subjects: LCSH: Fathers--Death--Fiction. |
                 Intelligence officers--United States--Fiction. |
                 Murder--Investigation--United States--Fiction. |
                 Sabotage--United States--Fiction. |
                 World War, 1939-1945--United States--Fiction. |
                 Trust--Fiction. | LCGFT: Historical fiction. |
                 Romance fiction, American. | Thrillers (Fiction)
Classification: LCC PS3618.I34 F76 2024 (print) |
                 LCC PS3618.I34 (ebook) |
                 DDC 813/.6--dc23

DEDICATION

For Japanese Americans, and all others before and since World War II who have been judged solely by the shape of their eyes, their religion, their country of origin, or the color of their skin, and then jailed without trial or adequate representation.

CHAPTER ONE

JANUARY 1926

Eight-year-old Laura Atweiler held tight to her foster-brother's hand. As she trotted to keep up with Jimmy Schoenfeld's long legs, she glanced fearfully over her shoulder. She hoped Daddy's friend, Mr. Arndt, hadn't seen them leave.

She didn't like Mr. Arndt. His red hair flopped in his eyes so Laura could never tell what he thought.

But Daddy said, "Arndt can teach a three-legged elephant to climb."

Daddy was a general in the United States Army. He'd hired Mr. Arndt to work with the Army's new special force of mountain men here in Colorado. And he invited Arndt to live with them.

Yesterday, Laura found Mr. Arndt in Daddy's office when Daddy wasn't home. That wasn't right. Arndt had pretended he'd been looking for Daddy. She knew he had watched her all the rest of the day.

Today, when Jimmy offered to take her ice-skating, she felt good to get away from Arndt. As they walked toward Little Lake, Laura guessed that Jimmy guarded a heavy secret. Most times her sixteen-year-old foster-brother strode out easily, but today he trudged. He smiled once, when he helped put on her new Christmas skates, so he didn't feel angry with her. But he didn't talk. Closed his mouth tight. Laura tried holding her mouth like Jimmy's. It hurt.

At the edge of lake, he picked her up as they skirted the long sedge grasses. He set Laura's feet on the frozen ice, held her left hand and steadied her. When they moved forward, Jimmy glided, solid and watching, but silent. Laura glanced up to see if he might tell her his secret. Her skates slid from under her. He swung around to keep her upright.

"Whoa there, Laurie. You can't go lookin' up or down. Changin' your head, it changes your balance."

"Where do I get to look?"

He turned her to face the pine and poplar woods. Beyond the lake, hovered iron peaks of the Rocky Mountains. He knelt down to see the world the way she saw it.

"See Old Eagle's nest, way out in that dead spar?" he asked.

"I see it." Laura laughed, proud to spot it so fast.

"Good," he said. "Find things at the same height. You look at them while you turn."

Laura found them: a prominent rock; a jabbering jay; a spruce branch; the last leaf on a poplar tree. She opened her arms, the way Jimmy did. How easy it looked when he skated free, head high, back straight, his thick blond hair flying to catch up.

Laura moved forward, her eyes on the jay and the spruce. She flung her arms overhead to pivot. Her wooly leggings scrubbed against her long winter coat. She fell face down.

Stupid ice.

"Oh, Laurie, that was going to be beautiful," Jimmy said. He picked her up by the waist and set her on the ice. She wiped her tears and straightened hurt feelings while Jimmy talked. "This dumb heavy coat stopped you." he said.

"My feet are too tight," Laura sniffed.

"Let's sit on the log and fix those boots," he said without looking at her. "Then I'll teach you how to skate backwards."

"Jimmy!" she cried, "I can't skate backwards. I can't even skate forwards without you."

He bit his lip in that way he had, like when he grew scared her Daddy wouldn't keep him 'cause he'd done something bad. He had lived with them almost a whole year, and he still thought Daddy might kick him out.

Suddenly, Jimmy picked Laura up and skated to the log where they'd left their lunch bag. He set her down, tossed his head to get his hair away from his eyes, and began untying her boots. She watched him, certain he would tell his secret soon.

She put her mittened hand on his shoulder, studying the pattern in the sunshine color of his hair – hair as different from her tight black curls as hair could be.

"Jimmy, your hair's like yellow threads, like that stuff that grows around the corn." He kept his head down, working the laces. She talked on. "Your hair goes in circles all around your head, 'cept these parts." Her mitten flicked his twin cowlicks. "These funny parts don't have anywhere to go."

He looked up, annoyed. And then, she saw the little hard place in his throat go down, like he swallowed big.

"Laurie," he started, but his voice went high suddenly. She smiled to encourage him. Whatever his secret, she knew she could help him. He did that lip biting again. What bad thing could Jimmy have done to make him so scared?

"Daddy loves you, Jimmy. He won't ever…"

"Laurie, I'm going away."

The way he said it made her scared, too. She gazed at their lunch bag, playing with the leather ties. "That's all right," she said, pretending it was. "I can eat my sandwich while you skate."

"That's not what I mean, Laurie. I'm leaving with Werner Arndt when he goes back to Germany."

"Mr. Arndt?" She stiffened but didn't look up. She just kept gazing at the canvas bag, afraid – afraid of Mr. Arndt who watched her from behind his bushy red eyebrows like she might be a cricket he wanted to step on – afraid of Jimmy's excitement whenever Mr. Arndt patted him on the back and called him "*Mein knabe*. Best climbing student."

"No!" She glared at him. "No, you can't go off with Mr. Arndt. He doesn't love you."

"I've talked to the General . . .," he began. "

Dad," she said firmly. "Call him Dad."

"Laurie, he's not my Daddy. He's yours. And I'm sixteen. I have to go out and start being a man. I have to learn how to be a mountain guide like Werner Arndt."

His eyes were rimmed in red. She tried not to sniff.

She said, "Daddy says Mr. Arndt's Germany is a sad country since the Great War. You'll be sad, too, Jimmy."

"I will, Laurie. This has been the best year of my life. I'll miss you. I'll miss the General, too."

Laura stomped her skate. "He's not your General, like a soldier. Daddy loves you, just like he loves me."

She saw then that she might keep him. He gazed at her hopefully. But, in the next moment, she lost him. He shook his head slowly and brushed her tears off her cheek with his thumbs.

"Write to me in Germany, Laura," he said gently. "And write in German too. You're getting very good at your German."

She sagged against his shoulder. "Will you write to me?" She felt him swallow again, felt his fingers comb her crazy hair.

"Sure, little Curly Top," he said. "I'll tell you about the mountains I climb." He kissed her forehead once and bent to retie her skate laces.

"You have to teach me to skate backwards," she said.

He laughed softly. "Right now, Your Highness?"

She nodded. He smiled. Then he put his hands around her waist and lifted her from the log to stand on the frozen pond. "You'll have to concentrate. We've only got today."

Looking up, she bit her lip. She copied his gesture, but it helped her not to cry. "How long will you be gone?" she asked.

He shrugged. "Werner says there are lots of mountains over there."

"You can climb three, James Schoenfeld," she ordered. "Then you must come home."

He laughed, but she hugged him around the waist and whispered through her tears, "Jimmy, I love *you* more than mountains."

He wrapped his arm around her back and pulled her closer.

CHAPTER TWO

COLORADO, UNITED STATES, SIXTEEN YEARS LATER

THURSDAY, MARCH 5TH, 1942

A hiss sliced across silent snow. Laura jerked out of fitful sleep. She flattened into her sleeping bag and listened.

Voices? Did I dream the voices?

Her stomach tightened around a shaft of cold fear. She fought panic as her father had taught her, breathing slowly, deeply. Silently. In the night, wood scraped on rock. An angry mutter rumbled briefly. And then the hiss again – the same sound, grown in intensity.

There are voices, people on the trail below me. Is it Dad? Uncle Banks?

She rose, thinking to call out, but a third enraged hiss stopped her.

General Arthur Atweiler could be a stern man, but he never demonstrated wrath. Laura sensed evil in the dreamed voices. There'd been a tone of derision. That sinister memory held her silent. She lay as flat as she could and listened for more. Only a muffled swish gave away cross-country skiers.

There could be others, a straggler. Laura waited.

She'd shunned the common trail as she skied up Longs Peak. A premonition told her to use all the tricks her father taught her. The same premonition had brought her alone up the vast slopes of the Rockies. It made her sleep lightly. Her pocket pistol lay on top of her pack where her left hand could find it with little movement. She had not lit a fire but had built a small tent of kindling and logs. A gas-soaked rag, wrapped on a stick, perched ready to fire against animal intruders, but Laura didn't fear animals. Their violence they reserved for self-defense.

The unknown skiers retreated farther down the hill, leaving behind them a feather-deep silence broken by the sleepy muttering of a bird as it subsided into small complaint and soft rustling. No other sound invaded the night except pounding pulse in her ears.

Trying to explain away her terror, Laura lay in her lonely bivouac. She conjured reasons why three or four men would ski down Longs Peak at night. None of her reasons were convincing.

Fifteen minutes passed. No straggler or rear guard made his way down the trail. Laura decided to take the risk, resuming her own journey. Her night vision had been rated excellent on the firing range. Her hearing was acute, and she knew how to move with little sound. She might as well be moving.

Sleep became impossible.

Within minutes, she packed and donned her skis. Instinct had called Laura Atweiler from Camp Springs Army Base to Longs Peak in northern Colorado. She'd sensed trouble when her father failed to meet her two days ago, on Tuesday. He'd left no message. That meant there'd been a week with no contact.

Yesterday, she'd asked Vibes, the Communications Specialist, to radio the training camp. All Vibes heard had been static, a storm, he guessed, making radio transmission difficult. The radio black-out added fuel to Laura's concern.

Even though she'd earned the job as Colonel Johnson's secretary, Vibes couldn't tell her the location of the new Tenth Division Ski- Mountaineers' training camp. Her father and his officers were scouting the location, getting ready to move the whole division from the slopes of Mount Rainier in Washington State to safer and drier quarters in Colorado.

As secret as it ought to be, Laura believed she knew the probable location. She'd camped with her father often enough to share his preferences. She knew a hidden valley, a beautiful isolation with definite advantages as location for a new training camp. Within a mile, the Ski- Mountaineers would have access to all types of climbing routes and a great shelter in the bargain.

So, here she'd come in silence, hoping she'd guessed correctly and would find the base camp. Laura could be sure of only one thing; something was not right.

Ever since the death of her foster-brother, James Schoenfeld, she'd sensed tension and distrust among the men close to her father. Her father had become increasingly secretive and protective of her in the last few months. In spite of the fact that she was now twenty-five years old and a responsible member of the army support staff, her father had not shared his thoughts with her.

She believed he'd grown suspicious of some member of his staff.

Since the officers at Camp Springs Army Base seemed not to trust each other, she'd become wary of them. The atmosphere of subterfuge made her undertake this quest alone.

She feared – not because she climbed this mountain by herself, but because she might reveal her worry to the wrong person, afraid of being seen and followed.

Her skis slid softly across the fall line as she skirted the deep well around an old pine. A thicket of Aspen loomed in front of her. As she turned aside to avoid it, rustling branches alerted her. She sensed another presence. Laura froze.

Man? Animal? To her right, naked tree limbs bobbed almost imperceptibly. The cause of the movement lay hidden by night. No breeze moved those branches. Laura shifted her pole and reached for her pistol. Withdrawing it slowly, she listened for that shadow of sound.

Tensed for an attack, she skied around the grove and turned uphill.

Laura forced herself up ever steeper slopes toward the cul-de-sac valley.

False dawn sent gray lights over the plains below her. Laura stopped to study her back-trail.

Crepuscule.

The thought intruded unbidden. Her heart tightened as her mind used her father's word for this part of the day. *Crepuscule.* He'd once explained the word's fascination.

'This half-light, Laura, it's an obscuring veil of crêpe between a dark night of evil and the light of day.'

Laura shoveled her fears beneath a flurry of action. She trained her glasses on the woods and then on the snow nearer and nearer her place among the Aspens. She saw many tracks of animals, but nothing moved. Not even birds were disturbed by the furtive presence she felt, yet the memory of a stealthy follower kept her neck hairs up.

And then she heard a low, guttural moan. Laura whipped about, searching into the elongated morning shadows for the hiding place of her pursuer. In the early sunshine, she found more tracks. Weasel slithers crossed marmot scamperings, tracks as fresh as if the small animals had passed moments before. But as she studied the terrain, she saw nothing of the animal that followed her.

The tracks of last night's skiers were below and to her right. Their deep marks headed away from the secret valley, not from the summit trail. However, the tracks were not made by her father's men. The skis were wider and heavier than those of the General's special forces.

Who could they be? This alpine valley could be known only by a trusted few besides herself, her father, and two native sheepherders who used it briefly each mid-summer. She neared home, and all seemed quiet. But the low moan, and the skiers' trail made a lie of peace.

Over the swaying branches of bare Aspens, she recognized the top of the cliff which made the secret valley a cul-de-sac. From the cliff's south side, she saw the upper part of the frozen waterfall, a series of giant icicles – water trapped in mid-plunge. If she could see the cliff from here, it meant the deep cave behind the frozen falls lay ten minutes farther. Those minutes would be a stiff uphill climb around short, lower falls and onto the valley floor.

Hopeful, wary, she set off at a fast clip. A small white rabbit bounded across the trail before her.

Laura frowned. Spring at this elevation could be weeks away. She saw nothing to entice animals out of their dens, certainly not the tight, cold buds of next years' leaves. Without food, only some great disturbance would awaken these burrow animals. An avalanche, an earthquake . . .

Driven by this new thought, Laura plunged up the slope to the left of the lower creek. The risen sun hovered over her destination. She scrambled through the scrub piñons to the valley floor. Across an expanse of snow, she saw the cave, wide and dark. No fire lit its recesses.

And then she stepped around the last pine and saw more. Between Laura and the cave lay the snow-whitened bodies of seven men, sprawled as if resting from a long hike. The white surrounding each body was tinged with pink – blood seeping into the soft, cold crystals.

Laura sank to her knees. Her self-centered reaction shamed her. Her father would expect action. Rescue. With her ski poles, she pushed herself up and forced her legs to drag toward the carnage. She moved stiff, tense, fearful, toward the quiet forest. Expecting at any moment to be shot, she worked her way across the field. She stopped at each body.

Major Wells, no pulse, no heartbeat, no breathing – shot through the neck.

She ticked it off as if she were a battlefield nurse – as if Major Wells had never danced with her, never looked at her with warmth and hope.

Sergeant Hospice, no pulse, no heartbeat, no breathing – shot in the back, exit from the chest.

"God, help him," she whispered, staring at the dried blood on the sergeant's jacket, on the snow, on everything near the beloved old man. Sergeant Hospice, a strutting little rooster, tough, unsophisticated, quick to anger and quick to love. She had to act clinical – had to force herself to note the causes of death like a disinterested coroner so she might remain alert, might find some still living.

Lieutenant-Colonel Temple, no pulse, no . . . no ring finger, but a gaping wound where his hand rested over his heart.

Laura let out a whimper.

No breathing.

She could not believe what she saw. Here, in the center of her homeland, buffered from the hostile world, good men dead as if on a bomb-cratered field in France.

Why were they attacked? Where are their attackers?

She knew where the murderers were, or at least some of them. They had skied out during the night, right below her camp. She took the wrist of the next man. No pumping motion rose through his cold skin.

Lieutenant Ashton. No life. Lieutenant Bond. No.

She tried to move on, tried not to think about Jenny Bond and the little boys who would never see their daddy again.

Ashton and Bond. Ashton and Bond, her mind kept repeating. No!

Peter Lethe, recruited from Switzerland to train the men in survival techniques – shot through the leg, and in the back of the head.

Laura's mind refused more. She lifted her face to the clear sky, inhaled the pungent odor of pine and ice. A gentle breeze carried away her lone cry. A long, despairing echo returned.

Oh, Peter, you should be at home in your village with Elsbet. Why did we bring you here, to this?

Don't quit, Laura, she thought in her father's clipped tones. Die in action.

Her head bowed, Laura moved her leaden skis toward the last man in the snow field, her father's aide-de-camp, Gregory Banks.

Uncle Banks . . . Banks worshipped her Dad like an older brother. He'd protected her father from life's small cares, supported him in his enormous responsibilities. Laura sank down, desperately hoping to find breath or pulse.

"Please, Uncle Banks, please breathe."

Banks – no survivors, her military training finished the list, while her woman's heart cried soundlessly. Then she spoke.

"Where is their commanding officer?"

She had to say it that way. *Commanding officer.* It felt so much easier to pretend that's what she looked for. She raised her head from Bank's silent chest and stared at the open cave. Perhaps some trace of the men who did this lay in there. Or had all of them left last night?

They're watching, crouching behind rifles. When will they shoot? She shook her head, trying to think. Gazing blindly toward the men at her feet, she realized she had to move to the cave in spite of fear. Then, she had to find her father. Pushing her body upright, she held her pistol at the ready and started to move, only to realize that her ski tips were under Bank's legs.

"Sorry," she whispered to the dead man, and then, "Sorry, so sorry. I should have come yesterday. I could have hidden in the trees. I could have stopped them. I could have ..."

Laura used the impossible could-haves to give her strength as she backed her skis away from Bank's body. She recited "could haves" over and over like so many Hail Maries, in order to propel herself toward the frozen waterfall and its dark cave.

"Where is he?" Laura whispered, "He should be here with his men. How can a commander lose his whole officer group and not be here? What is he doing?"

The more she sounded like a Courts Martial, the easier it became to ski toward the cave. Laura feigned anger. She kept other thoughts at bay for the duration of her pretense. Skirting the frozen pond at the base of the cliff, she glanced up. In the form of long icicles, the falls were cold and impersonal. During summer, the water tumbled, splashing noisily into the pond and running out into the creek toward the second falls – a laughing friend, someone to play with, to tease. Now, the ice was ominous, silent, waiting to pierce.

A gray figure moved out of the woods – an enormous dog. Laura chilled, watching him watch her. He approached the pond, his gaze never wavering from her. The whisper of his fur as it touched the dead branches had been the sound she'd heard all day. Blood had dried on his flank. He limped on frozen paws. His golden eyes glittered with hatred and hunger.

Vandal, she thought. Gone mad. Laura knew Vandal, more wild animal than dog. The murder of Uncle Banks cut the wolf's one connection with humankind. Head tucked low, the wolf stepped to the edge of the pond. He stared at Laura, at the icy pond surface, then back to Laura. She took a risk, loosed her pack and slid it down her arms.

Watching him warily, she yanked on the thong that tied one pocket. She withdrew two long pieces of beef jerky and laid them on the snow. Then she reached out with her ski pole and jabbed a hole in the ice on her side of the pond. A second jab widened it.

She stepped back from the ice and moved up the slope toward the cave. The dog watched her retreat and then, never taking his gaze off her, he limped around to the hole to drink. Three licks. Raise the head. Check her position. Three more licks.

He repeated this vigilant method as he attacked the jerky. Chewing, watching, chewing.

He'll be all right once he's slaked his hunger, she promised herself as she cautiously side-stepped up the talus slope toward the cave, watching the wolf watch her – both of them distrustful, both ready to pounce at the first sign of aggression in the other. Where the slope to the cave became too icy, Laura bent and took off her skis. Of long habit, she clapped them together and set them into a snowbank.

The clap of her skis sent Vandal skittering back toward the woods, but he stopped at the edge and turned to watch her again, his head lowered, offering trust.

"Come back, boy," she crooned. "Come on."

The wolf lifted sore paws high out of the snow. His gaze steadied, his muscles grew taut, but he moved slowly toward the beef jerky. Laura did not want Vandal at her back. Still, she had to enter the cave. She glanced at him often while she kick-stepped her way up the last incline to the shelter. As she turned to enter the darkness, Vandal stiffened, one paw on the last of the jerky. He moaned, a long, low rumble in his chest – the sound she'd heard this morning at dawn. Laura glanced back at him. He made no threat, merely stared into the vast blackness behind her.

Inside the mouth of the cave, she halted, noting the fire pit where white ash swirled and settled. Debris of firewood, pans, rucksacks and leather boot thongs lay to the left of the fire.

She ducked inside. In the darkened recesses, her eyes adjusted slowly. Then she began to make out the shadows of the rocky ledges where she used to keep tins of food when she and The General camped here. She glanced around the floor, stopping her perusal at each dark shape, a towel, an empty blanket, a pack spilling shirts and socks.

In the corner nearest her lay a dark huddle of cloth. She bent, pulling back the thin blanket. The small shape moaned.

"Dad? Daddy!"

His body slumped over sideways. As he fell, she caught his head and shoulders in her arms. Leaning back slightly, she let the thin gray light from the cave opening fall on him. Horrible burn marks covered his hands. His eyes were open, but sightless, the lashes burned away.

"Laura?" He had barely enough energy to say her name.

"Yes, Dad. I'll take you out on my skis. We'll make a sled out of…"

"No. Liss …" He reached for her with blackened fingers. "Lissss…"

"I'm listening, Dad."

"All … aren't … killed." His head lolled to one side. He seemed for a moment to lose consciousness again.

Laura tried to understand. Perhaps he hoped some of his men had survived. He turned his head toward her once more.

"Laura?"

She hesitated, and then told him the truth. "They're all dead, Dad. I found them."

He made himself speak. "Our James . . . danger."

"Our James?" Even as she asked, Laura's throat closed over a sob. Her father's mind became confused. James, her childhood idol, had left when she was eight. Three years ago, in Berlin, after thirteen years of guiding alpine climbs, James had died in a stupid fall down six flights of stairs.

Her father lapsed into merciful unconscious, tendrils of his white hair falling against her wrist.

Then he gasped awake. "Gov'ment camp," he said. "Soon. With James. Trap."

"A trap? Which government camp? Camp Springs? Our camp?"

A pain, deep within, twisted his body in her arms. "Aah . . ." For long moments, he concentrated on conquering his torment. His cracked, bleeding lips touched her ear. "Hess." He cried, desperate to make her understand. "Rudolf Hess."

Her mind cast about for a connection, "Hitler's secretary?"

He whispered, "Hitler's spy . . . Canada . . . controls aren't in States."

Her father made no sense now. Hess had been captured in Scotland almost a year ago, and the British kept him in prison. She gazed at his creased and graying face – the burn marks near his eyes festered and oozed. No wonder his mind wandered.

Her father's hand reached for his face but fell to his chest. "Cigarettes," he whispered. "Sticks from fire. I tell them. Everything . . . I tell."

She forced herself to take deep breaths, to search for a saving action instead of being sick at the carnage. She held him with care, wanting to give him love, knowing that every touch also brought agony.

After a moment, he rallied. "I told about camp, trap. James Schoen . . . danger."

There was no mistaking what he said, but he'd become delirious. "James Schoenfeld is dead, Dad."

"Look in files. Bee." He gestured feebly, as if drawing a rectangular shape in the fetid air.

She reached for his idea. "I'll search in my files under Bee."

His lips seemed to say "Good". The effort cost him moments of agony. Laura watched her own tears fall on his reddened eyelids.

"I'll check the files, Dad. First, we have to get you back to Camp Springs."

"No, leave next Banks. Ski after James."

Insensibility released him from pain. Laura's heart stood still until she felt his faint breath on her cheek.

"Soldier it out, Laura." That's what he would have said. "Chin up and march forward on the alert."

She stiffened against her need to cry, thinking, I will ski out . . . After Hess, or whoever did this.

"I'll take care of it, Dad," she said gently.

A moment later, he whispered, "Use. . . Johnson."

"Colonel Johnson will help."

Her father's head moved. He seemed to change his mind, whispering, "Tell James first."

Laura decided to pretend she could tell James whatever he wanted. "I'll tell him, Dad. And I'll find the file."

"Don' bury. Ski fast."

Laura felt the knot in her chest tighten. Gathering his body into her arms, she saw that his boots had been removed. The soles of his feet were burned, his legs swollen. Her stomach clinched, but she turned her face before he could see her.

He can't see anything, she realized.

Her mind had filed away the damage she saw on his body, not letting the many pieces add up to a whole. After hours of suffering, he must have given them information. His guilt tortured him more than his burns.

Arthur Atweiler had always been a small man, but now, her father's decimated body was so light she could lift him as if he were a child. She knew he'd never survive the trip to the nearest town. She would force herself to do as he asked, lay the General next to Banks. But she would await death with him.

Outside the cave, she heard Vandal's soft grief howl. Laura wanted to cry for both of them, but her father needed her to be strong. To bring down Hitler's spy from Canada, she'd have to be strong for a long time.

"I'll kill them," she whispered. "It will be taken care of."

"Laura!" he gasped, "Not you."

As she stepped into the cold sunlight, Laura hugged her father close to her shoulder. She moved down the slope toward the battlefield. "I'll be all right, Dad. I am your daughter."

CHAPTER THREE

FRIDAY MARCH 6, 1942

Laura's father sighed when she laid him down. One sigh, and he died. She sat between him and Banks, studying each burn mark on his body, memorized them as if by knowing all his agony, she could take it away. Pain left his body with his sigh – left him and entered her, crushing her, until she could feel her heart cease its everyday pumping.

Finally, Vandal nudged her toward action. She reached a hand to caress his side and found icy fur and blood. On her knees, she pawed through his fur to find its source. Worn and weak, he made little resistance to her search. He'd been raked by a bullet.

The sled she might have built for her father she built for the big dog. The skis that Peter Lethe would never again use became sled runners. She tied Aspen boughs to the skis with leather thongs pulled from blood- spattered boots. She did not cry, not even as she left the bodies of her father and his friends without burial. Their souls were consecrated by the bitter, vengeful prayers she'd whispered during her long vigil.

If she were going to catch them, her father's killers must never know she'd been here. To discover their betrayer, she had to do as her father told her. She must turn her back on them all and force herself down the mountain. Then she had to raise such questions with the communications specialist, Vibes, that he would insist a search be made. The Army itself must discover this massacre.

The first hours of her exodus were spent lurching downhill, losing control and pulling Vandal's sled away from the melt-wells around the trees. Twice she had to retie the make-shift sled. Near the place where she'd slept the previous night, the murderer's trail swept off to the north. A sudden rush of bile emptied her stomach. Vandal awoke. He whined, high and soft. His eyebrows twitched as he watched her double over.

Laura reached a hand to smooth his hackles. "I'm all right. We'll get going soon."

Her course veered south. By the time she arrived at the hidden trailhead, it was eleven o'clock at night. Exhausted, she approached her jeep with caution, searching for signs that anyone tampered with it. In the pale light reflected off the night clouds, she could discern no ski or boot tracks, nothing to indicate the murderers were aware she had been on the mountain.

Let them grow complacent, she seethed.

Laura drove back to Camp Springs, arriving in the dark hours of Friday morning. She carried Vandal into her home, built up a fire in the den, making him a bed near its heat. She cleaned his wounds and covered his paws so he couldn't chew on his toes.

She felt reluctant to leave the warmth of the house and the companionship of the wolf dog, yet she must follow her father's order to search her files. She changed out of her wool jacket and bloodstained boots, setting the boots on newspapers at the back of her clothes closet for later cleaning.

Downstairs again, Laura peered into the den, watching Vandal sleep.

With a long sigh, she pushed herself off the den's oak doorframe and forced herself out to the jeep once more.

She drove to the sheriff's office and parked, trying to convince herself it would be all right to ask for help. She wanted the bodies found soon. In her mind, she watched dark, ugly birds of prey sweep into the pristine valley, circling, landing. Raging and helpless, she knew she shouldn't have betrayed the men by leaving them. Deep down, she also knew the sheriff would have to turn the investigation over to the army. And then the world would know she'd been on the mountain the night the assassins skied away. As a witness, she would become the hunted, unable to surprise the murderers.

After tense minutes, Laura slumped against the steering wheel.

Lonely, but determined, she stiffened her spine, turned the car key and drove away from the sheriff and from any hope of help.

* *

FRIDAY, MARCH 6TH, 1942

Dieter Haupt grew more aware of how short his body and how thin his hair whenever he had an assignment with Gerbold Klaus. Gerbold had grown beyond big – monster shoulders and piano legs. But Dieter envied most Gerbold's thick blond hair. It didn't matter that Dieter was the smarter of the two of them; Gerbold made him feel insignificant.

This assignment in Colorado seemed no different.

The two of them trudged on opposite sides of a slushy street through the city-center of Denver. They pretended not to know each other.

Arrival at their destination must go unnoticed.

At the last corner before the hotel, Dieter raised his cold fingers, signaling Gerbold to stop. The big man nodded, then gazed into the frosty display window of Denver's J.C. Penney Store. Dieter figured Gerbold studied his reflection, not the merchandise. The guy loved to watch his own jaw muscles flex.

On his side of the street, Dieter dropped a nickel on the counter at the newsstand and picked up yesterday's *New York Times*. Transaction completed, each man continued his wet, cold journey toward the Brown Palace Hotel.

Dieter unfolded the front page. The aroma of ink floated out to join coffee odor from his frosty breath. He scanned the headlines: 'Mob in Charlotte Burns Catholic Church – six dead'; 'Race Riot in Detroit Kills Eight'. Another headline on the bottom of page one read, 'Racial Tension High Near San Diego Naval Base – five dead, scores injured'.

Dieter nodded his appreciation. Every detail reported. Every incident magnified with bold headlines. *The Times* helped sow fear.

"Fear is power." Werner Arndt often said.

Dieter thought about General Atweiler and his men on the mountain. Their courage had enraged Arndt. Even Lieutenant Banks' big wolf dog had bared his fangs at Gerbold before Banks' whispered order sent the dog scurrying away. The barrage of rifle shots had no doubt killed the dog.

During that recent morning on the mountain, they had surprised the General's bivouac camp with a complete takeover. Arndt had set a guard on the officers. Then he shoved General Atweiler into the cave where there lay a fire pit. By the fire, working the man over, Dieter realized he'd never seen Arndt so vicious. He grew so focused on heating coals to use in breaking Atweiler that after he gave orders about dealing with Atweiler's officers, Arndt completely abandoned them to Gerbold's infamous work. Each man had been tied to a different tree, all in view of the torture inflicted on the others.

And every one of them could hear Atweiler's screams. Fear is power.

They never found the dog's body. That fact gave Dieter the willies.

The animal had eyes that glittered with understanding.

Dieter shivered and returned his attention to the newspaper. As he walked along the snow-silenced street, he glanced inside the front section, hunting headlines for other events he and Arndt had recently set in motion.

'Explosion at Key Railroad Bridge in New Jersey.'

'Newly Launched Carrier Fleet Not Seaworthy'. A sub-headline read, 'Sabotage Suspected'.

Dieter smiled. Suspected? Arndt's men at the docks work hard. At the present rate of failure, the U.S. Navy will limp into war nine months too late to save England.

As he approached the hotel, Dieter hurried his walk. He was never anxious to be in the presence of Werner Arndt. Arndt, however, did not tolerate tardiness – not even when Dieter's missions were a stunning success – and certainly not when he had failed.

As he quickened his step, Dieter turned to the inside news section and read more closely. He found no mention of the Tenth Division Mountaineers, Allied Army Intelligence, or General Arthur Atweiler.

That was good.

He did find a small article, buried on page twelve. It concerned a certain aeroplane that mysteriously blew up as it took off from the Denver aero port. The news reporter believed that Brigadier General Groves and his guest, the Nobel Prize winning physicist, Enrico Fermi, had died in the tragic accident.

Dieter had prayed to see that in print. He hoped Arndt saw it, and believed it – last night's mission accomplished.

But Dieter knew he'd failed.

Last night, in a flush of pride over the successful destruction of General Atweiler, he had treated himself to one or two drinks before heading to the aero field. Once in the bar, a drunk he'd met the week before hailed him. He joined the man in a booth. They sat nursing their bottles while his buddy groused about Germans who were allowed to remain citizens in spite of the war.

"The U.S. of A. is getting all them Japs rounded up," the man said. "We should do them Gerries just the same."

Dieter nodded. His American accent proved good enough for a loud bar like this, but he didn't want to test it much. He'd about finished his third beer and his one hundredth nod of agreement when who should walk into the restaurant section but Enrico Fermi himself – and Brigadier General Groves – Dieter recognized them from Arndt's photo file.

Dieter quickly dropped American dollars on the table, preparing to leave. His drinking buddy pointed at the newcomer in the European-cut suit, and said, "There goes a Kraut, free as you please."

As Dieter shrugged into his worn American jacket, his gave an automatic response. "That guy is Italian." He hadn't noticed the sudden lull in noise as customer stares followed the dignified general.

Everybody nearby must have heard him. One of those people probably had figured out he should not recognize Fermi.

Much later last night, after placing the explosives, Dieter waited for Fermi and Groves to arrive at the aero port. They never came. In this morning's gray dawn, the plane took off and immediately blew up.

Watching the fireworks of his useless handiwork, Dieter became convinced that the general had whisked Fermi out of Denver by car. No doubt about it, the intended victims had been warned.

In that realization, came the genesis of the idea. Dieter knew it to be impossible, but his mind insisted on playing with it. His mind told him he had to get out. Arndt would know of failure. Failure meant death.

Dieter must disappear.

Dieter informed his naïve and wishful mind that there was nowhere to go. Arndt found every man and woman who ever tried to escape him.

Look at what he had done to the Schoenfeld kid.

*   *

Dieter folded the newspaper, turned the corner onto Seventeenth Street at Broadway and climbed the steps to the hotel, Denver's posh Brown Palace. Inside, he glanced at the doorman, one of Arndt's men. Then he caught the eye of the obsequious manager, lover of all things German – especially of power and fear. He glared at the man, forcing him to veer off from approaching. The man had no sense for secrecy; he wouldn't last long.

The great room of the hotel sparkled with crystal. Dark wood, burnished to a reflective shine, thick wool carpets and opulent furnishings made this hotel as gaudy as any Dieter had seen in Germany– a languorous, Victorian madam.

The pungent aroma of grilled beef washed over him. He grew suddenly sick to his stomach. Arndt loved fire as a means of torture and murder.

His burly friend, Gerbold, had entered by a side door and arrived near the elevator at the same time as Dieter, but didn't look at him. To any outsider, it would seem the two men knew nothing about each other.

Gerbold stepped first into the metal cage of the elevator. He asked the operator to go to the seventh floor. The operator's face went white as he closed the metal lattice door. Dieter figured the man knew who owned the seventh floor. For protection, and for the expected expansion of operations, the whole eighth floor belonged to Arndt, as well.

Dieter asked for the fifth. At five, he walked off and climbed the stairs to the seventh floor where he passed a guard and met Gerbold again. They walked down the green-carpeted hall together.

Two men guarded the door at the end of the plush hall, both as big as Gerbold.

"Why two guards?" Gerbold asked.

"Don't know," Dieter whispered. "Maybe Arndt is getting ready to make some changes." He could smell Gerbold's sweat. Or maybe his own.

"Last time there were two guards, it was Detroit," Gerbold muttered. Dieter remembered that afternoon – Detroit, hometown of the Jew-hating fanatic and radio orator, Father Coughlin. After setting off a huge race riot, one of Coughlin's obsessed followers, Becker, came demanding more seniority in the organization. It took two guards to haul Becker's body out to the garbage shaft. Becker had mistakenly thought having a German name made him an equal.

Gerbold and Dieter tried never to make that mistake with Arndt.

Even if he'd succeeded, Dieter didn't like finding two men at Arndt's door. It had to mean something went wrong. He and Gerbold lifted their arms, allowing the guards to frisk them.

"Kristoff," Dieter greeted the broad-shouldered, older man.

"Hello, Diet," Kristoff grunted as he watched the other guard take the Singer pistol from Gerbold's jacket pocket. Then Kristoff reached over and pulled a Finnish-made Luger-Lahti from Gerbold's heavy jacket lining. "Gerbold, you know better than to carry this," Kristoff said, "It's not American."

"Somebody attacks me," Gerbold said, "I'll definitely look American with that little bean-shooter Arndt issued us – a dead American."

Dieter shook his head at Gerbold's stubborn ways. Kristoff's partner took Dieter's own handgun – a Remington.

"You get these back on the way out, but not the Lahti," the man said to Gerbold.

"Ach! You will have me killed?"

"Orders," Kristoff said, and then turned toward Dieter. "He expects you."

The second guard opened the heavy door.

Before they entered the office of Werner Arndt, Dieter ironed worry from his face. Arndt never congratulated him on a job done well. Today, the best he could hope for would be no comment on last night's explosive fiasco. There was little possibility for no comment, however. When it came to failure, Arndt always knew.

The room Dieter and Gerbold entered seemed large and dark except for the window looking over Seventeenth Street. Along the walls stood tall bookshelves filled with English literature and American Law books, all bought on sale for cover, in case anyone came visiting or foolishly broke in.

Nothing in this room would have a Swastika, the black eagle or any other symbol of the Third Reich. And the papers Dieter saw stacked on the desk – those would be fake contracts for the purchase of shale-oil rights or some other American commodity.

The mahogany bookcases hid the files necessary to run U.S. Abwehr operations. They also hid wires to the radio antennae that Gerbold had affixed atop the hotel one dark night.

Werner Arndt's Colorado lair. Dieter knew this didn't compare to the opulence of the office in New York City and the one in Los Angeles.

Money from Nazi friends in the United States made it all possible.

He and Gerbold stopped in front of Arndt's big desk. Dieter's hand brushed the leaves of a potted plant – an evergreen shrub wrapped in decorative paper and sitting on the corner of the wide-open mahogany surface.

Odd, Dieter thought. Who would expect Arndt to decorate with a plant wrapped in pink?

Dieter stared at Arndt's hair. It had been dyed. Arndt was a big man, with a powerful head – difficult to disguise. However, the change of hair from red to black, and from curled to straight made him almost unrecognizable. After a moment, Dieter realized the change also included thick eyeglasses. Arndt's brows had been blacked as well.

He must intend to go somewhere he might be recognized. The idea made Dieter itchy. Arndt rarely allowed himself to be seen in public. The few times Dieter remembered had been visits to certain women. There was only one woman of interest in this area.

Arndt glanced up from his telephone conversation, and then returned his attention to the phone.

Kristoff, the bodyguard, leaned against the wall behind them. All these years, Dieter thought, and Arndt still employs a guard even when his faithful dog, Dieter Haupt, visits his Kommandant.

Nearby, at a small desk, a young man fiddled with the dials on a radio. The radio squealed as the kid twisted knobs, looking for some particular band of airwaves. Not far from the radio, a gray tarp of heavy sailcloth had been carefully spread on top of the carpet.

Gerbold glanced at Dieter. They had both seen tarps like that before.

Sweat beaded on Gerbold's forehead.

Behind his desk, Arndt continued his conversation.

"Steel?" he asked his caller.

After the reply, Arndt nodded and wrote numbers. "*Gut. Und munitions?*"

"*Und* the Remington-Singer trade?"

The other person must have given satisfactory information. Arndt smiled and said, "*Jah.* Invest."

Dieter relaxed a bit. Business here continued as usual. These were not investment orders, but coded recommendations of companies to hit with worker slow-downs, fires or mysteriously stolen shipments. Arndt hung up, and then, still without acknowledging their presence, dialed a second call. "Where is she?" Arndt asked.

Arndt nodded at the response. "She goes to her office? Or to the office of her father?"

Dieter guessed who they were talking about – Atweiler's daughter – sharp-looking, self-reliant, and far too smart for her own good.

Arndt reached across his blotter, absently fingering the pink paper on the potted shrub. To the person on the phone, he added. "You are to send a 'military detail' of your own choosing. Guard her until her father is found. Tell me where she goes, what she does."

Dieter heard some objection at the other end. Arndt's response grew impatient. "*Shist*! It matters not. Tell her you worry. He does not call the base, und so the American army is concerned for her safety – whatever."

Arndt's interest never seemed healthy for a woman. And the fellow at the other end of the phone line – presumably Arndt's man at Camp Springs – Arndt's bought spy – his days, too, were numbered. He better not blow the assignment to watch Atweiler's daughter.

Arndt hung up the phone, then lifted the line briefly before hanging up with care one final time.

"Gerbold," he said, "You must to change that phone line. Someone listens *noch einmal.*"

Again. Arndt always thought someone listened. No line Gerbold set up ever lasted more than three days.

"Haupt," Arndt nearly whispered Dieter's name, and then turned to observe him. Dieter kept his face under control. Arndt would never see him cringe. "*Ach,* Haupt, please sit down, both of you."

They both sat – soft, low chairs facing the expanse of Arndt's desk. In this position, Dieter, helpless and vulnerable, could not see past the desk except to look out the upper part of the window.

Arndt said, "That traitor Fermi and General Groves were not on the plane you so neatly blew up." His silky voice exuded sadness.

Ice gripped Dieter's spine.

Arndt continued. "How do you suppose the General knew he should not go to the aero port?"

Dieter shook his head. His breathing gave away his shakes. Arndt glanced at the bodyguard. Kristoff stopped leaning and stepped away from the wall. The kid at the radio sat immobile, watching. Next to Dieter, Gerbold leaned slightly away from his friend – separating himself from failure.

Now Dieter knew. Arndt had been told of Dieter's one slip. "Haupt!" Arndt's voice shattered the air. Panic wet Dieter's wool

pants. He clamped tight. Just smelling him, Arndt would know.

"Our people recently caught two more scientist defectors, Otto Blemming and Felix Abraham. They lie in the depths of the Saint Lawrence River."

A reproach. Fermi lived.

Arndt rose from his leather chair and slipped, cat-like, around to their side. Sitting on the corner of his desk near the potted plant, he bent a soulful gaze on Dieter and Gerbold.

"So," he said in that voice of his that should have been benign, "what have you two been doing in the last twenty-four hours?"

Gerbold's jaw relaxed, but Dieter knew better. Arndt toyed with him, the way he used to toy with his victims back home – put them off their guard, make them think for a while that they had escaped his wrath. But Dieter had watched it all: the fawning thankfulness; the hopeful rededication to work; the moment of horror; the swift death.

As Gerbold recounted his work of the previous twenty-four hours, the sweat of Dieter's fear trickled down his armpits. Next, Arndt would ask about the tavern last night, and then it would be over.

Dieter had the fleeting thought that he should welcome this end – swift, brutal and blessedly final – the only way he would ever escape Arndt.

Outside the office window, snow fell on the roofs of Denver, and beyond, the peaks of the Front Range stood hooded in white. Dieter inhaled. The earthy odor of the potted shrub reminded Dieter of his home, his mother.

Arndt's harsh voice brought him back to the present. "We could have murdered that wop," Arndt snarled. "Traitors like Enrico Fermi must die."

Dieter stiffened for the final blow. Beyond Arndt, the young man stopped playing with the radio transmitter. His blue eyes and baby skin seemed to light up with delight. For a moment, Dieter thought the kid relished watching him die.

Instead, he spoke.

"Ready," the boy said excitedly. "I have *die Abwehr*, Canada, online, sir – at thirty-two kilocycles."

As Arndt turned away from him and toward the radio, Dieter let out his breath. He thought, how green this *Knabe*. Only a sapling to be so enthralled making contact with Toronto agents. At least the boy's enthusiasm had put off the inevitable for another minute.

Arndt stepped smoothly around the desk, skirting the pink-wrapped potted shrub as gracefully as he always moved up the sheer face of a mountain. Dieter's attention riveted itself on the tarp – a rough shroud.

Arndt reached out to take the transmitter from the boy. He tapped out a message while the youth looked on in awe.

In the familiar code, Arndt tapped, "Change to the new band," After a brief 'Ja-wohl' from the Abwehr operator, Arndt signed off and turned the dials.

The boy looked uncomfortable. Dieter wondered why Arndt used this precaution. Did he not even trust this boy? When Arndt came back online, the first word he tapped out seemed short and clear. They all heard it. `H...E...S...S...'

Hess in Canada? Dieter had read the stories. He knew that someone who claimed to be Rudolph Hess, Hitler's deputy party leader, had been captured flying over Britain. So, who was this Hess?

After that opening name, the out-going message and the answers came so fast, Dieter couldn't keep track of the entire exchange, but he caught occasional mentions of munitions factories, shipyards, and railroad lines. He assumed all would soon be hit with explosives or fires started by the agents Arndt controlled throughout the North American hemisphere.

As abruptly as he began tapping, Arndt signed off.

He handed the apparatus to the boy. "We must use a different band next time. Hess is too slow."

Arndt turned back toward Dieter. "*Gerbold, heraus. Schnell.*" Dieter jumped with surprise.

Gerbold stood abruptly, as if catapulted from his chair. He stepped to Arndt's side.

"You were seen at the tavern last night." Arndt said.

Dieter stiffened. The final blow could not be delayed. Arndt would make Gerbold sweat and then, fun and games over, Arndt would attack Dieter.

Gerbold stammered. "*Nein. Es ist Wahrheit.* Who tells you these? Arndt punched him in the eye, a blow so swift and powerful that Gerbold collapsed, unconscious on the tarp. Hot red speckles of blood melted into the gray cloth.

His body as taut as a primed trigger, Dieter gave a moment's thought to bolting, but he didn't move. He knew, however, that when Arndt called him over there, he would obey.

Turning toward the boy who still sat next to the radio, Arndt spoke calmly, his hand now playing with change in his trouser pocket.

"*Knabe*, last night, at midnight, you spoke to General Groves' chauffeur. You covered your head in a wool cap, dressed in American Army fatigues, but Kristoff here, he knew it was you."

The older guard stepped forward, watching the boy with fascination.

The boy's eyes widened with alarm. He shook his head once before Arndt pulled a sharp blade from his pocket, slashing across the boy's throat. The boy barely had time to look startled before his head tilted at an improbable angle and the light left his eyes. Blood sprayed over the telegraphic radio and onto Arndt.

Arndt didn't even wait for the body to fall backward onto the tarp before he ripped off his bloody coat and tossed it on the boy's face. He turned on Dieter. Shining blood covered Arndt's visage.

His dripping hand gestured at Gerbold. "No one calls me crazy," Arndt said. Then, he pointed at the boy. "As soon as Gerbold wakes up, he and Kristoff must to carry this out back to the truck. In that cemetery at the edge of Camp Springs, there is an open grave near the tallest oak tree."

Arndt leaned toward his desk and lifted the pink-papered florist's pot. "Plant this shrub over the stupid *Knabe.*"

He shoved the pot into Dieter's trembling hands, adding, "I want to find that grave. We will use it again."

In a panic of relief and dread, Dieter nodded. His mind urged desperately.

Plan a way out.

As if one could plan to escape the inevitable.

CHAPTER FOUR

FRIDAY, MARCH 6, 1942

In the gray hours before dawn, Laura waved at the Camp Springs entry guard, drove through the gate and down the road until she was out of his sight, then turned onto a small side trail. She parked her jeep in the woods behind the main buildings. The jeep blended into the woodland background. None but the guard would realize she'd come to her office so early. Dog-tired, but determined, she studied the camp for activity. To her right were rows of wooden barracks, all dun colored. They showed no signs of early risers. Not even the latrine lights were on.

Outside her jeep, the trees swayed in winter gusts. Branches popped, bursting from within as ice expanded their cells. The clouds no longer reflected the white of snow or moon. Partially obscured by the brown leaves of a giant oak, the board and batten administration building loomed over the barracks and parade grounds. At this hour, the cold metal flagpole was barren. If she succeeded in convincing Vibes to call for a search, the flag soon would fly at half-mast.

Sitting still for the first time in many hours, she couldn't shake away the images graven into her mind. Through the frosted windshield, she imagined the front door of the administration building swing open.

Shadow figures filed out, joking with each other. Temple, Ashton, Bond, Wells, Hospice, Lethe, Banks, and the smallest one, the one they all looked up to, General Arthur Atweiler. The picture seemed real, the men lively. Laura dragged in a ragged breath, choking off a sob. She slumped over the wheel and closed her eyes. She could not let feelings control her now. It would take cold, careful planning to find the murderers and kill them. She could not even admit to grief.

She felt sure the murderers did not massacre her father and his men just to slow the training of the new Tenth Division. Something of even greater magnitude forced them to risk entering this country in search of the General. Her ignorance of their purpose made Laura's every action dangerous to herself, and to others. If she knew their goal, she could guess what they would do next. She had to get into the building unseen to search her files before she talked to Vibes. She must discover what Dad wanted her to find there.

Her father said `Use Johnson'. Colonel Johnson, attending a war-preparations meeting in Denver, was expected back next Tuesday. This couldn't wait. Father had urged her to tell James. Of course, she couldn't tell James Schoenfeld anything. Among the living, she had no idea who to trust besides Johnson. Laura had to learn as much as she could without arousing suspicion.

'Look in files. Under Bee," he said. Now was the time. She'd have the offices to herself for at least two hours. She checked her appearance – regulation suit, skirt and high heels for the office. A glance at the back of her legs showed only a slight misalignment of her silk- stocking seam – her disguise. As far as others might care, she was an inconspicuous secretary on a busy training base. None would know the grisly memories and deep hatred that ran through her. Into her parka pocket, she dropped a sheathed gutting knife. Someone on this base had betrayed her father. When she found him, she would show no mercy.

She pushed open the jeep door. The wind howled. A cold blast of air hit her exposed limbs. She pulled her hood over her head and ran through the wood, crossing stiff grass-stubble toward the administration building. As she passed the giant Bur Oak, a sudden noise made her leap. Her heel caught on a knobby root, throwing her into the outstretched arms of a shadow. She reached for her knife but could not move fast enough. The shadow held her immobile. A deep voice growled near her ear. "What are you doing out here in those stupid shoes?"

Fear gave her power. She reared back and banged her head against the stranger's throat, making him gasp for air. Breaking free of his arms, she shoved him against the tree trunk. "Back off, fellow," she yelled. Her mittened fist clenched the fish knife in front of his face.

His startled, deep brown eyes and a few strands of black hair were all she could see around his muffler and ski cap. He held one gloved hand to his throat as he pulled in short quick breaths. When he regained control of his throat, he opened his eyes. Laura felt an instant of burning intensity in his gaze.

He looked at her as if he'd been startled by what he saw, as if he had expected her to be someone he knew but found he did not know her at all. He stood not much taller than her, but broad-shouldered and long-armed. He was powerfully built, yet he put up his free hand in easy surrender as he eyed her knife.

Too easy.

"Deadly . . . aim," he gasped through his protective scarf. His gaze drifted lower, making Laura feel suddenly exposed. She knew this stratagem. Refusing to check her jacket buttons, she kept her attention on his eyes. As his glance moved over her body, his eyes widened.

"Who are you?" she demanded.

But he did not answer. He kept attempting to distract her with his study of her clothing. Near the edge of his scarf, the skin over his prominent cheekbones tightened as if in appreciation of a work of beauty. Very good, but she fell for none of it. She pressed the knifepoint into his chin.

"Answer me," she said.

"Sharp knife," he whispered, "And poison . . . those high heels?"

"You don't want to know."

"You need . . . no . . . mothering," He said, testing his voice with each syllable.

"You need to explain why you're lurking about these woods," she said, flicking the knife blade to catch the light and his attention.

His gaze caressed her face, making her alert to a trick. Then he smiled. "I'm bird watching," he said.

Every muscle in her body tensed at his suggestive chuckle. "Crows," she said, scraping the knife across his neck scarf, breaking threads in the tight plaid. "Ravens. That's all you'll see on this base."

He didn't even flinch. "Oh, I disagree," he said, his ink-black lashes lifted as his gaze took in the expansive fields behind her. "I've spotted some slow-witted pigeons out on the parade ground." He glanced back at her face. "And one, brave eaglet in the woods."

In that instant, with swift, concentrated grace, he caught both her wrists and pulled her against his chest. The suddenness of his motions startled her, but she was even more dismayed by the warmth of him. His dark eyes held her gaze. "You should be wearing warmer clothes," he whispered. And as suddenly, he let her go.

She straightened, but still held the knife pointed at his chest. "You should not be on this base. Identify yourself."

She watched mocking smile lines soften near his eyes as he studied her wild hair.

"Miss Atweiler, I have seen what I came to see. And now I will be gone." He ignored her knife, turned toward the deep woods and strode away. She knew there was barbed wire surrounding the woods in that direction.

"Wait."

He glanced over his shoulder. "Change your mind?" His eyebrow rose in puckish humor. "Want to see me again, do you?"

Stupidly, she wanted to capture him, haul him before the nearest drill sergeant, but she knew she should feel lucky he had not hurt her. "You can't get out that way," she said.

Lame, she thought. It sounds like you care.

"On the contrary, my dear," he said, raising a pair of fence clippers from a belt at his waist. "I shall be a few moments repairing my entrance, but I will have no trouble."

"The guard . . .," she began.

His eyes betrayed the devilish grin beneath his scarf. "That poor guard does not deal well with chloroform, but he will recover soon."

At that, the stranger disappeared behind the giant oak. By the time Laura scrambled to the far side of the tree, he was no longer in sight. She found hundreds of his boot prints, going all directions in the snow.

Clever, she thought. Holding the knife at the ready, she ran the two hundred yards to the fence, and yet saw no sign of him. Nor could she find signs of a hole in the fence. She did find a dazed and sick corporal emptying his stomach onto the ground.

"Corporal Rankin," Laura ordered, as if she had the right. "Come with me to the staff-sergeant. You must report this breach of the perimeter at once."

* *

Corporal Rankin's report roused the camp guards for a search of the grounds. No sign of the intruder could be found. The staff sergeant doubled the number of guards at the perimeter, while Lieutenant Brooks took her story and began an interrogation of the young corporal.

Forty-five minutes later, as she re-crossed the parade ground to the main building, Laura kept a wary eye out for the man in the woods. The more she thought about his presence, the more uneasy she felt. She had almost no idea of his appearance beyond those eyes – dark, smiling, teasing eyes. To the lieutenant's questions, she could only describe brown eyes, black hair and glossy, thick eyebrows.

For some reason, her mind kept returning to the warmth of the stranger's breath on her ear when she first fell into his arms. She did not, of course, mention that sensation to the lieutenant. Nor did she speak of the silly pride with which she recalled his remark about the eaglet he'd found in the woods.

At last, Laura approached the administration building. With only one hour left for her investigations, her hands were probably too cold to work with paper, and her feet were freezing in her high heels. Her whole body shivered with fatigue and with surreal memories of the secret valley on Longs Peak and her encounter under the oak. Gulping clear, cold air, Laura swallowed all emotion, ignored all sensation, shoved her key into the front door lock and set herself to the task at hand.

As she opened the door, it came to her. "He called me Miss Atweiler." And then she realized he'd as much as told her – he had come to see her. For a moment, the memory of his humorous eyes made her feel warmer, safer. Then reason replaced fatigue. She shivered with fear. The stranger knew her and watched. And she had no idea who he might be.

*   *

At the edge of the woods, lounging in the high branches of an ancient oak, a solidly built man waited. His dark eyes narrowed. He watched the slender figure of the woman. She hesitated before the door. Her shoulders slumped briefly before she straightened her back and grabbed for the handle. The man's leather jacket creaked as he stretched one hand to massage his thigh and hip joint – an habitual gesture, performed whenever he sat still for any length of time.

"She knows," he whispered to himself. "She knows too much."

CHAPTER FIVE

Inside the dank administration building, Laura headed straight for her office, closed the door and dug into her file cabinet, quietly sliding out the drawer marked A through C. Under Bee, nothing. Back to the beginning of the B section, she ran her fingers through the folders, hoping for a sign which would set off a memory alarm. *Baudouin, Bavaria, BBC, Beacon, Beau, Berlin, Bern. . .* Nothing. Everything she looked at reminded her of the war in Europe, but nothing jarred. She began again, poking into each folder.

Below, a door slammed. Footsteps on the stairs. An office door opened down the hall. Thinking the stranger of the woods might be resourceful enough to get in, Laura tip-toed to her door. She cracked it open and peered out, wishing she hadn't left her pistol in her hiking jacket at home. It wasn't regulation Army, because she was a woman, but she could have hidden it in her purse, maybe.

In the morning darkness she saw a light in the typing room at the end of the hall. Closing her door, Laura slid the lock into place and leaned her head against it. His face, the plaid scarf and his laughing eyes, appeared in her memory, taunted her. She pushed herself to work.

Back at her file cabinet, she studied each page, searching for something that didn't belong – a message from her father. The person down the hall came out, walking lightly toward Laura's door – not the stranger's deliberate tread. The steps hesitated.

Go on, go on, Laura willed the walker. The footsteps moved again, retreating down the hall. *I can't talk – I can't talk. Too much.*

Laura sagged against her cabinet. Tension brought back the memory of the silent field covered with bodies. Her loneliness and grief threatened to take over from her anger. She had to keep her anger alive to give her courage. She pushed herself to study individual files. The folder labeled 'BBC' had program listings and a review of a speech by Winston Churchill. The file 'Beacon' contained notes on a new radio transmitter able to send powerful signals from Boston to Nazi- dominated countries in Europe. The file labeled 'Beau' had only one slip of paper.

That stopped her. She pulled it out. On it someone had typed the words "See champ". She dropped to the drawer with C to H, pawing through the files. Under 'champ', she found a single sheet. The word 'Lenses' had been typed on it. She flipped back to the drawer where 'Lenses' would be filed and found a file with the word 'Lenin', but no 'Lenses'.

What's Dad trying to say?

Laura stood very still, her hand in the file drawer as she thought.

"Files, under Bee." He said "files", not exclusively mine . . . His office?

She closed her file cabinet and turned the combination lock. Her father's office lay two doors away. Between sat Colonel Johnson's office. As she passed it, Laura glanced at Bernard Johnson's door. She allowed herself a moment of self-pity and fatigue.

'Use Johnson', Dad said.

Bernard Johnson grew on you . . .as a soft-spoken, intelligent young man, not as the boyfriend he hoped to be. He'd become her father's second in command in spite of the fact that he might be only thirty- five years old. The war pushed young officers into heavy responsibilities. His responsibilities had him in Denver, and incommunicado. No help from that quarter. Laura straightened her back, absently pushed stray curls behind her left ear, passed Johnson's door and slipped into her father's office.

The fresh woods smell of the General's pipe tobacco hung in the air after weeks of his absence – as if he'd just left. Laura gripped the front of his desk and let out one long, painful breath.

The moment of weakness passed. She reached for his dictionary. Inside the front cover lay an inscription, 'To Arthur with love from Marjory'.

Her mother had given him this book because of his curiosity about words, a trait he'd shared with James. Below her mother's signature in the same ink color, but a different hand, she read what appeared to be a date: 12/14/26.

Her mother hadn't written the date. She had died before 12/14/26.

Finding these numbers had been an accident the first time, but it hadn't been hard to guess what that date in the dictionary really stood for. Laura had played enough games with her father to know how his mind worked. Laura used the numbers to open the combination lock on her father's files. In the upper drawer, she looked for 'Champ'. She found nothing, but she did find a 'Lenses' folder with one slip of paper. Numbers. '7312'

She took the slip out. Intending to copy the numbers and then replace them, she stuffed the slip in her pocket.

The smell of her father's pipe tobacco grew suddenly much stronger. Slowly, so as to appear unaware and guiltless, Laura closed the file drawer. She turned.

In the doorway between her father's office and his own, stood the camp comptroller, Major Richard Cameron, his pipe bowl gripped in his slender hand. Cameron looked at her through thick glasses, silently waiting.

"Richard, you're in early. Trip to Washington go okay?" asked Laura breezily.

"Yes," his answer seemed curt. "May I help you?"

"I hope so," she tried to smile, if only to stop the quivering of her lower lip. Watching how he held his pipe, as if imitating her father, she feared she might tell Richard Cameron what she'd found. She'd always admired Cameron's meticulous work and his apparent admiration for her father, but somebody close to the General had betrayed the location of the training camp.

Laura plopped down in her father's swivel chair, working to look comfortable. "Last time I saw Dad, he insisted I find a file on "Operation Bee". There's no such file in my cabinet, so I thought he must mean here in his office.

"You have his combination?"

"Sure." Laura said, as if every army brat carried her father's secrets in her head.

Major Cameron stared at his pipe, and then at her once more. His stooped shoulders pulled back slightly as he sighed.

Laura looked at him coldly.

I refuse to feel guilty, she thought. *And if you, Cameron, had anything to do with the murders on Longs Peak, then be damned.* Cameron walked slowly, as if he were debating with himself. She saw he might be reluctant to question her, yet unwilling to believe her father would breach protocol.

Dad knew I'd figured out his trick with the dictionary, she reminded herself. He never changed the lock and, until today, I've never taken even a curious peek.

Cameron twisted the combination quickly, opened the drawer and played his fingers through the folders. Laura saw his fingers hesitate in the area where 'Lenses' would be. The slip of paper seemed ready to pop out of her pocket. Cameron let his hand walk over the file before he closed the drawer and opened another.

"Nothing under 'Operation' or 'Bee' in here, Laura", he said after an efficient search. "Maybe you should wait until your Dad comes home."

"But he . . ."

"Better yet," he said, looking at her over his glasses, "ask him again next Tuesday."

Laura sank back into the chair. Did he taunt her? "I'll do that," she said, wondering if he knew there would be no more Tuesdays with her father.

Cameron seemed to wait for her to leave. He turned his head slightly toward the window and the play of light made a rainbow through his thick glasses. Laura sat up. She swiveled the chair away from him and looked out the window as well, saying, "That's all I need, Richard. Thanks."

Behind her, she heard him hesitate and then move softly toward the door. The quiet clip of his leather shoes had been the sound she'd heard earlier. Richard, and not the stranger from the woods, had hesitated outside her door this morning. Cameron and not her father had left the strong smell of tobacco in the office just before she came in. Why did he know her father's combination? What did he do in this office when the General left?

The rainbow reflection on his thick glasses . . . Was Dad's code name for him 'Lenses'?

*   *

Just before ten o'clock that night, Laura let herself out of the broom closet at the end of the second-floor hall. She'd stowed a flashlight and a blanket in the closet in the mid-afternoon then waited until only two officers were still in the building – Vibes, the head radio man, and Major Cameron who wrote a report of his meetings in Washington, D.C..

Pretending to leave around seven in the evening, she'd stepped in here instead, wrapped herself up among the smelly mops and brooms. She slept fitfully as she waited. Endless nightmares of stalking animals chased her through the woods. Always, as she came to the bur oak, her father reached for her just before a man wrapped in a plaid scarf stepped between them and cut her off – the stranger from the woods.

Waking, moments ago, she'd heard Richard and Vibes leave by the stairwell next to the closet. Laura wanted desperately to call out to them, to tell them about the bodies that needed burial. But she didn't. She had to find what her father sent her to find. Then, she could raise a hullabaloo about her father being missing.

Soon after the men left, Merle, the night-watchman had shuffled down the hall, giving each room a cursory look-in. Merle left. Now she could test her theory about Major Cameron. She hurried through her father's office into Major Cameron's connecting room. Laura slid the black-out shade down to the sill. From her bag, she pulled gloves and a flashlight. Careful to aim her flashlight away from the window, she found Cameron's file cabinet and tried the number. Left seven, right past seven to three, left again to twelve. She felt the tumblers fall. The drawer slid open.

'Lenses' is Cameron, then. Gently she drew out the drawer.

In her mind, the rasping voice of her dying father whispered, "James Schoenfeld. Under Bee." Laura had to stop a moment, breathe and listen for other sounds in the darkened building. She froze.

A jeep passed on the street below but continued on. Methodically, she hunted. The word 'Champ, J.B' flashed by. Playing the light over the heading, Laura pulled the 'Champ' file, dropping it on the desk. Inside were several pieces of paper. Most of the papers seemed to be letters typed and then edited with pencil marks like a decoded transmission.

The language of each letter was French, so she read them with ease. The topic of all of them seemed to be difficult climbs in the Swiss

Alps, France or Austria. She found one yellow sheet, a form with typed words filling designated spaces. Brief phrases described J.B. Champ – brown hair, brown eyes, five foot ten inches tall, weighing one hundred sixty- five pounds.

Laura sighed. The yellow paper gave Champ's age as thirty-nine – Tarascon, Provence, France, so a Frenchman. The town name seemed familiar to Laura. At the bottom of the page, she saw Champ's signature. In the waning light of the electric torch, the name became hard to make out Something like Jacques Barcleigh Champ.

This man, Champ, seemed to be one of Dad's sources of climbing information, nothing more.

Outside the dark office building, a jeep changed gears and started up the hill toward the Camp Springs exit gate. Laura listened tensely and then relaxed as the sound receded. She turned back to the 'Champ' folder on the desk. Leafing through it, she noticed a half-sheet telegram that had escaped her attention the first time. The type looked small and worn, making it difficult to read in this light, but, unlike everything else in the file, it was in English, and dated three weeks ago – more recently than any of the letters.

> *"Sir,*
>
> *The real Lascaux is undiscovered. Be all gone by March. Nice skiing near camp. At three fifteen I test attraction for sadistic flies on Abner's facade."*
>
> *Columbine and Black-eyed Susan."*

The English should have made sense, but of course the very appearance of sense that made no sense indicated a code. She'd have to decipher it later. It appeared unlikely that this one sheet would be missed if she took the telegram home and left the rest of the folder in its usual place. Laura laid the telegram on the desk and put the Champ folder back in Major Cameron's files.

A sudden need to know about James came over Laura. She wondered if Cameron's files would yield information on James's last years with Arndt. Dropping to her knees on the floor, she pulled out the file drawer Q through T. There in the wavering circle of her dying light, halfway back in the drawer, was a file clearly marked `Schoenfeld, James Burke". Hesitating only a moment, Laura lifted the file. Her breath caught as she let the folder fall open. A large photo of James dropped into her lap. She had never before seen this portrait. He seemed to be about twenty-eight or nine. His hair shone bright blond, straight and long across his forehead. The shy smile of his boyhood had become dazzlingly confident. He gazed at the photographer, his left hand gripping a walking stick. His other arm hung loosely at his side, but the tense right angle between his thumb and fingers made Laura believe his nonchalance feigned. James looked excited about the day's plans.

He seemed to have turned, saying something funny to the cameraman just before he struck off on a hike toward the golden spire of rock behind him. His long blond bangs blew across his slender face, partially obscuring one eye. His brows rose in question – brows so dark they seemed out of place next to startling blond hair.

The photographer had captured him at the moment of joy when he started another adventure. The focus seemed so clear that Laura reached out to touch his thick, brown lashes and soft, smiling lips. It seemed possible to smell the dust of his path, feel the heat of nearby rocks.

He'd become slender, but not weak. His arms emerged from his short-sleeved shirt showing long, sinewy muscles. Below his lederhosen, his leather shorts, the strength of his legs appeared as clearly defined.

He'd grown taller, yet lighter than the description of Jacques Champ. In fact, she remembered one of his last letters telling her he was so skinny he could stand behind a sapling and be in hiding. "I'm

Kate Smith's shadow," he'd quipped, teasing Laura about her radio favorite, the hefty "songbird of the south." It had been over three years since he wrote that letter.

Laura looked at his face for a few moments before she set the photo on the desk next to the Champ telegram and went back to the papers in the 'Schoenfeld' folder. There were several medical bills, marked paid and dated January, 1939, for services from a hospital in Berlin. Attached she found a death certificate from that hospital. Next, a bill for an air flight for two to Paris, in February, 1939.

Was one ticket for James's coffin? Anguish seared Laura's throat, but she pushed on. Behind the flight bill sat another invoice, this one from a Paris apartment for six months' rent. Marked paid, it had been signed in General Arthur Atweiler's Spencerian script.

Last in the folder she found the same kind of official Army-yellow paper Laura had seen in the 'Champ' file. It described James as six feet two inches tall, one hundred- fifty pounds, blond hair, brown eyes. Across the sheet the word 'Deceased' had been stamped. Underneath, in her father's handwriting, he'd penciled "died of injuries from a fall."

"Deceased," she whispered. Before Laura's eyes swam the faces of all the men she'd found in the meadow on Longs Peak. As hot tears coursed down her cheeks, she saw once again the tortured and distorted body of her father sighing into release of life. And then there appeared a vision of James, falling over and over down long flights of stairs to a slow, agonizing death.

"Jimmy. My Jimmy," she cried out, hugging the folder to her chest. Laura rocked back and forth, back and forth, sobbing out her grief. The note about James's death released the wrenching anguish she'd held at bay during the long trek down the mountain. All night, her heart had been as cold as silent snow. All day she'd worked at her desk, sometimes pretending it hadn't happened, at other times vowing revenge on the murderers for the sadistic way they'd killed her father. At last, she could cry into the darkness. Loss and loneliness closed around her.

Her torchlight flickered one last time and then died. Outside, another jeep shifted gears, but this one did not recede into the night. It pulled into the parking lot below Major Cameron's window. Its lights flashed across the black-out shade and then went off.

Stunned, she heard the jeep motor sputter. A metal door squealed open. She had to get out of here before someone found her. She closed the folder and returned it to the drawer, frantically hoping that in the dark she hadn't left it too far from its rightful place. She shut the drawer, twisted the combination lock and grabbed up the photo and Champ telegram from the desk. One silent dash allowed her to roll up Cameron's shade before she heard a door open at the end of the hall.

Taking the photo and telegram with her, she hurried into her father's office. There stood a small, wooden coat locker near his washstand. She had fit into it when she was a child. It would have to do for now. Laura squeezed into the cramped locker and tried to pull the door shut. Her shoulder wouldn't allow it to close completely.

In the hall, someone opened and closed several doors, drawing nearer. In what Laura felt certain was her own office, he spent a long time before retreating to the hall. Laura knew he would shortly arrive at this room. Her throat still hurt from crying. After wiping at her puffy eyes, she had to regrab the inner door handle of the inadequate coat locker.

In Bernard's office, she heard a file drawer being opened, then later shut. A methodical thief, she thought. He'll come here next and I've only the knife. Of all the days to leave the gun.

Bernard's door opened and re-shut. As she held her breath, her father's office door opened. She heard the scriff of gabardine cloth as someone moved into the room. The thin beam of a flashlight played across the window and the wall. Through the opening in the closet, she could barely make out the back of a man. He wore a heavy jacket, not army issue. A Balaclava cap with its facemask hugged his head.

It has to be that guy from the woods. Arrogant, gutsy, aggravating!

The man opened the combination lock with ease. It occurred to Laura that he must have known her own file combination.

That's why he spent so long in my office. But I've told no one my combination, not even Colonel Johnson.

Looking only in the top drawer, the man worked as though he knew these files well. Laura could hear his fingers flip over the folders, stopping a few times to look within.

With my revolver I could have him red-handed. Instead, I'm about to be trapped.

Her nose tickled. Wiggling it to keep from sneezing, she felt sure he could hear every move she made. Once, he pulled out a folder, glanced in her direction and then turned toward the window. He played the flashlight over the contents of the file. The facemask covered even his eyebrows, so she couldn't be sure it was the same man. His eyes were barely visible. He held the papers very close to his face as if he were having difficulty reading them.

After a moment, he plopped the folder back in place and let the drawer roll shut. The man stepped out of sight toward the door, allowing his flashlight beam to wander around the room. It seemed to Laura that he played the light twice over the closet. Sure he had found her hiding place, she stiffened for that moment when he would yank open the door and pull her out onto the floor, a barn mouse cornered by the cat.

Instead, he softly turned the handle of her father's office door and went into the hall. She let out a long, slow breath and waited. The belief that he waited for her to make a stupid mistake kept her tense as he checked Major Cameron's files next door. Once, she thought she heard him groan and then swear. An abrupt bang announced the closing of Cameron's file drawer. The man exited into the hall. He hurried toward the stairwell and down to the entrance door.

Laura knocked her head on the top of the coat closet as she dragged her tight and painful muscles out of the small space. She ran to the window to get a glimpse into the parking lot, arriving just in time to see the short man jump into a U.S. Army jeep. The area was dark. She couldn't see any identifying marks on the vehicle. He revved the engine and pulled out without ever removing his Balaclava. With sinking hopes, she watched the jeep turn left toward the heavily populated barracks area. Now it would be impossible to find out who the intruder might be.

She realized that he'd been looking in the same drawer where she'd started – the drawer where 'Beau' would be. And 'Beau' led her to 'Lenses'. And in her father's files 'Lenses' gave her the combination for Cameron's files where she'd found 'Champ' and James's own file.

Laura opened that drawer in her father's files where the intruder had been. Sure enough, toward the back of the drawer, a file had been unsuccessfully crammed among its fellows, above the rest by a good quarter inch. Expecting it to be the 'Beau' file, Laura pulled it out, leaving the one behind it raised so that in the dark she could replace it properly. The folder felt too full to be what she'd thought. As she turned it into the low light at the window, she saw that the title contained the words 'Verheerung Anrichten'.

"To cause Verheerung, catastrophe," she whispered the translation. Inside the file every page had been typed in German. At the top of the first page she saw a penciled note, again in her father's distinctive script. "from J.B. Vital!"

That guy in the Balaclava was on an entirely different trail through these file cabinets, she thought. But J.B. could be this fellow Jacques Champ. And Verheerung, vital . . . She stopped all motion, thinking, This! This is why they killed Dad. Why else would that man appear tonight, so soon after the deaths in the mountain?

"There's no other way to know," Laura said to herself. Carefully, she removed all the papers from the file onto the desk. She grabbed clean papers from next to the typewriter and stuffed them into the 'Verheerung' folder before placing it back into the drawer as even with its brothers as she could make it in the darkened room.

Afraid, distrustful of every noise, Laura pushed the Verheerung papers, the photograph of James and the mysterious telegram about the caves at Lascaux into a nearby mailing envelope. She slipped out into the hall and worked her way past the sleeping Merle to the exit in the back of the building. She pulled her knife from her purse in case the stranger waited in the woods.

I should have used it on him this morning, she told herself, but she'd had her chance and blown it.

Whipped by cool air and isolation, Laura ran across a grassy field and into the woods where her jeep waited. As she lay the envelope on the car seat, she elbowed the lock down on the door and started the motor. She blew out a breath of relief, glad to get out without running into the man in the plaid scarf and leather jacket.

Glancing at the envelope, Laura thanked God her father had insisted, for the sake of their European skiing friends, that she become fluent in both French and German as she grew up.

You were right father, for all our sakes.

She'd have to translate quickly. No telling how often this file could be referred to. She would decipher these papers tonight and have them back in the office in the morning. Since it said 'vital', someone besides the intruder could be looking for it at any time.

CHAPTER SIX

SATURDAY MORNING, MARCH 7TH

Sleep had become impossible. Laura stood at her bedroom window and watched the false dawn. When the eastern sky turned metal-silver, she dropped her embroidered linen curtain and faced the papers once more. The 'Verheerung anrichten' reports were spread over her bedroom floor where she'd read through the night.

Her father died because he knew too much. Now, she also had seen the papers, the Organization at work. *Verheerung anrichten* was a frightening scheme – an ingenious way to throw U.S. planning into turmoil. According to one report:

> *'Verheerung agents are well-placed and already sabotage industries. February 13: They have blown up one dock at the San Diego shipyard. Five times in the last three weeks they've successfully disrupted train transport along the East Coast.*
>
> *February 12, 18, 21 and 25: incited riots between Navy personnel and civilians in both Baltimore and San Diego.*

January and February: infiltrated the United States Marines warehousing and transport system on seven occasions, diverting arms shipments as well as foodstuffs and winter survival equipment to an unknown destination.'

Laura's throat tightened. She'd read about some of these incidents in local newspapers, reported as if they were totally unrelated to each other. Even the press had not seen a pattern. Anxious to know as much as possible, Laura reread the reports.

'The Verheerung organization provides financing for the Bundist-Nazi agents in North American radio and news. The Verheerung disrupt and usurp our communications systems. They spread distrust and fear, and endanger all citizens by blaming our military and economic disruption on minority groups.'

No trouble finding believers for such lies, Laura thought.

For years, Father Coughlin filled the radio waves with his rabid

anti-Semite tirades. Everywhere on the radio dial, Nazi-aping American Bundists and some German-American societies spent their spittle spouting anger at Jews, Catholics, Negroes, Asians . . .

Recent news broadcasts recounted outbreaks of violence against Japanese Americans since last December's attack on Pearl Harbor. Three weeks back, the President signed Executive Order 9066 forcing the relocation of all with Japanese ancestry away from the coasts.

Laura bit her lip. "Hatred is already dividing us."

According to the mass of papers on her floor, Nazi-controlled hate mongers in newspapers and radio practiced two types of attack. Some agents roused racial hatreds. Others attempted to lull the population into believing Hitler their friend. The editor of a New York newspaper for German-born citizens extolled the virtues and "passionately peaceful" nature of Hitler's plans for the future of all Germans in the world.

One frightening fact stuck in Laura's mind: the energetic editor of that small newspaper presently negotiated to buy several prominent English-language news companies on the East Coast.

"Where did he get the money for such a bid?" she asked herself, and then she found a possible answer. According to J.B.'s report, the *Verheerung anrichten* had a new central control located somewhere outside of Toronto, Canada – an unknown man, apparently enjoying the financial support and confidence of Hitler and the Nazi Party. This man directed spies in Canada and kept close contact with the network leader in the United States.

Her father's informant, the mysterious 'J.B.', had discovered *Verheerung* in November, 1941. From their correspondence, Laura deduced that J.B. and her father had been warning key generals in the armed services. They tried to convince them that the organization's agents were poised, waiting for the signal to gear up to higher levels of activity. For the most part, it appeared that their warnings had been brushed aside, ignored.

The only man who seemed to take their message seriously was an American diplomat who cabled them from Switzerland, a man named Allen Dulles. His cable lay in her lap.

> *'Your man correct. U.S. Verheerung answers to Werner Arndt since early February, 1942. Arndt a central figure, Europe network since '33.'*

Laura's hand shook as she lifted the cable. *Arndt.* The very name sent black clouds across her vision. *Not grief,* she told herself. Rage.

Arndt has been doing this for a very long time. Nineteen thirty-three . . .

An unwelcome realization hit Laura.

James! Did James help set up Verheerung before he died?

Sick to her stomach, Laura admitted a possibility.

My letters – were my childhood letters to James just another way for Arndt to learn about Dad?

Arndt might have read and laughed at them.

"James wouldn't," she said firmly. "He couldn't have."

Trying to put such thoughts behind her, Laura knelt over the papers, picking up the transcribed Verheerung messages in chronological order, getting them ready to take back to her father's file cabinet. One paper felt stiff. As she handled it, she realized it was two papers stuck together. When she pried the two apart, some of the face of the second was destroyed, but most of the writing was still readable. Her father's Spencerian script.

> *'December 3, 1941, news from J.B. Hess, Rudolf: Left Germany, May 1941. Tracked through Denmark. Hess expert aviator, flying Messerschmidt with number 1545-VJOQ. Man caught in Scotland imposter. Claims birth in 1899. Real date 1894. Did not recognize photograph of own son. Appears to be Hess, but flies airplane without Hess's skill. Couldn't even figure out how to avoid radar across North Sea. Plane which crashed in Scotland was Messerschmidt, number 1545-NJC11. What happened to VJOQ? Who is the man in the British jail? Where is Hess?'*

Farther down the page, in pencil instead of ink was another note in her father's script.

> *Small plane landed in a field in Iceland, May 1941. Flyer stole fuel from barn. Farmer gave chase, was shot, wounded.*

German-made bullets retrieved by doctor. Flight took off toward west. Not able to track, flew too low for radar.

Laura sat very still, re-reading the note and thinking.

Dad said 'Hess, Rudolf Hess'. I thought Dad was losing his mind. Yet, everything he said to me made some kind of sense — except that part about warning James . . .

Not a muscle in her body moved. She let hope steal over her for a moment, let it slide between her fingers and into her pores, let it expand her heart for long seconds before she clamped down on it. Banished it.

No! James died of injuries from a fall down stairs.

The very incongruity of it, the absurdity of a skilled mountain climber falling down stairs made it believable. Laura yanked the reins of her mind back into practical thoughts.

Who was the man in the Balaclava last night? He knew this file existed.

If he was an agent of Verheerung, why didn't he take this?

"And this character J.B.", she whispered, "Is he merely another informant?"

Laura hugged the papers to her, trying to stop the shaking brought on by fatigue and fear. She adjusted her heart to encompass an abrupt shift in the Truth of her life. Her father had been more than a military general working with mountain troops. On reading J.B.'s reports, it became clear that Arthur Atweiler had also run a network of spies in Europe since long before the war. She had never known this second life.

How had she missed that through all the years? Even as Colonel Johnson's secretary she should have seen some hint of this other activity. Nothing had crossed her desk even smelling like military intelligence operations. She had been aware of General Atweiler's deepening levels of anxiety, but unaware of the cause. Yet, her father's strong fear of the *Verheerung anrichten* organization was clear from his marginal notes in the reports.

'Pray God J.B. finds what we need to stop this.'

She imagined the dangers J.B. faced to dig out this information. How desperately he'd struggled to prove to a deaf government, to Army Intelligence and recently to the Central Office of Intelligence that Verheerung was at work.

Between November 1941 and February 1942, J.B. disclosed the identities of more than two hundred Verheerung agents in the United States. Laura had copied those names and their stations.

J.B.'s most recent coded radio message had been transcribed as,

'I can now discredit Muscles with Nazi high command. Show you proof. Arrange time. Usual place.'

"Who the Devil is Muscles?" a frustrated Laura asked the absent J.B. "And where is `the usual place' Dad would have met you?"

Next to J.B.'s statement, her father had written jubilantly.

"With this discovery, the Verheerung network will be destroyed."

The un-named discovery seemed to be the last wireless telegraph communication from J.B. It was dated February 15, 1942 – three weeks before her father was killed.

Did Arndt wrench the proof back from Dad on Longs Peak?

Bastard! Is that what Dad told when you tortured him?

Torture!

Determined not to give in to the terrible pictures in her memory, Laura worked with efficient speed, replacing Verheerung papers in the innocuous looking envelope. Her short-hand notes and her handwritten copy of the puzzling telegram from the *Champ* file went into a smaller envelope. She hid the smaller envelope among her ski sweaters. This morning, she would return the Verheerung files to her father's office. She'd have to get the mysterious telegram back into Cameron's *Champ* file when he was not working. She was so far unable to decipher it, yet Laura felt an inexplicable urgency whenever she studied it.

With great care, Laura set the new photo of James on her highboy chest of drawers. Next to it stood a photo, taken by her father, of James and her eight-year-old self. In the photo, sixteen-year old James was teaching her to skate on the ice at Little Lake. Near that photo stood a portrait of her father and Gregory Banks a picture taken with her Kodak Brownie Box the previous summer at their camp in the canyon on Longs Peak.

She stared at the three photos, people she loved, all at a high moment in life, all now dead.

Never forget. Never, she keened. Arndt tortured Dad!

She wanted to cry, but couldn't. Ice seemed to have formed over her emotions, rendering her capable only of concentrating on the task.

Find Arndt. Revenge the murders.

Stop *Verheerung Anrichten*. Stop the Verheerung.

*   *

SATURDAY MORNING, MARCH 7TH

Laura walked purposefully down the stairs, ready to leave for the office.

As she grabbed for her coat, the doorbell rang. She nearly dropped the envelope of papers. Six in the morning. A rush of hope made her believe Vibes or Major Cameron had already decided to search for the General and his men.

Swiftly she hid the envelope under a hatbox in the coat closet, and tried to calm her nerves before she strode toward the oak front door. She gained a moment's grace by leaning her head on the wooden doorframe. Breathing deeply, Laura straightened her back, squared herself and twisted the heavy brass handle.

Facing her stood a dark-haired man in civilian clothes. His brown eyes gazed back at her and blinked as if he were equally surprised with what he'd found on the other side of her door. Neither of them spoke for a moment, she assessing him as he assessed her.

He appeared to be only about two inches taller than she, but because of the power in his shoulders and his long arms, he appeared much bigger.

His arms hung loosely at his sides, but something about the tense way he stood reminded her of Tom Mix in the moving pictures – ready to go for a gun at the slightest provocation. His gray and brown beard almost succeeded in camouflaging a jagged white scar that began next to his right eye and continued down his jaw line onto his throat. Streaks of gray in his beard followed the scar.

That cut must have come close to killing him, she thought.

He must have seen her eyes follow the scar. His full mouth tightened into a hard line and his chin jutted out before he broke the silence.

"Miss Laura Atweiler?" At the low sound of his voice, a quick memory of the man in the woods came to her. She held the door ready to close swiftly, but he made no move to barge in, and something about his wide brown eyes made her want to know why he was here.

"I'm Miss Atweiler. Who are you?"

He had his billfold at hand, anticipating the question. "Agent Ian McKay," he said crisply, flipping it open to an official looking identification card. "From COI. Donovan sent me. I'm sorry to bother you on a Saturday morning, but this is urgent. May I come in?"

Laura didn't answer him. She snaked her hand out the door and grabbed his proffered billfold. "Wait here," she said, closing and locking the door between them. Inside the house, she placed a telephone call to Washington, D.C., the new Central Office of Intelligence. When she finally reached the agency, she questioned several people before she found a secretary with authority to divulge any of the agency's hard-earned intelligence.

"I have a man at my door," Laura began, "He claims to be one of your sleuths named Ian McKay. Do you have such an agent? If so, what does he look like?"

"We *may* have such an agent," said a throaty female voice. "It is against policy to tell you anything about him."

"In that case, I will send him away. I don't deal with mysterious strangers."

"This is government business," the voice became imperious. "You must answer his questions."

"Have you folks read the Bill of Rights lately?" Laura asked, "especially article number four?"

"Oh, but ma'am," the voice rose a few decibels. "He's flown all that way. . ."

Laura took advantage of her upper hand. "Supposing, Miss," she began, "this is purely conjecture, mind you – supposing the real Ian McKay were bumped off enroute to my town and this is his murderer at my door, using his identification."

"Well . . ."

*   *

When Laura reopened the door, Ian McKay lounged against one of the pseudo-Greek posts that held up her porch roof. His eyes narrowed.

"Do I check out?"

"Vivien says you sound like you."

He raised a dark brown eyebrow and whistled. "You got pretty far up the ladder. Points for perseverance. May I come in?"

Laura opened the door wider and stood aside for him. He sauntered in and turned toward the parlor. Two things she noticed right away. He had a slight limp, and he knew the correct direction to the parlor.

McKay brought himself up short of the parlor door and looked back at her, explaining, "I used to work under General Arthur Atweiler. I knew your father and your house, but you must have been away at school."

Possible. She had been in Greeley at the Normal School for two years before the war.

He filled in the blanks, "1938 and '39." She nodded. "I was gone then."

He opened the parlor door and stood aside for her. As she passed him, she glanced up and saw a small encouraging smile, the type used as you lead a lamb to slaughter. Suddenly alert, she remembered McKay's past tense reference to her father.

"You *knew* my dad?"

"Haven't seen him for a while, Miss Atweiler. I've been in Europe mostly, since the Germans invaded Poland." After a moment, he said curtly, "Laura, sit down."

She stopped short, heard him bite off his phrase as if aware that he'd been too familiar. Faced off, they engaged in a silent battle of wills – he, very quietly waiting for her to comply, she equally determined to assert herself. To this stranger, she should remain "Miss Atweiler". Furthermore, she was certainly not a sweet little woman whom anybody ordered to "sit down" before launching into an interrogation.

He broke off the stubborn engagement and outflanked her with gentlemanly manners. "Miss Atweiler, I need to sit down, at any rate."

Remembering his limp, she nodded. He sighed and took one of the overstuffed chairs that stood between the fireplace and the child's rocker. In the rocker sat her watchful old Teddy Bear.

"Do you mind?" McKay asked, gesturing that she also sit.

"I don't," she said, yet she sank slowly into the matching chair. He watched her, his face a mask except for the lowering of thick lashes as his gaze followed her motion. When she settled back, he seemed to breathe again.

"Miss Atweiler, COI sent me because our communication with your father has been cut off since last Sunday. I myself tried to reach him from . . . from Europe. Others have been trying since then – I became concerned."

Laura's face grew hot with a flood of loneliness and anger. Avoiding his gaze, she glanced toward the unlit fire, trying to decide how much to tell him. Horrible memories weighed her down. Her discovery of the Nazi spy network had given her an enormous responsibility. She wanted to dump her fears and worries on someone, but she couldn't take the chance. She'd never heard of Ian McKay. He knew her father. He knew her house. But she didn't know him.

Laura decided to play ignorant yet concerned. "I'm worried, Mr. McKay. Dad normally meets me for an outing on Tuesdays, or he notifies me if that's not possible. Last Tuesday, he wasn't there."

"There being where . . .?" McKay absently stretched out his arm and touched the head of her old Teddy Bear.

"Last Tuesday we were to meet in the little town of Manitou," she said. "Dad likes to ski cross-country there."

Ian McKay's face seemed to stiffen. Then he glanced toward the worn bear in the rocker. Laura thought the bear's presence seemed to reassure him. Once again, she thought of the man in the wood yesterday. McKay's voice seemed similar. His eyes the same dark brown. And the way his tension relaxed around his eyes reminded her of that moment in the woods when he pulled her to his chest. She grew certain he was the same man.

And she grew more reluctant to tell him the truth.

Caressing Teddy's soft ear, he asked, "When your father didn't show up, what did you do?"

She thought fast. He might know some of her actions already, but she believed no one knew she'd gone to Longs Peak. She would have to mix the truth and a lie with care so that he believed it all.

"I waited in Manitou," she said, "thinking Dad had been delayed. I drove home, and Wednesday morning I asked Vibes – I mean Robert Nelson, our communications specialist, to radio Dad. He got no reply. Since Colonel Johnson, my boss, was away in Denver and I had some vacation days coming, I went back to Manitou on Wednesday and Thursday to look for him."

Laura hoped he would believe her account of where she'd been Wednesday and Thursday. She would not tell him she'd spoken with her father as he died. Laura shook with weariness and with the desire to spill out the truth. But she couldn't do it.

Maybe the COI secretary thought Agent McKay was one of Wild Bill Donovan's top people, but Laura couldn't trust him. Her father had never mentioned working with him. She had yet to digest the fact that there could be many things her father never told her. Perhaps her father had a connection with the Central Office of Intelligence.

Did Dad trust this man?

Or is McKay apt to pull crazy stunts? she wondered.

She remembered Bernard Johnson's tales of COI agents taking unnecessary risks. She refused to trust McKay with information that might endanger her life – not before she caught Arndt.

"You came back here Thursday night?" he pursued.

Laura swallowed hard, deliberately making herself resent his touching her stuffed bear. She wanted to be angry enough not to cry.

"Thursday night I came home, hoping Dad might call here. He didn't call. I went back to work Friday – yesterday."

McKay leaned forward intently, "Did you tell anyone about your concern?"

"Vibes, of course. He tried the camp again but figures they're on maneuvers somewhere. I wish someone would just go look for him – he's never gone this long without a call or radio contact."

McKay's next question came slowly, so slowly that she could almost imagine him puffing on a pipe while he thought about whether to ask it. "Were you aware, Miss Atweiler," he said, gazing directly at her, "of any member of your father's staff who worried him in any way?"

She frowned, still unsure of how much her father would want her to say.

"I understand," he said encouragingly, "that you will not want to name anyone – that you would want your father to handle my questions. But since something seems to have kept your father from communicating with either you or me. Perhaps you could help me by simply telling me if he felt any member of his staff might be untrustworthy."

At last, she nodded. "I don't know who, but he suspected someone. Of what, I have no idea."

"Why aren't Major Cameron or Colonel Johnson more concerned about not hearing from the General?"

"Only Vibes is aware that there hasn't been communication. Colonel Johnson has been at a staff training in Denver since last Saturday – a week ago. Major Cameron just returned from Washington D.C."

"Ah, I see," said McKay as he stood. "I have taken up your time and worried you – unduly, I'm sure. Please accept my apologies."

Laura stood to show him out, wanting to ask, she didn't know what. "Mr. McKay."

He thrust out his hand, offering to shake hers. She took it, found it surprising in its length and warmth. "Miss Atweiler," he said. "I appreciate your help. I will keep you informed as I learn anything."

She was thankful that he asked her no more questions, but also reluctant to have him go. The need to tell someone the truth, to search for help became an ache in her tired body. If she knew him better, she could lay the whole story in his lap and let him decide what to do.

But she didn't know him at all.

*   *

One half-hour later, Laura sat in her office. By seven thirty in the morning, she'd pirated the *Verheerung* papers safely back into her father's file cabinet.

The offices were full of activity by eight a.m.. This might be Saturday, but her father's staff worked overtime preparing for the next recruit training. The base hummed with activity. To anyone looking in, Laura appeared to be hard at work repairing her stubborn Underwood typewriter with a hair pin, but inside, her soul shrank at the mental image of bodies lying in the snow, prey to scavenging animals.

She flipped on the radio beside her desk. On National Broadcasting, Harriet Hilliard sang with Ozzie Nelson's orchestra. Laura tried to hum along, if only to keep herself awake since she'd slept only two hours last night.

Vibes came in at nine-thirty. He reported no luck in raising General Atweiler on the camp radio. He looked upset, but tried to hide his concern.

How ironic, Laura thought. Vibes is probably protecting me from worry.

"I'm sorry, Miss Atweiler," he said, edging toward the door. "I'm sure there's some good explanation. They expect their first recruits for the new training camp in a couple of weeks, so your Dad's probably just up to his ears in things to do."

Laura nodded, numbly aware that she made Vibes nervous.

"I'd go up there myself," he continued. "But I can't very well do that without authorization. Major Cameron and Colonel Johnson are the only ones who can give that."

I understand," she answered. "Let me know as soon as Major Cameron gets in this morning, will you?"

"Yes ma'am."

The truth was, she didn't want to deal with Cameron's penetrating and glass-magnified stare again. Yet, waiting for Monday when Bernard Johnson had been scheduled to come back from the Denver meeting would take too long.

She'd have to face Cameron. When she explained her worry over not hearing from her father, she hoped Cameron would try again to raise the camp by radio. Silence from the broken radio receiver in the cave should alert him that there had to be a problem. Then finally he'd send someone to Longs Peak.

. . . unless Cameron were Arndt's man.

By 8:15 a.m., she decided to go looking for Cameron herself. Laura reached to flick off her radio when a newscaster interrupted the orchestra music.

"This is Walter Winchell bringing news of national importance. The Federal Bureau of Investigations has just announced the arrest of more than twenty Nazi spies in the state of New York. The FBI states that it has been assisted in its investigations by a loyal American immigrant, German-born William Sebold. Sebold, who has actually been working for the FBI, posed as the central figure in this spy ring since late 1939.

"More on this development as we get it. We now return you to the Ozzie Nelson orchestra."

Laura thought. Swell, let's all add to the list of people we can't trust.

Anyone searching for scapegoats to hate, the suspect-citizens list now included those with a German sounding name, a name like

Atweiler. She considered the list of names she'd copied last night, certainly plenty of German surnames, but just as many of Scots, English, French and other origins. J.B. had discovered at least thirty spies in New York alone. Had he gotten his information from Sebold as well? Or had he seen a more thorough list which the Nazis had compiled at their end?

The arrests Walter Winchell announced confirmed J.B.'s assertion that careful infiltration had begun long ago. It also told her that she should send a letter and a copy of her list to the FBI and let them handle the investigations since the COI had done nothing with her father's reports.

Or should she give Agent McKay a copy? She wasn't sure how far to trust the man. The memory of him caressing her Teddy bear unsettled. The memory of his eyes disturbed her more. He had watched her every motion, assessing her, gauging her honesty.

Ozzie Nelson had just struck up Stardust, when a metallic squeak announced that a visitor had opened Laura's office door. Glancing up, Laura saw the dark uniform and the engaging smile of Colonel Bernard Johnson. Relief washed through her at the sight of his friendly face.

"Bernard! You're back early."

"Missed you, Laura. Had to come back."

Bernard looked well, she thought, tanned and rested. He stepped into the office and towered over her desk, peering down at her handiwork. "That typewriter giving you trouble again? You shouldn't have to get all dirty trying to make equipment work properly. That's a job for . . ."

"Buck Rogers?" she joked, a bit flatly. "Except Buck has gone to the Twenty-fifth century and I'm stuck doing the old-fashioned bobby-pin repair."

Bernard realized right away that something more was the matter. "Laura, what happened?"

She tried to stand, but her legs went limp with gratitude. Bernard had become the one in command here now, even though he was, as yet, unaware of it. Her worry spilled out of her in a rush.

"I haven't heard from Dad. It's got me worried, Bernard. He's never missed without some kind of word – a call or a radio message," she said. "Vibes hasn't been able to reach anyone at the camp. He's tried and tried."

Bernard reached over the Underwood and took her hand in his strong fingers. "You must be worried sick, Laura. Come on down the hall with me. We'll get this straightened out."

She let him pull her from the chair. It seemed so good to have someone else take the load that she just about fell into his arms. All the way down the hall, she thought about how good it would be to stop pretending and tell Bernard exactly what had happened.

But as they approached Communications, Laura's relief evaporated. She had held in for so many days already that it had grown difficult to convince herself to trust. Bernard seemed as honest as any man she knew, but since he was, perhaps, more trusting than she, he might not be as careful about guarding her secrets.

By the time they got to Vibes' office, she had refrozen her feelings and locked Bernard Johnson out of them.

CHAPTER SEVEN

SATURDAY, MARCH 7TH

Late that afternoon, Laura paced throughout the house. Her exhausted mind felt like blank fuzz, blank enough to be roaming through her subconscious.

General Purpose vehicles, she thought. Jeeps. How like the army to give the little car a pompous name. And equally like the troops to turn the pompous into something inanely funny.

Her father and his friends died, and four crazy little jeeps now were bouncing up the rutted roads on Longs Peak toward their bodies. Laura's guilt weighed. She wondered how she would face their wives and children. She'd lied to them, left the men lying there for almost two days after she knew they were murdered.

What if their bodies have been mutilated? What if they can't be found?

Laura glanced at her dresser. Atop it sat the file about Jacques Champ which she had stolen again from Cameron's office. He seemed to be Dad's informant about mountains and other going's on in Europe. She'd gone in to get these from the offices this morning, as soon as Cameron and Colonel Johnson left for Longs Peak, but she had no energy to read the papers. Her hands rubbed at her temples. She closed her eyes.

The taut state of her emotions had left her drained. Always playing in the back of her mind ran a jerky movie showing Richard Cameron and Bernard Johnson finding the bodies of her father and the other men.

They would search without success for clues. Then, discouraged and outraged, they would load the bodies into canvas bags and wedge them into the jeeps for the awful ride home.

She couldn't think while this film drummed its insistent funereal rhythm through her brain. She felt as cold as meadow snow. Laura wrapped her arms around herself for warmth. She pushed open her closet and grabbed a warmer shirt, an old boy's flannel shirt, cast off years ago by a growing James. She stuffed the Champ file into an envelope and carried it downstairs to the den in the house she and her father had shared for twenty-five years.

Downstairs, Vandal greeted Laura. The dog lifted his big head and whimpered mournfully. He'd been Gregory Banks sole companion for five years and now the man would never return to scratch his ears and share a tussle. Vandal hadn't enough energy to chew the wraps she used on his paws. Laura tended to his cuts, rebound them and fed him. All the time, she talked softly to him.

"I'm sorry I'm not Uncle Banks. It's not the same without your old friend is it, Vandal?"

In order to keep an eye on the dog, and offer a companionable presence, she lit a fire in the den fireplace. Then she sat down at her father's desk to read the Champ file. Vandal moaned as he put his head on his paws. His eyes followed her every gesture.

"Good boy," she crooned. "You'll get better soon. You'll be running after butterflies next summer when we all go camping –"

Her voice broke as she realized that the 'We' who went camping every summer were dead – save herself and this poor beast. Laura blinked her dry eyes. Now that she had the privacy to cry, she couldn't let go of her control. She'd grown empty. Empty.

She turned back to the Champ papers. At first glance, the bond of the sheets all looked the same, but close examination in this light showed a subtle difference. Flipping through, she saw that several reports looked like they'd been retyped on a different typewriter than the others. The paper felt cheaper. It had no watermark.

The first of the reports on cheap paper seemed nothing more than a chatty letter. Yet, it was an obvious copy of a letter with the date and the original signature removed. As she leafed through the others, she saw that this curious disguise had been practiced on all of the retyped documents.

Someone had hidden the dates and the signatures.

Even the salutations are gone, so you can't tell who received them.

Nothing handwritten appeared on these sheets. Laura wondered if she would have recognized the script style of the original writer.

She read the first report, translating the French with ease.

"While camping near the village of Annecy, I got in a good long- distance ski. Beautiful lake. Hiking by myself above the village, I found Muscles peering into a cave. He didn't see me, though he looked around to make sure no one was near before he went in. I figured Muscles didn't want me to see that he'd found the cave. I thought he probably wanted to use it to scare Kirsten and me, so I pretended not to have been there."

"Muscles," said Laura. "In the Verheerung reports, J.B. called someone Muscles . . . the man whose credibility he planned to ruin."

She read on.

"Later, when Muscles came back to camp, he asked me lots of questions about where I'd been. I gave him to understand that I'd been on the far side of the lake from him. (I had been there the day before, so I knew the terrain quite well.) He seemed to believe me. Wouldn't it be fun if K and I use his secret cave to put the scare into him instead?"

What a childish letter for a colleague of Dad's, Laura mused, turning to the next letter. With growing awareness, through each letter, she felt she was reading about the growth of a teasing boy into a serious human being. As he grew, so grew his ability to be awed by the beauty and power of the world around him. Laura became drawn into that world more and more by Champ's ability to laugh at himself while yet displaying a finely tuned sense of honor and awareness.

Hours later, she grew sure that these were actually copies of James Schoenfeld's letters to her father because some of the incidents in these letters were those James had also mentioned in letters to her. Also, though in his letters to her, he had often referred to Arndt's 'daughter', the letters to her father made it clear that "K" or Kirsten was Arndt's young mistress.

Writing as Jacques Champ to her father, he had been more detailed about climbing tools and techniques. In James's letters to her, he had tended to make light of dangers which he spelled out for her father. He'd been very protective of her naivete – of her childhood.

So, she reasoned, Jacques Champ had been used as a pseudonym for James.

But why, she wondered, did James need a pseudonym? And why did her father insist she search for this file and yet never mentioned the more vital Verheerung report?

Laura decided her father also had been trying to protect her by keeping her ignorant of his intelligence operations. She'd found the

Verheerung report only because of the man who invaded the Admin Building last night. There seems to be no connection between James-Jacques and Verheerung.

Laura tasted the salt of great excitement. A renewed hope welled up.

There was a new possibility. What if her father hadn't been merely delirious? James might be alive. The Verheerung reports could have been written by James who must also be J.B.

Slow down here, Laura, she warned herself.

The reports by J.B. on Verheerung were written by a distrustful man. Even J.B.'s rare display of wit seemed acerbic and double-edged where James or Jacques would have been merely droll. The only common thread between James and J.B. is the reference to the man called Muscles and the climbing.

Another plausible, yet disappointing explanation for the change of character to J.B. occurred to her. Someone else had taken over the Jacques Champ or 'J.B.' identity after James died in 1939.

Once the possibility of life for James had entered her mind a second time, it became shocking, and painful to give up. Yet to capture Arndt and stop Verheerung, she had to be realistic. If James did die, she had to figure out how to recognize the more cynical 'J.B.' who followed in his footsteps.

Discouraged, Laura turned to the last Champ letter from James/Jacques. She gasped as she recognized the story. James's last letter to her, written a few days before he died, had mentioned this adventure. To her, he had written a brief letter, but enclosed two newspaper articles about it from *Paris-Le Monde*.

The story, as written to her father, seemed much more complete.

James had been twenty-nine years old then. The letter's style gave the feeling he'd become a mature man. Its first sentence cleared up the identity of Muscles.

Dear General,

Last Monday, we both nearly died. Werner, (who proved he deserves the nickname Muscles, as you shall see) – Werner and I had just hammered pitons into the rock face near the top of l'Aiguille, the Needle, above Chamonix. We'd put our belay lines through the pitons and tied off, forming a safety rail. Both of us hooked our waist harnesses to the line, preparing to bivouac for the night on the ledge we had found. Our ledge was the top of a separate, tall pedestal connected to the main vertical pillar at several key points.

You can see that we were following your first law of climbing, General. "Plan for the worst so the worst can never happen."

While getting ready to hook in my climbing tools and extra boots, I leaned far out over the rock ledge. Below me, the sheer wall of The Needle shown gold in the late afternoon sun. The shadows from the low light emphasized the striations of l'Aiguille's vertical blocks. It was an awesome sight – the power of rock to stand against wind and rain for millennia. I said a prayer to the god of rock, the most permanent thing I knew.

Your nonchalant buddy, Werner leaned back and smoked a Gaulois, gazing out over the view. I had begun to reel in my climbing tools so that I could untie them from my belt and hook them to the belay line for the night. Suddenly our ledge and the column of rock which for centuries had held it up, collapsed – rock plunging down two thousand feet of vertical drop in a few seconds. My body plunged sickeningly and then hit the end of my short rope, bouncing back and throwing me hard into the pillar wall.

I tensed for the death I knew was coming. Our sudden weight would rip the pitons from the rock face above us, hurtling the two of us onto the boulders hundreds of feet below.

I was suspended only by the harness at my middle. Twisting violently in the cool air, I breathed in a fine rock dust — the very rocks on which moments before, I had sat. I knew the pitons could not hold against this strain.

A tremendous thunder echoed up at me long after the boulders had settled at the bottom of the Needle. The sound had to have carried clear to the village. In those first moments of sheer terror, I couldn't remember if Werner had clipped his harness into the safety rail. I imagined him already down there, buried under the newly fallen rock.

Stunned. Tons of granite had chosen that moment to break away from this ancient up thrust. I had leaned out, and that slight shift of a few pounds nearly brought my life to an end.

I might still be brought to a slow and tortured death if I couldn't manage to stop twisting in the cold evening breeze and use my hard-won skills to save myself.

I glanced left and, to my relief, saw that Werner was hanging as I was. Like two pigs at the butcher shop, we were.

"Look at the pitons, boy," he growled. "Are they holding?" (I am always a boy to his giant self.)

It was quite a strain to turn my head far enough so that I could see the pitons. I did it slowly. I didn't want to jerk one of them out. I can't tell you, sir, how much more slowly I twisted back.

And by then, I was praying to the ephemeral god of fragile metal. "They're holding," I answered him, "but mine is bent down."

General, I bet you've seen Werner swear so quietly that large men will back away. Well, sir, he chose that moment to employ his considerable verbal abilities. At the same time, he reeled in his ice pick which was still hanging from his harness and reached carefully into his pockets for more pitons.

Then with his usual arrogance, he ordered, "Get your pick ready, boy. We're going to get you out of this."

I looked down. A Miracle. My pick was still attached to my harness by its thin leather thong. Beyond the pick, the fallen rock still seemed golden.

Laura read on, fascinated by the determination of Werner Arndt and James Schoenfeld. Through a sub-zero night and the morning hours of the next day Werner and James worked together, employing all their skill, a single one hundred-foot rope and the few tools which had not fallen with the rock ledge.

Toward the end, on the last precarious descent of about eighty feet, James went down first while Werner sat above, paying out the safety rope.

James wrote, "Without even a cry, he dropped me thirty feet. I thought he'd lost his bracing and was falling from above me. I don't remember feeling fear. I only remember thinking 'what a shame to die now that we've accomplished so much together.'"

Suddenly, I jerked to a stop. A few rocks tumbled down, one hitting me on the shoulder. I went numb for a few seconds. The pain when it came was great, but when I recovered a bit, I could hear voices below me.

Hanging there, trying to get oriented, I looked up. Werner was still sitting, still braced as he had been. I couldn't figure out what had gone wrong.

I looked down and saw twenty to thirty people about fifty feet below me. They must have been there for some time, but neither of us had seen them, so intent were we on survival. The people from the village must have heard the rock-fall the night before. They'd come to see and stayed to pray.

At this point, in the margin of the story, a note in crabbed handwriting said.

'Get over there, sir, before it's too late.'

Laura read the section near this comment again, and could not see what caused the reader to urge her father toward Europe. Did he sense that James was truly about to die? Who wrote that marginal note?

Far from unraveling the puzzle, she continued reading James's story.

I hung there, looking for a perch from which to belay Werner. In another few feet, when I found the right ledge, I climbed into it.

'Ready." I signaled him. I couldn't see him, but I could hear him as he doubled our rope through his karabiner, looped it around his body and prepared to come down to me.

When Werner climbed into the new ledge, he said nothing about having dropped me, just showed me his ripped gloves and asked, "Where'd all these circus spectators come from?"

Without waiting for an answer, he set about getting himself ready to let me down the last fifty feet.

By noon of that second day, we belayed each other down the sheer wall of the pinnacle and into the waiting arms of the towns' people and the French press. Our progress since sunrise had been watched with binoculars and cameras. The newspapers and radio stations had decided to make both of us into heroes.

Heroes they were. It was a tale of friendship and courage which all of Europe would read. James's version of the story was told with gripping horror tempered by a humorous view of the two of them as ants in the overall scheme of the universe. While reading it, Laura alternated between sweating terror and soft laughter.

At the end of the letter, her father had written, 'Will this blind him with debt? Can we still trust him when the time comes?'

Laura frowned at her father's question. In contrast to the boy of the first letter, the Jacques Champ or James who had written this last story was mature, a man in spite of Arndt's diminutive 'Knabe' nickname for him. James had clung to any chance to continue living. As he put it, "I wanted to finish playing my bit part in the earthly comedy."

James did not take himself too seriously, but he did view with great sobriety his obligation to save his friend Arndt.

"Trust him," Laura heard herself say aloud. Yes, she was sure of it, "Trust him."

At that moment, Vandal whined, making Laura jump. The doorbell rang.

"Hush boy, I'll get it."

She didn't want anyone to know Vandal was here – at least not anyone who knew he'd gone to Longs Peak with Gregory Banks. Laura shoved the Champ papers into the desk and closed the den door before she hurried to answer the second ring.

She had dreaded this moment from the first.

CHAPTER EIGHT

Her visitor would be Bernard Johnson, nervous and concerned. He would come, looking very grave, and tell her everything she already knew. Her father and his friends had been found dead. Or maybe he would avoid telling her everything in an effort to spare her the worst; she would have to go on pretending she hadn't memorized the minute details of that ice-cold tableau.

Laura braced herself to answer the door and the reality. She grasped the brass knob and pulled.

Lounging against her pillar stood Agent Ian McKay. He had one hand up, holding his identification card. A crooked smile played across his face.

"Want this again?" he asked, wagging the I.D. card. "Once is enough," she said.

"You were hoping for better company," he commented. "Not better. Different. What can I do for you Mr. McKay?"

He shrugged as if he had no idea what he wanted. "How about letting me in?"

"Is there a reason for this visit?"

He pushed back on his short hair, as if it were in his eyes, and then smiled at her. "There are several reasons, Miss Atweiler. The most important one is that there seemed to be a lot of activity at the base around nine o'clock this morning and most of it ended up heading north. I thought maybe you could tell me about that."

Laura looked away from his questioning eyes. The jerky movie of death played through her mind again.

"Miss Atweiler?" Ian stepped toward her.

Instinct made her back away from him, but she saw that his face registered only concern for her.

"What is it?" he asked.

She grabbed at the doorframe for support and pretended to be just fine. "Why don't you come in, Mr. McKay? We can talk in the parlor."

This time he followed her, though she knew from this morning's visit that he could have found it himself. She gestured him to the chair he'd used earlier, but she went to stand at the mantel.

*   *

Ian McKay didn't like the pallor of Laura's skin or the wary look she gave him. He knew she'd been up all of Friday night. He'd seen the light in her room. Eleven on Saturday night and still awake. She had to be fatigued, frightened and waiting for word from the camp – in no shape to be interrogated. Yet in just this fragile condition he would most likely to break her down. He must find out just how much she knew.

What had her father told her?

How close had she come to the danger James Schoenfeld had brought on them all?

He watched her lean against the mantel. It hit her across the middle of her shoulder blades, pushing her breasts tight against the faded boy-shirt. He wondered if she wore that old shirt whenever she needed comfort.

Her worn corduroy pants lay flat against her abdomen and then hung straight almost to the floor. She'd once rolled the cuffs to fit her length, but the left one had unrolled, almost hiding her toes. He hadn't expected her small body to make him feel so aware. If he'd thought this would happen, he might have sent someone else to talk to her. Now that he'd seen her himself, he'd be damned if he'd let any other man interrogate her.

She moved restively. He had to start the unpleasant business. "What's happening at the base?" He tried to keep his voice non-threatening.

"Colonel Johnson came back early," she said. "– this morning in fact. I told him I was worried about Dad. Johnson tried to get the camp on the radio. He couldn't . . ."

She turned abruptly, seeming to push away the sudden urge to cry.

McKay's eyes narrowed as he watched her wander the length of the fireplace. After a moment, she stopped. She must have thought to avoid his scrutiny by keeping her back to him. However, using the mirror, he kept his gaze on the tell-tale color which tension brought to her cheeks. She began talking again, her voice brittle. All the while, she rearranged her mother's porcelain ladies.

"Johnson couldn't raise them by radio," she said, "so he took several men up to Longs Peak to see what's going on."

"Johnson went to Longs Peak?" he asked gently.

Ian saw that she realized her error at once. She shouldn't have known where they'd gone. She glanced up and found him watching her in the mirror. Mutely, Laura nodded.

"How long does it take to get up there?" he asked.

She hesitated. He hoped she would consider telling him the rest of the truth. Instead, she looked at the breakable dolls and evaded. "Depends on what part of the mountain the camp is on," she said. "It's a big mountain."

His jaw tightened with frustration. "Which officers know the camp location?"

She seemed to weigh the propriety of telling him. To his relief, she said, "Bernard . . . that's Colonel Johnson – he seems to know. Major Cameron and Vibes Nelson are the ones down here who probably know. Up there, there were eight men, including Dad."

He noticed the past tense, but decided not to push her, yet. "Did you know the location?"

"Dad never told me," she said.

Another evasion, he thought.

"When I worked with him, your father took me to a summer camp in a box canyon on Longs Peak. Have you been there?"

She crumpled. Across the room, he could hear the air rush from her lungs. Her head went down to her hands on the mantle, one hand grabbing onto a doll for support.

McKay's concern brought him out of his chair and across the room.

*   *

Feeling him suddenly so close behind her, Laura flinched, but stood still, her hand ready on the heaviest statue. He never touched her, but regarded her reflection in the mantle-mirror. His gaze pierced her thin armor. Laura couldn't take her eyes away from his dark visage.

Understanding – too much understanding, as if he were reading her thoughts merely by looking at her.

Agony. She was afraid – afraid of him, afraid of herself for wanting to confide in him. In the mirror, she felt him hypnotizing her, pulling her into the depths of his mind. She was too anguished to resist.

He knows, she thought. How can he know that unless he was there himself?

Looking at her own reflection, she saw what he saw. Sleepless nights had left her skin even more pale than usual, her black curls lay about her face and shoulders in unkempt wildness, her dark eyes were fully dilated– the picture of a distracted, overwrought woman on the edge of hysteria.

He couldn't know she'd been there. He just had to look at her to know she was about to fall apart. She had to get ahold of herself, or she would tell the wrong person too much.

The truth was she knew too much and yet not enough. She presented a danger to Arndt, but, in her state of ignorance, she was an even greater danger to herself. She needed more information.

She needed rest.

Seeing what she believed might be compassion in McKay's gaze, Laura felt the urge to let this man take the burden of the search from her, so that she could let out her grief. Perhaps if she told McKay . . .

The doorbell rang.

"Colonel Johnson," she whispered, noticing McKay's startled reaction. He glanced at the lace-curtained window, then back at her reflection, his expression unreadable.

"I want to talk to you again," he said. "Can you keep him out of here?"

"Out of the parlor? Yes," she replied. "But it's just Colonel Johnson. Why can't you be seen by him?"

"At this stage of the investigation, the fewer people who know what I am, the better." He seemed taut, wary. Moments ago, she'd been sure he had been leaning toward her, overpowering her resolve with his own.

She took a deep, relieved breath. "I'll take Bernard into the kitchen."

She figured it might seem disrespectful to take one's boss into the kitchen, but it was the only place left.

"How about the den?" McKay asked. "Wouldn't that seem more natural?"

Not in the den with Vandal, she thought.

But she said, "The kitchen is more natural this time of night, since I'll be making dinner." She moved on sluggish legs toward the parlor door as the doorbell chimed once more.

Behind her, McKay's gentle voice asked, "Laura, what do you know about Verheerung?"

Shaken to the core, Laura halted, and then without looking at him, continued toward the door, groping for a sufficiently evasive line. "Verheerung?" she said, "War creates Verheerung. If any more secretive strangers come into my life, it too will be in Verheerung."

Under control at last, she turned back to face him. "If you must hide behind my curtains, keep your boots out of sight and do beware of the mirror."

He gave her a slow smile and stepped away from the mantle.

This time it took several deep breaths to steady her nerves. In the den behind her, she heard Vandal growl deep in his throat, then whine and thump his tail.

"Quiet." She ordered, hoping Mr. McKay thought she ordered him. She waited another few seconds. When she felt stronger, she opened the door to Bernard Johnson and the news he brought. She'd been right; Bernard was tense. He was also slow in getting to the point.

"Where's Dad?"

"Let's go inside, Laura."

"Bernard . . ."

"Laura, I want to talk to you inside."

He startled her by taking her arm in a tight grip and pushing her inside. He refused to say anything more until they were in the kitchen. Laura gestured him to a chair in the breakfast nook while she pretended to create biscuits and beef gravy, the only supper she could make without thinking.

Bernard avoided the central issue. He also avoided looking at her directly, recounting how he, Major Cameron and several junior officers drove over miles of unfinished roads, how they hiked the last few miles and found a box canyon. She knew he was coming to the deaths, but she grew afraid of how she would react when he actually told her. He must have seen that she tensed for it.

"Laura, please sit down."

She did. He took her hand. Though his hand still felt cold from the outdoors, she left her hand in his. She figured it would be easier for him to tell her about it if he held onto her.

"Laura, we found your father and his men. They've all been murdered."

Unexpectedly, her body jerked upright. Her hand, which had been in his, went instinctively to her throat. At last. Bernard's saying it made the whole nightmare solid. She felt she'd been alone in a dream since the moment she stepped into the meadow and saw the bodies. But now, they were in a nightmare.

She felt empty. Cold.

"I'm sorry, Laura. I have no idea why this happened – no idea." Bernard leaned toward her, his attempt at gentleness going somehow awry as his big hand firmly took her chin and forced Laura to face him. "I don't know what to say," he said in a harsh whisper. "I feel responsible somehow. I should have had a guard up there, some kind of watch."

Laura found her voice. "Murdered? How?"

He pulled her hands together in front of him. "Most of the men were shot. Garand Rifles I think – you know, those M1's we started training with last summer."

"My father?"

His glance met hers for an instant, but he evaded. "He died, too."

Laura watched Bernard with pity. He'd never be able to tell her what he'd found. She felt guilty for putting him through this charade, for even having to send him up there to see that sight in the first place. At thirty, he was so young compared to the other officers. He'd never even fought in a war, never seen death as final reality.

"Where?" she asked. "I can't tell you that."

"Oh, of course," she said. "I meant where is his body?"

He glanced at his big hands and gathered himself to say what he should. "Cameron and the men are bringing them into the base. I'm supposed to bring you with me. I have to talk to the wives."

He stood and fiddled with his service cap for a moment, finally slapping it against his thigh, he said tightly, "Laura. I'm sorry. This should never have happened. I can't figure it out. I can't …"

Laura rose from the kitchen table and laid a hand on his arm. "It's all part of the Verheerung war wreaks on us, Bernard. You couldn't have foreseen it."

His head jerked up and he stared blankly at her as if he couldn't focus on the image she presented. "Laura. How do you … How can you be so calm?"

She felt anything but calm. She ached inside, a pain ran across her back and another seemed to strangle her. With enormous effort, she excused herself. "Eat the biscuits, Bernard. I have to get my coat. Wait here."

She walked swiftly across the hall to the den. The need to get away from his sorrowful eyes became overwhelming. She closed the den door, heard a moan start deep inside her and grabbed at a nearby bookcase for support. Instead, her arm collided with the chest of a man. Unbelieving, she looked into the liquid brown eyes of Ian McKay and let him fold her in his embrace.

"You have to cry, Laura," he whispered into her ear. "Don't hold back."

She almost let him take over. Her body sagged against his strength for a moment. His arms surrounded her, one hand pulling her head to his shoulder. She felt his mouth push into her hair, and she actually sobbed with relief. She needed his strength, needed him to surround her with warmth. She rested against his solid power for several foolish moments before she regained self-control.

He was a stranger – a stranger with the ability to make her drop her instinctive barriers. Laura pushed away from him.

"How did you get in here?" she whispered.

He stiffened. Holding her at arm's length, he answered in low clipped tones, "You've become just like your father, have you? Bury emotions. Always guard yourself."

She blinked, then felt anger surmount surprise. "I asked how you got in here."

"Quietly, during the long minutes while you gathered the courage to let Johnson in. Did you know what he was going to say to you? Is that why it took so long to open the door?"

She wouldn't rise to that bait. "How could you have heard?" she whispered. "The kitchen is so far ..."

"The kitchen stove pipe brings sound in," he said in a low voice, gesturing toward the chimney. "But I didn't need to hear. Your reaction tells me what he found."

"Why are you in my den?" she whispered.

"You said 'If any more secretive strangers ...' I wanted to know what secretive stranger you had hidden in this room." McKay pointed toward the dog. "How did he injure those feet?"

Vandal lay on his back, his body completely relaxed, comatose. "What have you done to him?" Laura pulled from McKay's hands and fell on her knees next to the dog.

McKay followed her down to the rug. "I scratched where he itched," he said, reaching over her shoulder to touch a paw. The bandage had been chewed off. "Those look like ice cuts and a bit of frost bite."

She knocked his hand away. Vandal stretched his paw toward Ian before flopping over on his side. Letting out a satisfied `woof', he closed his eyes again. Laura knelt beside him, allowing herself to rest a moment before she got enough energy to kick McKay out.

"How did he get into this condition, Laura?"

Laura slumped. "I kept him out too long at Manitou."

The man behind her drew in a deep, patient breath. She didn't dare look at him.

"You'd better get back to Johnson before he comes looking for you," he whispered.

"You," she growled, "Get out of my house."

He frowned down at her. "This window will do when the time comes. First, I need to know what is your relationship to this Colonel?"

She rounded on him, fists tight. "Why should you care?"

From her knees, she was at a disadvantage. He easily stepped beyond her reach.

His eyes narrowed and his jaw stiffened. "I'm suddenly investigating a murder – several murders," he whispered harshly. "What relationship do you have with Johnson?"

Grinding out each word, she said, "He . . . is . . . my . . . boss."

"My sources tell me you two are like . . ." He crossed two fingers, suggestively.

"Your sources stink. Once in a great while, we go together to social events on the base."

"That's it?"

"Get out."

McKay stood very still, watching Laura rise from the dog. When she reached toward the fireplace poker, he put up one hand.

"No need," he whispered. "I'm leaving."

She lifted the iron handle. Ian didn't seem to move, but in one snake-like motion, he had her wrists in a vice grip. She winced as he pulled her toward him.

"Let me warn you," he whispered. "Tell no one I've been here."

Laura, mesmerized by his concentrated power, felt herself tremble uncontrollably.

"I'll do what I think is best," she said as evenly as possible. She was angry at her body for betraying her fear. Stiffening in an effort to stop, she only made it worse.

He glanced significantly at the dog and then back at her for a long moment. The muscles of his jaw tightened. His eyes seemed to become opaque.

"You know more than you tell. That could mean your death."

She scoffed, "I suppose I should trust you."

His grip on her wrists loosened tentatively and his hands moved slowly up her arms. She controlled the futile impulse to jerk free as he moved in on her. His eyes searched her face as if for some sign. Laura swallowed hard, bracing herself to fight him.

"That's good," he whispered. "Trust no one."

Almost without moving, McKay took the poker from her hand. He backed toward the window and had climbed half out when he pointed the sharp tool at her. "I'll be back. And I'll be watching."

CHAPTER NINE

SATURDAY NIGHT, MARCH 7TH

Two days before, she'd been in the sub-zero cold of the looming mountains. Now, a balmy warmth spread over the plains east of the Rockies. By the time Laura left her house with Colonel Johnson, midnight rains had washed the air clean.

As she closed the front door, Laura heard Vandal's guttural growl clear from the den. Bernard Johnson seemed not to have heard it. She glanced around expecting to spot Ian McKay lurking, rousing the dog's ire. She saw no sign of him. Bernard ushered her into his jeep and drove to the Camp Springs base.

They pulled into the wet-dirt parking lot. The base lights were all on, as if, at this unusual hour, the men sensed the impending news. Officers and Master-Sergeants clustered around the muddy carpark whispering and waiting. Laura noticed a civilian among the gathering crowd. In the dark and rain, she thought she recognized him. When he began to walk, she grew certain – Agent Ian McKay. She wondered what violence had left him with the limp. She also wondered how he'd arrived so quickly.

McKay walked across the street, deep in conversation with Chaplain Father McClellan, but he appeared to be keeping an eye on the wives and close friends of the dead men as they came to the administrative building. Laura swung her legs over the low side wall of the jeep and started to jump when Bernard rushed to lift her down. She realized McKay watched Johnson's familiarity.

Well, this will raise his eyebrows.

Bernard didn't seem to notice the man. He whispered urgently as he steered her inside the building, "Laura, I don't want you alone in your house until we get the investigation cleared up."

"Why?"

"The murderers," he said, turning toward her almost protectively. "I'm afraid they were after something, some information up there at . . . at the training camp. If they didn't get what they wanted, they may come looking for it down here. I can guard the ad-min building, but they may decide to see if the General had it at home. Your house is hard to watch."

"I am trained, Bernard," she replied as they entered the big front door. Her tone of indignant independence felt forced. Overriding her self-doubts, she announced, "I've gone through the defense exercises as if I were a son. You know – rifles, handguns, obstacle courses, hand to hand combat, the works."

Bernard snorted and pulled her away from prying eyes into an empty instruction room off the main floor hall. He twisted her toward him.

"You're not a son, Laura," he whispered harshly, "You're a woman." Frowning down at her, his big hands gripped her shoulders a little too hard. In his urgency, he didn't seem to notice that he bruised her. "These guys, the way they killed, I mean, they won't stop at anything and I'm afraid for you."

Laura watched Bernard desperately scan her face. He swallowed hard, "If you'd marry me, I could move you into . . ."

"Bernard. Please, this isn't the time to discuss marriage again. I appreciate your concern, but . . ."

He shook her as if to make her think more clearly. "Laura, you can't keep me at arm's length. Not at a dangerous time like this."

She dropped her head. So tired. So tired – and now to have to fight this. "I won't marry you for protection, Bernard," she said firmly.

Suddenly, he realized how hard he pressed on her shoulder. Relaxing his grip, he shrugged uncomfortably, "Isn't there someone – a girlfriend you could stay with? a relative?"

Laura glanced away, across the classroom to the window. Outside, McKay still talked to the chaplain, but had turned to face the scene in this room. She and Bernard were standing in the pool of light from the hallway, not so isolated from prying eyes as Bernard had hoped.

Drat! she thought, this little picture will provide fuel for McKay's assumptions.

Then she wondered what her relationship with any man had to do with Ian McKay's investigation. Bernard's renewed grip on her shoulders brought her mind back to his worries.

"Where can you go, Laura?" he asked.

A solution came, one which would allay Bernard's fears for her. At the same time, she'd get away from watchers like McKay so that she could do some investigating of her own. It was worth a try.

"There is someone. After the funeral, I'll visit my Aunt Melany in Helena, Montana," she suggested. "Dad's sister ... She's too frail to travel here for the service. She'll be ... well, a visit would help her, too."

Bernard looked relieved. "I could arrange a seat on troop transport, maybe even on a commercial flight."

"Thanks, Bernard."

"The sooner, the better. I want you out of that house." He looked around distractedly. "Guess we'd better get upstairs and meet the others."

"Bernard."

"Yes?"

"Don't try to polish up death for these people. They need the truth."

He looked harried. "I can't tell them everything. It would hamper the investigation."

* *

Later that evening, in the administration building's third floor, two men talked.

"I keep getting this weird signal late at night." said Vibes Nelson, frowning and twisting his radio dials. "It's not Morse code, but it's a definite pattern."

Major Cameron didn't exactly listen, but Vibes didn't mind ruminating to himself. "Weather's been strange lately," he thought aloud, "Could be sunspots, I 'spose."

Major Cameron grunted.

"Seems like it's too regular for sunspots," Vibes went on, holding one side of the headphones to his ear, "but it's a darn strong signal."

Cameron leaned forward, gazing out the window into the darkness. "She arrived, and on Johnson's arm."

Vibes' smile became tinged with sadness. He knew 'she' was Laura Atweiler. He didn't mind moving to that subject for Cameron's sake. "She's going to be lost without that old man," Vibes commented as he tapped out a routine message on his radio transmitter. "Sheer loneliness may drive her into Johnson's bed after all."

"Not that woman," said Cameron, "She's tough. But I wish I'd seen her reaction to the news. Laura Atweiler knows more than she tells, I'm sure of it."

Vibes snorted. "She knows nothing except that the General didn't meet her, and I couldn't get him on the radio."

Cameron retreated from the window, perched on the corner of a table, and leaned over Vibes Nelson's clacking code key as he talked.

"She knows enough to suspect more. Why else would she be snooping in her father's files the day before the murders are discovered?"

"How could she know?" Vibes asked while he transcribed an in-coming message. "I by-gum didn't tell her how to find that camp."

"Vibes, that lady's been skiing and camping with her father since she was a tike – knows the Rocky Mountains better than any of us. And the General's body had been moved from the cave to the field."

Vibes' head jerked up. His machine chattered on without him. "Footprints," explained Cameron. "It was damned cold up there, but it hadn't snowed since the murders."

"Did anyone else see the prints?"

Cameron shook his head. "I got there first."

Vibes gazed at Major Cameron with renewed respect. The Major had never been a strong man. It would have taken enormous willpower to plow up that snow-bound trail ahead of everyone else. "You tampered with evidence." Vibes stated.

"Everybody else was too sick to notice," said Cameron. "Hell, I was sick myself – they'd been dead several days."

"The footprints . . .?" Vibes urged.

"The General had been carried out by somebody wearing small boots – carried out and laid next to Banks. And, judging by the depth of the sit mark there, that person sat between them in the snow for a long time."

"Not her. She'd a' raged back down here and raised an alarm you'd a heard back in D.C.," said Vibes.

"Unless she didn't know who to trust."

Vibes rocked back from his beloved radio and put his hands behind his head. "Now who wouldn't trust little ol' me?"

Cameron looked at him through thick lenses, "Any girl whose daddy's just been murdered in the slowest possible way."

Vibes' chair hit the floor. He stood, pacing to the small office window. "What was she lookin' for in them files?"

"I wish I knew."

Vibes looked over his shoulder at his companion. "Be careful, Cam. She's sharp. Could blow this whole thing to bits if she gets curious in the wrong directions."

"I know."

"What'll we do about J.B.?" Vibes asked. "This could make him dangerous."

Cameron nodded. "I'm due to call Austria tonight. Maybe we can curtail him a little."

"Unlikely!"

* *

The man figured he had only forty-five minutes before Miss Atweiler came home from Camp Springs base. He figured the bereaved would console each other for thirty minutes. Then they'd allow the good Colonel to plan a funeral for them. They'd console each other a little more and then depart for empty homes. Forty-five minutes to an hour, tops. By one thirty in the morning he had to be gone.

That ought to be enough time. One toe hold was a bit precarious due to broken mortar, but he had a firm grip on the sill to the second story window. She'd been thoughtful enough to leave most of the house lights off.

Not much chance of detection, but he always worked with care. The first mistake was often the last in his business. As he'd hoped, Miss Atweiler had not been interested in second floor locks. The window slid open easily. He pulled himself inside, shut the window and turned on his torch. The room had a masculine touch. Dark wood bedstead and chest, suit valet by the closet door, painted hunting scenes and photos of mountains on the walls.

In one framed photo stood an ominous mountain – a mountain he knew well. Its craggy top was lit by the rising sun glinting off a massive wall of rock to the west and slightly below the summit. One small cloud seemed to be brushing past the summit. The man looked closely at the photo and could barely make out a climber, suspended mid-way down the west wall in the first sunlight of that day.

Frowning, the man turned off his torch and moved into the hall. He paused at the next room, pushed open the door with his unlit torch. Out wafted the scent of pine needles and fresh air. His frown deepened when he saw that the window to this room was not only unlocked, but open.

Just beyond it stood a huge Himalayan Pine – even easier access than the chimney bricks at the back of the house – too easy for his taste, but others might find it tempting.

He closed the bedroom door and opened the attic door across the hall.

He stepped lightly in the wood shavings that were scattered with seeming abandon over everything. He climbed the stairs and strode silently to the workbench. On the worn and much gouged top were several carved pieces: a chess set whose pawns had drear faces like street people from the dark days of the Great Depression; a dog of wolf-like proportions; a woman standing on a rock, cradling a child in her arms as she faced into the wind.

The man lifted the carving of the woman for a better look at her features. As he studied the carver's strokes, his jaw tightened. His fingers clasped the piece so closely they threatened to break the flying tresses of her hair. Abruptly, he set the piece on the table and pushed away from it.

Perpendicular to the workbench, nearer the attic window stood a small table covered in shavings and dust as the rest of the garret space. In the center of the table stood a large toolbox of metal. He wrenched open the top of the box. It contained a shelf of gouges and knives.

Beneath the tools lay a headset, telegraph key and an antenna coil – exactly what he had expected to find.

He lifted out the apparatus. Underneath, he found a small book filled with closely spaced Spencerian handwriting – seventy pages of names, addresses and dates.

Satisfied, the man closed the lid of the box, and took it all – tools, radio set and book with him down the attic stairs.

As he neared the door to the hallway, he stopped long enough to wipe his boots. Shining the torch on them, he smiled grimly. No telltale sawdust remained. Opening the door, he peered out, and made his exit, unaware of the shavings that wafted out into the hall in his wake.

Passing her bedroom with its open window, he felt compelled to step in. He listened for the sound of a jeep (which might be delivering Miss Atweiler home), or of her quick-paced tread (if she'd dared to deliver herself). He hoped she'd come alone.

This had to be her room – flowers on the wallpaper and lace on the curtains made that undeniable. He read the titles in the neat stacks of books on the shelf above her desk – Rabelais, de Maupassant, Rilke – she loved reading French and German works, he knew. He lifted the roll-top and shone his torch on the papers inside the desk. A few letters from friends and the beginning of a shopping list met his gloved fingers. Searching further, he opened each of the drawers, coming at last to the drawer that held file folders upright. Inside the last unmarked folder, he found the telegram from Champ to General Atweiler.

"Damn!" he whispered harshly. He took it, stuffed it into his jacket pocket and returned to his search. Finding nothing else of interest in the desk, he moved to the highboy chest.

On top of the chest, he picked up and studied each of the photographs, one of Major Gregory Banks and Miss Atweiler's father posing in the mountains. This one he looked at long and hard, as if memorizing the features of those captured there. The second photo he looked at only briefly, a photo of James Schoenfeld beginning a hike. The man in the photo and the man looking at the photo were like day and night to each other, the one slender, blond and smiling, the other stocky, dark of hair and dark of outlook. The darker man scowled at the naivete exhibited in the blond man's exuberance.

The third photo held the intruder's attention the longest. A very young man and a dark-haired girl-child smiled bravely at the camera, each seeming to put on a front of happiness for the other, and for the world.

When he looked closely, the man could see that the two occupants of the photo wore skates and stood near a log at the edge of a pond. The child's arms wrapped around the young man's skinny waist.

At last, the man set the photos back exactly as he had found them, gave the chest of drawers a cursory search and headed toward the closet where he slid a wooden door on a well-oiled metal track. Shining his torch inside, he found a few pressed dresses and two pair of dress shoes. Reaching toward the back end of the closet that was covered by the sliding door, he found what he sought. Two worn leather boots, caked with mud, sat on newspaper, waiting attention which was long overdue to them. Hanging on the rack above was a short woolen jacket.

The intruder pulled the jacket out into the room where he could shine his light on it more easily. There, the dark stains revealed themselves unmistakably as the brown of dried blood. His fingers probed deeply in the weft and found that not all of the tell-tale blood had dried even yet.

His eyes blazed with anger and then smoldered with decisiveness. He thrust the jacket back into its place on the rack and yanked the door closed.

Turning on his booted heel, he had barely stepped out of the room when the sound of a soft click alerted him to the unlocking of the front door.

CHAPTER TEN

Laura halted in the doorway. She'd heard one thump. That was it – one thump. After slipping away from the hovering Bernard and walking herself home, she felt foolish to be frightened.

Lord save us from things that go bump in the night, she managed to joke with herself.

Just Vandal's tail.

In the den, the dog proved her right. When she knelt down to greet him and check his paws, he thumped his tail once more and then whined. He glanced up at her soulfully. Vandal did much better. He'd chewed off his bandages. She herself was exhausted, not having slept much since last Tuesday. She blamed her noddled head for a stupid wish to confide in strangers such as Ian McKay. Tired as she felt, it helped clear her head to walk Vandal to the back yard, then feed him before she started upstairs to bed.

She stumbled toward her room, planning to throw herself on the welcoming bed. Instead, she forced her feet to make a stop in the bathroom where she splashed cold water on her face and brushed her teeth. She didn't even look at herself in the mirror.

I'll look sick. If I see it, I'll feel sicker.

Out in the unlit hall again, she leaned on the doorjamb and tried to capture a scent that niggled her subconscious.

Pine and Cherry wood, she thought.

"Pine, from the tree outside, but why Cherry?" she muttered and shoved away from the wall, retreating to her room.

As she opened the bedroom door, the smell of Cherry became stronger. "Pipe tobacco?" she whispered.

Like a thunderbolt, it hit her. Someone had been here. Stupidly, she'd left her window open. The Himalayan Pine made an easy ladder if the intruder didn't mind pitch and sharp needles. Suddenly afraid, Laura felt a strong presence. She looked over her room. A few things had been moved, but nothing taken – her jewel boxes not even opened.

Dumbly, she faced the truth. The intruder was not after jewels, he sought something more important – information. Johnson had warned her. Sure of what she would discover, Laura pulled out the file drawer of her desk. In the unmarked last file, nothing.

The Champ telegram! Gone.

"Arndt!" she whispered, "But what could he learn from that piece of nonsense?" She jumped up and began to fish furiously for the copy she'd made yesterday and filed among her sweaters in the highboy. Then, she forced herself to stop.

He might still be in the house.

She fumbled, nervously pushing up the roll top on her desk. From one of the cubby holes, she withdrew several rolls of stamps. Behind the stamps, her fingers found the handle of her pistol. She'd left it loaded since her return from Longs Peak.

"A brilliant lady," she whispered to herself, putting her back to the massive desk, warily eyeing the closet. If he hid in there, she'd have him.

I want him stuck in the guardhouse while I decipher the telegram. If Arndt's gone to the trouble to steal it, it must be important.

She side-stepped to the closet. Holding the revolver in her left hand, she steeled herself and yanked on the door. Slamming her free hand onto the gun butt, she aimed it into the back of the closet. Her bloody jacket hung, innocently swaying in empty space.

One look at the brown stain and the whole scene rushed back attacking her senses – all the blood on Gregory Bank's chest, her father's agonized words.

"James . . . Danger"

Danger. She shook off the powerful memory. Danger had come into her house. He hasn't gone downstairs. The dog would have made a racket. Where is he?

She needed sleep and she had a ridiculous desire to lie down with the gun in hand and just wait for him to come.

No ma'am, she ordered herself. Route him out. Hand him over to McKay or Johnson. I'm too tired to care which.

Leaving the closet open, Laura pushed her dresses in front of her jacket back where she couldn't see it easily again. She slipped off her high-heeled shoes and moved silently out into the hall. Here, the smell of Cherry wood was much fainter.

He spent a long time in my room and very little in the hall, she deduced.

The other bedroom door in the hall had been her father's. Ordinarily, she kept it closed to conserve heat. The door gaped open. Laura believed he could be behind that door. She moved to the open side of her father's bedroom door. Reaching out with one foot, she kicked the door back into the wall behind it. She found no one there, not even in the closet.

She moved to the attic fairly certain that her back was safe. When she glanced down the hall, she noted tell-tale wood shavings dusting the floor near the attic door.

He's up there for sure.

A moment later, Laura stood off to one side of the door to the attic stairwell. She pulled. It swung quietly at first, then opened further with an ominous squall. Laura frowned, wondering why the dog hadn't heard this noise and put up a howling racket. When the echo of metal hinges died, there was only silence in the darkened stairwell. The attic had always been her father's private lair, where he carved figurines of wood. For years, he'd insisted that this area be his alone. She should not even clean it. Laura had always assumed that he needed this place to hide from the heavy responsibilities of generalship.

As she stepped into the attic stairwell, Laura became fully aware of two things. First, her father had never spent any of his hours up here wielding a broom, and second that she 'd be vulnerable from above along the whole length of the stair opening. She paid more attention to the last thought as she crept up the steps, pistol cocked and ready.

The light switch was at the top of the stairs on the left wall. Laura's night vision had often proven as good as the best marksmen on the base, so she kept to the center of the stairs and let her peripheral awareness watch for any shadow of movement. The smell of Cherry wood was stronger up here, and each step she took stirred it up even more. Not tobacco, she realized. Her father's wood shavings.

He's been carving pieces from the old cherry, the one we cut down before Mom died.

She crouched, knowing her head would top the sides of the stairwell by the sixth step. Seemingly empty black space surrounded her on both sides. She wished she'd brought Vandal with her, but knew that would put him in danger.

You're trained for this, Laura. Do your job.

Her mind mimicked her father's voice.

A breeze of cool night air crossed her face and lifted her hair slightly. Laura shivered, whether from fear or cold, she wouldn't allow herself to guess. Only facts were allowed to assert themselves.

The window must be open.

She rose step by step, becoming a better target with each rise. At the eighth step, she flung her hand toward the post at the head of the stairs. In one motion, Laura flicked on the light and ducked down into the protection of the stairwell. No gunfire followed this flood of light. No sound of startled movement or furtive retreat could be heard above her.

The Buzzard is too smart for that!

An ache of tension shot through her back as she crouched on the stairs. Her stocking feet stuck to scattered wood shavings. Through her shirt, the unfinished planks of the wall rubbed into her back. Her ears were alert for the smallest sound, but her own breathing seemed to reverberate across the empty spaces. Above her, all seemed brightly lit, like the sun on a benign spring morning. Yet, the smell of cherry wood denied the calm. The man who had whittled that wood had been murdered. For her, nothing would be peaceful until she caught his murderer – a murderer who'd also invaded her home.

She listened, ready to shoot at his first move. She knew he wouldn't move. He'd wait until Laura showed herself above the steps, and then he would open fire. If it was to be a battle of wills, she would win. She settled in for the wait.

After twenty silent and nerve-wracking minutes, an even worse possibility occurred to her.

He's gone.

Slowly, she rose far enough to take a look. A quick glance and she ducked down. Still, no one moved or fired. She rose again.

There were no shadowed places in which to hide, only the rafters converging at the high roof beam and sloping away toward the floor on all sides. Two tables sat at right angles to each other under the open window. Relieved and disappointed, Laura stepped onto the gray, wide floorboards. Each footstep creaked, telling Laura that her quarry had been gone before she came to the second floor or she would have heard his every step.

However, his every footstep could be seen in the sawdust. From the looks of them, he'd been to the window and back to the stairs twice. The lugs in the soles of his boots left a pattern she'd never seen before, not even in the snow at Longs Peak. The lugs were lozenge shaped with a semi-circular bite out of the flat end.

She looked at one of them closely, hoping for a maker's mark. On the ball of each print, she found a circle with what seemed to be a worn crown inside of it. She certainly didn't remember that symbol from any of the companies who did business with the U.S. Army.

At the window, she found what she'd expected to find if Arndt were her intruder – the mark of a hefty rope which had once been wrapped around a rafter. As it had been pulled out of its temporary hold, the rope had worn grooves in the rafter and abraded the dark green paint off the outer edge of the windowsill. Laura could bet that if she looked in the morning, she'd see dirt and sawdust footprints down the white-board siding of her home.

She glanced out into the night and felt herself being watched. Hastily, she backed up from the window, chilled by her own stupidity.

Think defensively, Atweiler! Your anger doesn't make you immune.

Arndt would kill you without blinking.

As she calmed down, her attention moved to the two tables nearby. The small one directly under the window held only dust. In its center shone a clean spot, rectangular in shape, about twelve inches wide by sixteen inches long. The spot seemed so clean, that the object protecting it had to have been removed in the last few minutes.

Its removal was part of the growing puzzle which, when pieced together, should explain why her father had been killed. What had been in the clean space, Laura couldn't even guess, but the missing object had been important to the man who'd stolen into her home tonight.

The longer table, closest to her, was cluttered with tools and with shavings and carved pieces. One statue had been lifted up, and put back down, not quite in its original place in the dust. Laura ducked down to look at it without touching it, hoping that Colonel Johnson or someone could get fingerprints off of it later.

The little statue was of a woman carrying a child in her arms. The woman's hair had been blown away from her face. Laura could see the care with which her father had carved the curls in the darkest part of the Cherry wood. She recognized the woman's face immediately – herself.

Startled, she blinked and backed away. From this more removed perspective, she realized what had happened. The small statue had been based on an old photo her father had treasured, a sepia and tattered image of her mother carrying her. Without being aware of it, Laura had grown to look like this beautiful and vaguely remembered woman.

Blinded by unshed tears, she pushed the attic window closed, latching it angrily. She locked every window in the house and brought Vandal upstairs before she could fall into bed. Even then, the vision of the woman and child invaded her restless dreams. But in her mind, the woman stood next to an attentive young boy with corn silk hair. Behind the boy, James, she could see the scarred and wary visage of Agent Ian McKay.

*   *

Two miles away, in his third-floor apartment, Richard Cameron leaned furtively over a foot thick, gutted dictionary, trying yet one more time to reach his contact in Austria. The radio transmitter-receiver hidden inside the *Webster's Universal and Unabridged* transmitted Cameron's terror. In return, he received absolutely no assurances, only the empty static of electrically noisy space.

Added to that came the annoyance of a tree branch tapping on his third-floor window. Tap, tap, tap. Swish, swish, swish. Tap, tap, tap.

"S.O.S," he thought vaguely. Cameron jerked to attention. There were no trees close to his apartment. That's why his antennae had been strung on the bath exhaust pipe. He closed his dictionary and turned slowly toward the window.

Outside his windowpane he discovered a bearded face, grinning broadly.

Cameron lunged for the window, unlocked it and jerked it open. "What the dickens . . .," he sputtered.

"Took your time about it, Major." Cameron's visitor said. Hoisting himself over the sill, Ian McKay dropped a black toolbox onto the floor and, tucking his lithe body, performed a neat roll into the room.

"Good. No house plants to knock over," McKay mumbled.

"I've a door," said Cameron, smiling at the dark-haired man. "And nosy neighbors," McKay reminded him. He stretched worn back muscles and shook out his stiffened left leg. "Besides, I have to keep in practice. You trying to reach me with that thing?" he asked, pointing to the transmitter.

"Yes. Why are you here?"

"I missed you," Ian McKay replied, and then added somberly, "I also missed the boss."

Cameron's earlier terror returned with a start. He fumbled to explain.

But McKay interrupted, saying, "I know what happened on the mountain. And I've seen her."

"Laura Atweiler? Did she see you?"

"Yes, but she doesn't know who I am. I want to keep it that way for now."

"You have changed, all right," said Cameron, eyeing his friend's powerful build critically. "The weight lifting, the beard ..."

"The short leg, the scar," added his visitor. "She hardly saw past the surface damage."

Cameron nodded, "Yes, the scar. Still, you took a big chance letting her see you."

"I had to know what he's told her. I also did a second story job on her house while you were at the meeting of the bereaved. She came home alone – nearly walked in on me."

Cameron nervously pushed at his glasses. "You cut things too thin. Why snoop around there?"

McKay held out a yellowed telegram. "She had this in her desk."

Cameron glanced at the telegram and knew right away what it must be. "The trap! Did she understand it?"

"I didn't wait around to ask her. But you told me last summer that she's become a very smart lady."

Cameron frowned. "Maybe she hasn't had time to figure it out. That must be what she took from her father's files on Friday, when I found her in his office."

"When did it arrive?" McKay asked.

"The day before. I filed it right away." Cameron glanced up, very puzzled. "But I filed it in my office. How could she have gotten my combination?"

"Maybe she has talents no one has fathomed," said McKay suggestively.

Cameron raised an eyebrow. "Are you asking?"

At first, McKay tried to look belligerent, then, reluctantly, he nodded. "No man has fathomed her talents," said Cameron quietly. "She's certainly never seduced me, for the combination or for anything else. She radiates 'hands off'. On the base, only Johnson keeps trying. All that most men know is that she's a darned smart secretary, a gutsy climber, and on skis, she can't be caught."

After a moment's silence, McKay let out pent-up air and tried to change the subject. "So, if she had this telegram, what other files has she seen?"

"Took you by surprise, didn't it?" Cameron said.

McKay glanced up, and recognized Cam's steady understanding. "She's not . . . Is . . . Is this wrong, what I'm feeling?"

Cam shook his head. "Doesn't matter that she's related to him, or that you thought you knew all about her. You just met the real thing."

McKay held Cam's gaze and nodded slowly. "So smart, so strong, courageous, and so much in pain."

"Yep," Cam said, "So, let's focus on keeping her safe." "If she'll let us. What other files?"

Cameron shrugged. "According to Vibes, Laura hadn't been in the building since Tuesday, March third, except for the few minutes early Wednesday morning, when she asked him to radio the camp. She came back to work Friday morning."

"You checked the Verheerung file?" McKay asked.

"Last night – Friday night. Because she'd been in his files, I drove in around midnight and looked in all the offices to make sure no files were unlocked. The Verheerung file hadn't been touched. I looked again today after we brought in the bodies. It's still there."

"So, even if she did understand this telegram, she's not likely to know about Verheerung."

"Not at all," Cameron answered.

"Unless her father told her," McKay said.

Cameron stiffened, anticipating confirmation of his own suspicions. "Why would Atweiler tell her about Verheerung?" he asked.

"Because he was dying," said McKay. "I think she climbed up there, probably Wednesday night or Thursday sometime."

Cameron let out a long, frustrated breath and then said, "I feared that might be Laura."

McKay looked up, expectantly.

"When I arrived at the box canyon," said Cameron, "there were footprints in the snow – small ones near the cave entrance. The ones coming out were deeper than the ones going in. Most footprints had been brushed away, but I also found a sitz mark near the bodies. Looked like she'd sat between them long enough to melt a space deeper than the bodies. But her father's body was different than the rest – not covered with a dust of snow as they were. And he'd been … he'd been worked over more than the others."

Both of them sat in a silence of dark memory. Finally, McKay leaned forward, "Anyone else know all this?"

"Only Vibes. I erased the evidence just before the others arrived." McKay gave him a close study. "That took some hustling."

Cameron colored slightly, but nodded. "Yeah. Some hustling."

McKay frowned and methodically listed their evidence, counting on his fingers to emphasize each point. "Laura Atweiler has Gregory Bank's very sick and injured dog in her den, mud on her ski boots and blood still drying on her jacket. You find that her father had been moved after the murders and after a snowfall. He's laid next to Banks, his staunchest friend. The person who moved him seems to have held a long vigil between the two bodies."

Cameron's somber face grew taut.

McKay summed up emphatically. "Laura Atweiler never waited for her father at Manitou. She went looking for him. When she found him, he may not have been dead. There's no telling what she may have learned. She has to be watched."

Major Cameron slumped.

"I'll watch her after the funeral and tomorrow night. Then I leave. Will you watch her while I'm gone?" asked McKay.

After a moment's hesitation, Cameron nodded, "She's slippery." "She sure is," said McKay wearily. "But I want her taken care of

while I take care of this." He waved the telegram toward Cameron. "I will."

"Thanks." Without waiting to be invited, Ian McKay picked up the toolbox and headed for the extra bedroom that Cameron kept ready for him.

CHAPTER ELEVEN

MONDAY, MARCH 9TH

Laura stood at the edge of the open meadow and looked out over the flowers. Beside each bouquet stood a white cross. The dirt mounded gently over three new graves like chocolate colored comforters over sleeping children.

Not sleeping, but buried beneath the sandy loam were

Lieutenant-Colonel Robert Temple, Major Gregory Banks and General Arthur Atweiler. Yesterday, the bodies of Sergeant Hospice and four other men had been drummed onto transport planes, destined for their grieving hometowns.

And still Laura couldn't cry. Nor could she bring herself to talk to anyone.

Who can I trust? One of the men who came to the funeral betrayed these dead to that monster.

The funeral service had been dignified and somber, but it hadn't blunted her horror. It had not been the comfort Bernard said it would be. She hadn't let it comfort her. She meant to kill Arndt in the way he'd killed her father, slowly and painfully, inch by inch.

She shuddered and fingered the matches and cigarettes she'd begun keeping in her raincoat pocket, just in case. In her other pocket lay the aeroplane ticket to Helena, Montana. Bernard had given it to her as he drove her home after the funeral. She'd thanked him, but, to his obvious disappointment, she had not invited him in.

Laura kicked at a dead Aspen log, rotting at the edge of the meadow. Walking back to the cemetery had been a mistake, she thought, irritably. I should have stayed at home – tried to decipher the copy of the telegram from the Champ file.

Since two days before, when the original telegram had been stolen, there'd been no more intruders in her home. Vandal now slept next to her bed. At night, her gun rested under the false tissue box she placed on the nightstand. Though she hadn't told him about the missing telegram and rectangular shaped object, she had told Bernard someone had invaded her house. As a result, Bernard had stationed an enlisted man in her living room. Today's guard thought she still lay in her bedroom, recuperating from the funeral service.

Instead, she'd climbed out the window and down the Himalayan Pine. Her loaded gun weighed down her purse. Something heavier weighed on her soul. It made breathing difficult, thinking impossible. Returning to the cemetery, Laura hoped to bury the lump of hard hate in her chest. If she could cry it would dissolve. Then she might concentrate. She could do what she had to do.

But she stood here, staring at the ice-encrusted flowers, at the white crosses like bedsteads marking each dirt quilt. Nothing came.

Nothing.

"Miss Atweiler."

She whirled toward the voice. In the Aspen woods, hands in his pockets, baggy jacket stretched across his wide shoulders, stood Agent Ian McKay.

"Have you got a gun in that jacket?" she blurted.

He laughed, "Do you ever dissemble?"

"Have you?"

"Sure," he shrugged. "Numerous times."

"You're evading now," she pointed out. "I meant 'Have you a gun?'"

He smiled and held the jacket open. The gun was strapped across his shoulder. "You're foolish to walk alone in a cemetery," he said calmly. "What'd you plan to do? Go in the front door, kissing Colonel Johnson good-bye, and come out the back door hoping to attract the man who killed your father?"

Laura stuffed her hands deep into her coat pockets and walked away from him. "Your informant is incorrect," she said, over her shoulder. "I do not kiss Colonel Johnson 'Good-bye'. Or even 'Hello'."

"But the gun in your bag is intended for use on the murderer, isn't it?" She slowed down at that.

How does he know? Or is he just guessing?

McKay went on. "And the matches and the cigarettes in your coat are not there for smoking, are they?"

Laura glared at him while she thought back through the day. There'd been no time when either her coat or her purse were not with her.

He supplied the answer. "The attendant at the funeral home. You remember. He was so solicitous that he nearly lifted the coat off your shoulders before you waved him away. He has very fast hands. That's what I hired him for."

She pulled the long gray coat more closely about her throat and asked, "Did he rifle my bag with his left hand while he pick-pocketed the coat with his right?"

"Not quite, I guessed about the gun," McKay said as he closed the gap between them. "The bag weighs you down. You saw something this morning that put you on your guard, didn't you?"

"Were you there? I didn't see . . . "

He shook his head. "Too risky to attend the funeral myself."

"So, you hired the accomplice with the funereal voice and the fast hands . . ."

McKay shrugged, "I told my friend to watch for anyone who didn't look like a mourning relative. Did you notice the same one?"

"The big guy with the black hair." As soon as it was out, she wished she hadn't said it. He already knew too much, but she seemed to have an uncontrollable wish to tell him even more.

Ian's gaze came back to her face. "You see a lot, don't you? Out of hundreds, why did you pick out that one man?"

She shrugged and decided to go with her instincts. "No one greeted him afterwards. And he didn't make efforts to greet anyone either. Also, he had red beard stubble – not very common with black hair."

McKay's face went gray.

"What do you know about him, Mr. McKay?"

McKay pretended to study new buds on the nearest Aspen.

"Mr. McKay, I have been honest with you. You can return the favor." He shook his head slowly and moved closer, looking down at her.

"No," he began. "No, Laura Atweiler. You haven't been honest with me. You know how your father died. Apparently without ever seeing his body, you know. The matches and cigarettes prove that. I want you to forget the ugly revenge on which you've set your cold little heart. Trust me to take care of it. Take that ticket to Montana – the one Colonel Johnson gave you. Get out of this before you get hurt."

"You were at Longs Peak," she accused.

"Out Laura."

"Are you threatening me?"

He studied her face a moment before he answered, "Yes. There is no doubt in my mind that if you persist, you will be dead. Painfully, ignobly dead. Go to Montana."

"Go home little girl," she mimicked. "Go home and let Big Brother take care of everything." She saw his eyes widen, startled, but she went on angrily. "Everyone claims they'll take care of it. You, Johnson, Cameron, the Chaplain . . . There's only one problem. We're discussing my father. I'm the one with the reason to risk everything."

Cursing, McKay grabbed her arms, shaking her. "What will that get you? When you are dead, will revenge taste good then?"

She glared up at him, dizzy from the suddenness of his anger. "What do you care?" she rasped out.

McKay released her so fast that her head snapped forward. "I knew him well, Laura. I care . . ." He turned his face away from her. "I . . . care." His voice broke. "Laurie, leave this to me."

Laura backed away, straightening her coat. She stared at him, transfixed by the power of his pain and anger. She thought him unstable, maybe even dangerous. As she watched for a chance to escape, he muttered harshly to himself and tossed his head to one side as if to clear his hair from his eyes. Laura held her breath, trying to remember something. Perhaps she had met him when he worked with her father, sometime when she visited from college. Before she had time to figure it out, he let out a long, exasperated whistle.

He stepped further from her, saying gently. "I'm not a maniac, Miss Atweiler. Please stop thinking about finding a hole to hide in."

"Convince me."

"My anger is fear for you. I followed you here to see you safe home again." He must have seen her teetering between distrust and belief. "May I walk you home?" he urged. "I'll leave you at the door. Promise."

She thought a moment and decided that keeping an eye on him as they walked would be more comfortable than a prickly awareness that he followed her. As she nodded assent, Laura switched her purse to her right arm and held the clasp with her left.

He smiled, a little lopsided because of that scar. "I know you're lefthanded, Miss Atweiler. You won't need the gun with me, but hang on to it, if it makes you feel safer."

"It does."

He offered his arm. She shook her head. He bowed with mock gentility, and they started back toward her house. At first, they were warily silent, then merely quiet as they walked. After the first mile, Ian McKay finally spoke.

"I don't know how much you know about what your father did for the Army, Miss Atweiler," he said. "I'm going to tell you, so you'll understand why it's imperative that you leave the investigation to me." McKay glanced at her but she gave him no sign of the curiosity which built inside her.

"First, your father worked as the center of a network of Army Intelligence Officers in Germany, Austria and Switzerland. They worked for him well before the war, keeping the U.S. informed of Nazi military plans and the build-up of war machines."

He studied the effect of this news – only a raised eyebrow from her. "You'd guessed?" he said.

She nodded, "Only recently," she said, feeling more cut off from her father by his secret life than by his death.

McKay must have heard her sadness. Gently he added, "General Atweiler compartmentalized his life – a time for work, a time for love."

Laura swallowed hard. It was true. She had known only one part of her father.

"Unfortunately," McKay said, "Some of his men found it lucrative to work for the Nazis as well. Early on, your father was too straight, too idealistic to comprehend duplicity – not a good spy. But he learned distrust. In 1939, one of these double agents killed or caused the death of several of his colleagues. The man even murdered his own mistress because he believed she might know too much. His mistress, Kirsten Ciezki's body was found naked in a colleague's bed. Her murder had been a set up. The double-agent blamed her death on the other man and used his supposed grief as an excuse to knife his friend before throwing him down a stairwell, six stories to his death."

Laura stopped moving. She knew he talked about James – the true story. It had never made sense that he merely fell down those stairs.

"What is it, Laura?" McKay stepped closer.

She reached out blindly for his coat front, grabbing for something solid. "James," she murmured. "Arndt killed James."

"Yes," McKay said softly, steadying her with his hands.

"But they saved each other on l'Aiguille," she said, looking up at him. "Only a few days before." Even Laura could hear the rising hysteria in her voice. "They saved each other – If Arndt wanted him dead, he could have done it then."

McKay's jaw muscles went taut. "I . . . We'll never know why he passed up that chance. But Arndt must have believed James had guessed his double-agent set up." He leveled his gaze at her and spoke emphatically. "Arndt never leaves a doubtful ally alive."

Laura swallowed hard, admitting to herself that seeking revenge against Arndt would be a frightening goal. She remembered the letter detailing the climb down l'Aiguille, the Needle. In that moment, she knew exactly when Arndt realized he couldn't kill James on the descent – that unexplained drop toward the end of the climb – Arndt had started to let go. In the midst of committing murder, he'd seen the witnesses and ripped his gloves and his palms in order to stop the rope.

Laura looked up at Ian. Groping for some hope, she asked, "If James is really dead, then who is Jacques?"

McKay bit his lower lip and said blankly, "Jacques? Oh, yes. Jacques was James's code name, before . . ."

"But J.B. writes about things after 1939, after James died. And he sounds like James . . . I know he's bitter, more cynical, but still…"

McKay snapped to a new level of alertness. "J.B.? How did you hear about J.B.?"

Laura couldn't believe she had been so forthcoming with this man.

She tried to pull from his arms, but he held tight, searching her face. She tried to bluff, knew she didn't half convince him.

"J.B. is someone Dad corresponded with," she began. "He radios his stuff from Switzerland. Dad had me transcribe some of it a long time ago, maybe last year . . . last spring."

She could see her lie didn't work. McKay's face became a mask again. He let go of her, backed up and reassessed her. His eyes narrowed as he moved away, and she became aware of a stupid thought.

His thumbs don't rest on his fingers when he's tense. They stick out, almost at right angles – trigger happy, maybe. How far is it to his gun? Her left hand grasped the clip on her purse, ready. They stood there, each vigilantly aware of the least motion in the other. Several frozen moments passed before his thumbs relaxed against his palms. Laura took an uneasy breath.

"Have it your way, Miss Atweiler," he said coldly. "But remember that Werner Arndt is no fool. And above him is someone even more evil. Don't try to outguess them. Stay out of their way."

"And let the big boys take care of it all."

He raised one brow at her before merely taking her arm to hurry her homeward.

*   *

Through the lace curtains of her parlor, Laura watched Agent McKay stride out of her front gate. Once on the other side of her fence, he shrugged his broad shoulders more comfortably into his gun belt, shook his head as if to swing long hair out of his eyes and disappeared down the street.

That, she thought, is what James used to do with his long, blond hair.

She remembered that last day at the frozen pond. He'd skated across the ice toward her, showing her how to start a turn. James' skates sprayed her with a shower of ice crystals as he halted. He faced her with a tentative smile and tossed his head to clear the bright blond hair from his eyes. The same gesture informed her that Ian McKay once must have had long hair as well. Dark hair, but long like James's. Laura wondered how long a habit like that stayed with a man.

Behind Laura, her nervous young bodyguard paced the parlor. She would have to put his fears to rest now that he'd discovered her roaming habit. She should be disgusted with herself. She'd let her instincts get the better of her, let herself trust Ian McKay. At the cemetery, she had believed he cared what happened to her, but now she grew certain he just pumped her for information. With a shiver she remembered what he said about Arndt.

He never leaves a doubtful ally alive.

Is that also true of Ian McKay, she wondered? He lives by his wits and his strength. The limp and scar show he almost died that way. I'm a means to a goal for him. What if I become an obstacle?

The soldier, standing nervously behind her, moved his feet. "You shouldna gone out without me, Miss. Colonel thinks the guys that killed …Well, he thinks they're after you, too."

She looked around at him apologetically, "I'm sorry I worried you. I was with an old friend, so pretty safe. You want some dinner, Corporal Myer?"

The corporal loosened up enough to grin. "Sure would, ma'am – that is, if it wouldn' be no trouble."

"No trouble at all," she said and took her things to the kitchen.

While making dinner, she placed her second call to the Central Office of Intelligence. This time, her last name and the information about the man with the red beard stubble got her as far as Wild Bill Donovan himself. The director sounded guarded because of possible listeners.

"The man you describe is very dangerous, Miss Atweiler. Allow our man there to deal with the threat."

"Sir," she said, frustrated by the need to be oblique, "What happened here appears to be part of a much bigger plan – related to a small airplane in a farmer's field in Iceland. It will take more than this one man to deal with that."

He paused. When he spoke next, Donovan seemed stunned. "What is your source?"

"J.B." she said.

Another long pause told her eloquently that she'd hit a nerve. Finally, he said softly, "You do your homework, Miss Atweiler."

To make it clear her father had not breached Donovan's trust, she added, "I did my homework after my father died – because my father died, sir."

"I understand," he said. "Now please, for the next two weeks, lay low and let my man and his colleagues do their job."

Laura couldn't promise the impossible. "I will not interfere with him, Sir," she said. As close to the truth as she could come.

After serving Corporal Myer a steak and potatoes dinner at his post near the front door, Laura returned briefly to the kitchen. She took the matches and cigarettes out of her coat pocket, stowing them in her pack for tomorrow's journey to Helena, Montana. The purse with the revolver, she took to the bedroom. Tonight, she'd decipher the Champ telegram.

Tomorrow, she'd fly to Aunt Melany's. From there, she'd go wherever Arndt might be hiding.

* *

An hour later, Laura had a crick in her neck and no clue as to why the Champ telegram was significant. Laura reread it for the hundredth time.

For three days, I've studied this blamed thing.

Individual words and phrases made sense, but not the whole. When she applied ordinary ciphering techniques, the thing made no sense at all.

"Sir, the real Lascaux is undiscovered. All else is in place. Be all gone by March. Nice skiing near camp. At three fifteen, I test attraction for sadistic flies on Abner's facade.

Your Columbine and Black-eyed Susans."

Only the sign-off was significant to Laura. Blue Columbines and Black-eyed Susans were among the most prominent meadow flowers of the mountain parks of Colorado. They created beauty. Schön, beautiful and Feld, meadow or field. With James's penchant for word play, this could be another twist on his name.

But it couldn't be James. It was sent only three weeks ago. Still, the telegram had been in the file on Champ.

Of course, she thought, Champs – meadows, fields in French.
And before that Jacques Barcleigh – leigh is meadow in Gaelic.

McKay had admitted the connection between Champ and James. Champ replaced James. Champ was both shorter, stronger and darker than her childhood image of James.

Her mind wandered back to her encounter with McKay in the cemetery.

Why does he want me gone to Helena?

On the surface, she understood the professional agent's wish to have an amateur stay out of the way, but Ian McKay seemed to put it more personally. She wondered if he wanted her safe, or hoped to get her out of the way so he could cover up what he did here. While Laura reflected on that sobering thought, another occurred to her.

Is it possible he actually hopes to revenge my father's death himself? Why would he care so much? He does know Dad very well. What did he say . . . ? A time to work, a time to love. A time to play too. Ian missed that part.

She understood at last that The General had kept work separate for her own safety, but she had known his love and shared his play – mountain climbing, sharp-shooting, skiing.

Except when he carved. I never knew about the statue of Mother.

A sudden desire to be where he spent all those solitary hours made her rise. Needing an excuse, she found a broom and dustpan before she started up the attic stairs. The messiness of the place struck her fully this time. He'd been a meticulous man. Even their campsites were clean and orderly.

This room is almost deliberately strewn with shavings. How could he work here?

The footsteps, her own and the intruder's, seemed to punctuate her question.

Her father didn't just carve up here. He hid things here, secret things.

He needed to know the minute someone invaded this room.

On the table under the window, the empty rectangle already filled with dust.

What was there before? A file box? A book of codes?

She knew she should tell someone it was gone, but who?

Bernard will know what to do with the information. He won't do anything with it himself, but he'll know where to send it.

No doubt she did him a disservice. Even though he seemed a coward when it came to plain speaking for the bereaved, he must have physical and moral courage. How else could he have become a colonel at such a young age? She decided to tell him about the empty space when he took her to the airport in the morning.

In the meantime, she wanted to know what else might have been up here when Arndt invaded. Arndt had picked up the statue. Perhaps there were papers hidden inside the carvings.

She turned over each figure and found them solid. Glancing around, she saw nothing else in the room but cobwebs and sawdust. She checked each rafter, running her fingers around the hard to see places. Nothing was hidden between the rafters and the roofing. She knelt down, testing the lowest corners where rafters rested on the framing timbers for the second level of the house. As she backed out of the last corner, a tight space near the window dormer where two roof angles met the attic floor, her eye caught a glimpse of white at the edge of the flooring. Reaching for it, she got down on her stomach. Slowly, so as not to tear it, she pulled an old envelope from between the unfinished floorboards and the wall.

The strong, rounded handwriting made her cry out.

James!

She stared at it as if he himself had come into the room. Slowly backing into the light, she couldn't take her eyes off of it. The envelope had been addressed to 'A.T. Hamlet' at a post box in nearby Colorado Springs.

This is how the Champ letters arrived.

Laura began to laugh and cry at the same moment. The writing was James's. The joke was her father's.

'Weiler' means town or hamlet, she incanted, just as her father had said it when she first asked him about their funny name. And there was a special connection to James in this pun. The year James lived with them, they'd read Shakespeare's *Hamlet* aloud in the evenings, because it was a school assignment for James.

She hadn't understood most of the story then, though she'd loved sitting next to her father and feeling his voice rumble through his body. James had always lain on the floor, feeding the fire and occasionally asking why Hamlet didn't 'Do Something'.

Laura sniffed and stared at the dusty paper through a film of tears.

For God's sake why can't I get that boy out of my mind? He's been dead for three years.

She knew the answer. She'd worshipped him as a child. As a teenager, her letters to him, and his to her, were a shared growing up – separate, but somehow intimate. She'd begun to recognize that he was no longer the boy she'd been writing to, but a deeply thoughtful man.

Her father's long trip to Europe while she attended college, in 1939, coincided with the mysterious cessation of James's letters and the beginning of a certain distance in her father's writings to her.

Three months later, her father had come back to the states, but not to Colorado. He'd spent three weeks climbing in Oregon before he showed up at her university rooms in Greeley. Over dinner, he explained that James had died and that he, the fearless general of armies, had detoured to Oregon to get up the courage to tell her so.

But since her conversation with McKay, she realized that her father hadn't told her the whole truth. Arndt had killed James.

Then, three years later, Arndt killed her father.

Why doesn't Laura Do Something?

Daughter, square your shoulders and march forth on the alert.

Laura wiped her eyes and started to get up. Then she noticed the torn corner of the envelope. Her father always opened envelopes that way, tearing off a small part of the upper right-hand corner, slipping a pointer finger into the hole and ripping down the side.

Part of the cancellation stamp was gone, but Laura saw clearly that this letter had been mailed 12/30/40 – almost two years after James's death.

She sat down, hard.

James is alive.

The idea seemed hard to grasp, but this was James's writing. This was James.

What was it her father said? "James . . . killed . . . danger." Later he'd said, "Find James Save Werner."

I thought he meant save Werner. But he shook his head. He meant save James from Werner.

She stood quickly, bumping her head on the rafter. Rubbing her crown, she left the attic and carried the envelope back to her room. There, on her desk sat her copy of the mysterious telegram.

If James is alive, she thought, this telegram is from him.

Excitement rose in her body, making her hands tremble, her mind race with anticipation. Believing James was alive, and knowing how

James's mind worked, she might be able to decipher the Champ telegram after all.

Today is Monday, she thought, four days since I found Dad. Arndt's had four days! I have to find James before Arndt traps him.

CHAPTER TWELVE

MONDAY, MARCH 9, 1942

The crackle of a radio receiver drowned out automobile noises from the street below. Nine o'clock Monday night and all day Werner Arndt's powerful body had been hunched over a small black suitcase. Arndt's red beard stubble grew again into a full healthy beard and his blackened hair showed its natural gold-red color at the roots. Dieter Haupt knew others thought Arndt a handsome giant of a man – the epitome of the Nazi ideal.

Only when an observer looked into his blue eyes did he notice a certain emptiness behind the color. The beautiful blue veiled an infinite void. Most men did not look at his eyes more than once. They didn't want to envision so clearly the future into which he led them.

As he worked in another part of the apartment, Dieter watched Arndt lean close to the suitcase that concealed a radio receiver. He transcribed a tap-code message. He could transcribe and send at far greater than thirty words a minute, even in unusual codes. The sender at the other end halted along at a bare thirteen words per minute. Arndt's left-over energy and tension could barely take the stress of waiting. His impatience showed in the sideways wag of his over-large head.

The battered suitcase-radio sat on the floor. No other furniture existed in the apartment, only blankets, climbing packs and the debris of several meals. Dieter plowed through papers on the floor, past communications, searching for evidence of their successes.

On the wall next to the doorway hung Dieter Haupt's large map of the United States. Dieter stoically pushed pins into the map in places dictated by information the third man gleaned from the papers. Dieter's white hair stood on end from repeated rakings with a greasy hand. He was exhausted, but he couldn't stop until Arndt rested.

All day, Arndt had been communicating with men and women in the major cities across the United States. He wiggled his shoulders with impatience as he listened to the tapped-out message that seemed interminable. As soon as the sender finished his message, Arndt began hammering a reply on the keys with fury.

"Gott im Himmel. Esel!"

Arndt continued haranguing his distant audience with the transmitter key and his persuasive voice, not so much unaware as uncaring about his bleak surroundings. He worked feverishly, communicating with several stations over the next hour. He tapped out messages to a drug store owner in Detroit, in Los Angeles to a seamstress, a Grand Dragon in Macon. He cajoled, harangued, threatened. He advised, blew on the coals of latent racism, mentioned the beloved fatherland or the natural supremacy of whiteness.

Dieter no longer trusted this man, hadn't trusted him for a long time because he now understood that in Arndt's life, only Arndt mattered.

Everyone else? Expendable.

At last, Arndt turned from the radio and glanced at the room – a blanket for a bed, carefully laid out in an alcove that couldn't be seen from the entry. No pictures, no books and no lamp. Not even torn wallpaper to relieve the cold plaster. He didn't seem to notice the lack. Arndt never amused himself with anything but work – and twisting others to his will.

Dieter took one notebook of coded phone numbers and slid it under a pile of discarded food and paper. He couldn't even explain to himself why he made that move, but he knew if anyone else found that notebook, it would spell doom for all the work that he and Arndt had done in the United States.

A final message was sent by Arndt to Toronto. The reply returned and the sign-off – W.R.R.H.

"Wilhelm Richard Rudolf Hess," muttered Arndt as he transcribed the message. "He wants the world blown up yesterday. I am willing to plan and to wait for tomorrow."

Grabbing up the heavy black telephone that sat behind him, he dialed a seven-digit number. Dieter knew Arndt's brain held a memory bank of phone numbers. He wouldn't be looking for the notebook any time soon, and if he did, Dieter could produce it in a flurry of pretended searching.

As soon as the other party answered the phone, Arndt launched into his message.

"They're sending the next mission into New York Harbor on a U2 under the command of Gottfrau," he spat out. "That prick can't even read a map." Arndt needed no reply. His phone companion in an unusual display of wisdom remained silent. "At least they've got Brehmen and three others landing in Florida," Arndt went on. "A good explosives man. They'll do the job on the shipyards of the southern coast."

The man at the other end of the phone line said. "Pouf! All gone by the end of the week."

Arndt scowled. "Nothing so childish. Brehmen will merely undermine the foundation piers of the slipway, or cause a small flood in the hull at launch time, anything to slow progress."

"What about this traitor Sebold, in New York?" the man asked.

"Not my problem. I didn't recruit him."

"He's exposed at least twenty men. More each day. They go on trial next month."

"They were stupid not to spot the camera set-up in his office – the clock, the mirror aimed right at their faces . . . What did they think that mirror was there for? Their vanity?"

The other man tried flattery. "At least you've stopped Military Intelligence – dead in the snow, so to speak,"

Flattery fell on contemptuous ears. Arndt needed no one else to tell him his value.

"Stopped Military Intelligence, hah!" Arndt snorted in disgust. "You always hope for the easy ending, don't you? Atweiler is dead, but Schoenfeld is still out there."

"What tipped you that he might be alive?"

"Never mind how I know. I know. Schoenfeld thinks he's set a trap. I need a little bait of my own. Miss Atweiler ought to do the trick. She still under guard?"

"Very."

"Take care of that guard. I'll want to meet this little beauty alone – tonight."

The voice at the other end sounded pinched. "It's not that easy. If I call off the guard, my connection with what happens after will be clear."

"Only if either the guard or Miss Atweiler is alive to talk."

"He's a mere boy."

"So much easier to take care of. I will take care of Miss Atweiler."

"I can't just murder him, that would expose me to . . ."

"Warum nicht? Do I have to remind you of the importance of certain photographs in my file?"

"Werner . . . It's already ten o'clock."

"Herr Arndt to you," snapped Arndt. "Little Lottie is prepared to say all kinds of things about your time together in Berlin – what you did, what you talked about . . ."

"I'll take care of the guard."

"Do it soon. No guard after midnight. By two o'clock in the morning, I will have young Fraulein Atweiler caught in a spider's web that even Schoenfeld won't be able to cut."

"And after you've caught her?" "I become the spider."

CHAPTER THIRTEEN

MONDAY, MARCH 9, 1942

By eleven o'clock that night, Laura had very little time left and nothing to show for hours of work. She had to leave for Aunt Melany's in the morning and still had no idea where to look for Arndt. In spite of her assumption that the telegram was sent recently by a resurrected James, she became lost in a jumble of allusions for which she had no background. She knew James's mind. Yet, from the opening line to the last, the Champ telegram left her stumped.

> *"Sir,*
>
> *The real Lascaux is undiscovered."*

Army Intelligence reports had hinted at mysterious cave paintings, recently discovered at Lascaux, France. However, Laura wasn't even sure of the subject of the Lascaux paintings or how they could be related to Verheerung.

After the reference to Lascaux, the rest seemed to make sense, but didn't.

"Be all gone by March," it read. "Nice skiing near camp. At three fifteen I test attraction for sadistic flies on Abner's facade."

James! Could you be any more inane? Why didn't you use the code instead of these senseless phrases? Where are you?

Desperate, Laura paced her floor, re-reading the note. Through filmy bedroom curtains, the heavy darkness of night weighed down her mind. After several more efforts, she resorted to reading aloud. Hearing the words 'all gone', she stopped.

That's it.

Years ago, just before he embarked for Europe, James had sent her a joke postcard showing a map of a huge state of New York with all the other states in 'proper perspective'. The other states, drawn small, had also been renamed to seem like cultural backwoods. Colorado had become 'Cold 'n Ratty'.

And the state of Oregon had become 'All Gone'.

James would have remembered that post card as well as she. At sixteen, he would have pored over it, savoring each silly pun.

All Gone! So, James will be in Oregon by March. It's March ninth already. When in March? Where?

"At three fifteen I test attraction for sadistic flies on Abner's facade."

Laura ran from her room so fast, she banged the door against the wall. Flying down the stairs, she calculated. "Three fifteen – on March fifteen. I have only five days left. I've wasted so much time trying to understand."

Downstairs, she passed the young corporal, half asleep in his straight-backed chair. Hazily, he arose as she entered the room.

"Have a seat, Corporal Myer," she said. "I'm just searching for something in the library. Won't bother you a bit."

"You wouldn't be climbing out of any more windows, now would you ma'am?" he asked.

"Not yet," she laughed. "I'll let you know." Hurrying into the library, she stepped over the dog. Vandal raised his head and then stood, sensing her urgency.

"I've got to find it, Vandal. It's got to be in here."

In a drawer at the left end of the bookshelves, her father's maps were in order, thin folders for Ohio and Oklahoma, followed by two fat files for Oregon.

"Not much mountain climbing in Ohio and Oklahoma," she mumbled to the dog. Vandal grunted.

The files for Oregon were heavy.

Too much climbing in Oregon. How'm I going to find the right one tonight?

She glanced at her watch. *Eleven-fifteen.*

As she opened the first file folder, the phone on the desk rang. Annoyed, she snatched it up. Private First-Class Smith asked for Corporal Myer.

When she called him, the sheepish Myer entered the library, watching the dog. Vandal growled low in his throat as he did every time anyone other than Laura entered the room. Laura calmed the dog. "Friend," she announced and handed the phone to Corporal Myer as the dog subsided at her feet.

It occurred to Laura that only Agent Ian McKay had gotten away with massaging Vandal's belly. There'd been no growls and distrust when he'd snuck into this room yesterday. She wondered how Ian calmed Vandal.

Corporal Myer eyed the dog all the time he stood in the room. He spoke diffidently into the phone and seemed flattered to have the attention of a mere private. Laura wondered how any boy came to be so unsure of himself. Myer seemed a polite young man, but he lacked confidence.

Hanging up, he explained, "My buddy says Sarge says I'm to go on back to barracks, ma'am. He's got an officer already hidden in your garage in case you have any intruders during the night."

Laura glanced up from the maps and gave the young man a warm smile. "I appreciate your vigilance, Corporal. Get a good night's sleep."

"Yes ma'am." Out of habit, he saluted her, then grinned and backed out of the room. In a moment, she heard the front door close behind him. She glanced after him, feeling the emptiness of the house without his awkward presence. Then she hauled herself back to work, slapped another 'Oregon Climbs' folder down on the big desk and glanced through.

Mount Jefferson, Crater Lake on Mount Mazama, Thielson, Three Sisters, McLaughlin, Three Fingered Jack, Sacajawea Peak, Mount Hood.

She remembered the climbing photos in her father's bedroom. The one of Mount Hood had been framed and hung within the last two years, since James's supposed death. She remembered its craggy basalt top lit by the rising sun. A flag of peach colored clouds flew around its summit. Her father had gone to Oregon three years ago. Since then, he'd visited Oregon three or four times a year supposedly testing climbing equipment in the heavy, wetter snow of the Cascades.

In the Verheerung papers, James's last communication (as J.B.) had proclaimed jubilantly, "I found a way to discredit Muscles with the Nazi high command. I'll show you the proof next time I'm in the states. Could you arrange time away from the base to meet me in the usual place?"

Is Mount Hood your usual place?

Laura plucked the contour map for Mount Hood out of the pile.

Flattening it, she started pointing her finger at the summit, then following down the several summit routes for climbers which were marked with dashed lines. Steel Ridge, Newton Clark Glacier, Cathedral Spire, on the east.

Her finger returned to the apex each time.

South side, Hawkins Cliffs, Reid Glacier, Yocum Ridge, Sandy Glacier.

Her finger returned to Yocum Ridge. No climber's route had been marked.

Impossible. Too steep, too many obstacles, too exposed. . .

But the multi-swoop profile was comic character L'il Abner Yokum's major characteristic. And the impossible climb was James's trademark.

"I test attraction for sadistic flies on Abner's facade," he'd said.

Arndt must be the sadistic fly James wanted to attract? Did he intend to get him out in the open by announcing that he would be on this impossible ridge on the Ides of March?

After thirteen years together, Arndt would know James's penchant for allusive word play. He wanted Arndt to understand this telegram.

Laura sat back in the big leather chair. I have to think it all the way through. First, James is alive.

She hugged that thought to herself for a moment before returning to puzzle out the situation. She sighed as she listed the next factors.

James became a spy for Dad. James's code name was Champ. Arndt was a part of the network too. Also, Arndt's mistress, Kirsten Cieski, I suppose. But Arndt also sells information to the Nazis.

Ian McKay's story of James's death returned to her mind, vividly underlining Arndt's vicious nature. Arndt suspects James and Kirsten have discovered his Nazi connection. He has Kirsten killed in James's bed while he and James are climbing l'Aiguille, the Needle.

Laura realized Arndt tried to kill James during the last descent of the Needle, but stopped, seeing that there were witnesses. That had been the reason for the unexplained drop during the last eighty feet. James was not supposed to live to defend himself.

So, easy to pin Kirsten's murder on him if he can't protest.

But Arndt became stymied in that plan by the villagers near l'Aiguille who 'came to see and stayed to pray.' Instead, when James and Arndt returned to Berlin, Arndt used the discovery of Kirsten's death as an excuse to fly into a jealous rage, stabbed James and threw him down the stairs.

Someone – neighbors perhaps – prevented Arndt from finishing the job. Yet, even in the hospital, James would still be in danger from Arndt.

There had been, she recalled, an urgent note to her dad from a colleague in the margin of James's letter about that climb. The General flew to Europe and found James near death in the Berlin hospital. He convinced some doctor to sign a death certificate. With James dead, Arndt had believed himself safe.

Remembering those pre-war times, Laura understood how precarious the next step must have been. Barely months before the Germans invade Poland, traveling was not yet completely restricted, but she could imagine how tight it was, getting an invalid through German borders.

Somehow her father had flown James to a hospital in Paris to recover.

Then Dad took James to Oregon for rehabilitation.

"Why didn't Dad tell me? Why did he let me go through all that anger and pain?"

She answered the question herself. "Arndt has a spy at Camp Springs. Dad had to convince that man I believed James was dead."

"Why didn't they tell me the truth later?"

She knew that, too.

James returned to spying. He is J.B. who sent the Verheerung reports.

There would be every chance he would, indeed, die after all.

She shook off self-pity and returned to the present. Recently Arndt discovered that James is alive. James, realizing Arndt is after him, tries to draw him out – tries to attract the `sadistic fly' to Mount Hood.

The chivalrous assumptions of that plan convinced her its author was James Schoenfeld.

Great! James, did you think Arndt would show up alone to do gentleman's battle with the Green Knight?

James! Do you even know that Dad's been murdered? Dad's supposed to meet you.

She shivered, thinking of James alone, expecting help from her father. He had no back-up, inadequate information.

No one to meet you – So I will meet you. Where? Abner Yokum's profile on Mount Hood.

Quickly, Laura returned her attention to the map. Until given close scrutiny, Yocum Ridge appeared to be like any other rock on the mountaintop. However, the elevation rose from eight thousand to eleven thousand feet so rapidly that the contour lines seemed to be stacked on each other. The one ridge on which there were no dotted lines indicating climbers' routes. On either side of it, there were numerous crevasse markings in the glaciers. A fall would mean death.

What the devil do you think you're doing, James? Climb an unknown route? Advertise it to Arndt and let him pick you off with his stolen Garand? Where's your common sense?

She noticed how readily she'd slipped back into the habit of talking to James Schoenfeld. She knew he was alive, as if he had come into the room himself. Alive and in danger. That's what her father had tried to tell her.

On the map, her finger ran down the Yocum Ridge to an abrupt waterfall below Timberline. Following the contour lines back to the east, she came across the name "Government Camp" indicating a small settlement of cabins.

"Nice skiing near camp," she whispered and studied the nearby areas. At least two ski trails from the famous Timberline Lodge ended near the little town. She glanced at her copy of the telegram again.

"Be all gone by March. Nice skiing near camp. At three fifteen, I test attraction for sadistic flies on Abner's Facade."

Laura blew a long slow and exasperated breath. "The man's crazy," she said. "But that's what he plans to do. And I must get there."

She glanced at her watch. Five after twelve – the shy Corporal Myer had been gone almost an hour. Vaguely, she wondered why the new guard had been stationed in her garage instead of her house.

The guard's probably a grown man. Bernard Johnson's so protective of my reputation – it's almost as if I were his wife.

Not a chance.

She folded the map and stuffed it in her pack. She put away the other maps and pulled out a road atlas for the western states. Studying it, she decided that she'd be way ahead to take off in the jeep tonight. It would be lots faster than waiting until tomorrow morning, flying to Montana and driving from there.

"It's a good thing the jeep is outside the garage," she said to herself. "I can imagine what Bernard's guard would say as I drive away. I'll just have to pack quietly."

Her mind back on the maps, she decided to head north to Wyoming and then cross Idaho and eastern Oregon. With all her winter driving experience, she wouldn't be stopped by the high pass in Wyoming though it might still snow there. She could drive straight on through and arrive at Government Camp in about forty hours.

The dog beside her whined and leaned against her leg. Studying him, she realized what a help it would be to have some kind of ally. He seemed to be recovering from his ordeal on Longs Peak.

"You can come too, boy," she crooned, rubbing his ears. "Let's get ready."

*   *

TUESDAY, MARCH 10, 1942

By one thirty in the morning, she'd thrown all the blankets and food they'd need into the jeep. Her skis were tied on top. She was a little surprised that the guard in the garage hadn't come out to stop her, but she assumed he'd gone to sleep. She stayed long enough to leave the unused airline ticket inside the screen door. He'd find it when she didn't answer in the morning.

A call to Aunt Melany had informed her not to expect Laura for several days. Aunt Melany also knew what Laura planned. She hardly approved, but the old lady was a lot like her niece and her brother, Arthur – stubborn and independent. She understood. In fact, though bed-ridden, she wanted to come, too.

Aunt Melany possessed Agent Ian McKay's identity in case anything happened. She'd promised to ring phones until they jumped off desks in both the COI and the FBI if Laura didn't call Helena, Montana within six days.

Vandal seemed frisky for the first time since she'd brought him down from Longs Peak. He leaped through the unsnapped isinglass window at the right side of the jeep and made himself comfortable in the passenger's seat. Laura climbed into the driver's side and started the motor.

Suddenly, the passenger door opened. A darkly clad shape appeared in the doorway. One wide hand reached in toward the dog's head.

Laura's heart stopped as a low voice resonated, "Scoot to the back, Beast."

Vandal barked once and then jumped to the cramped back seat. He sat there panting and staring at the dark image of a man who pulled a rifle from behind him.

Laura yanked on the latch at her door, intending to roll out and run, but the man slung the rifle and an ammunition belt over the seat to the floor behind her, even as his other hand pulled her right arm, preventing her exit. He put his knee into the right front seat.

Ian McKay folded himself into the small front seat, saying, "Let's go. We're all settled in."

"You!" Laura croaked. "Get out."

"Can't." He closed his door. "You'd take off. And then where would I be?"

"I want to go skiing by myself," Laura began lamely. She had to convince him of her benign intentions. She didn't want random COI agents like Ian McKay finding out that James was alive. "I just need to get away and . . ."

Her heart froze.

Ian was waving the original Champ telegram in front of her. "They told me you'd become a smart lady."

She grew silent – flushed, and trembling with anger.

"I figured you'd understand this sooner or later," he said, looking at the telegram in the darkened car. "Sooner than I expected," he concluded. "However, you can't go off on this expedition by yourself. It wouldn't be safe."

Glancing at him, she started the motor and eased off the clutch, thinking fast – thinking about the unbuttoned plastic window next to him and whether she and the dog could survive a roll in the jeep.

"I'm glad you decided to drive instead of fly," he went on. "I don't have a Daddy Warbucks to hand me airplane tickets, but then, I expect I don't bat my eyelashes in the accepted way."

"You are rude and disgusting." She pushed down on the accelerator and glanced at the dog in the mirror. He circled to lie down in the back seat.

"Me rude?" McKay said, mockingly polite. "You were going to leave without a word to those of us who care the most."

Laura slammed on the brakes. Ian's hands slapped the dash as his head made contact with the windshield. His body rocketed back into his seat just as the dog hurtled into the back of him. Vandal howled. The motor choked off. Laura turned to see what damage had been done to the animal.

Ian grabbed her wrists. In the light of the streetlamp, she could see blood streaming down his forehead and across one eye. His other eye glinted at her through a narrowed slit.

"You want to get the man who killed your father?"

"Yes," she ground out.

Slowly, emphatically, he said, "So... do... I."

Vandal had reclaimed his place in the back seat. He slumped down onto it. Laura noticed all this out of the corner of her eye as Ian held her.

Ian's anger seemed to send shock waves through the air, yet the dog merely lay down. Vandal was no protection.

At least her stupid ploy hadn't hurt the dog, but it had clearly hurt the man. No telling what he would do to her.

"Miss Atweiler, I'm going to let you go," he said between tightly clamped jaws. "You are going to start the car and get us to Oregon in record time without further mishap. Do you understand me?"

"Your forehead . . ."

"I'll take care of it as soon as I have your word."

She hesitated. His grip tightened. Glancing down at his big hands, she noticed the crumpled telegram on the seat between them. Its significance finally hit her.

"You broke into my house," she said.

"Yes."

"Not Arndt."

"God, I hope not."

She stared at him long and thoughtfully before she made up her mind. "I'll drive." She omitted that she'd dump him at the first opportunity. He let go of her arms and fell back into the seat, closing his eyes.

After a moment, he reached inside his coat and pulled out an envelope. With it, he wiped his forehead.

"That's my aeroplane ticket," she commented.

"Nobody is to know where we're going. It'll be tough enough to do it right with just the three of us getting in each other's way."

Laura decided not to mention that Aunt Melany knew. She frowned. "Three of us? You, me and Vandal?"

He opened one eye and gave her an unfocused glare. "I guess it's actually four. You, me, James and the dog, here."

"Oh. James." She thought, how does he know about James?

"How come my dog doesn't even growl at you?" she asked.

"I'm lovable. Could we get on the road, please? It's already after one-thirty in the morning."

As she started the motor, he zipped up the isinglass window and turned on his left side so he could watch her and rest his injured head at the same time. "It's going to be one chilly drive," he commented and fell asleep.

CHAPTER FOURTEEN

TUESDAY, MARCH 10TH

At one forty-five in the morning, the bare bulb of the Atweiler's attic light shone on Werner Arndt. In one hand, he held a crumpled piece of paper on which the controlled swirls of Laura's handwriting could be seen. Arndt's other hand caressed the rounded contours of a Cherry- wood statue. His eyes were hard, gray as gunmetal and glaring at Colonel Bernard Johnson.

"This is Laura Atweiler?"

"It looks like her," said Johnson. "Is the child Schoenfeld's?"

"There is no child."

"As far as you know." Arndt's thumb ran across the woman's abdomen and rested, almost lovingly, next to the arm that held the child.

Johnson winced as he watched the fragile statue in the meaty hand.

Arndt's power filled the room, fascinating and repelling Johnson. "Where is she?" Arndt asked softly.

"I don't know. She was supposed to get on that flight tomorrow morning, but tonight . . ."

"Her jeep is gone," Arndt began, "Her room is neat. However, there are no boots, no winter jacket in her closet or in the basement storage area."

Arndt's voice softened ominously as he continued the list. "No sleeping bag stored in the camping equipment, no tent, no tarp, no skis, no crampons, no icepick, no rope. Where do you think she goes?"

"She escapes into the mountains sometimes, to be alone."

"Longs Peak?" Arndt became deafening in his controlled whisper.

"She could go there. But the bodies are already gone. There's nothing there..."

"Where was she last Wednesday? Last Thursday?"

"At home, on vaca ..." Johnson saw at once the folly of guessing, "I don't know for sure."

"So," said Arndt, "she could have been up there."

"But the location was top secret."

"She is the General's daughter, nein?"

"Of course."

"She is stupid?"

"No," Johnson answered reluctantly.

"You said she asked Vibes to call the camp when the General did not turn up. Do you think she then merely sat in front of the fire waiting? She, who escapes to the mountains?"

"Perhaps not, but ..."

"Tell me what you found when you returned to Long's Peak."

Johnson hesitated.

"Tell me."

"The bodies were in the field, exactly as we left them, except that Atweiler had crawled out of the cave and died next to Major Banks."

Arndt hissed, "Crawled out? We left him in no condition to puke, much less crawl."

"His body was out there."

"You have not before told this!" Arndt's voice rose and his perfect English twisted with his anger. His hand clenched the statue.

"I saw the trail where he crawled."

"You were first to the meadow?"

"Major Cameron arrived ahead of us by about half an hour."

"And this Cameron, was he in the cave when you arrived?"

"Yes. He'd checked all the bodies. Made a sketch of their location. Said he'd followed Atweiler's trail back to the cave. He had Major Well's roommate, Major Farr, start bagging the bodies almost as soon as we came on the scene. It was getting late."

"What condition did you find Cameron – his uniform?"

"Pretty done-in, I can tell you. He practically ran up that trail. Said he fell several times. That's why he gotten so wet and had to change to civies before we left the camp."

"His uniform was wet?"

"Yes." said Johnson, puzzled.

Arndt's face twisted as he glared at Johnson. Johnson stepped away from the menacing grimace. Without even glancing at the statue, Arndt flicked his thumb and cracked off the woman's arm. The arm and child fell on the floor.

Johnson's eyes widened in fear.

"First," hissed Arndt, "Tonight, we surprise Major Cameron with a visit."

"Yes, sir."

"Then you come with me to Oregon. You and Dieter Haupt will make a stop in a little town called Madras. There's something in Madras needs finishing. After that, you meet me at Mount Hood. I believe Miss Atweiler will be there and need your soothing presence."

"But my men? Tomorrow begins a new Boot Camp."

"They will learn to parade without you," said Arndt.

As Arndt turned to leave, his boot reached out and smashed the Cherry-wood child into the floorboards.

* *

TUESDAY, MARCH 10, 1942

Ian McKay asked Laura to stop at a phone booth on the edge of Denver. As soon as she pulled over, Ian took the keys from the steering column. He climbed out and made a call he didn't tell her about. And Laura refused to give him the satisfaction of asking, but in the snow, she saw that the mark of his boot was the same as the marks made in her father's attic wood shavings.

After that phone call, Ian McKay slept deeply.

In the darkest hours before dawn, Laura pulled over to the side of the road, unable to keep her eyes open any longer. The man beside her awoke with a start.

"Stopped? Where are we?" he asked, stretching his body so thoroughly that she backed into the isinglass window beside her.

"I thought you were in a coma," she said sarcastically.

"People in a coma don't snore."

"You don't snore."

"I didn't used to, but I could hear snores even in my sleep. I think hitting your windshield deviated my septum."

"Deviated what?"

He grabbed his nose and leered at her.

"Oh," she said, fiddling with the gearshift. She looked out over the darkened road. "We're somewhere in Wyoming. The junction to Saratoga is ten miles ahead."

"Where the hell is Saratoga, Wyoming?" muttered Ian.

The dog behind them turned and snored in his sleep.

They glanced at each other. McKay looked startled. Laura burst into laughter – the kind of crazy release exhaustion requires. While she wiped her tired eyes, Ian took the keys from the ignition again, and opened his door.

"Hey," she said, grabbing for his jacket.

"Back in a minute, Love."

She recoiled.

He turned back, chuckling. "A mere figure of speech, Miss Atweiler."

Two minutes later, she wished he would come back. The jeep grew cold and the night dark. He was at least another intelligent human being with whom to share the road. Laura wondered why she wanted to share the road with Agent Ian McKay when she knew so little about him except that he always seemed to know what she would do. She knew he worked for the new and somewhat suspect Central Office of Intelligence.

And he climbs into houses and paws through drawers. He hires pickpockets. He's fixed it so I'm traveling with him, but no one else knows where I am. He lives on the edge of violence . . . but he claims to care about Dad – enough to seek revenge.

This last fact had made her drive all these hours next to his silent, sleeping form, carrying them both toward Oregon and whatever situation James had set up to trap Arndt. Ian McKay seemed to want Arndt as badly as she and James did. But she could not be sure. She would not trust him until James told her to trust.

She peered out into the darkness, wondering where McKay had gone. Was he meeting someone? Someone he didn't want her to know about? She reached into the back for her pack. In the seat behind her, the dog turned around once and stopped snoring. Outside the silent car, the wind had kicked up in the last few seconds, sending dust swirling. She could smell the odor of new sage needles and hear the rustle of wind through Juniper trees. Through the windshield, she saw a tumbleweed roll into the left fender and huddle there, making a soft scratching sound.

Something larger hit the isinglass beside her. Laura jerked awake. A looming shadow reached toward the yellowed window. She gasped and grabbed frantically for the nearest hard object just as the door yanked open.

Ian's eyes grew wide as she brought the business end of her pack swinging toward him. He ducked and grabbed at the strap.

"What the . . ."

"Oh. I thought you were someone else."

He held onto the strap and glared at her, opening the door wide so she could get a feel for the vast emptiness behind him. "Who else did you have in mind, Lady?"

"I just meant . . . You were gone so long, I thought . . ."

"It's tough to find an appropriate bush around here," he explained. "Hop out. It's your turn. I won't look."

It took her a second to understand. Then she held out her hand. He reluctantly deposited the key in it as she emerged from behind the wheel.

"We trust each other so thoroughly," he said and slid into the driver's seat, closing the door.

Laura gazed into the darkness, searching vainly for enough underbrush to offer a modest escape. She grew cold. The wind created eerie sounds as it whistled through the stunted trees. Off in the distant hills, a mountain lion squalled like a baby. Laura took a few hurried steps off the highway and decided to believe Ian wouldn't look.

CHAPTER FIFTEEN

Ian's mistake, he figured, had been to glance at Laura as she slept. She'd backed into the far corner, leaning against the passenger door. Her eyes had closed an hour ago – long sable lashes brushing her pale skin as she finally gave in to exhaustion.

He shouldn't have looked at her. After that fatal glance, he tried to get his mind back on driving. His mind wouldn't cooperate. The shadowed mystery of her pulled at him. And beyond the jeep window, the clear winter night contributed to his discomfort – the moon lighting her finely shaped cheek bones, the Milky Way haloing her curls, the midnight shadows revealing the contours of her chin, her breasts, her hips. He tried to ignore these distracting details, tried to tell himself how wrong it would be to think of her this way when she had just lived through a horrible ordeal.

He tried, God knew he tried. But all he wanted was to hold her in his arms, touch the peak of her lips with his thumb, awaken her with the lightest kiss.

He disgusted himself. His body ached with lust.

And then, the road swerved right. The motion of the jeep brought her head and shoulders away from the window frame. Unsupported by anything but the back of the seat, she lolled like a soft doll. Keeping an eye on the road, he reached out to steady her, accidentally caught his little finger in her rolled-up sleeve and pulled his hand toward him to get it out. His finger came free with a tug. She toppled.

As her head landed in his lap, Ian knew he was in trouble. He knew it by the heat in his loins and the throbbing hollow at the base of his throat. He knew he should push her upright before too late.

Instead, he wrapped one curl of her black hair around his forefinger and rested his hand in the shining depths of her tresses.

*   *

Dawn rose behind them as they traveled toward the Idaho border.

Ian's humming brought Laura out of her stupor. As soon as she opened her eyes and realized where she was, she figured she had trouble.

Her head lay in his lap. She could watch the motion of the steering wheel, a mere inch above her right ear. Her left ear had grown numb. Absolutely still, she thought fast.

If only I'd locked the jeep before I started driving. . .

She hadn't locked it. She was stuck with him. Still, it seemed the height of folly to have allowed her head to rest in his lap. She must have been stupidly sleeping when she intended to keep silent vigil. She'd closed her eyes for such a short time – back when it was deepest dark.

His long fingers rhythmically combed her curls and hummed as he drove. Above her, the black steering wheel turned slightly clockwise, then counter-clockwise. The bump and hum of the road matched the tuneless humming of the driver. She decided to wait until Ian's song ended before rising so as not to startle him while he drove.

But his tune never seemed to end. She had plenty of time to become acquainted with the view of his thigh covered in dark green gabardine. His muscles were hard.

No wonder my ear is numb.

She gazed at his knees, sideways. Laura closed one eye. She alternated eyes and then looked again with both. There was no doubt about it. His left knee was a good deal farther from the dashboard than his right.

That accounts for the limp, she thought.

She knew she should sit up, but the warmth of his hand on her head and the rhythmic motion of his fingers were oddly comforting. She told herself she'd been foolish to trust any man. The Verheerung papers showed that her father's trust had been betrayed. Ian McKay could be the Judas.

At the very least, he was an enigma. He knew too much about her, though she'd never met him before. She knew nothing about him. He claimed to have worked with her dad in Army Intelligence during the only years she lived somewhere else. He knew how to get around the house as well as she did; it was he who took the telegram from her room.

Suddenly she tensed, realizing Ian had stolen the rectangle-shaped thing from the attic table. Ian must have felt her tension. His hand stopped its caressing motion and returned to the steering wheel.

"Laura," he said softly, "We're going to have to stop and get gas. Watch your head as you get up."

Get gas, she thought, I'll get rid of him then.

She ducked out from under the wheel. "Sorry," she said, barely looking at him. "I didn't realize . . . ."

"No problem." He glanced at her disheveled hair and clothes.

She thought she detected a smile lurking behind his eyes. She didn't like feeling vulnerable, so she sat up straighter and ran her fingers through her hair. As she did so, she caught him looking at her again. For the space of one second, his gaze was openly sensuous. Then he saw her eyes watching his. Silent laughter lifted his dark eyebrows.

"Caught," he said, adding, "You've become a beautiful woman, Laura Atweiler. I'm sure I'm not the first to notice."

Flustered and embarrassed, she lowered her hands and tugged at her wrinkled flannel blouse. "I . . . please." She couldn't seem to make her voice come out.

He watched her a moment, then looked back at the highway. "Believe me," he said, "You are beautiful. The men on the base have noticed, but they've also noticed that you don't want to be looked at that way. I'm sorry I've made you uncomfortable."

His apology made her even more uncomfortable. "Well . . . Yes. I shouldn't have fallen asleep. I . . ."

She knew she sounded stupid.

"The car swerved," he said. "Falling wasn't your fault."

She took a deep breath, then wished she hadn't and crossed her arms over her flannel shirt. He glanced away, out at the flatlands, as if interested in tumbleweed.

Determined to move the conversation away from herself, Laura asked, "Why do you want to help me find Werner Arndt?"

"All right," he sighed, his gaze returning to her. "Why help you?

"First, what do you really know about James Schoenfeld?"

She felt trapped. Ian claimed to be an ally, yet perhaps he was not. Anything she told him about James could put James in danger. Still, James was going to need help.

She decided to answer his question with a question. "How did you interpret the telegram?"

Ian steered the jeep around a coal wagon pulled by two sway-backed horses, and then he glanced at her.

"Laura, if you go after Arndt on your own, I guarantee you will lose. The man kills on very little provocation. If he wonders about you, he'll kill you, just in case."

"And you? Why should I trust you?" she asked.

"First, because I understand James. You want a demonstration?" He pulled out the telegram, waving it toward her and saying, "The Lascaux reference is obscure. It's not relevant until later. What does matter is that a man who signs off as field flowers, is planning to attract a sadist to a mountain in Oregon. The mountain has a ridge with a name like a famous cartoon character. It also has good skiing near a camp. How'm I doing so far?"

She turned toward him. "What mountain and why?"

"I'm not sure. That's where you come in."

"Who signs off as field flowers?"

"Schoenfeld, of course. The poor guy can't seem to stray far from his real name even for his own good."

Laura stiffened at the implied criticism.

"It's okay, Laura. We all have our little weaknesses. Schoenfeld has this one. Otherwise, he's one of the world's best mountain climbers and a gutsy spy. Loyal too. I must add. Never a whiff of double-dealing with regards to your James."

She was silent. And she was thankful he'd confirmed James character.

After a moment, he asked, "What mountain, Laura?"

"Who sent you?"

"I didn't hear from The General at the usual time. I knew the relay was working. I'd had other messages through that system. Donovan, head of COI, gave permission to abandon my post, but my own concern brought me to Colorado."

"What do you know about James Schoenfeld's death?" Laura asked.

"It was faked. He did almost die, don't get me wrong about that. But the General spirited him out of Berlin and left behind a death certificate and a box of bones and ashes."

"So, Arndt won't be expecting to see him?"

Ian shook his head slowly. "Not so. Arndt has recently figured out the ruse. Three weeks ago, James got something on Arndt. Arndt realized only James could have found this evidence, so he struck swiftly to stop the spread of that information."

"How?"

There was a moment's hesitation. When Ian answered, his voice was low and rough. "Arndt knew if James were alive, he would be in contact with the General. Since he didn't know where to find James, Arndt couldn't take a chance on the next link in the information chain."

"So, he killed Dad," she filled in what Ian was reluctant to say.

"Yes." He spoke as if treading on glass. "At about the same time, James discovered that Arndt knew he was alive. In an effort to distract Arndt, he sent this telegram. He made sure Arndt got a copy of it, so that Arndt would come after him instead of anyone else. But the telegram was too late."

Knowing all too well what 'too late' meant, Laura shifted, turning her face from Ian's view. Silent moments later, she drew a deep breath. "James doesn't know how many men Arndt has with him," she said.

Ian eyed her sharply. "Do you?"

"I think at least three, maybe more. I saw four tracks in the snow leaving Longs Peak."

"Laura," he whispered, "I wish you hadn't seen . . ."

"Dad waited for me," she said quickly, hoping that if she spoke fast, her voice wouldn't break. "Dad couldn't die until he warned me about Arndt and about Rudolf Hess. He tried to tell me James was in danger, but I didn't understand him at the time."

Laura was grateful that Ian watched the road as she talked. Her throat tightened around each word, choking her with unremitting tension.

Ian's hand reached out, tentatively taking hers. "Laura," he whispered.

The warmth of his hand eased her tension a little, enough to let one strangled sob escape before she clamped her lips shut.

At the brief sound, his fingers tightened then relaxed around hers. He steered through the absurdly sunny morning, demanding nothing, giving his strength to her. Ten miles later, Ian pulled the car abruptly off the road toward a lone, ramshackle building. The one gas pump stood at the side, covered with road dust.

"Have to gas up," he explained hoarsely.

Opening the door, he started to escape the tense atmosphere of the jeep, but turned back a moment, saying, "I should have nailed Arndt in Austria when I had the chance, but I thought 'better the snake you know than the snake you don't', and I let him go."

Ian rolled out the door before the pounding in Laura's head forced a cry. She slumped down against the side window, stifling deep moans into the wool of her jacket sleeve.

I'll kill him. I'll kill him, her mind declared over and over.

She didn't know if she meant Arndt, or Ian McKay who'd left Arndt free to torture others.

Minutes later, her anguish spent, she felt Vandal's rough tongue licking her ear. Jerking around, she faced long fangs and a dripping grin. He lifted one heavy paw and set it gently on her shoulder before whining. It took a moment for her to understand. Finally, Laura opened the jeep door and stepped out, followed by a desperate dog. Vandal raced to the nearest tree and did quick preliminary sniffing.

McKay stood in the dilapidated phone booth at the side of the building, just then hanging up the phone. She felt panic rise in her.

Who's he calling? He knows I was at Longs Peak. He knows . . . too much.

Dad said, "Hess, Hitler's spy, Canada, controls aren't in the U.S." Is that spy Ian?

Laura tried to regain control of fear, gulping in deep breaths of cold air. Distrust flooded into her heart. Once there, it froze her tears. She turned her back on Ian and watched Vandal.

"I guess we forgot his needs back there in Wyoming," Ian said behind her.

Laura felt her spine tighten at the sound of his voice. He was still on the phone, but had opened the door. She needed an ally, but did she need a man she barely knew? How much of what he said had been designed to gain her confidence? – to wreak Verheerung with her emotions?

He seemed, merely a green COI agent who had mistakenly let Arndt live, or, as she felt, could he be something more – a clever man who tested her, searching for the depths of her knowledge before he decided what to do with her?

Who did he telephone?

How could she trust such a man? Why did she want so desperately to trust him? Why had she let herself fall asleep on his lap?

He opened the booth door wider, and said to the other party, "Arndt will be after you. Now." He hung up.

She thought his last comment had been planned to put her off the idea that he might communicate with Arndt. She shouldn't believe all she heard.

As he approached, he waved a newspaper he had gotten from somewhere in this forsaken place.

"Have we left Wyoming?" she asked, trying to decide whether to rid herself of this man – and how.

"Yep," he answered. "It was about eight o'clock this morning when we crossed from Wyoming sagebrush into Idaho tumbleweed. You had to look quick to note the spot. We're nearing Twin Falls."

"I'll drive," she said quickly.

Laura climbed back into the car and waited for Ian to corral Vandal. She thought about driving off, but watched the dog jump up and lick the man. Brusquely, she told herself she couldn't leave anybody in this

God-forsaken spot. Then she realized he still held the car keys.

*   *

TUESDAY, MARCH 10, 1942, NOON

As they bumped along a graveled portion of the highway, Ian read aloud from the Tuesday, *Denver Times*. "The Army has been summoned to Detroit's Sojourner Truth Housing Project, Monday, March 9th," Ian read in a quiet tone. "During the night, soldiers with fixed bayonets and tear gas attempted to quell rioting which began Sunday. It is alleged that a white man picked a fight with a Negro outside a local Red Cross Center. A policeman who attempted to intervene was shot with his own gun, setting off a race riot of unprecedented proportions.

"Martial law has been declared by Governor Harry Kelly. As the riot comes under military control, twenty-five Negroes and nine Whites have died of gunshot wounds. Hundreds have been injured. The number of arrested individuals rises hourly."

Ian's voice trailed off. Laura could feel him watching for a reaction. Why read this to me?

Laura kept her face stone cold and immobile, her eyes following the road as she drove. But her heart pumped hard and fast. She knew why he read it.

He thinks I know about Verheerung.

She recognized Verheerung at work in each news article Ian had read to her this morning: cross burnings on the lawns of prominent Jewish families in Massachusetts; the lynching of a negro man in one of the border states; fights between Mexican-born U.S. citizens and white sailors in Los Angeles – all the signs were there. Arndt heated things up. Americans died, hating each other. And Nazi Germany reaped the benefit.

She was frightened by what he read, but too unsure of him to talk about it.

He works for the COI. They ignored Dad's warnings about Verheerung. Is even the COI subverted by Arndt's organization?

Somehow, Ian made her want to confide in him. She couldn't allow herself to be that foolish. She had to be strong for James. If Ian McKay were the wrong person to trust, telling him she knew about Verheerung would spell her doom. If he were Arndt's spy, she wouldn't be allowed to stay alive long enough to get to Mount Hood. James needed her to be there.

Ian folded the paper carefully and laid it in his lap. He remained silent for twenty miles. Laura began to relax, but when he spoke again, his voice was distant and cold.

"There is one more interesting story, Laura. It has to do with the mysterious death of a Corporal Myer. He was found near the Camp Springs Army Base early this morning. He'd been knifed in the face and then stabbed in the heart. According to Colonel Bernard Johnson, Corporal Myer had been guarding a witness to several murders. That witness is now missing."

Horror chilled Laura. She glanced at Ian.

He's the only one who took advantage of Corporal Myer's absence.

Did he kill the guard in the garage as well?

Ian seemed to read her mind. He leaned forward where she could see his face as he ticked off her activities of the evening before.

"I started watching your house at dusk. You were all over that house, turning lights on and off in the attic, your room, the library. Soon after you entered the library, the phone rang. Then the young corporal left.

You stayed in the library a little longer and then went to the storage area in the basement."

She drove in silence. As she thought back, all that he said was true. Ian could have been there all that time and observed exactly what he related. On the other hand, he could have watched until the corporal left, followed him and then come back to guess the rest – and to see her packing and leaving. His intuition could supply her activities of the missing minutes it would take to kill a boy.

Corporal Myer. What terror he must have felt at the last moment. Oh God, care for him. He was killed because of me – because they think I might have told him something . . . something about Arndt, or Verheerung.

Ian's voice halted her self-rebuke.

"Laura," he said harshly, "that day in the cemetery, you said you transcribed some of J.B.'s radio messages to your father. The only messages James sent under the code name 'J.B.' dealt with evidence that the Nazis had a Verheerung organization in place. I know you understand the importance of the stories I just read to you."

Laura's throat constricted. She had no defense against all that he knew. It was her own fault. She had mentioned J.B.'s reports.

He waited. She drove on, blindly following the road which blindly followed Bear River toward Pocatello. The sun hovered overhead, the air warmed leaving Laura cold. As cold as a young man, murdered because of contact with her. As cold as seven bodies in a snow field.

Ten miles went by in silence as she thought about the boy and the men, about the people who suffered all over the nation because of Arndt and his spies. How could she trust anyone with all that she knew? – only James. She had to get to James before even he was murdered.

At last, Ian reached out and touched her shoulder. Surprised, she jerked, but he let his hand rest firmly on her, his thumb brushing her clavicle.

"You have to trust someone, Laura. Arndt is vicious. He's smarter than either of us. But I know his weaknesses better than any man alive."

She stared straight ahead, feeling the warmth of his hand. He didn't move it, didn't caress her, just sat there letting the strength of his personality seep into her as he talked. She was frightened of herself for wanting to talk to him. She had to talk. Fear, anger, grief were mounting in her soul – an avalanche ready to crash down on her at the slightest noise.

Ian's voice came to her distantly. "You might as well throw those matches and cigarettes out of your pack at the next stop," he said gently. "You couldn't do it anyway."

The heavy swell of emotions burst out of her at that moment.

Pounding one hand on the steering wheel, she gulped down tears. "I can. He did . . . He did it to Dad . . ."

"Stop Laura," Ian grabbed at the steering wheel.

But Laura was beyond noticing. "Inch by . . . the way he burned . . ."

Ian's elbow came down, knocking her arm off the wheel. She covered her eyes from the image inside her head. "Daddy! God don't let Daddy die! Fire . . . just like . . ."

Ian held tight to the wheel, kicking her foot off the gas pedal at the same moment. Oblivious of the road, Laura's fist ground an imaginary brand into her thigh. "He burned his eyes, his hands, his feet . . ."

The jeep slid into a field of sage, throwing Laura into Ian's arm where it crossed the steering wheel. He grunted at the impact, but held the jeep to its course until the momentum died and they skidded to a halt.

Both of them bounced forward again, but Ian's arm blunted the blow for Laura one more time. Ian stretched at an awkward angle across the seat. His body swung around the steering column, his right shoulder hit the dash, but he managed to hang on and not be thrown into the windshield. He ended in a heap on the floorboards, his upper body next to her legs. Laura slammed back into the seat. Seconds passed before either of them could get breath.

Ian crawled up into the seat, his gaunt and scarred face hovered close to hers, but Laura didn't have the strength to pull away or fight back. His hand circled her throat, his thumb crossing her windpipe, fingers pushing beneath her hair to feel her fragile neck bones.

She gazed dumbly at him, waiting for his hands to squeeze the life from her.

"Cry, damn you. Cry," he whispered hoarsely.

She came out of her stupor, throwing off his hand with a wild swing of her arm.

"Get off me." She grabbed for the car keys, but his hand beat her to them. "Give me those," she yelled. "I have to get to James. Give them to me, do you hear?"

He held them aloft, smiling slightly. "So, you're alive," he said.

She lunged. He wrapped his arms around her, holding tight. "Laura," he said softly, "Why don't you kick me too?"

"I will, if you don't give me those keys."

"In my own good time," he held her close so she couldn't get any telling blows into his body. After a few moments, she slumped against him crying silently from anger and frustration.

"That's what I want," he whispered. "You've been to hell and back." His hands caressed her back, soothing and encouraging.

"How long has it been?" he asked as she buried her sobs against his shirt. "Over a week since you found them dead in the snow field. Except I'm told you couldn't have found your father in the field. He'd been moved from the cave. Did you lay him there, next to Uncle Banks?"

She cried silently now. As Ian massaged her back, she pictured her father and Banks as they lay next to her on that day in the meadow.

Uncle Banks? she thought, how does Ian know he is my Uncle Banks?

Before her thought congealed, Ian spoke in gentling tones. "Your father was still alive. He tried to tell you things you could hardly believe. But then searching through the files, you found he'd been correct – someone you knew had betrayed him. And ever since, you haven't known who to trust."

Fatigue and grief robbed her voice of strength, but she asked one question. "You took something from Dad's carving room?"

She could feel the tension increase in his arms. "If I tell you about that, Laura, you'll be in greater danger than you are now. Just leave it."

"How can I trust you?" she asked through a barely stifled sob.

"You've no choice," Ian said. "I'm all the help you'll get. Stop fighting it and trust so we can work together. Otherwise, we'll both die separately."

"There's James."

"Ah, James," Ian's sighing breath warmed her ear. "James has changed. You'd hardly recognize him. You put your finger on it the other day. As J.B., he's become a cynic, hard."

"That won't keep him from climbing the ridge and getting Arndt out into the open," she defended angrily. "James's courage hasn't faltered."

"Courage," Ian whispered. He leaned back against the jeep door, pulling her with him so that she wasn't cramped behind the steering wheel.

"Sometimes brazen arrogance looks like courage," he said, "but it's mere foolishness. James sent the telegram and threw down the gauntlet, before, when he thought he had nothing to live for. He would die and take Arndt with him – a meteoric death for both."

"What makes you think you can speak for his motives?" she asked indignantly.

Ian's laughter seemed sad. "Have you become the defender of your big brother?"

"I just got him back," she cried, "resurrected. I'm going to help him, not judge him."

Ian glanced down at Laura's upturned face, the muscles around his dark eyes softening. He moved slightly, bringing her closer, bent his head and touched her lips with his. His feathery caress deepened in seconds.

In spite of herself, Laura melted into him. Her hands moved to his shoulders, pulling him closer still. His mouth gently insisted, his hands urgent as they explored the sensuous contours of her back and hips. The more he touched her, the more she wanted to be touched by him, only by this man, this persistent, arrogant man.

"Laura," he groaned. His lips touched her cheek and began trailing a warm, moist path down her throat.

How could I have thought him capable of murder? Of course, he watched my house. I should have known. I should have trusted him from the first. It was just that he was so secretive.

Ian sat up abruptly.

Laura was chagrinned by his retreat.

He's playing with me, she thought. Now backing off to enjoy his little triumph.

Scrambling to recover her dignity, she bumped her hip into the steering wheel.

Ian caught her wrists and pulled her back down to endure his appreciative scrutiny.

"Please, Ian," she moaned. "Don't make fun of me."

An enormous gray paw descended on Ian's shoulder. A rough tongue scraped across his neck leaving a slick wet mark. Ian ducked his head away from Vandal.

"Laura," Ian whispered. "It was our dog who stopped me. He wants attention too." Ian's brown eyes watched the rise and fall of her breathing. "You've become a powerful woman, Laura Atweiler – courageous, sensuous and so unaware of your effect."

"Ian, I didn't mean to . . ."

"Laura," he shushed her, "I meant to. Since that morning when you absconded with my wallet and checked me out, I've wanted to know how it felt to hold you close. His voice became soft, "I've wanted . . . Laura, I've lost so much."

Laura watched the heat of his gaze become introspective. He seemed less imposing, in spite of the fact that he still held her wrists. She felt less like escaping, more like taking him in her arms and comforting him. It didn't take much effort to wrap him into her embrace. She felt nothing sexual about their coming together this time, merely his need and her giving. After moments of warmth, he pulled back slightly, carefully not looking her in the eye.

"There's a train station in Twin Falls," he said, as if they'd reached some tacit agreement. "I'll put you on a train to your aunt in Helena. When this is all over, someone will come get you, bring you home."

"Someone?" she asked, rising to sit behind the steering wheel again, "You don't expect to survive this do you?"

He shrugged and pretended to look out his side window.

"I happen to know," she said, "that the view through scratched isinglass is not great. Look at me Ian McKay and be honest."

He turned slowly to face her, his brown eyes somber, "I expect to have the fight of my life on that mountain. I may die, but I'll bring Arndt down with me, one way or another."

"And James?"

He frowned.

She fumed, "If you think I'm going to let you and James tackle that monster by yourselves, you know nothing about me."

He pushed his short hair off his forehead – a desperate and unnecessary gesture. "Laura, I need to know . . . James and I need to know that you're safe. If something should happen to you . . . if Arndt traps you or threatens you, I won't be able to get at him."

"I'm not exactly Gracie Allen," she began heatedly. "I'm not stumbling in, opened-eyed and naive where Arndt is concerned."

"Now Gracie . . .," Ian snorted in a fair imitation of the comedian George Burns.

"I climb," Laura interrupted. "I ski. I'm a crack shot. I've been trained as well as any man on Dad's staff."

"No!" his voice was knife sharp. "That's final. No. I won't have you within miles of that man."

Laura opened her mouth, shut it and sat very quietly behind the wheel. After a moment, she took hold of the steering wheel and staring straight ahead, said, "Ian, You're asking me to trust James's life to you alone. I can't do that."

Ian stared at her fingers. From the way his eyebrows pinched toward each other, Laura was sure he wrestled with telling her something. After a moment, he let out a frustrated sigh.

"Laura, James's life is as important to me as my own. I would do anything to keep him alive and to get Arndt off his back."

"That makes two of us," she replied quickly. "So, let's get moving and get there in time."

Ian pursed his lips, concentrating on a decision he found hard to make. Laura waited, a little impatiently, but as quietly as possible, willing him to hear her thoughts.

I'm not just a frantic woman, rushing off without control.

Chagrin forced her to admit she'd displayed a clear inability to control her attraction to him, a man she barely knew and shouldn't rely on.

At last she said softly, "I do have a plan."

He looked up, surprised. "And what might that be?"

"I'll tell you the plan when I can trust you."

He smiled, sardonically. "How will you know that?"

"I'll know."

"Then let's go," he said, with obvious reservations. Laura felt certain he would try to find some way to keep her away from Yocum Ridge.

Her plan included evading his plans.

Ian glanced at her flushed and tear-stained face. "Are you all right to drive?"

"Are we stuck in this field, or can I just back out?" She asked.

"Here. Try backing first." He handed her the keys.

CHAPTER SIXTEEN

TUESDAY, MARCH 10TH, AFTERNOON

Arndt maintained a tense silence after they landed at the private aeroport in Bend, Oregon. Dieter Haupt said nothing as they moved the ski and climbing gear from the aeroplane to two trucks. All nine men were well equipped for the days ahead. They expected Schoenfeld to lay a trap, but they were confident. They would kill him.

With Schoenfeld and Atweiler both dead, the men in these two trucks would be the only people who knew the scope of Nazi infiltration into U.S. industry, politics and community hatred. They would be free to work unhindered.

Except that Dieter didn't trust Johnson. He trusted Arndt. Arndt would act as he always had – throwing away what was no longer useful. Arndt could be trusted to throw away Johnson soon. Dieter planned to remain useful forever.

Once the trucks were packed, the men climbed into them. Arndt gestured Dieter and Johnson into the lead truck. As he turned to hoist himself into the cab, Dieter saw the owner of the aeroport salute Arndt with a stiff arm and raised fist. Arndt grabbed the fawning man's arm and pulled it down into an American style handshake.

"Fool," Arndt hissed as he climbed into the driver's seat.

"Why didn't you kill him?" said Johnson. "He will talk."

Arndt stared at Johnson coldly before answering, "I need him for when we take off again."

Johnson shifted uncomfortably in his seat.

Dieter made himself small between them. Silently, Arndt drove north along the eastern edge of the Cascade mountain range. On their left, awesome white peaks jabbed into the gray sky. Heavy drops of rain spattered the windshield. Even the hypnotic clip-swish of the wipers didn't help Dieter relax next to the power and cunning of Werner Arndt.

*   *

TUESDAY, MARCH 10TH, AFTERNOON

Edgy and unsure of each other, Laura and Ian rode in silence through the beauty of an Idaho spring. At three o'clock, when it was Ian's turn to drive, Laura took the keys, handing them back as she climbed in the passenger's side.

"No trust yet," he commented.

As Ian drove, Laura mentally catalogued two coyotes, one fox, five Pronghorns, and one enormous jack rabbit bounding through the sage. Her other thoughts, the ones whirring around in her head were the ones she didn't want to face.

But she couldn't help remembering with embarrassment how she'd responded to his kiss. She never let her guard down around the men on the base. The only way she could explain her weakness this time was exhaustion. She'd have to get some sleep in the next few hours.

Another puzzle. Ian claimed he cared enough to give his life for James, yet he warned her to be wary of James. Unable to think clearly about this two-faced attitude, Laura slept, carefully facing away from him.

Ian woke her as he drove into Twin Falls, Idaho. They bought sandwiches and the weekly *Twin Falls Times*. Reading aloud, Laura came across several racial incidents which took place during the recent week – the murder of a Japanese restaurant owner, fighting between whites and Mexican-born farm laborers, the mob murder of a lone black cobbler in a white farm community. She closed the paper, trying push away fear.

"Is this happening everywhere?" she asked.

Hearing her voice break with emotion, Ian reached a hand to grip hers. "It's hard to tell how much of this can be blamed on Arndt. Some hatred already worked in these communities before he came."

"I know," she whispered. "When the first Negro platoons were assigned to Camp Collins, there was a lot of talk, a lot of distrust."

"People shoved together," said Ian, "establishing top dogs and under dogs."

Laura shook her head, her voice sharp. "It doesn't have to stay that way, though. After a few months, led by the attitude of their officers and sergeants, the men got on. By the time they finished basic training, there were some abiding friendships between the white and colored troops."

"That can happen," said Ian, "but only when folks are forced to stick it out and get beyond their fears. Arndt knows that doesn't happen in most places. He knows how to make fear turn to hatred. Hatred will spread on its own."

Laura thumped the newspaper with her fist. "What if we can't stop the chain-reaction?"

Ian became silent, biting his lower lip in thought. After moments he answered her. "What we do, Laura, will be done for the General, and each other."

"And for James," she added.

He glanced at her. "And for James," he nodded. "After that, it's up to all our people to stop the hatred and the rioting."

They drove through Mountain Home and Boise, heading toward Dorset, following the trail of the pioneers across Idaho. Laura took her turn driving while Ian stared at sleek mountain cats and delicate-boned deer that moved in silence through the snow-drifted land.

*   *

Ian glanced at her pale face, thinking about her response to his kiss. It had been warmth welling up, melting cold distrust. He was afraid she'd been vulnerable because of grief. But he prayed her warmth truly could be meant for him. God, he hoped so. Still, he decided against telling her the whole truth about James. Maybe later. He'd tell her all of it when she knew Ian McKay better.

His glance became a longing. He studied her as she drove. Laura's finely-modeled nose ended in a slight flare that made her look determined. Yet, he knew her to be fragile compared to the enormous ugliness into which they were driving.

He had met Hess, the nerve center of a network of professional haters and spies. And he understood Arndt's undiluted greed and venom.

Ian stared out at the long-shadowed land and planned how to save Laura. First, he had to make sure she never reached their destination – never came near Werner Arndt.

*   *

Near sundown, Laura slowed for a traffic tie-up in Dorset, Idaho.

Two chevron-striped armatures lowered, keeping the wagons and trucks from crossing the railroad tracks. A claxon warned of an approaching train. Laura thumped on the wheel in frustration.

"These people lined up here as if a train arrival were entertainment," she said. "They weren't even trying to get across the tracks."

Ian glanced behind them. A maroon Packard sedan pulled into the line behind them. From behind the Packard, Ian could see a phalanx of men marching up the street toward the railroad crossing. Every one of them was carrying a pitch-fork, axe or a shovel.

"Laura, turn the car around and drive out of here slowly."

"We have to cross the track to get to Oregon," she pointed out reasonably.

"Damn it, Laura. There isn't time to argue. Do as I say."

"Who are you? The General?" Laura glared at him.

He saw it was too late. The train pulled into town, stopping at the station with a hiss. The crowd surged around them. Glancing ahead at the train, Ian could see the small faces of two little girls peeking out of the windows of the nearest passenger car. Their straight black hair created a sharp contrast with the pale smoothness of their skin. Ian had a moment's impression of curiosity in their expressions – curiosity which turned to wide-eyed fear just before they were pulled back from the passenger car window by a frantic woman.

The crowd closed in around the jeep. One large man whacked Laura's side of the jeep with his rake as he passed by.

"Lock your door," Ian ordered Laura. He reached for his lock button.

But Laura had stepped out already, and carried the keys.

"Aw shit," he mumbled and rolled out, leaving the wolf dog in the back seat. He caught up with her as she shouldered her way to the front of the crowd. "What are you doing?" he asked as he took her by the elbow.

She ignored him. Instead, she turned to the big boned woman next to her. "Why is this train attracting so much attention?" she asked.

"This is the third train to come through here in the last week," the woman snapped. "And every time, them Japs gets off and uses our station."

"For what?"

"Bathrooms. Some even wanted to buy food."

"Proves they're human, doesn't it?" Laura's voice became sharp- edged.

Ian pulled her close to him. "Shut up," he whispered.

The woman eyed Laura and Ian closely. "Who're you?"

He answered, hoping Laura would keep herself under control, "We're on our way to Fort Lewis, near Olympia, Washington. Special assignment."

Laura jerked her head toward him, her eyes wide with surprise. He knew what she thought. Fort Lewis had been where her father and his colleagues had been working with the ski mountaineers before Pearl Harbor. Though he'd startled Laura, Ian's announcement had the desired effect on the big woman. She looked at him with less suspicion and even a hint of respect. He plunged on, "There any side road that'll help us get around behind this train? I'm concerned about being late for my ship-out date."

"This train ain't staying here any length of time," the woman assured him. "Water up and move out. That's what we're here to make 'em do."

Laura frowned at the woman and started to say something when the crowd began to jeer. The doors on the train passenger cars swung open. Train personnel poured out – several Negro porters, one Negro ticket master and a Caucasian fellow in coveralls. They were followed by young men in Army uniforms carrying rifles.

Wet behind the ears, Ian thought, Semi-trained recruits for guards.

Ian saw they were privates, every one of them. Barely out of boot camp, he guessed.

Behind the young men, crowded in the exit steps of the car were several passengers, hanging back, yet being pushed forward by the anxious people behind them. The man in front wore a business suit, brown with small stripes, a brimmed hat, oxford shirt and a tie of diagonal stripes. He looked like any other American businessman, except for the fear in his dark oriental eyes.

Ian recognized the man immediately – from Hood River, on the north flank of Mount Hood. The father of his friend Takehiko Okada. Ian willed the man to stay inside that train.

Mr. Okada seemed to have the same thought. He shouted over his shoulder in Japanese and then in English. "My people, sit down. There is trouble here."

Inside the passenger car, a few heard Okada's order and sat down. Ian began to hope for no confrontation.

Down the track to the right, Ian noticed a second lieutenant disembark and saunter into the station gift shop. Beyond, the gift shop, on the roof of the small train station, another man swung the water- tower armature into place over the train, twisted the valve open and delivered water to the engine's storage tank. Neither the army officer nor the water-tower worker paid any attention to the crowd gathered four car-lengths away.

Ian glanced at Laura again. Her attention riveted on the scene at the passenger platform. The train seemed filled with Japanese families, all hoping to get out and stretch their legs for a moment before they continued their enforced journey to a relocation camp in Wyoming.

Taking advantage of Laura's distraction, Ian lifted the car keys from her hand. "We need to move the jeep. Come with me," he urged.

She shook her head, "Those poor frightened people," she said, standing stubbornly still.

"Laura, we have a job to do. Don't become part of this mob."

She rounded on him, "This mob is here to harm them. How can you just walk away?"

"Someone killed the General," Ian reminded her in a whisper. "Someone intends to kill James. If you get caught up in this we may never spring the trap on Arndt."

"Hey," shouted the lady on Laura's left, "You Jap, get back in that train."

The rest of the crowd took up her strident call. Ian glanced back at the train. Okada had been pushed out onto the platform by the crush of people behind him. The young soldiers were in confusion with no leadership. Some soldiers faced the train, others faced the crowd. Their rifles, most of them held in one hand, would be easy prey for the mob. A fellow on Ian's right raised his pitchfork toward the oriental passenger. Seeing the threat to his life, Okada seemed to empty himself of all fear. He turned to face his aggressor, looking the man in the eye.

Ian, all thought of leaving pushed from his mind, shoved his way to the front of the crowd. He slapped his boots together, thrust out his chin as he'd seen General Atweiler do many times. He called out "Atten . . . hut!"

Two soldiers who faced him stood at immediate attention – their rifle butts on the ground, the rifles close to their side.

"Fall . . . in!" Ian hollered as he pivoted to face the crowd with military crispness.

A chain reaction of obedience took over the platoon behind him. All turned to face the direction of their comrades – out toward the angry crowd.

"Hey," yelled the big woman. "Who's that?"

From further back in the crowd, Ian heard Laura's voice reply, "That's General McClelland. I've seen him in the papers." The eyes of the nearest soldier cut briefly toward Ian.

Ian shouted, "Port . . . arms!" Every rifle rose to be cradled at a forty-five-degree angle. The man with the pitchfork backed up. Ian felt the collective retreat of the mob.

But the woman's voice yelled, "You army bastard, make them Japs get back on that train."

Ian called out, "Porters, please seat the passengers."

The ticket master said, "Yes . . . sir!" and pushed his way onto the first step among the frozen faces of the Japanese families. The ticket master called out in a very good imitation of Ian's manner, "Passengers . . . find your seats."

A sudden scurrying inside the train allowed the ticket master to push his way further and further up the steps. Okada followed him inside as soon as it was possible. In the stairwell, Okada turned to face the crowd with dignity and courage, a sentry guarding the safety of his loved ones.

Ian saw the second lieutenant meander out of the station cafeteria, lighting a cigarette. The paunchy man showed no awareness, no concern for his passengers' safety, nor for the safety of his platoon. Ian figured he'd better finish this maneuver before the man realized his command had been taken from him. In a clash of egos, these poor soldiers wouldn't know whose orders to follow.

"Order . . . arms!" Ian shouted. The platoon slapped rifles down to their sides. "When I give the command to board the train, you will board the train. About . . . face!"

The platoon turned as one. The lazy second lieutenant pulled the cigarette from his mouth and stared at his men.

"Port . . . arms!" Ian shouted.

"Just a bloody . . ." yelled the second lieutenant.

"Board the train," called Ian. The platoon poised. "Move!" Ian's voice grew urgent. The platoon double-timed it up the steps and into the passenger cars.

The second lieutenant bellowed, racing toward Ian. "What the devil are you doing?"

Laura's voice sang out, "Lieutenant Idle, are you people gonna ever stop in Dorset again?"

At her question, the officer jerked to attention.

The strident woman leaned close, flicking at a pin on the Second Lieutenant's uniform.

"Says here you're a sharpshooter. That make you a leader of men?"

A man demanded, "Idle, you wait to get water from Nampa after this, you hear?"

The lieutenant, whatever his real name, was besieged by angry suggestions for what to do with his passengers. Ian had only moments to get the train going before the diversion Laura created fell apart.

He reached into the train stairs to shake hands with a fellow citizen. "I'm sorry about this scene, Mr. Okada."

The man glanced at him. "McKay."

"Yes, sir."

"Tell Takehiko his mother is bearing up."

"I will," Ian promised. "I will tell him, sir. Safe journey."

Okada grabbed the rail and hoisted himself into the passenger car. At the front end of the train, Ian saw the water-tower armature swing away from the train. He noticed the engineer's worried glance down the length of the train toward the commotion at the passenger cars. Ian studied the train windows, watching for Takehiko's father.

Behind Ian, the crowd yelled at the Lieutenant. "Don't bring 'em here again."

Okada appeared near the window. He put his arms around his wife, soothing her cries. Then he turned her to look outside. Speaking quickly, he pointed at Ian. His wife turned, a small smile lighting her tears. She bowed toward Ian several times. Ian bowed in return, then waved as he stepped back into the crowd.

"Keep this train moving," shouted a voice near his left shoulder. "Don't bring those traitors to Dorset."

Ian backed into the crowd. Off to his right, he saw the second lieutenant drop his cigarette. A tall porter reached out from the doorway and grabbed the officer's arm, saying, "Best get on right here, sir. I'm closing up."

The lieutenant swung on board, his eyes bulging with fear. The porter glanced at Ian, winked and shut the door. Laura caught Ian's arm as the crowd pushed toward the train.

"Let's get in the jeep," she said.

When they turned, the woman who had been near Laura stood in their path, glaring at them. "Who are you?" she demanded.

"Actually, I'm just a Major. Major John McClelland ma'am. I'm an officer in civies, on my way to the Pacific through Fort Lewis."

"Well thanks for your help here today." She reached out to pump Ian's hand up and down in her sweaty grip. "Yes sir, you sure got them Japs back on that train in a hurry."

Ian had trouble controlling his own expression, but worse, he saw that Laura's eyes were narrowing. He knew her well enough to be afraid of what would happen next.

Years back, he'd seen her eyes narrow that way at James. Then her head would lower, and she would charge head first into James's stomach. Knocked him flat, every time. Ian had to stop Laura from tackling this obnoxious woman.

"Interesting to meet you, ma'am," he hurried to say. "Let me introduce my wife, Honey." He pulled Laura close. He hoped it looked like an affectionate gesture. "Honey here is going to work at the shipyard in Portland, Oregon while I'm shipped out."

"All for the war effort" the woman grinned at Laura. "That's admirable, Mrs. McClelland."

Figuring to get out while they could, Ian and Laura said tight-lipped goodbyes and hurried back into the jeep. Vandal had become so frantic that he'd slobbered all over the windows. They wiped the car down with Ian's plaid neck scarf. Ian sat in the back seat to calm the dog.

Laura and Ian said nothing to each other, but their silence filled with tension. Later, as they drove across the tracks and out of Dorset, Laura glanced into the rearview mirror. Only the maroon Packard, a farm truck and a black Ford trailed them out of town.

While she kept an eye on the trailing cars, Laura thought about what she'd seen. Ian McKay had known exactly what to do. He'd supplied leadership at the moment it was most needed. His action saved the people in the train from the hateful mob. He saved the mob from itself. As she had watched him, she felt such warmth in her chest, such pride for him. During those moments, she came to know she could trust him.

She remembered during the year that James lived with her and her father, James and his friends played soldier. The habit of leadership developed in the boys through those games – leadership and teamwork.

James also had been a natural leader, so adept at it that he could convince the older boys to let Laura play as guidon for the platoon. She'd loved her big brother for that. And now she'd seen the value of that kind of leadership in a dangerous situation. She admired how Ian McKay had put his skills to use for everyone in Dorset Train Station.

Laura admired. Maybe, she thought, she trusted. But that was all.

There could be, she told herself, nothing more, in spite of the sagebrush field where she'd nearly killed them with her crazy anger and her explosion of grief. The kiss they had shared in that field meant nothing. She would see that it didn't.

Within miles of Dorset, the Packard and the truck behind them turned off at their home-farm driveways. Laura pushed down the gas pedal and pulled the Jeep away from the one remaining car, the black Ford.

"What are you evading?" Ian asked, glancing behind them. "Black Ford sedan. It has Colorado license plates."

"They weren't back there until the incident at the train station. Maybe it's just a coincidence they're from Colorado," he said.

"Maybe," Laura said. "Maybe." She kept glancing into the rearview mirror, but the Ford seemed to be receding into the distance as the hour wore on. She began to think Ian had been right. After all, this was one of the few routes open between Colorado and the western states this early in the spring.

As afternoon cooled toward dusk, the car no longer appeared behind them. Laura finally relaxed. "I suppose you could have proven you were a major, if that woman had asked," she said.

"I've got all kinds of identities. Why?"

"Didn't that Japanese man at the train know you?"

"His son is a friend."

"A spy? Part of Dad's group?"

"I'm not free to comment."

"Free to make up all kinds of lies, but not free to tell the truth," she commented.

"At least, not a truth which might endanger another person."

Laura said nothing.

They traded drivers again toward sunset. As usual, Laura took the keys around the car with her. Ian accepted the key exchange without comment. Once she and the dog were settled, Ian relaxed into the driver's seat. He glanced at Laura and said, "Thanks for your help with the crowd, Laura. You were perfect."

"Maybe a little mouthy," she said.

"You got it under control, though."

She thawed, chuckling softly, "Yeah, I can tell lies, too."

He flicked her a smile. Suddenly neither of them could stop laughing. She crowed, "Did you see that guy's pitchfork droop?"

Ian gave a startled guffaw. "Why Laura Atweiler," he laughed. "I thought you a lady."

Laura's eyes widened. She opened her mouth to protest her innocence, but the whole situation struck her as absurd. She collapsed against the isinglass window, once more helplessly laughing.

*   *

Grinning, Ian drove onto the bridge that crossed the Snake River Canyon. They passed through the town of Ontario, Oregon and drove upward, toward the lowering sun and onto the volcanic plateau of Eastern Oregon. Once, in the mirror, Ian saw one dark car, a mile or so behind them. Otherwise, the road was empty.

As they climbed, Ian spotted a lone spire of golden rock, miles away, across the flat upland.

L'Aiguille, he thought bitterly. James . . . trusted him then.

Minutes later, the highway took them along the edge of a deep arroyo. The sunset colored the canyon walls red-orange and purple. Afterglow seemed a light of fire in a thick-needled Juniper Tree. The air freshened with warmed sage, Juniper and dust. Beside Ian, Laura slept.

He let his mind caress the jet-black tangle of her curls, her smooth brow and black lashes. Asleep, she was a pleasure to look at. Awake, nothing but trouble, a fact he should have expected. He had an idea how to ditch her before they reached Mount Hood. She'd be safe at Labbé's.

CHAPTER SEVENTEEN

TUESDAY MARCH 10TH, EVENING

Arndt pulled his convoy to the side of the road five miles south of Madras, Oregon. Dieter got out and steered himself well away from Arndt. Arndt barked orders to the men. After rearranging equipment and passengers to suit himself, he motioned to Dieter and Johnson. Dieter was not happy to have the attention.

"You remember Moses Labbé?" Arndt asked.

Dieter nodded. "That huge Indian who guarded the American embassy, Berlin, 1939."

"Ja wohl," Arndt said, then staring at Johnson, he added, "Labbé is the one who found Johnson's codes ..."

Johnson interrupted, "We'd changed codes by that time."

Arndt pinned him with a glare which left Johnson writhing. "Labbé understood the messages you left," he said. "Labbé began the hunt for double-agents. Labbé warned Atweiler about me."

Johnson's white face became immobile except for one twitching muscle in his eyelid. Dieter hoped Johnson would just shut up. Johnson made excuses, like a kid whose mother forgave the most dimwitted actions.

"Madras, Oregon," said the implacable Arndt, "is Moses Labbé's hometown. He lives with his father and brothers on a ranch two miles north of Madras. Last fall, we tried to eliminate him, but we brought down only one screeching old woman. She stepped in front of her son at the last moment."

Johnson essayed an easy tone, "I remember. Big Labbé lost an arm. The woman died. Atweiler flew out for her wake."

Arndt looked through him, cold, contemptuous. "Atweiler's attendance warned us. Labbé still works for Atweiler's intelligence operation."

Johnson had the sense to close his mouth.

Arndt shifted his weight closer to Dieter. Dieter knew what was coming. Arndt tested him.

"I want you two to finish him by Wednesday night," said Arndt. "Start tonight. Use the townspeople. Make it look like another racial incident."

Dieter heard the unspoken message. When this "incident" was over, Johnson should also be dead.

*   *

WEDNESDAY, MARCH 11TH

Laura drove northwest on the highway that cut diagonally across Oregon's volcanic plateau toward the town of Redmond. As they moved through the tawny shadows of pre-dawn in the high desert, either their experience at the train station, or a new level of trust seemed to make Ian almost loquacious.

"Laura," he said, "were you in love with James?" His question stunned her.

"I . . . uh . . . James has been gone since I was eight."

"But you wrote. Often. And he wrote, too. As you grew, you must have sensed how important you were to him."

"Important, yes. But still only eight years old in his thoughts."

He gazed at her in the light of an oncoming car. "James did not think of you as a child of when your letters and photographs were clearly those of a grown woman."

"How would you know that?"

He looked away as he answered, "James and I were together in some tight spots. At such times, a man talks about what's vital to him."

"He didn't share my letters."

"Of course, not. Were you in love with him?"

Laura drove silently, trying to understand herself. Finally, she said, "I loved James, but I never imagined myself in love with him."

Ian asked the next question slowly, as if not sure he wanted to hear the answer. "Did no one live up to the General?"

Laura glared at him, "That's just Freud-schlock."

He burst into laughter. She heard the edge of sadness in his subsiding chuckle. Afraid to confront their mutual sorrow, she continued to rail at him.

"Where do you get off analyzing?" she spat out. "What do you know about women, or love, or fathers?"

Silence answered her – a silence so thick she felt its weight surround her. She took her gaze off the road to look at him. Ian McKay stared through her, beyond her. The bleak look in his eyes so desperate and empty she wanted to grab his arm and shake him.

She didn't touch him. Instead, she glanced back at the road, holding tightly to the steering wheel in her desperate need to control her sudden fear of the intense man beside her.

At last, Ian whispered, "Nothing. I know nothing."

* *

Ian drove through Redmond as Laura slept. He turned north on the highway to Madras and the Labbé Ranch, determined to leave Laura in the safety of the Labbé family. He envisioned her reception there – the rough and tumble Labbé boys trying to reign in their noise and act like gentlemen. They would love her. He imagined how they would all sit down to a hot breakfast cooked up by Papa John. Ian would excuse himself for a trip to the outhouse, and never return. Once out of sight, he could take off in the Jeep and meet Arndt without worrying about Laura.

A warming fantasy. And heartbreaking. Afterward, Ian never expected to see Laura again. But he sat next to her for at least another few hours. He didn't even try to keep himself from taking small advantage of her closeness. He swerved the jeep, just a little, enough so her relaxed body fell against his shoulder. She didn't awaken, but snuggled contentedly against him. He couldn't help smiling as she sighed into sleep. His heart thumped with happiness.

He refused to think how temporary this happiness was. And he didn't think about what would happen once she knew the truth about James.

Instead, he breathed in the woman scent of her, noted how each curl turned toward her face or touched her throat. After long years of loneliness, he savored this moment. In between quick glances at her, he drove toward their destiny, gathering memories of the feel of her trusting body next to his.

Later, she awoke and was embarrassed by her position. She pulled herself upright and sat there stiff and silent. He felt the few inches between them become like a concrete wall. They rode for long miles across the dark plateau.

Then, as the sun rose, Laura reached across from the passenger's seat. She touched his shoulder. The intimacy of her gesture startled him. When he glanced at her, she pointed to the northwest. There was the Cascade Mountain Range, looming ivory and black in the new morning – isolated silhouettes, each pristine white from timberline to the jagged exposed rock at the peak: Mount Washington, Mount Jefferson and further north, Mount Hood.

The sight of Mount Hood made him shudder. He expected to die there, taking Arndt down with him. Arndt's death would avenge the General, but he feared it was too late to stop Nazi sabotage of U.S. industries. And from what he'd seen in Idaho, the racial hatred Arndt set off would live and grow – hatred feeding on itself.

Ian drove, fully aware of Laura beside him. Her worn plaid flannel shirt, her corduroy men's pants, the curve of her hips, these were etched into his mind. The memory of their kiss and of her softness still caused his fingers to itch. The Laura of her letters had been intelligent, witty, and very opinionated. Laura in the flesh was all of that, and more.

Courageous, exciting, and vulnerable.

For his own sanity, he refused to look at her again. Instead, he watched the mountain, his old friend, the place where he had challenged Arndt to one last duel of wits.

He wished he'd known the real Laura before he'd issued that foolhardy challenge. Yet he'd been forced to get Arndt's attention, to wave the red cape in front of him in a desperate effort to save General Atweiler. As it turned out, even the challenge had been too late. One false act on Ian's part had doomed the only man he'd ever fully trusted.

Laura was right, he admitted to himself. Of love and fathers, I know nothing at all.

He drove on through the morning, moving toward Warm Springs Indian Reservation, land set aside to contain the once wide-ranging Columbia River tribes – the Wascos, Paiutes, Teninos, Bannocks, and even Shoshones were brought from Montana and Nevada.

Just outside the reservation, Ian drove through the cattle and wheat- trading center of Madras, Oregon. They passed the Madras Jug, the one establishment still open in the early morning. Outside the tavern, men with old Winchester Repeaters and Springfields slung over their arms milled around at the sides of the dusty road. Two ancient farm trucks and a black Ford sedan were parked haphazardly near the tavern entrance.

"Must be planning a hunting trip," Ian commented.

*   *

Two miles north of Madras, Laura was surprised when Ian pulled the dusty jeep onto a side road. He muttered, "First, I have to see a friend."

She asked no questions as he turned into the rock-covered road. He drove past a small pine forest before taking a right-hand turn onto the driveway of a neatly kept log house. Laura didn't need to ask questions. She felt certain this detour was part of Ian's plan to keep her off the mountain. She planned to stick close to the car so as not to be left behind.

She saw that it had rained here sometime during the past night. The roof of the big house glistened in the sun. Water beaded at the tips of drooping pine needles. Laura unsnapped a corner of the isinglass window and inhaled the aroma of wet bark and drenched volcanic pumice.

In front of the house, the driveway ran parallel to an irrigation ditch whose sluggish water gurgled down from the pine forest they'd passed. The ditch and driveway both turned beyond the corner of the house. A tall, wood-framed barn stood forty yards behind the house, towering over the small home.

*   *

When Ian climbed out of the jeep, a sudden wariness made him pause. Without knowing why, he retrieved his ammunition clips and his Garand semi-automatic from the floor behind the driver's seat. He approached the front of the two-story house, climbed the steps to the veranda and walked around the old swing from which Papa and Christina Labbé used to watch the setting sun. Ian's knock on the oak door brought only echoes in reply. He lifted his hand to knock again. Startled to see a spray pattern of bullets around the lock, Ian's back stiffened with fear for Labbé. He saw that the windows nearby gave back no reflection. They were empty of glass. Yet there was no glass on the porch. He strode to the end of the porch, studying the area around the house.

None of the usual farm sounds met him. Ian remembered noisy afternoons here three years ago – afternoons when his own doctor had brought him down from Government Camp for visits with Moses Labbé, the one friend who knew him before the knife scarred his face and betrayal scarred his soul. Back then, the Labbé family had filled the air with their energy. Steaming horses stamped and nipped each other in the corrals, and the sound of machinery or a scythe had filled the vast grassland.

On this afternoon, as he sought any sign of the Labbés, nothing moved. Behind the barn, Ian glimpsed only the tall cottonwood tree at the creek bed and the edge of the peach orchard between the house and the barn. On a hillside, far from the house, Christina's old sway-backed mare nuzzled new grass. No other animal was in sight.

It was the silence that had made him uneasy – made him pick up his rifle.

Laura climbed out of the jeep. Ian hurried down the porch steps toward her.

"Stay near the dog and the jeep," he said. "Something's not right here."

She glanced around the house warily. He saw her eyes widen the moment she realized there were bullet holes in the door.

"Is your friend inside?"

"Knowing Labbé, I'd guess he's outside, hiding, watching for whoever did this to return. Maybe he's near the barn."

"The guys who did this could be in the barn," she said, eyeing its imposing height. "That loft window is a perfect place to get a bead on you."

"I'm counting on the cleaned-up broken windows. Owners clean up. Not vandals."

Laura exhaled a deep breath, frowned up at him and said, "You carrying any ammo for that rifle?"

Ian nodded, warmed by her practical concern. "I'll be careful."

"I'll be covering you from porch." Laura's hand went inside her jacket pocket. Ian saw the bulged of a small caliber pistol against the fabric.

"Stay down," He ordered and raced a zigzag pattern toward the barn. As he rounded the empty corral, a dark shadow appeared inside the wide barn door. Ian halted near the corner post of the corral, cocking his rifle. The door swung slowly out, its iron hinges creaking against the weight of its heavy frame. The elder Labbé ambled out of the barn.

Ian's breath rushed out in relief at the sight of the stocky man.

Labbé wore his work overalls. His leather jacket and blue chambray shirt were caked with mud and straw. His hair, usually immaculate and braided, was loose. Sweat beaded at his hairline. The skin around his eyes darkened with fatigue and wary alertness. Perched on his shoulder, Ian recognized Christina Labbé's favorite, cantankerous rooster, Hephaestus.

Labbé carried his buffalo rifle slung over his arm with apparent nonchalance.

Ian wasn't fooled.

"You expected trouble, Chief?" he asked.

Labbé nodded, "Last night some o' my good buddies decided they didn't like Indians. Won't be the last time." Labbé nodded in the direction of his peach orchard behind the house. A dead cow and two dead horses lay in the field.

Ian's mouth went dry. The gruesome picture resembled the field of bodies at Longs Peak. He didn't want Laura to see this.

"Did they kill all your stock?" he asked. Chief John Labbé made a living with his packhorses.

"Nope. The boys have most of 'em on a log-hauling job over towards Olallie Butte."

Ian's shoulders relaxed at the news that the Labbé boys were safe. "When will they return?" he asked.

"The Runt's going to bring the boys back just before he heads up to meet you at Government Camp."

The Runt was Moses, John Labbé's youngest and most enormous son.

Papa Labbé had liked the joke for twenty-five years. The Runt's peers called him The Big Labbé.

"You know who did this?" Ian asked.

"Same crappy bunch it always is. Anybody wants to make trouble just has to talk loud and nasty at the Madras Jug. I saw one new fella – drifter I suppose, just over for the excitement."

"What'd he look like?"

"Very tight mouth, straight across like this," Labbé pulled his mouth into a thin line. "White hair, but young skin."

Ian smiled at that description. Though Labbé neared seventy years old, his French and Shoshone complexion was still taut over his round cheeks.

Labbé poked Ian in the chest with a stubby finger. "What's your goal here, soldier? You didn't come all the way from Austria to save an old man from drunk bigots."

"I came to ask a favor," said Ian, "but now I'm not sure it's a good idea." He and Labbé started back toward Labbé's log home. The rooster flapped, shifting weight to face Ian.

"That bird still mean?" Ian asked.

"Still goes after folks ears if they don't watch out."

Ian pulled up his jacket collar to protect himself.

Ian and Labbé rounded the corner toward the front of the house. Labbé halted. He stared at Laura. Her profile turned to him and she leaned down to hold the dog, her wild hair blowing in the March breeze as she watched for a sign that Ian needed her.

"Atweiler's daughter," Labbé stated. "And Bank's dog."

Ian started.

Labbé looked up and chuckled. His cheeks met his eyelids in a smile. "No Indian magic, McKay. I met Banks and Vandal when Atweiler first brought you out here, back when you were nothing but a broken hoe."

Ian raised an eyebrow in question, jerking his thumb toward Laura.

"Her?" said Labbé. "I saw her picture in Atweiler's wallet. Also, saw her in my dream."

"What dream?"

"The one where you died again, buried in a deep blue grotto – very beautiful."

Ian tensed. How did Labbé know his plans?

Labbé laughed. "Don't look so worried, my friend. You were resurrected for another go-round. The gods won't let you stay dead 'til you finish what you're here for."

"And Laura Atweiler?"

"She won't let you go either."

Ian was deeply embarrassed by the man's shrewd guesses. Ian glanced at his boots, trying to gather his wits and control his hopeful reaction to Labbé's predictions. He forced himself to stop grasping at the vision of returning to Laura. He made himself gaze at her standing on the porch, her hand in her pocket, waiting to be sure she didn't need that pistol for his sake.

Chuckling, he said "Labbé, if I left Laura Atweiler here to defend you, your tavern buddies wouldn't last long."

Labbé began walking toward Laura, whispering, "Then take her. I want to keep my local entertainment alive, at least 'til I know which one shot Christina."

Ian saw from Labbé's closed expression that he wanted no sympathy about his wife's death last year. Ian took a light tack. "If things get dull down here, Chief, come to the Battle Axe Inn. March sixteenth. All of Government Camp will be celebrating."

Laying a hand on Ian's shoulder, Labbé asked in a low voice, "Will you come down from the mountain top for the party?"

Ian's glance caressed Laura. He grew afraid for her – he who had been willing to throw his life away in order to stop Arndt. He wanted to return from the trap alive if only to keep Laura safe. He glanced at the chief. "I'll do my best to come off the mountain."

Ian was sure Labbé caught the undertone of desire in his voice. Labbé nodded. "Worth coming back to, that one," he said.

Beneath his gray and black beard, Agent Ian McKay felt his face flush. The corners of the old man's mouth twitched.

They both heard it at the same time. Out on the highway, the distant rattle of metal and the jouncing of rubber tires alerted them to new traffic. Both men turned toward the sound. With war restrictions on gasoline, any traffic out this far from trading centers like Madras was unusual. Ian listened attentively, watched dust rise on the road south of the ranch and recognized that a convoy of battered trucks must be approaching Labbé's – the men from the Madras Jug.

"Hot damn!" shouted Labbé. "Get your woman to the creek bed. Stay as far from the barn as possible. I got a surprise for these fellows in there."

Laura had already understood the danger. She urged Vandal away from the jeep and locked its doors even while Ian ran toward her. The trucks raised enough dust to make following their progress easy. They had turned on the secondary road and were only a mile away when he reached her.

"Labbé wants you at the creek behind the barn. Let's go." "The jeep. They'll know someone's here . . ."

"Maybe they'll think it belongs here. We've got no time. Come." They both lit out with the dog loping ahead of them. Ian assumed that Labbé ran for the creek as well, but the man stood stock still in front of the barn door. Vandal began to leap at the man in friendly greeting, but Labbé put out one hand and the dog sat obediently.

Behind them, Ian could hear the trucks change gears for the last climb up the driveway.

"Chief, what can we do. What's your plan?"

"You're going to hide as far from the barn as possible. I'm going to stand here until they see me, then I disappear into the barn and hope they follow."

Glancing over his shoulder, Ian saw the nose of the first truck as it topped the rise to the ranch. Soon the invaders would be able to see them all. "Quick," he urged Labbé, "How can I help?"

Labbé glared at the truck and stepped between Laura and the view from the moving vehicle. "Get her out of here. Lay low. Stay put."

Ian grabbed Laura by the arm and hauled her around the side of the barn toward the creek and its high shrubs and grasses. Vandal bounded on toward the creek bed.

"Ian," Laura called as she ran. "What is going on?"

"Those boys outside the tavern . . ."

"Back in Madras?"

"They were here last night."

At that moment, Laura caught sight of the dead horse and the cow lying in the field of melting snow. She halted in her tracks. Her face paled. Ian saw deep grief glaze her eyes. He knew she faced again the memory of the field at Long's Peak, her dying father and his murdered officers. Ian slung his rifle strap over his shoulder and caught her up in his arms as she stumbled. He hugged her unconscious body to him and ran, reaching the creek bed fifty yards behind the barn just as the trucks braked. He trudged through the creek. On the other side, he lay Laura on his jacket in the new spring grasses beneath the huge cottonwood tree.

Vandal, whining, inched toward her on his belly, his eyebrows twitching in puzzled question.

Ian hovered over Laura, trying to keep her from the breeze that crossed the open field behind them. The nearest shelter was a shed, back toward the highway, and Labbé always padlocked it. Ian touched Laura's throat and her forehead. Her skin didn't feel cold, but he was surprised she hadn't come to while he carried her. Then he remembered their days of little sleep and scant rations. Exhausted, undernourished and on an emotional tightrope. He leaned closer and felt her breath stir the hairs on his face. Without guilt, he touched his lips to hers and found her warm.

A rusty door screeched open on one of the trucks. Ian jerked back from Laura. He pulled his jacket closer about her throat, buttoning it. Then he left her safely hidden. Hunkering down, he re-crossed the creek and hid in the shrubs, waiting to see what happened when Labbé disappeared.

Several men with long rifles piled out of two trucks at the front of the house. They were agile, fast, and ready for action. A broad-shouldered man slapped the hood of Laura's jeep and shouted, "The Big Labbé is here all right, boys. Here's his jeep."

A second hollered, "Come on out, Labbé. Stand up like a man, you one-armed bastard."

"Seen one of them. The old man," yelled another. "Backed into the barn like a coward."

"Wills, this side. Paulson take the west side of the house." These orders were shouted by a man with white hair and a surprisingly young face. Ian realized that had to be the fellow Labbé described to him – the one who was here last night.

"Yes, sir, Deets!" A broad-beamed fellow shouted. He saluted the white-haired man with a stiff arm, as if he were a private and Deets the sergeant.

Deets yelled to the others, "They're sneaky. Cover the exits."

The men spread out around the house. Some worked toward the barn, covering each other from safe position to position as if trained to do this type of siege. Ian was surprised, however, to watch one tall man slink backwards, toward the last truck. Something familiar about the man caught Ian's eye. He dressed for the mountain, not this balmy day on the plain, completely covered with a heavy coat and stocking cap. As the

man made his move away from the action, he seemed to watch only the fellow called Deets.

Laura touched Ian's arm. His body jerked with surprise. "Is your friend well hidden?" she asked, crawling up next to him behind the scrubby wild alder.

"Can't tell." Ian kept himself and his gun down out of the afternoon sun as he watched. Laura wrapped his jacket about his shoulders. He wanted to pull her close, to keep her warm, but he had to keep his attention on the men. Laura huddled down near him in the brittle grass.

"I'm sorry about giving out in the field there," she whispered, her wary glance on the men in the driveway.

Ian shoved back his short black hair and glanced at her. He was relieved to see some color in her face again. "You're tired," he said.

Laura said nothing, just bit her upper lip. Her almond-eyed gaze darted about the barn and house, avoiding the dead animals in the gruesome field. "There are two men on the porch," she said, "and one on the far side of the house."

He answered her unspoken question. "At least two fellows went into the barn after Labbé." As Ian talked, he caught sight of Vandal slinking around the far side of the house. He wondered how he got way over there, and why the dog would bother.

Laura didn't seem to have noticed the dog's absence, and since Ian didn't want her to worry, he said nothing. Laura pointed to the back end of the barn where the ground dropped in elevation providing headroom for an enclosed space under the main floor. The door on the west wall of that lower space stood open, showing raised boxes hanging from the walls. The boxes were stuffed with straw.

"Anybody go in below?" she asked.

"Not from this side. But there is another door to that chicken coop on the other side, over where the creek turns north."

"Have I missed one of them?"

Ian shook his head, "There's at least one you haven't seen. He's been inching his way back toward that last truck. Looks like he doesn't want to be part of this action."

"Let's hope he gets away, then."

"I wish Labbé would get the hell . . . the heck out here."

Laura asked. "Labbé. He's the one you were going to leave me with?"

Ian kept his voice low. "The Labbés took care of me when others thought I died."

He tried to keep track of the men, but he wanted to gauge her reaction. He didn't have to glance at her to find out how she felt. She lay the back of her slender hand against his dark beard.

"They are good people," she whispered. "But I'm sticking with you until we get Arndt."

Though he said nothing about her declaration, Ian wanted her to leave that cooling hand right where it lay for a long time. Her slender fingers followed the scar beneath his beard. His whole body tightened in reaction.

"You gotta see this," a man yelled from inside the barn, making her withdraw her hand and jab it into her jacket pocket. Ian heard solid oak bang against siding as the man in the barn swung open the loft doors over the driveway.

The man called out, "Y'all get yer butts up here and help me."

The men in the driveway charged toward the barn. Back at the roadway, the tall, heavily coated man took advantage of the distraction and jumped into the truck.

Ian felt Laura tense beside him. Then he saw the wolf dog race at the truck. The dog's bark attracted the attention of the men in the driveway.

The nearest man, the one with the white hair called Deets, hollered "Stop him!" and raced back toward the front of the house, cocking his rifle. The escaping man started the truck motor and drove crazy-fast in reverse down the driveway toward the road. Deets fired after the vehicle. The shot barely missed the leaping dog. The bullet smashed the windshield. The truck, roaring backwards, wobbled from one side of the road to the other, nearly rolling into the ditch. As it passed the porch, all Ian could see were the driver's hands whipping the steering wheel, turning against the slide of the truck. The truck teetered on the edge of the ditch. Vandal caught up with the truck.

The dog's muscles bunched. He sprang into the air, landing on the hood. His toenails screeched across the slick surface. He managed to hold himself on top by digging into the windshield-wiper well. He snarled, and barked, and pawed at the shattered windshield. At the last moment before the truck would have careened into the ditch, the driver seemed to get control. Gunning the motor, he pointed the truck face out, turning sharply to the right.

As the truck surged toward the highway, Vandal's body flew off the hood. His yelp of pain made Laura cry out. Ian grabbed her to keep her down. Vandal rolled over in the middle of the road, knocking down Deets who dashed down the drive. The wolf dog snarled at Deets, rose and tore off after the truck once more.

Laura gasped. "I've never seen him like that."

Ian frowned. There was something, he thought, something about the gangly, all-elbows way the guy had moved that seemed familiar.

He couldn't place it, and didn't have time to worry it. He worried enough about what Laura would do if the gang caught the dog.

"I think I got Labbé cornered," shouted the fellow in the barn loft.

Ian tensed, listening to the sound of men running on the main floor of the barn, above the chicken roost. He heard at least one man climb up the loft ladder. "Look it that!" shouted the first man. And then Deets, running back toward the barn, yelled "Don't touch it. Don't touch anything!"

Ian noticed the little five-shot twenty-two pocket pistol Laura had pulled from her jacket. It was so small he hadn't felt it when he carried her.

"That pea shooter stops nothing," he grunted, listening intently to the sway of the loft doors against their hinges.

"Stopped moose with it." She stared out at the activity near the barn front, then glanced to where the dog had disappeared.

Deets still yelled not to touching anything when the first man shouted, "I've got it!"

"They've caught him," she rasped.

"Nope," Ian chuckled. "Look below the barn. In the chicken roost."

There in the shadow of the coop stood Labbé giving him the thumbs-up sign, grinning.

Labbé waved and then noticed a russet colored rooster running toward the door. Ian recognized Christina's Hephaestus. Labbé raised his foot to stop the rooster, but the bird darted around him and dashed for home under the barn.

"No don't!" Ian shouted. "Damn that bird!"

But Labbé darted back into the cavern after Christina's favorite. From the loft they heard, "Help me lift it, you jackass."

A muffled boom reverberated from the inside of the barn. A man's scream cut off in mid-rise.

"Oh, God," Ian prayed. "Get out, Papa." As the barn roof appeared to slump inward and the loft doors slammed shut, Ian yelled, "Papa! Get out!"

The explosion hurled the loft doors off their hinges and down the driveway. Deets already ran away from the barn, a look of horror on his face. He stumbled. The doors flew over his head. Splintered timbers blasted through a fresh hole in the roof and sprayed across the sky. Deets rolled over, pushed up to his feet and sped off around the front of the house and down the drive toward the highway.

Laura tackled Ian from behind, below the knees, knocking him back into the grasses before he ran three feet.

"What the hell?" he yelled. "I've got to ..."

"Lay low. Stuff is flying. He'll need you alive."

CHAPTER EIGHTEEN

By the time the debris settled, Deets had disappeared around the front of the house. Laura had a feeling he hid in the small woodland between the cabin and the highway. She expected him to begin shooting if either Ian or Labbé showed his face. Deets didn't seem to care what happened to the men he'd brought from the tavern. Those who hadn't been in the barn when it blew up were running toward it. Flames consumed the barn. Laura could feel the heat clear back by the creek. Black smoke billowed out the imploded roof.

When the wind shifted to the south bringing the smoke toward Laura. She could hardly see farther than the end of her arm. Ian buried her head against his chest, whispering, "We've got to get back across the creek, out of this pall."

The wind shifted again, toward the east this time, and Laura glanced beyond the flaming barn and down the driveway. Three men sprawled in the gravel of the driveway, probably hit by flying debris. It looked to Laura as if one of them might be dead. The other two were screaming.

She couldn't imagine anyone inside the barn surviving the initial explosion. From the crash of timbers she heard below the main floor, chances for Labbé didn't look good either.

As more wood broke through to the chicken coop, Ian's arm tensed around her shoulder. She heard him swallow a moan. Laura was certain Ian's next move would be to crawl under that bombed out and precarious structure trying to save Labbé. She figured she might as well do what she could to clear the path between here and there for him.

As she started to rise, Ian grabbed her arm. "You are going nowhere with that pop gun."

"There are only three, maybe four guys outside," she pointed out. "Right now, they're dazed."

"Well gee, Let's round 'em up." As he dripped this bit of sarcasm, she saw Ian studying the land between the creek and the burning barn.

"Round 'em up. Right," she said checking her pistol.

"Wrong," he said, shoving a clip into his Garand. "You stay here with this and cover my back. I'm getting Labbé out." He shoved his rifle into her arms.

"Oh sure. 'Excuse me gentlemen," she mocked, "I'm just passing through . . ."

He pulled three ammunitions clips from his jacket as he replied. "I'm scooting down the creek bed to where it swings close by the barn."

She took his carbine and clips. He took her pistol. Ian touched her chin, bringing her gaze away from the inferno. He held her attention. "You will stay hidden. Shoot anyone who interferes with either you or me. And then move quickly to a new location under cover of the creek- bed shrubs."

She glanced at the flaming barn. He pressured her chin up. In order to allay his concern, she said, "Yes, sir. Now go."

He zigzagged across the open field between the creek and the back of the barn, heading toward the far side, disappearing around the corner while the men on the drive checked the bodies of those left outside.

Between them, two of the men carried one shrieking fellow back to the truck that was left. The third man stayed behind to check the others.

Laura saw him turn quickly as if hearing something. He pulled up his rifle and ran toward Ian's side of the barn.

And all Ian had was her joke of a pistol. Laura hoisted Ian's Garand. She checked its clip as she raced across the field toward the back of the barn. Since the other two men were busy at the truck, she didn't worry about being seen. Deets, she couldn't think about. She did worry about arriving too late.

As she ran, the raging barn fire gave off skin-searing heat. Dry wood popped, alerting Laura to a shower of roof shingles. She dodged the fiery meteors and raced through black smoke to cut off the guy who stalked Ian.

Laura rounded the far corner of the barn in time to see the fellow raise his sharpshooter and aim it toward the under belly of the barn. Laura shot from the hip. Her bullet snagged the dirt in front of the guy, but it stopped him from shooting where Ian dodged inside. Instead, the man turned on her. She two-stepped to the right, pulling the trigger as she raised Ian's carbine to her shoulder. Her bullet hit the guy in the leg. His bullet slammed into the barn wall.

He raised his rifle for another shot even as his leg crumpled under him. Laura pulled the trigger once more. She heard his gasp, but didn't stand still to take inventory. The two men from the truck were running and shooting at her. As she wheeled back toward the creek, a bullet snicked into a rock six inches from her boot.

*　*

Ian had to get Labbé. Smoke billowed from the upper story of the barn. His eyes were stinging. Ian cupped his hands around his eyes, trying to clear his vision for the darkness that greeted him.

"Chief." Ian called as he slithered along the empty coops.

"I like Papa better," whispered the old man from somewhere in the north corner. His voice weakened as he went on, "Papa is coming, Christina."

Ian pocketed Laura's pistol and fought his way through the maze of empty roost boxes. The heat from above seared, making him wet his lips often. The whirling of cold air into the space brought chicken feathers flying out of the roosts. In an attempt to keep Labbé alert, Ian talked.

"Damned chicken feathers."

"Feathers soft," Labbé's voice was tight with pain.

"Papa, where are the birds?"

"Chickens very smart," came the faint reply. "Know when to leave."

"Yeah. But not roosters . . ." Ian stumbled into a length of fallen two by ten – a beam from the ceiling under the main floor. On the floor under the lumber lay Labbé, pinned by debris.

"Why the hell did you blow up the barn?"

"Twenty years I've been paying insurance on this old bchemoth," Labbé sobbed even as he tried for a light touch. "Need to expand."

In the dim light, Ian recognized that the crashing beam had brought parts of the loft down through the barn floor. Ian threw loose boards into the next carrel, clearing a path for himself and Labbé.

"Planted a bucket o' gold nuggets on a pressure release bomb?" Ian asked, trying to keep Labbé's mind in the present.

"Nah," grunted Labbé. "A chest full of Christina's beaded rejects – her seconds. Thought she ought to have some revenge."

Ian shook his head as he yanked lumber off of Labbé. Christina's beadwork had a value near gold in Northeastern art galleries. Above them, through the hole in the first floor, Ian could see flames burning the posts and the hay stores. Fire climbed the back wall. At the edge of the overhead hole, Ian caught sight of a dead man, his hand dangling toward the chicken coop. No way from down here to tell how many others had died.

Air sucked in from the doorway, past his face and up to feed the fires. "Papa," Ian said as he pried the pile apart. "We've got to move."

"I hope I killed the right one," said Labbé, still splayed on his back. Ian grunted, "Christina knows you tried."

Labbé sat up, trying to lift the two-by-ten.

"Wait," ordered Ian. With methodical, quick motions, he got a grip on the beam. "Now," he said. "One, two, three."

At the moment, they began straining against the weight, shots cracked outside. The second shot was the distinctive sound of Ian's own Garand. He forced himself not to think about Laura, just kept lifting the beam.

"Roll out," he shouted. Labbé rolled. Ian dropped the end of the lumber and reached for Labbé's arm.

Labbé stood, cradling a limp, rust-feathered rooster in his arm. He hobbled toward Ian, crooning to the bird, "Damn you, Hephaestus."

Three more shots sang out just beyond the side of the barn. Labbé glanced up at Ian. Their eyes met in the gray light of the roosts. Ian heard boot steps running. More gunfire, not the sound of the Garand. His throat tightened.

"Get out. Find her," said Labbé.

Ian gritted his teeth and pulled Labbé through the maze after him. Above them, the spit and whack of exploding wood announced the advance of the fire across the main floor.

Under the framing timbers, Ian could see daylight and the upper branches of the Cottonwood tree beyond the barn. A flame of gunfire shot through the shrubbery at the edge of the creek. His Garand.

"She fights," said Labbé. "Let's go." He hobbled ahead of Ian toward the light.

Above them, the floorboards groaned. Off to their right, the corner post twisted with the movement of weight above it. Ian caught up

Labbé's arm and hurried him toward the opening nearest the creek. The south wall above and below the main floor split open. Christina Labbé's bird struggled and squawked. The southeast post and both framing beams supporting the main floor walls collapsed.

As Labbé and Ian limped toward the understory door, the lintel above the exit came down, bringing heavy fire-blackened timbers from above to block their escape.

Outside, Ian heard his Garand crack once more. Labbé's rooster flew through the small opening left in the doorway. Labbé pulled Ian down into the dust. The ceiling above them bulged.

"Damn chicken feathers," spat Labbé.

The whole back wall above ripped from the sill plate, taking the barn roof down with it.

*   *

As the barn roof fell, Laura back-pedaled so fast she slipped in the blood of her third attacker. She dropped his bayoneted Austrian rifle, rolled over, scrambled to her feet and ran for the open field. The roof crashed into the Cottonwood. Branches and embers flew like shrapnel. She felt embers hit and burn through her jacket and shirt. As she charged across wheat stubble, Laura found she was crying. All the time she fought for her life, Ian and his friend had made no sound. She'd seen no sign of either in the few moments she was close to the barn. And now the entire structure had caved in on them. They were trapped in that burning hell.

She pivoted in mid-stride, landing with her face toward the hissing, fiery ruin. She couldn't hide when Ian needed her help getting out of that damned chicken coop under the barn. As she passed it, Laura scooped up Ian's rifle again. Running past glowing timbers, she leapt the creek.

She glanced about, checking for Deets and any more of the Madras gang. The east wall of the first floor, the only part of the barn left standing on the level above the coop, had become a wall of flames. It hovered, held up by two blackened posts, threatening to topple into the chicken roosts and near the door where she hoped to find Ian.

Laura gasped when she saw the mess blocking the doorway. Charred lumber and timber crisscrossed the opening. He was in there, under all that heat and weight.

Her knees caved in. "Ian!"

"Get a damned shovel."

Laura raised her head. "What?"

His reply came from deep in the space beneath the barn. "Help dig." She heard hands working in the muck on the other side.

Laura's breath burst out. Hope and fear tightened the back of her throat. "Kick the boards," she yelled.

"Tried that," Ian grunted as he dug.

"Built it . . . of . . . Ironwood," said Labbé from the far side of the wall. "Prevents . . . chicken thieves."

"Where are the shovels?" she coughed out.

"Ferget shovels," said Labbé. "Shovel's in the barn."

"If you hear timber falling, you back off," Ian ordered.

"Yeah. Sure," she called as she ran to the body of the first man she'd shot. She picked up his rifle. Even as she lifted it, it's silhouette seemed familiar, a Mannlicher with a bayonet.

The wall above her moaned. She glanced up. The heavy beam at the top of the wall twisted. The warped rectangle leaned toward her. She didn't have time to worry about the weight of it. Laura drove the bayonet into the earth under the wall and began cutting. As soon as she had cut a square in the peaty turf, she fell down on her hands and knees ripping it out.

The wind took the smoke south toward the Cottonwood and the creek. The air was a cloud of hissing steam – hot timber landing in puddles. She jabbed the bayonet into the earth. Within minutes, she could see Labbé's big hands scrabbling at the earth beneath the lower wood sill. She'd turned up a good-sized rock and slipped it through between the earth and the lower frame of the wall.

"Use this," she said. "Digs better."

Ian grasped it. She returned to cutting the turf.

Above, the moan of the wind grew louder.

"Get away, Laura." Ian shouted.

"It's not coming down," she yelled. The truth was she didn't dare take time to look up. If it really came down, she figured she would hear that difference in time to jump – or it wouldn't matter.

From out of the hissing, smoking cloud, Vandal trotted up to Laura. He began scrabbling at the dirt under the wall, too, throwing it behind him and into Laura.

Vandal dripped a grin at Laura. She moved her digging next to the dog's.

Labbé crowed, "I found another good dig rock. Do like dog."

Laura heard the difference in their digging. They were making faster progress. Straddling her work and, using the butt of the Mannlicher as a dull shovel, pitched turf and packed soil behind her, getting deeper and deeper under the sill of the chicken coop wall.

The wall above screamed against its nails. When the hole below deepened, Ian shouted, "Get out, Papa."

Labbé's head appeared between the soil and the sill plate. Lying on his back, he pushed through up to his waist. Laura hauled on his shoulders as he scrambled. His silver belt buckle caught once. He sucked in his gut and popped out. Laura pulled him up and went right back to digging. So did Labbé.

"Okay, okay," shouted Ian. "I'm coming."

Lying on his back, his shoulders wriggled until his hands could get a purchase on the sill plate. Ian pushed. The south post of the wall on the main floor popped. The post plummeted into the dirt.

"Run," shouted Ian.

The dog barked frantically, prancing away from the heat.

Laura and Labbé each grabbed a shoulder and yanked Ian through.

Burning lumber dropped near Ian's legs. Laura kicked it away from him. They hauled on him, running until he wrenched himself from their grasp.

"Trying to kill me?" he rasped. Behind them, the rest of the burning wall fell into the yard, covering their hole, covering the body of the dead man, covering his bayonet-rifle-shovel.

"Where's Deets?" Ian yelled, "Where's my gun?"

Laura dashed back toward the wall. The Garand stood there, its stock visible up to the breech. She pulled it out of the charred pile. The clip was gone. She suddenly remembered hearing it pop out, spent, just after she shot the last man, the man she'd had to bayonet because he wouldn't give up.

Shaking from the memory, Laura found a fresh clip in her jacket pocket and shoved it in the Garand. She charged back to Ian. "Run to the Creek bed," she urged. "Deets will see us."

Vandal led the way. It wasn't until they dropped into the cover of the wetland shrubs that Laura had time to think. Fury raged through her body. Ian reached for his Garand. He must have seen her anger. He jerked back.

"You nearly died," she cried, whacking him in the jaw with her fist. "You stupid, stupid, you. . ."

Ian dodged her next blow and pulled her into his arms, "Yes. Stupid," he soothed as she broke into sobs. "And you covered for me, love."

Laura fought him, but he held her until she cried into his shoulder. "I killed them. I shot and shot. I could feel his flesh give against the knife. They . . .."

"You had to do it, Laura," Ian whispered. "They forced you to do it." She rocked within his arms. In minutes, exhaustion overcame her.

"Don't ever go without me," she whispered. "Don't go . . ."

Ian nuzzled her forehead with his nose. "I love you, sweetheart."

"Don't, "she said again, then fell asleep.

As Laura slumbered in Ian's embrace, Labbé turned from his watch for Deets and said, "That damned Hephaestus is eating my wheat seed."

"I'd shoot him," growled Ian, "but I'm busy."

CHAPTER NINETEEN

An hour after sunset, when an automobile rattled up the highway, Laura, Ian and Labbé were still lying in wait among the trees near the creek. The car noise made Vandal whine. Laura stirred awake in Ian's arms. Vandal moved off into the orchard behind the house, keeping his body low to the ground, running in swift vengeful silence.

Labbé lifted his rifle and nodded to Ian before he too slipped out to the woods near the highway. As he left, Ian glanced at Laura. She didn't move, but watched the shadow of Labbé slink into the woods. They heard the auto approach the ranch road. Ian felt Laura's neck tense against his forearm when the car slowed. Off in the distance, the dog snarled with intense hatred. A man yelled. A car door slammed. Laura glanced up at Ian.

He whispered, "Vandal's all right. Still barking. But we'd better get ready for anything."

She nodded, rolled from his warmth and reached inside her jacket for her pistol. "Take this," he said, handing her his Garand.

As she took it, she whispered. "You?"

"I've got this," Ian said, lifting a rifle with a bayonet. She flinched. In the light reflected off the clouds, Ian saw blood dried on the bayonet. He'd found this rifle and ammo near the body of a man who lay sprawled in the field behind them.

"Do you want to tell me about it?" he asked.

She stared at the blade, then long at him, before she shook her head. "I want to listen for Labbé and Vandal," she said and turned onto her stomach to watch the place where Labbé had disappeared.

Ten minutes later Labbé returned. "Black Ford sedan," he whispered, "Colorado license plates. It slowed near our road and that white-haired fellow ran out of the woods not forty yards north of my position. Dog hurtled only yards behind him, snarling something vicious. As the man jumped into the passenger's seat, the dog leapt. That fellow shrieked as he slammed the door – yelled something that sounded like 'Karl. Rouse. Shell.'"

Laura said, "Schnell. Karl, get out of here, quick."

"German?" Labbé asked.

"Yes. Vandal?"

"Racing up the road after the car. He'll be back."

Ian whispered, "That's probably the Ford that followed our trail since the train station in Dorset."

Laura shook her head. "He'd stopped already in Madras when we drove through. Must have known a short cut – a back road from the last canyon into the town."

"He knew that Deets fellow was here," Labbé pointed out. "Knew he'd need a way out."

"I'm freezing," Ian said. "If Deets is gone, let's try holing up inside your house while we ponder the meaning of Black Ford sedans."

"Busted windows," Labbé said. "Not exactly balmy in there."

"Nevertheless, let's get Vandal and get out of the wind," Laura whispered rising to her knees.

Concerned, Ian touched her shoulder. "There may yet be one of the Madras gang out there."

"Follow me," said Labbé and took off in a circuitous route through the orchard.

Ian followed Labbé and Laura, watching their backs for any sign of ambush. The three of them stole across the creek. Within moments, Vandal raced at them from across the wheat field. Ian put a hand on the dog's head as he passed. The slobber of anger covered Vandal's muzzle, but Vandal ran straight for Laura and brushed his head against her thigh. Minutes later, the four of them took refuge from the cold spring night in Labbé's log cabin. Using shielded candles to hide their movements, they climbed the stairs. Ian noticed that Laura had a bit of trouble climbing, as if she'd strained a muscle, or maybe was just too exhausted to lift her left foot high enough to clear the steps. The dog whined and nudged her, like a parent encouraging one of his pups.

In the upstairs hall Labbé opened a cedar chest filled with quilts, handing each of them two. As he straightened from the chest, his arms around two quilts for himself, Labbé smiled at Laura. "Vandal and I will be downstairs."

Ian noticed Laura's back stiffen. Through her shivers, she protested, "I should take the first watch. I slept already, outside."

Labbé ignored her offer, but glanced at Ian. "It is warmer together. Use the front room."

Laura's head ducked, hiding her face. As she watched Vandal clip downstairs with Labbé, Ian reached out and lifted her chin with his forefinger.

"He's teasing us," Ian said, watching her reaction. She tried a brief shivery smile. "You take this big room," he directed, "but first, let me check the bed for broken glass."

"I can do that," she whispered, but he walked past her, leaned his rifle in the corner and placed his candle on the dresser. She still shivered in the hall, so he took the Garand from her hands and laid it on the dresser as well. She stood in eerie quiet, watching his movements. He felt clumsy, scarred, wooden.

To escape her assessing eyes, he busied himself with checking the room. The window was covered with drapes. No wind blew the fabric, so he stepped around the double bed and pulled the drapes back. With relief, he saw a reflection of his candle on the dresser, and of her piquant face behind his shoulder. The glass had escaped gunshot. As he turned to leave, she stood in his way.

"This is the only room we've seen that has unbroken windows," she said.

He studied her solemn eyes. They gave no hint of wavering, but he feared he read too much into her simple statement. "Yes," he whispered. "Sleep well."

She touched his arm. "Ian, I'm cold."

The breath rushed from him as he pulled her into his arms. "I'll keep you warm." His voice came out rough and brittle as she burrowed into him. "Come," he whispered, "lie down. Be safe."

She let him lift her into the middle of the bed. After he'd covered her shoulders with a quilt, he took hold of her slim foot and untied her boot. Then one by one, he loosened the laces and pulled the boots off her feet. Shaking with what he preferred to think might be a chill, he unfurled the other quilts over her, and hastened to remove his own boots.

"My pistol," she said, holding it out toward him.

He took it from her and placed it on the bed stand nearest her. "Can you see it?"

She nodded. Her eyes were dark pools of unreadable emotion. He remembered the bayonet covered with frozen blood and reminded himself that he had promised her safety in this bed. He glanced behind him checking that the bayonet was not within her view. He moved his Garand from the dresser to the floor under the bed and within his reach. As he lifted the quilts, he talked, distracting her, he hoped, from his actions.

"Laura, thank you for getting us out from under the barn."

"But I . . ."

He reached out and touched her lips with his fingers. "Shh. Thank you."

She nodded. He bit his lip, fighting his reaction to the soft motion of her lips against his palm.

"Get in," she whispered. "Your hands are cold, too."

He slid in, taking her small body in his arms, covering her back as he pulled her toward his chest. She came with ease, as if she trusted him fully. Her cold toes touched his arch, sending shivers up his calves to his groin. To stop her motion, he wrapped his legs around hers and tried not to think about the knee she rested against his thigh.

"Lie still," he growled. "Sleep and be warm."

As she settled her head under his chin, he allowed himself to taste the tress that tickled his mouth. His tongue brought him the flavor of fresh pine and warm grass – a combination he found he craved. He moved his nose down into her curls. "Laurie," he whispered. "Laurie."

His answer was her deep, even breathing and the trusting weight of her head as it lolled back. Her breath fluttered softly against his throat. In the sliver of cloud-light beyond the slightly open drape, he watched her face in sleep – dark slash of eyebrow against porcelain skin, mouth relaxed into sensitive softness.

Temptation held him in its thrall. He thought long about tasting her lips, about encouraging her to give him all of herself. She could be his, now. Damn the future and what she would think when she found out how much of this situation had been his fault. Right now, he could stroke her back, touch her lips and bring response – and he needed that response, needed to feel connected, intimate.

Even as he lowered his head toward her, he condemned himself. He kissed the corner of her mouth. She moaned softly and moved her body toward his, her breasts brushing against his chest. Heat rose in him, urgent and desperate. He thrust his fingers into her hair and touched her mouth with his tongue. Her lips opened, slightly as her tongue licked away the tickling sensation. Her heavy lids lifted briefly, then dropped closed on a sigh.

Desire shot through him, and he knew he danced with disaster, for her and for him. Still, the draw of her mouth became undeniable. He kissed her, deeply, possessively. He felt her awaken to the gentle invasion of his tongue. Her head jerked back, resisting him at first, then she softened, inviting him further. He pressed the length of his body against hers.

The answering arch of her back warned him. He could achieve that response, that intimacy, but he would be damned ever afterward by his own conscience.

He pulled back. Her eyes opened, unfocussed, at first, then aware of his position.

"I want you," he whispered, "but not now. Not until this is over."

Laura seemed to blink the sleep-fog from her mind. "I'll be there," she said. "You better come back."

He smiled, "Now sleep." He raised one eyebrow in self-mockery. "I've got to get at least a little rest."

She smiled even as her eyelids dropped again. Within minutes she'd returned to exhausted sleep. She trusted him to keep her safe and warm. He would not betray that trust. Ian watched her head relax into the crook of his elbow. Her pulse beat an even tattoo at the base of her throat. Her breasts rose and fell within her flannel shirt.

Moments later, he dropped his head to the pillow and watched the sliver of night sky darken, then gray, then hint at pink.

Hours later, he slipped his arm from under her shoulders and rolled from her bed, leaving her warm and enticing body beneath the Star of Bethlehem, the quilt that Christina Labbé had helped him make, back when a needle and thread was about the heaviest thing he could lift.

*   *

THURSDAY, MARCH 12TH

The next morning, Laura woke alone in a wide bed. The sun rose as she ran her fingers through her tangled hair and re-buttoned her flannel shirt over her cotton camisole. Brown bloodstains stiffened her shirt and her wrinkled corduroys. She tried to ignore the memories triggered by the blood. She had nothing else to wear.

She remembered begging Ian to sleep with her. She remembered his gentleness as he warmed her. She remembered closing her eyes in complete trust. She was not at all sure how the flannel shirt had come more unbuttoned, but she felt certain Ian never took advantage of her. Instead, she feared she had undressed in her wanton dream about him – a dream of swimming naked in some tropically warm waters.

With a firm tug, Laura closed the topmost button on her shirt. She checked the buttons on her corduroys before she grabbed up her boots and tiptoed into the hallway. Halfway down the stairs, she heard Ian's voice from the room below.

"She's been through enough, Papa. Three dead men out there – she had to shoot them."

"Seems to me, son, you found evidence Laura Atweiler can take care of herself."

"I want her safe."

"Then, McKay, I recommend you keep her armed and close at hand."

Laura shuddered, assailed by a memory. She'd run a bayonet through the last and most determined man – his own bayonet. She closed her eyes, but still saw the man's startled blue gaze, his look of comprehension and terror in that moment before he toppled onto her.

She gripped the banister tightly to regain control of her shaking body.

Moments later, she continued down the stairs, speaking so that Ian would know she'd overheard him talking about her.

"Deets has me worried," she said, and Ian whipped about. "Why didn't he stay to finish what he started?"

Surprise and embarrassment flushed Ian's face, but he recovered quickly. "I believe Deets had other things on his mind," he said.

"Killing my family wasn't Deet's main goal," Labbé added. "Seems like he lost all interest in us when that tall fellow took off in the truck."

Laura studied Ian as she strode across the living room. In the warm sunlight from the window holes, she could see that Ian's scar had grown pale underneath his beard. His eyes were surrounded by darkness. She felt guilty for having gotten some sleep.

"You've been up all night watching for Deets to return," she said. "I'll drive the rest of the way."

Lacing his boots, Labbé raised an eyebrow toward Ian, but said nothing.

Laura asked, "Papa Labbé, are your sons planning to come home through Madras?"

He glanced up at her as he yanked the laces tight. "My sons, they won't return that way if I can head them off. I've got the Runt's – I mean Moses's truck in the shed. I'm off to warn the boys soon as you both clear out of here."

"We'll be gone then. Ian?" she started packing her pistol into her jacket.

Ian gazed at her. "Where are we going, Laura?"

"To find James," she said impatiently. "To warn him that Arndt has accomplices. And Arndt has smuggled weapons into the country."

Ian's eyes narrowed, "Smuggled weapons?"

"Those bayoneted rifles, those were Austrian Mannlichers," said Laura. "You can't buy Mannlichers in the local gun shop. Deets is Arndt's man."

At that moment, the phone rang. All three of them jumped at the unexpected sound of the outside world. Labbé recovered first, lifting the receiver, "Yo," he said gruffly. "He's here."

Labbé gestured to Ian. Laura busied herself with straightening an exquisite beaded centerpiece on the dining table while Ian listened to the caller. Ian mumbled, "They're sure it's him? What time?" A moment later, he said, "We'll be watching. Thanks."

Off the phone, Ian stretched his shoulders, rubbed his temple with a weary gesture, then said "Hess flew out of Toronto this morning. They've tracked him as far as Idaho, but now he's fallen off the radar screen – probably flying low."

"Rudolph Hess!" Laura said, "Why fly to Idaho?"

"He's coming here, Laura," Ian said. "Wants to make sure James dies."

Laura stared at him. "Is James's death that important to the Nazis?"

"They believe it is."

Laura realized what this meant to all of them. She turned toward Labbé. "Mr. Labbé, did you work for my father?"

Labbé's boot thumped the floor. He glanced at Ian, a question in his eyes. Ian nodded. Labbé said, "What makes you think I have a connection with your father?"

Laura took a deep breath, determined not to let her emotions surface as she answered, "One week ago, my father was murdered on Longs Peak."

Labbé paled. "Yes, Ian told me."

Laura's voice caught, but she pushed on, "Werner Arndt and others murdered him. I think the tall man who stole the truck yesterday may have been there. I believe that's why Vandal tried to kill him as he escaped. Vandal was on Longs Peak when it all happened."

Her next words were carefully measured. "I believe Deets came to your ranch for the same reason that Arndt went to the mountains.

Deets urged those Madras drunks to kill. He charged them up. He led them."

Labbé's jaw muscles tightened. He rose from his chair and strode to the western window, a window in which bullets had left three haloes of cracked glass.

Ian moved close to Laura, as if ready to offer support. She flashed him a tight look. Across the living room, she could feel Labbé's tension.

Labbé turned toward Laura and asked, "Why would Werner Arndt be interested in my family?"

Laura understood Labbé's wary hedging. He did not want to reveal his family connection to Army Intelligence. She answered as calmly as she could, "Arndt is ridding himself of all who know about his infiltration of our war industries. Up to now, except for the murders of the Tenth Division Officer Corp, Arndt has been able to make each killing look like an accident of racial hatred."

Labbé leaned heavily against the window frame. "His officers, too?" He glanced at Ian who nodded. Then Labbé asked, "How does Arndt know about my Moses?"

"Scopolamine," Ian's voice was so soft that Laura barely heard the word. Ian took Laura's shoulders in his hands. Gauging her reaction, he spoke in gentle tones. "They found Scopolamine in his blood, Laura. It's a new drug – a truth serum. Your father didn't break because of the torture. The drug doesn't let a man lie."

The image of her father's burnt eyelids rose from Laura's heart. "Dad," she whispered, "Dad." After a moment, she was able to speak. "They know about everyone who reported to him."

"We don't know what they know," said Ian. "We have to assume they know it all."

"We have to get to James," she said.

She saw Labbé start and then stop himself. He watched Ian closely.

Ian's gaze slid away from hers as he answered. "James is prepared. He understands the risks. He expects me to be there."

Laura squared her shoulders. "Then let's go," she said.

*   *

The massive slopes of Mount Hood loomed above the town of Government Camp as Laura drove their jeep through drifts of snow into the small settlement. On the mountain, she could see snow and ice spread out from dark summit rocks. To the left of a wide glacial fan, Ian pointed out a jutting intrusion of ragged cliffs.

"Those cliffs are called Castle Crags, "Ian explained, "And further west, beyond those crags stands Yocum Ridge."

Laura glanced up at the cliffs, but her attention returned to the road as she maneuvered around a parked snowplow. Ian continued to explain the mountain. "The granite on Yocum is even more rotten than what you see on the crags."

"You knew all along where we were going, didn't you?" Laura kept her voice as ice cool as she could. "You even know which route James is climbing."

"I knew, but I hoped you didn't," Ian said. "If you told me you thought James would be on Mount Jefferson, I would have allowed you to leave me in the dust."

Laura stared at him. "You'd have let me go crashing about in that wilderness alone?"

"With you haring off to Mount Jefferson," he said, "I would have been free to worry about Arndt, not you. At Jefferson, only nature would have been your enemy."

"What about James?"

"James and I will be up there together," Ian gestured vaguely toward the mountain.

Laura wished she knew where to begin looking for James. She knew Ian McKay wasn't going to give her that information. He made it sound as though James camped alone on the mountain, waiting for March fifteenth.

"McKay, you are an arrogant turtle brain." Her voice grew tight with frustration. "Arndt is going to suspect a trap."

"Arndt knows it's a trap," Ian said with a smile. "What he doesn't know is that James did not set it alone."

"He'd be an idiot not to suspect. He'd be crazy to come all the way up here to kill James."

She waved one hand back down toward the reservation, toward Labbé's ranch and all of the western states across which they had driven. "He could kill James in any town, and he could make it appear to be another incident."

"No, he couldn't. Arndt has no idea what James looks . . . where James hangs out. He knows only that James is waving the red cape at him and will be on that mountain three days from now."

"Red handkerchief," she scoffed.

"One thing I know about Arndt," said Ian quietly, "His ego drives him. He's been made to look the fool, thinking he'd killed James three years ago. Arndt wants to squash James, and he'll go to great lengths to do it."

Exasperated, Laura jerked the jeep into the space near the Texaco pump in front of the general store. She figured they had about two drops of gas. As she jerked out the pump nozzle, Laura said a silent prayer for Labbé and his sons.

Scopolamine. Laura had no doubt the General told Arndt about Moses Labbé, as well as about James. No one who worked for her father's intelligence ring was safe.

Laura glanced over her shoulder for signs of Deets and Arndt. From the other side of the jeep, Ian seemed to read her fear. "In this town, Arndt wouldn't last three minutes," Ian assured her. "These people refuse to hate each other."

Laura wondered if Ian knew these people as well as he thought. She decided to keep a wary eye out for Arndt in spite of his assurances. As she waited for the tank to fill, Ian dove into the back seat, saying, "Move aside, dog. I want to repack my gear."

Vandal bounded out of the jeep, heading for the nearest tree. Laura studied the settlement. Government Camp sat just below timberline elevation on one of the highest mountains in the Cascade Range. The town consisted of a few two and three-story buildings constructed along the edge of a meadow. On the far side of the meadow rose low, wooded hills. Through nearby trees, she saw scattered cabins.

Closer, along the highway, small buildings housed a grocery, a post office and gift shop, and a restaurant. Most of the buildings seemed to have extra rooms on the second floor. One window had a placard advertising "Special Room Rates for Skiers". The country was at war. Gasoline was hard to get. Very few skiers would be visiting. A dark-green Chevrolet truck had parked in front of the post office. On its door, someone had painted a Pippin apple and the words *Hood River's Finest*.

Ian glanced up from inventorying their gear. "Could you pick up some dog food?" he asked. "I'll settle the gas account."

"Sure." Laura clicked the nozzle and hung it up. As she stepped onto the porch of the small grocery store, Laura glanced toward the ski shop next door. A man lounged in the porch swing. He puffed away, intent on puffing up the fire in his deep-bellied Meerschaum pipe. Warily, Laura wondered if the man belonged to this town. Perhaps he sat there to watch for James's arrival and report it to Arndt.

At that moment, a plump woman stepped out of the ski shop. She hailed the pipe smoker and rested on the porch rail to exchange pleasantries with him. Laura slipped into the grocers', but hovered near the front window to watch the man and woman talk. The woman laughed, then she hoisted her round body from the rail and continued down the street to the east.

Laura breathed easier. The woman knew the man. He must be a regular. Still, Laura loitered near the store window, watching the woman's progress down the street. The woman waved heartily at two more neighbors before stopping at the apple truck. The truck door swung open. A young Japanese man climbed down from the truck driver's seat. He shook the plump woman's hand and then gestured for her to look at the boxes he had in the truck bed. Vandal waggle-tailed his way into their conversation.

Laura was glad to see the woman's easy acceptance of the young Japanese man. She wondered how the man managed to stay behind when all West Coast Japanese were supposed to have moved inland. A strong image came to her of the brave man in the doorway of the train in Dorset.

With the dog's happy yip, Laura's attention returned to the main street of Government Camp. The woman laughed at the dog's antics.

After petting the dog for a moment, the woman and man lifted boxes from the truck and carried them into the nearby building – a two-story log structure of strength and dignity – The Battle Axe Inn.

When the woman entered the Inn, Vandal stopped following her. He bounded back up the street toward the man with the pipe. The man and dog tussled in a friendly greeting until Ian called Vandal back to the jeep. The dog obeyed immediately, as if he belonged to Ian.

Laura frowned. Vandal's friendliness puzzled her. He was never so open with total strangers.

After a moment, she recalled her chore, and hunted up the dog food. Outside again, Laura dropped the food into the back seat of the jeep. She slapped her hands together to keep them warm. The air near Labbé's ranch had been cold, but dry. Most of their trip had been through cold, dry air. However, here at the pass, air from the Pacific

Ocean brought mixed rain and snow. Wet air penetrated Laura's coat. It seeped into her lungs and through her bones.

And wet air brought heavy snow to this side of the mountain. Behind the store, on the other side of the meadow, Laura saw the effect of wet cold. Black green Douglas Fir and softer green Hemlock branches sagged under the weight of arm-length icicles. Over the town and its meadow, lay a blanket of heavy, new snow. Pristine whiteness lent a surreal quality to Laura's ever-present apprehension.

It seemed impossible that anything evil could touch this town. Yet, across the western states, she'd seen how easily Werner Arndt and Rudolf Hess fanned Nazi-bred hatred into riotous fires among her own people.

Is Arndt here? Rudolph Hess? Are they watching us?

Ian paid for the gas, then glanced over the top of the vehicle at Laura. "We've reservations in the *Battle Axe Inn*," he said. "You take the jeep on down and I'll see about some climbing equipment at Langendorff's Ski Pole." He poked his thumb in the direction of the shop with the porch swing, adding, "I'll help unpack when I meet you."

Reservations! Laura thought. Just how well does he know this town?

Without comment to Ian, Laura drove the jeep toward the *Battle Axe Inn*. She followed Ian's expectations except for one quick side trip.

While he was in the *Ski Pole*, she stopped on the far side of the inn. Hurriedly, she untied her skiing equipment and pulled her snow tent and sleeping bag out of the jeep. These she stashed behind the *Battle Axe Inn* under the tarp that covered the woodpile. She could tell which portion of the woodpile had been used and hid her things at the far end.

"Find that, you Turkey Ian McKay!" she muttered. "When I want to find James, you're not going to have a thing to say about it, Mr. Bossy."

As she finished her job, she glanced up to find the young Japanese man from Hood River watching her. She hesitated, knowing he would wonder what she might be up to. After all, he was a friend of the owner of this woodpile. Behind her, she could hear the tarp flapping loose. The young man took a step toward her and extended his hand. In it lay a length of twine.

"You want to tie the tarp, Miss?" he asked, smiling. "This should be long enough. Don't want your skis to be covered in snow."

She took the twine. "Thank you, sir. Uhm..."

"Okada," he filled in. "Takehiko Okada."

"Thank you, Mr. Okada," she said. He gave a slight formal bow and returned to his truck. His helpful disinterest puzzled her. In fact, there was something strange about much of this little settlement. Each of the people she'd seen seemed to be very carefully not watching or paying attention to her. Yet she and Ian were the only thing happening in this town, other than Mr. Okada's apple delivery. Laura sensed that she and Ian were the focus of alert non-attention. With a prickly awareness, she headed toward the front door of the inn.

Entering the *Battle Axe Inn*, Laura found a low-ceilinged lobby. The room filled with light from two walls of windows. Overhead, pine-log beams were exposed. At the far end of the lobby, a fire blazed in the stone fireplace.

Laura stepped around the open jaws of a Black Bear rug. Vandal plopped down on the fur. Laura frowned at the dog's nonchalant acceptance of the unmoving bear. She thought he would at least give it an exploratory bark. Instead, the dog rolled to his side on the back of the bearskin and huffed a sigh of relief as if at home.

"Your name, Miss?" asked the clerk.

Laura was startled by his sudden appearance. "Oh! Uhm. Atweiler. Laura Atweiler."

The young man's head whipped up. He stared at her, open-mouthed.

His reaction surprised Laura. She wondered if she had suddenly developed two left eyes – or forgotten to button her blouse. She checked.

After an awkward moment, the clerk found his voice. "Atweiler. Yes. Mr. McKay called ahead and asked for two rooms. They'll be numbers five and six, right up front on the second floor, Miss Atweiler. Five looks out on the mountain as well as the highway."

Laura didn't want to share adjacent rooms with Ian McKay. She felt too vulnerable to his touch, especially after falling asleep last night in Labbé's double bed cradled in Ian's arms. Besides that, she wanted freedom to come and go without his interference. She wanted to find James.

"I'd really like something more toward the back of the lodge," she said to the clerk. The young man colored. His head bobbed down and he gazed rather blindly at the registration book.

"I'm not sure I've got two back there, Miss."

"Oh, you can leave Mr. McKay in room five. Just please find a room away from the street side for me."

"Well," he hesitated, glancing around as if hoping someone with more authority would come in the door. None came. "I guess I could give you number eight. It's at the back looking over the meadow, but it's near the kitchen annex," he warned.

"I'll take it."

By the time Ian returned, she and Vandal were moved in. Actually, Vandal stood at the head of the stairs watching his newfound interest, a wary Saint Bernard named Lady.

She could tell Ian was frustrated by the change of rooms. "I'll get your skis," he offered.

"Already taken care of, thanks," she said.

"Why don't you store your skis in the back room?" he persisted. "Mrs. Leszinski keeps them pretty safe there."

"Oh, really? Thanks. Maybe later. Right now, I think I need a nap."

Ian frowned. She watched him absorb the fact that he was being dismissed. He didn't give up easy. "Shall I call for you for dinner? I could move your skis then."

"Seven o'clock?"

He nodded, waited and then backed away from her door, a puzzled frown dragged his eyebrows down. Laura closed her door, and locked it.

CHAPTER TWENTY

Safe in the knowledge that Laura napped, Ian knocked on the door of a small log cabin. The cabin lay hidden in the woods east and uphill from Government Camp. He knew from the chimney smoke that the cabin was inhabited, and he hoped he knew who was at home. But just in case, Ian drew his gun.

"Put down the gun, McKay," said a familiar voice. "It's just us chickens in here."

The door swung open and Major Richard Cameron appeared, backed by a blazing fireplace. "Come in before someone sees you."

Ian smiled and pulled his tired left leg up onto the porch.

"I don't know how you can climb with that bum leg," the Major remarked.

"Climbing's fine. It's sitting does me in. I've spent almost three days packed in an Army Jeep."

"With the girl of your dreams."

"Who doesn't trust me."

"Any more than you trust her."

"Oh, I trust her all right. I trust her to blunder up that mountain looking for her long-lost brother. I trust her to become another victim of Arndt's sadism."

"Which is why you need me watching her."

"I'd like you to hog tie her. Better yet, I'd like you to slit the laces on her climbing boots, rip the edges off her skis, bend her ski poles over your knees . . ."

"It must be love," murmured Cameron. "Would you like to ask how my day was?"

That slowed Ian down. "You got away . . .," he said.

"Close. Thanks for the phone call," said Cameron. "I dumped out the back window with Atweiler's master list and my special dictionary when Arndt drove up to the front door. He wasn't alone either."

"Dieter Haupt?"

"Hang dog and fretful, but still heeling," said Cameron, "How'd you guess?"

"Dieter Haupt visited Labbé's ranch two nights ago, long enough to kill two horses and a cow." Ian didn't try to explain to Cameron about last night's craziness: Labbé's silent rage; his careful plan to revenge Christina's murder by destroying his own barn – who knew what other insanity Labbé had in mind?

"How's Labbé'?"

"He's gone to warn his sons at Olallie Butte," Ian said, then admitted, "Labbé's pissed off, ready to do murder."

Cameron nodded, "He's got a right. Christina was a wonderful woman." Cameron pulled a red stocking cap from his pocket. "You left this in my guest bedroom."

"Thanks. How did you get out here from Colorado so fast?" "Forged my own orders and hopped a troop transport. Bussed up from Portland yesterday." Cameron headed toward the small kitchen saying over his shoulder, "No sign of Arndt yet, though Langendorff and Mrs. Leszinski have got the whole town on the look-out for him. There are some cabins a little way west of town I've been keeping an eye on, but no one seems to be using them."

"Good," said Ian as he slumped into a Mission Oak rocking chair near the fireplace. Cameron handed Ian a cup of tea.

Ian sighed, "Seemed like every town we drove through banged around in some kind of inter-racial argument."

Cameron snorted. "Argument? McKay, you are a master of understatement. Just this evening, the news is that the Navy had to declare Los Angeles off limits to port sailors because of fights breaking out with the Zoot-Suiter gangs. Two deaths, so far."

"Well surprise," said Ian. "There was never any doubt in my mind that Arndt could get hate to flare up anywhere he wanted." He hugged the teacup to his chest for warmth. "After Pearl Harbor, the job would be a piece of cake. People are scared and angry – looking for someone to blame."

"And you haven't heard the worst." Cameron sat in a wicker armchair, but leaned toward Ian to emphasize the news. "General McArthur had to abandon the Philippines today. We're losing ground fast in the Pacific. People don't like losing."

Ian nodded glumly. "Defeat enflames fear and bigotry."

"And in Europe, things aren't going well," Cameron added, carefully choosing his words, "Arndt's way ahead of his schedule though. He wasn't supposed to turn on these riots until summer."

"I set him off," said Ian, staring into the chattering flames. "He knows the Nazi High Command suspects he has a stash of art treasures somewhere. To counteract their suspicions, he's racking up points by creating Verheerung here. And Arndt has already moved the art works to a new hiding place. He's making sure Admiral Canaris and the Abwehr won't believe he'd sell them out."

Major Cameron folded himself back into the chair by the hearth and watched his friend's morose staring into his tea. Cameron knew nothing could lessen Ian's guilt in this matter. Ian had roused the sleeping monster with one fatal miss-step.

Ian gazed into the fire, remembering an even older decision he'd made — a decision with far-reaching consequences for all of them. He'd been a different person then, a boy named James Schoenfeld, an interloper in a home too good for him.

Laura had been eight years old. That moment had proved the one instance in that year as family when Laura's childlike primness had been breached. He'd been standing at the dresser near the open door of his bedroom. He cleaned out his pockets in preparation for going to bed. Laura's door burst open. Glancing down the hall, he watched as she darted toward the stairwell.

She cried, swiping at her unwanted tears with the sleeve of her robe. Her frantic speed amazed Ian. She leapt down the stairs two and three at a time, crying, "No. No. No. I'm coming. Wait for me. I'll get you."

Worried, James went to the head of the stairs and started down. Then he heard Laura find what she sought.

"Teddy," she cried, her voice carrying up from the living room. "I thought you were upstairs. I'd never leave you alone in the rocker. I'll hold you tight, Teddy. Nothing will hurt you."

James hastened back to his room. He knew it would embarrass the little girl if she were seen with red-rimmed eyes and a runny nose. As she climbed the stairs, he looked out and listened.

"I'm sorry," she whispered as she ran up. "I'm sorry Teddy. Now you can sleep safe."

She came into view, her face wet, her concentration on the beloved lump of worn bear. She held it tenderly, crooning it to sleep as she disappeared into her room.

The bear, Ian knew, had been in the burning car with Laura on the day her mother died. Since that day, the General had told him, Laura never let her frightened Teddy sleep alone. James closed his bedroom door, leaned into the wall and wept for Laura's fears. He hadn't cried since his drunken mother abandoned him on the streets of Denver. That night, crying in a bedroom that didn't belong to him, he realized he cared too much. Loving this family was a risk he couldn't face. He had to leave, before they discovered how little he deserved them.

Sixteen years later, he'd discovered that Teddy now slept in a place of honor, the same child's rocking chair in Laura's living room. Laura had become stronger, even annoyingly self-reliant. However, neither James Schoenfeld nor his scarred, shorter, stronger but limping alter-ego, Ian McKay, were worthy of the family he'd left. The father he'd abandoned was murdered because of a rash decision Ian made. The child he'd been afraid to care about had become a woman – her body still fragile, but strong and amazingly fearless.

Unfortunately, this time, he more than cared. During the last week, he'd stupidly fallen in love with the lady.

Love!

The admission jolted him. Scrambling fast, he found a way to keep it from overwhelming him. Acknowledged, he said to himself with military detachment. Duly noted and factored into the plans.

And don't ever tell her.

But he knew he'd shown his love in many ways, especially during the night at Labbés. How could he relieve her of that if he died?

Ian leaned back, resting his head against the slats of the rocking chair.

Bringing his mind back from his memories, he glanced up at his silent friend. "Cam, you've got to keep Laura off the mountain," he said. "I'll be watching her tomorrow, the thirteenth. But on the fourteenth, I need you at the hotel with her. And I wasn't joking about the bootstraps and skis. . ."

"And poles," finished Cameron.

"Do whatever you have to. If you turn your back, she'll be up there. Once she deciphered the damn telegram, she became desperate to get James out of this safely."

"Only James? Why don't you tell her the truth about James?"

Ian's face became hard, "Because there is no James any longer. He is gone. Metamorphosed. If I live, I don't want her looking for what once was. If I die, the death of Ian McKay will not be such a wrenching loss."

Cameron snorted, "Don't count on it."

*　*

At four-thirty in the afternoon, Laura hung one set of clothes to dry after washing blood out of them in the cold water of the pitcher and basin. When she finished, she relaxed by staring out the window of her hotel room. Laura watched Ian enter a small cabin behind the hotel. Her curiosity had been piqued. He clearly knew someone in this settlement. She wondered who. Should she be trusting him? He said and did the right things, but he kept secrets as well. She would keep an eye on him.

While he stayed in the little cabin, Laura raised her gaze to the rest of the mountain. A wide swath of sparkling snow showed her where one of the ski trails descended to Government Camp. The trail began up at what looked like a large ski lodge. Laura rummaged about for her binoculars and took a better look through the trees to the upper part of the trail. She found herself staring at the cedar shake roof of the lodge.

It came back to her then, a painful memory. One evening in 1937, she had gone with friends to a cinema in Colorado Springs. The opening newsreel showed President Franklin Delano Roosevelt motoring up to Timberline Lodge, this same and very famous WPA building project in Oregon. During the film of ceremonies at the opening of the lodge, Laura was shocked to see her father's face on the silver screen. At the time, she believed her father supposedly trained troops in the Rocky Mountains, yet there he stood, in Oregon. Not part of the cheering crowd along the highway or with the VIP's near the massive, carved front door. General Arthur Atweiler was standing on the roof, near the central chimney. He carried an M-1 rifle and scanned the crowd.

Days later, her father came home from his training camp, or so he said. When Laura asked him why he'd been at Timberline Lodge in Oregon, the General merely smiled and told her she must have been mistaken.

She wasn't mistaken. She'd seen the film again the next night and he was there. However, after she asked him, she saw the newsreel once more. The footage that panned the lodge roof had an awkward hiccup where she knew her father had been edited out.

Now, at last she understood. Even then he'd been part of Army Intelligence. He'd come to Oregon on a clandestine trip, expecting sabotage or an attempt on the President's life – something forced him onto that roof. Something forced him to have the newsreel edited. He'd even been forced to lie to her. Now, five years later, war had forced the closure of the lodge.

"Dad," she whispered, "Why were you here? What should I know?" Laura's gaze rose above the lodge. A mile higher, on the Palmer Snow Field, stood Silcox Hut, a beautiful climber's refuge. Silcox had been built as the upper end of the famous Magic Mile, the second ski lift built in the United States. Since the ski lift didn't operate during the war, Silcox Hut also was closed.

Through Laura's binoculars, the rock façade of Silcox Hut seemed a tiny gray rectangle its roof covered with snow except for one dark circle where snow had melted away from the chimney. As she gazed at the hut, she saw a sudden flash of light from just below the roof. She looked again. The light was gone. She tried to hold very still, watching to see if that flash repeated itself. It did not.

At last, she convinced herself that what she witnessed must have been a last flash of setting sunlight on a window.

She removed the binoculars and readjusted her eyes to the nearer view. A few minutes later, Ian McKay left the warmth of the little cabin, buttoned up his mackinaw and pulled down a bright red stocking cap she'd never seen before. Perhaps the person he visited made the cap especially for him. A woman?

Why should I care, she admonished herself. Of course, he knows a few women. And I've got better things to worry about.

Unbidden came the memory of his kiss – was it only two days ago? She remembered the stalled jeep, a field of Idaho tumbleweeds, and the softness of his caress.

And then there had been last night, so cold, and so afraid of her memories that she had begged him to stay in her bed. She couldn't afford to ponder her motives for acting like a hussy. Killing Arndt ought to be enough to keep her mind busy. She felt Arndt was not far away – Arndt and a lot of Nazi cronies.

Except the three she had killed yesterday in Labbé's wheat fields.

She stopped remembering, forced herself to plan ahead. When Ian returned to the lodge, she had to make him tell her his plans. If she didn't know what he and James were doing, she might go out there and bumble into something. Ian was too arrogantly protective to tell her what he should tell. He acted as if he and James could capture Arndt by themselves.

Drat the man and his male attitude, she fumed. This is war – I'm not going to sit at home wringing my handkerchief.

Out the window, she watched Ian ski down from the isolated cabin. In spite of his injured leg, he skied smoothly, even gracefully. He and his new red cap disappeared among the trees for a moment. Schussing between Douglas fir trees, he reappeared from the woods, then disappeared again under the eves' overhang at the back of the inn.

Laura decided to make sure he didn't come to her room and find her skis were missing. She would get ready for dinner quickly and meet him at his door. Not much getting ready to do. A third of her clothes were drying on the make-shift rack next to the sink. She'd packed in a hurry. A choice of red or green flannel shirts and gray or brown corduroy pants – that seemed to be the extent of her fashion possibilities for evening wear.

"Oh yes," she reminded herself, "and boots, either clean or dirty." She grabbed her boot brush and held her lug soles over the trash can as she scrubbed.

*   *

At six o'clock, she'd heard Ian greet the dogs in the lobby. Then he gave the innkeeper, the plump Mrs. Leszinski, his compliments on the tantalizing odors from the kitchen. Soon after, he climbed the stairs, and unlocked his door. When she had even been able to hear him pouring water into his wash basin, Laura realized how small the Inn really was.

She calculated the time it might take for him to clean up and dress. Then she pre-empted him. At six-twenty that evening, Laura walked to Ian's door, only three rooms away from hers. She rapped sharply on the wood.

Ian opened carefully, his gun at ready. Looking a bit shaken for aiming it at her, he didn't seem to notice that he hadn't buttoned his shirt.

"Laura."

"I didn't mean to startle you, Ian. Were you expecting Arndt to barge into your room?"

"I'm careful. You're early."

"I'll wait downstairs," she said and glanced at his shirt.

He noticed his state of dress and began fumbling with buttons. "No. Come in a minute. I don't want you wandering around by yourself."

She was too embarrassed to say anything about his bossiness.

He stepped back, holding the door open. Laura edged into the room.

Ian glanced down at the gun in his hand, shrugged and reached to lay the gun on the dresser. The gesture opened his shirt, giving her a startling view of his taut nipples.

Flustered, she tried to keep her gaze anywhere except on his chest.

He groaned softly. Looking up, she realized that he was no longer buttoning the shirt, he slowly peeled it off, and he was watching her reaction.

Her reaction mortified her. A flush of heat rose into her cheeks. She tried, but couldn't stop looking at the sharply defined muscles of his shoulders and arms. His beauty lay in the contrast of unmistakable power with the softness of his warm skin.

Ian moved slowly toward her. "It's true," he said, "You've never done this before have you?"

She swallowed dry nothing. "I'm not doing anything," she declared in a strangely hollow voice.

"Your eyes are. They're telling me everything, of how frightened you are – frightened yet curious," he said as he moved closer. "You can't help being a curious woman. Curiosity fills you with courage."

"I'm . . . not courageous."

"I promised myself not to do this," he said.

"Then don't."

"But the way you looked at me – didn't look at me, just now ..."

She glanced toward the door, gauging the distance, back at him, gauging the intent. The heady odor of roast beef arose from the kitchen. "Aren't you hungry?" she asked desperately.

"Very," he took her arms in his hands. "There's not much time left for us."

Her breath caught in a sob. "Oh, Ian."

She needed to say no more. He leaned forward and kissed her very softly, leading her to ask with her lips for all that he held in check.

Laura leaned into him, frustrated, frightened, demanding.

* *

Days of wanting either to love or walk away from her made Ian pull Laura against him, kissing her with ever-growing power, caressing her with greater intensity. He could feel the contours of her breasts against his naked chest. Running his hands down her hips, he pulled her firmly against his body, then raised one hand to invade the back of her sweater. The supple smoothness of her back aroused him more swiftly than he expected. It was as if, with that brief contact, he had stripped her completely.

Laura surprised him by letting her hands explore his arms and then, as he touched her skin, by holding tightly to his shoulders, her lids lowered, her head arched back, her black curls falling away from her face. He pushed aside her loose collar and buried his face in her throat, inhaling the heady fragrance of her warm skin and tweedy sweater. His eyes closed against the fragile bones of her shoulder. He trembled with the recognition that he wanted her love, not the mere physical excitement that other women afforded him. He wanted her understanding and forgiveness.

Still, he couldn't tell her the truth about himself and James. If she knew, she'd see him as a brother. Since that startling moment when first he'd caught her in the woods behind Camp Springs, he'd had not one brotherly feeling toward this woman. Yet, he'd caused the death of her father. He was no more worthy of her now than he had been as a boy.

Ian pulled his head up abruptly. "No. I'm not going to do this," he whispered. "I want you – have wanted you since we first met last week, but we've so little time and there's something I want even more."

Laura's body leaned into his, her hands gliding through the white gold hairs of his chest. He closed his eyes and tried to breathe deeply.

The breath was a mistake. It made the desire aroused by her fingers race through his body.

"There are," she whispered, "only two things I want more than making love with you."

Fighting desperately to damp his physical reaction, he barely heard her response.

He rushed to apologize for his taunting strip-tease, "I'm sorry, Laura. Your evident fear enticed me. 'She needs this,' I said to myself like any stupid autocrat. 'I must teach her these things,' I told myself. 'Anyone else would bungle it'."

Laura talked through his apology, "First, I want you safe," she said. "Second, I want Arndt dead."

"Arrogant male attitude, right?" He went on, "No one else can do this as well as I."

Ignoring his self-reproach, she reached up on tiptoe to kiss his throat.

He jerked back, but since his arms were tightly around her, she continued to un-nerve him with her soft lips. "Laura, don't do that. You've no idea..."

"You changed your mind?" she asked, her fingers and her gaze lingering on his chest.

Startled, he looked down at her, noticed her puzzled frown and the direction of her curious gaze. Her lips descended to his breast and he lost all concentration.

"Yes!" he whispered harshly. "I mean no. I mean, I want to have a sexual memory of you, but more even than that, I want to have had your trust. I want you to say 'He was stronger, but he treated me as an equal, as an adult – a human being...'"

Her hands slipped down his rib cage and around to his hips, pulling him ever closer. "You treated me as an equal. A colleague?" she asked, her black curls entwining with the gold hairs of his chest.

"Exactly," he said roughly, "Not as an object of my fantasies" His breathing became quick as she settled her hips against his. "God knows I have fantasies about you," he whispered.

She looked up at him. Her dark eyes were translucent pools, apparently unaware of the torture her body put him through.

"You want my trust. You trust me," she stated, her hands retracing their path from his hips to his chest.

Ian leaned back against the wall, hoping that by holding her tightly, he could stop what she so naively did to him. It was hard for him to think, but he managed one clear idea. "If what you remember between us is trust, Darling, all other memories will be good and deep."

She reached up to kiss his ear, whispering "Trust between us will be good and very deep."

Ian could stand it no longer. Ducking his head, he touched her lips, managing to be gentle only for the first brushing contact. Then his shaky control gave way to passion.

Her whole being seemed to respond to his urgency. Her arms clasped him to her, her hands playing over his back in tantalizing circles. She pressed herself to him, accepting the explorations of his tongue and his hands as if exulting in his intimacy.

Over the years, he'd had many women, Arndt had seen to that. "You, *knabe*, prove yourself a man."

Those had been exotic women skilled in erotic arts, nothing to him, as he was nothing to them.

But he'd never known a woman so complex and yet so freely giving of herself – never one so unlike the shy girl he'd expected to find. He wanted to explore this woman, body and mind.

He lifted her in his arms and carried her to his bed. Laying her gently in the cotton flannel sheets, he bent to kiss her again, but she touched his lips with her fingers.

"If you trust me," she whispered, "let me help you capture Arndt."

He stood abruptly, "No! God no. He's vicious."

"You think I don't know that?" She rose on her knees. "Trust me to know how to take care of myself out there. Trust me to be my father's daughter."

Aching with unspent desire, fearful of what she contemplated, he plunged his hands into her thick hair, holding her head so that he could look at her face. Before his eyes was the woman in the photograph he'd found in the cave at Annecy, the photograph he couldn't stand to let Arndt look at even one more time.

She looked up at him expectantly, just as she had looked at the photographer. Her dark hair and chocolate eyes contrasted sharply with her creamy skin. Her delicate aquiline nose drew his gaze to softly peaked lips and a firm rounded chin. He never wanted Arndt to touch this woman, never wanted him near her.

His voice was steady and sure, "Arndt will kill you."

She held his forearms, swallowing back desperate tears, "Who are you kidding, Ian? Either we work together, or we'll die separately. We came here together. When he knows that, he'll assume we're both dangerous to him. If we separate, he'll kill you and James and then come for me."

"I can take care of him better if I know you're down here," he insisted.

"Arndt has at least three cronies," she said, "maybe more. You and James will attract them up to this un-climbable ridge for what? For what? So, they can shoot at you? You're bait for the most . . . Oh Ian! He tortured Dad. He didn't need to. Arndt had the scopolamine. He had all his answers, but he went on torturing him. On and on, and then left him to die."

Ian felt her body tremble. He saw terror in her eyes. His hands spanned her waist as he tried to convince her. "I know how to capture Arndt up there. I know this ridge, Laura. I've been up it several times in the last three winters, testing equipment for your father. Of course, it isn't marked on the climbers' map. I don't advertise my work. Nobody climbs that ridge but me. The rock is rotten. It's too dangerous unless you know what I know about it."

"But Arndt has your skills," she said. "Everything you know…"

"Not everything. Before I came to Colorado, friends helped me booby trap the area."

"You weren't in Austria?"

"I had been. I made sure Arndt saw a copy of the telegram and I came to Oregon to get things ready. I went to Colorado because your father didn't respond to his copy of the telegram when I expected him to."

"And James stayed here to watch over things?" she asked.

Ian nodded. He didn't want to tell her that it was actually the whole village watching over things, especially his climbing friend Joe Patton who'd been keeping an eye on the ridge from his tent camp in the high forests.

"Everywhere Arndt turns, he will be on my territory, on my terms. But if you're there, everything I've planned will come crashing down on you."

"James can be there, but not me?"

He hesitated, then plunged forth. "James knows everything I know. We set these traps together."

"Ian, think. Two men? Against how many? Arndt is evil, not stupid."

Ian stared at her for a long moment. At last he let out a sigh, choosing a plunge into risk.

"All right," he said. "I have to tell you so you'll stay the hell out of danger. Come over to my map."

Ian lifted her down from the bed. He grabbed his shirt, stuffing his arms in it as he walked over to the desk. When he turned to show her his plan, the shirt was already buttoned. Laura felt relieved, and extremely let down.

CHAPTER TWENTY-ONE

Dieter Haupt stood as close to the door of the darkened cabin as possible – as far from Arndt as the small room would allow.

"The big Labbé was gone," he reported. "The whole family. Gone. We killed nothing – a horse and an old cow, maybe."

"Did you torch the house? Fire the barn?" asked Arndt.

"The barn is destroyed." Dieter didn't bother to explain how. "Those drunks shot up the house and then wanted to crawl back in their warm trucks. When they saw they couldn't lynch any big Indians, the party died." Dieter felt himself blanch at the truth of that statement.

"When did Johnson disappear?"

Dieter tried to keep the shaking of his body from showing as he lied.

Men did not fail Arndt and live. "Johnson rode to Labbé's place in a separate truck. He must have taken the guy's keys. The owner of the truck was found dead about a mile from the tavern. Johnson's running for his life."

Arndt turned his impressive head toward Dieter for the first time. His eyes were the color of ice – deep, white, blue. "The question, Dieter, is where? Is he running from or toward?"

"Toward? Why would Johnson run toward you?"

"Being a big colonel – it is all he has. To continue being a big man, he must get rid of those who know what he really is."

"But his truck was seen going south, back toward Bend."

"Johnson may have gone south first," said Arndt patiently, "but given time to think, he will come back. He is out there. He waits to get rid of the evidence. You and me, Haupt. He waits to kill you and me."

"But he has bent to your will for five years. Why would he get courage now?"

"He has no choice. I planned to kill him."

Dieter sat in silence. He had known Arndt would dispose of Johnson when he was no longer useful. Probably Johnson knew that, too. But how had Johnson recognized the time? How would Dieter Haupt recognize it when it came?

Arndt stood up, pacing the small cabin floor. Dieter recoiled from the bigness of the man, the caged animal smell of him. Arndt's red beard and hair were growing out again, the hair he'd dyed to visit Atweiler's funeral. No respect had been paid by that visit. Arndt simply wanted to see Atweiler's daughter in the flesh.

Something about Laura Atweiler fascinated Arndt. Dieter couldn't understand it. Ever since Arndt had killed, or thought he'd killed Schoenfeld, the man had talked about the little package Schoenfeld had hidden away from him. He'd fantasized about getting at her for three years. When Johnson's bungling allowed her to slip away before Arndt arrived, Johnson was doomed.

Now Dieter Haupt had bungled. He had to think fast to redeem himself.

"Arndt," Dieter forced himself to speak, to hold his voice steady. "I can find Johnson. He's too weak to hide out in the snow – wouldn't even think of it. Colonel Johnson faces no hardship he can postpone."

Arndt stopped pacing. "Weak," he laughed. "Yes. You are correct." Dieter knew Arndt remembered how easily he'd compromised Johnson's career by offering one beautiful woman. Bedded, blackmailed and betrayed while he was an attaché to the American embassy in Germany – it had been so easy to buy Johnson's cooperation. Arndt's connections in the U.S. military made sure that Johnson, Arndt's bought man, became a colonel in the United States Army and had been assigned to work with General Atweiler.

Arndt no longer chuckled. He leaned toward Dieter. "But now Johnson has changed. He has been forced into a corner like a yellow dog. And his only escape is to kill. You must find him," he whispered. "You bury that one so that we have only Schoenfeld to worry about by the fifteenth."

Dieter held his breath. He didn't want his quaking to be recognized in his ragged inhale. As soon as Arndt turned away, Dieter marched purposefully out the door.

Arndt's voice held him one last time. "Haupt, be aware he may have gone south to get help. He may not be alone."

"I'll watch for that, sir."

"Now, send in Karl," said Arndt, dismissing him. "I need him to find Schoenfeld and this woman."

*   *

Four in the morning, but Laura was wide-eyed, thinking about the strange turn events had taken the night before. She lay in bed alone in a beautiful old hotel. For the first time in her life, she wished not to sleep alone.

They had eaten Mrs. Leszinski's wonderful dinner by the fire. Afterward, they'd sat together on the leather couch in front of the fireplace, talking and sipping Brandy. She remembered touching his boot with hers, and then abruptly, Ian stood, said a stiff goodnight and climbed to his room and shut the door. Laura knew the depths of his desire for her. She'd turned it to her advantage when convincing him to share his plans. However, except for that crazy few moments before dinner, when he stripped off his shirt and carried her to his bed, he held himself back, as if afraid. It seemed he believed he had no right to her love.

She knew he trusted her at last. Last evening, he told her all about the ridge on Mount Hood – the location of every trap, of every village man who waited in the timber to capture Arndt. Ian told her about the avalanche areas and the range of Arndt's favorite rifles. Laura rolled over in her bed, realizing the one thing he'd kept secret. He'd explained everything except where to find James.

She leapt out of bed in a moment, dancing on the cold plank floor, trying to keep her bare feet warm as she pulled on shirts and a wool sweater.

He visited James in that little cabin.

She pulled on wool pants, buckling the ankles to keep out snow. Her boots seemed to take forever. She had to splice one bootlace back together because she pulled too hard and found its weak spot. She grabbed her pack, and at the last minute, her binoculars. Dressed at last, she crept toward the stairs.

As she passed his darkened room, Laura hoped Ian slept soundly.

Outside, in the pre-dawn dark, she pulled her skis from under the tarp on the woodpile. In minutes, she'd skied uphill, approaching the little cabin from its backside. She saw a light in one of the cabin rooms. When she left the lodge, she'd had no doubt that she'd find James here, but the minutes of hushed silence while she skied had taught her caution. She would make sure it was James before she knocked on the door or window.

A shade had been pulled down over most of the window. Only the bottom four inches were open. She trained her binoculars on the little she could see there – a man's arm leaned on top of a table or desk.

Dark arm hairs. Not James. But whose?

She took off her skis, leaned them and her poles against a tree and crept closer. As she approached the house, she found a small evergreen shrub between herself and the window. Laura squeezed between the shrub and the cabin. In this space, she was hidden from anyone else who might be out this night. At the same time, she could see a great deal more of what happened in the cabin.

Major Richard Cameron, slender forearms covered with dark hair, was seated at a desk in what appeared to be a small bedroom and office in the cabin. He leafed through a fat dictionary, the type her mother once used as a high-chair booster for her. Richard turned a few pages in the foot-thick dictionary and reached into the body of the book. Out of a cavity cut through the pages, he pulled a battery-operated radio set.

Within moments, he had un-coiled the antennae, attaching it to a wire whose path Laura's gaze followed. The wire exited through a small opening in the very window where she stood. She glanced up, tracing the wire along the outside wall of the cabin and across open space where, against the white night clouds, she lost sight of it in a tall fir. She guessed Richard had climbed the tree sometime earlier and tied the wire up as high as he could go. With this device, he could send and receive messages quite a long distance.

She returned her attention to Cameron who transmitted a message. Laura listened, recognized the code for Vibes back in Camp Springs, Colorado. However, she couldn't keep up with the rest. She'd never gotten much chance to practice Morse code in her training with the army or with her father. Besides, she knew Cameron would be keying an encrypted message. Since Pearl Harbor, all radio messages were monitored on the West Coast. Any civilian with a radio set might be listening.

If Cameron glanced to his right, he would see her eyes through the slightly opened window, but he concentrated on writing down the code being sent back to him. His face was grim. When the message ended, he stood quickly and left the small room. A moment later, the room door swung wide open and Cameron returned, followed by Ian who carried her father's big toolbox.

That's the rectangular object from the attic. Why did he act as if it were something more sinister?

Laura watched, nearly forgetting the possibility she might be seen. Ian opened the box and removed the tool shelf. Underneath, he pulled out another radio, a false bottom and a sheaf of papers.

"What were the names?" Ian asked, thumbing through the papers. "Williams, in Leipzig, Kniepper in Brussels, Zelinka in Warsaw," Cameron had a hard time going on.

"All dead?" Ian rasped.

Cameron nodded. "Others are listed as missing. Probably in hiding."

Ian seemed to sway, then grab for a chair. "I did this," he said. "I doomed them, everyone … That one stupid minute."

Cameron dropped his headphone. "Arndt already knew who they were," Cameron stabbed the air with his pencil for emphasis. "He had every one of them picked out. This had nothing to do with your visit to the cave. He planned to point the finger at them all, and soon."

Ian glared at Cameron. "But I'm the one who gave him the reason. I threatened his safety by taking that letter and her photo from the cave. He knew his secret had been discovered. That's what set him off. That's what pushed his timetable forward. I killed them – all of them, and the first was Atweiler."

Laura's legs lost all strength as she understood what he said. She sank down from the windowsill, truncated thoughts racing through her.

Dad . . . his network gone. . . all dead. . .Ian. . .. that cave – 'The real Lascaux'. . ."

She stumbled away from the window. She couldn't think, couldn't find her skis, couldn't see clearly what to do. Laura feared – afraid for Labbé and his sons, for any in her father's intelligence network who were on the run. Most of all, she feared for Ian McKay. Ian would never escape these deaths. His guilt over her father's death would weigh on his heart forever. Guilt would prevent him from trusting himself – make him reckless, dangerous to himself and to James.

It was still dark, but seemed like hours later when by some roundabout way, Laura re-entered the back door of the inn and flung herself on her bed. She'd become even more exhausted, but couldn't sleep. The death of her father replayed itself in her mind. He had different faces each time, Williams in Leipzig, Kniepper in Brussels, Zelinka in Warsaw, Banks, Wells, Hospicc, Temple, Bond, Peter Regens and young, frightened Corporal Myer.

Is James Schoenfeld on the list as well? Of course, he is.

Laura moaned. Trying to erase the thought, she opened her eyes and came to grips with the fact that Ian had never talked freely about James.

He had only answered her questions about him when she asked point-blank. Something already had happened to James, and Ian McKay knew what.

*   *

Something had happened to Laura between last night's dinner and this morning's breakfast, but Ian was damned if he could figure out what. He became aware only that Laura avoided him all morning.

Hell, I've been avoiding myself.

After what he'd learned last night, he could hardly look himself in the mirror. He was filled with self-loathing for his part in so many deaths.

But he knew no reason why Laura would be feeling the same way – unless she had stumbled on the same information about him.

No! He dismissed the possibility.

She doesn't know. Even I learned the whole of it only last night.

Standing on the porch of the Curio Shop and waiting for the snowplow to pass him, Ian kept an eye on Laura who was across the street. He waved at Lige Coleman who ran the plow. Lige darted the plow in toward the porch of the Post Office and Curio Shop, creating an opening for each of the village's few storefronts. As he pulled the plow back, Lige pointed at Laura and gave the thumbs-up sign. Ian put a warning finger to his lips and received Lige's nod of understanding in return. Lige turned from the porch and plowed on, building an enclosed hallway of steep snowbanks on both sides of the street.

So far this morning, Laura had been out to Langendorff's Ski Pole as soon as it opened, skipping breakfast. He'd been following her path discretely. Everywhere she went, she asked the merchants if they had seen the man shown in a photo she carried. The photo showed a young, very blond and lanky man – a man these people said they'd never known. Late morning, when the ski shop was empty, Ian asked Ole Langendorff and Doc Hendricks what they'd told Laura about the photo.

Langendorff winked as he leaned over the counter and whispered, "I told the young lady that once, a few years back, I saw a young man, kind of peak-ed looking like that picture, but I don't recall his name."

Doc Hendricks, as usual lounging in Langendorff's, looked up from his newspaper. "I sure wouldn't have known him," he said around the stem of his Meerschaum pipe. "The young man like that whom I knew, has grown a beard. His hair got darker somehow. He's gotten more filled out in the shoulders and chest. And he's a lot shorter than he once had been. You'd never know him from that old picture. Lifted weights for a couple of years, I imagine."

The good doctor returned his attention to the news, a smug look on his face.

In spite of his worry, Ian smiled. Doc Hendricks had been Ian's strength during the first year after his near death. Much of his recovery had been due to the man's ingenuity in designing exercises to rebuild a mangled body.

The one feature Doc didn't bother to mention was the long scar. Its effect had completely changed his face. It drew down the corner of the eye it had come near to taking. Covering scar tissue with a graying beard gave him a bear-like appearance that clean-cut James never had. No one ever mentioned the scar, but it represented the central moment in his life. The instant Arndt cut him had changed his face, and more deeply, his soul, forever.

"I hope," Ian said, "that the rest of the settlement is as coy with Miss Atweiler as you two."

Doc Hendricks folded his newspaper and gave Ian the once-over. "Nobody's going to tell her anything until this is all over," he said, "but if you don't latch onto that one afterward, you're a fool."

Ian glanced out the ski shop window, watching Laura step confidently into the grocer's. Langendorff humphed, "She's too smart to get caught by an old mountain man."

Ian, his back to the two men as he kept an eye on the grocer's door, whispered, "I hope she's not too smart for her own good." Behind him, Doc and Ole were silent as Ian worked up a casual saunter to propel himself out the Ski Pole. He crossed the street as Lige gunned the snowplow into its last turn of the day.

An hour later, Laura came out of the Post Office and Curio Shop, ducked around the idling snowplow and headed back to the hotel, probably for lunch. She'd had no luck, Ian knew. He'd watched her from several vantage points and could tell from the slump of her shoulders how discouraged she was.

He holed up in Al LeGuin's grocery, following her progress through the front window when two strangers entered the store. One was a thickset man with black hair, the other looked taller and had stiff, beetly eyebrows poking out from beneath his ski cap. Ian glanced at them, wondering what brought them to this wayside. He decided to listen to their conversation with Al as he watched Laura. He glanced back outside.

Something had gone wrong. Laura had been walking toward him, but she seemed to be no farther from the snowplow than when she started. In fact, she was closer to it.

Or it was closer to her. He pushed past the two men who were between him and the door.

"Hey, you dumb Palooka," yelled the man with the thick eyebrows, grabbing at Ian's jacket.

He left the jacket in the man's hand and rushed out the door, yelling, "Laura. Laura, run."

She looked up, puzzled. He realized she couldn't hear him. And the sound that covered his voice seemed non-threatening to her. They'd been hearing it off and on all day.

"Run. The plow," he yelled, pointing and charging up the snow- banked street toward her. The plow roared only fifteen feet behind her.

Laura stopped, glanced over her shoulder and understood what he said. At that moment, the engine of the plow raced, the blade lifted, throwing snow and rocks into her face.

Ian's heart pumped in rhythm with the revving plow. His legs pumped faster.

Laura screamed, lunging to cut away from the line of the blade, but seemed blinded by the debris. Sunlight flashed on the arc of the blade as it lifted above her head. Ian knew the treads followed by a bare five feet. The bile of fear filled his throat. His legs seemed filled with weights. He knew he moved, but knew he would be too late. Her safety was beyond him. She ran, too, but the snowbanks on either side hemmed her in. She dodged toward the opening into the porch of the hotel. She must have seen Mrs. Leszinski who stood paralyzed near the doorway. Laura turned again to take the plow's enormous treads away from the hotel.

Trying to turn toward the hotel and back to the street slowed the plow. Laura had a chance.

Ian gained. He heard others running behind him. Off to his right, he saw Lige Coleman jump out the Post Office door and race toward the plow, as well. Laura was forced by the walls of snow to run down the street toward him. The plow picked up speed. She might outrun it for a short time, but if she slipped on the snow before the next store front opening ...

Through the windshield, Ian saw the bulk of a man. His hate-twisted face concentrated on rolling over Laura.

Ian yelled, "To the Post Office. No people there." He saw her veer toward the Post Office. Ian clambered up the steep snowbank on his left. He pivoted in time to leap from the snow across the wide treads of the plow. He grabbed for the roll bar at the side of the cab and caught it with one hand. Slapping his other hand onto the top of the cab, his feet cleared the treads by inches. He swung his legs into the cab, kicking the man at the controls. The man grabbed the shift lever and held on tight. Ian landed on top of him, knocking him into a second lever beyond the big steering wheel. The engine roared even faster.

Ian grabbed the man's thick jacket and yanked him off the pedals. The fellow came up swinging, and punched Ian in the face. The power of the blow sent Ian back into the frame of the cab. He grasped the bar, his back hanging over the tread. As he grabbed for purchase, he heard Laura scream. The sound was all that told him she still lived.

He rose, holding the cab frame long enough to lever himself toward the driver. Ian drilled his left fist into the man's face. The man gasped and flailed behind him for a solid purchase. Ian pushed the tread stick toward the dashboard. The tread on Ian's side came to a sudden halt, but the tread on the far side continued forward turning the plow into the snowbank. Ian yanked the keys from the ignition. The engine died. The sudden lurching threw the other man into the horizontal steering wheel, but the man lashed out with his foot, knocking Ian off balance. The man turned, grabbed the roll bar on his side of the cab and swung out into the snowbank.

His hulk materialized out of a spray of snow. The big fellow clambered along the snowbank, but soon stumbled and rolled down into the street. He rose and dashed toward the end of the village.

Laura rushed out of the Post Office and Curio Shop, running toward him, unaware she ran toward her enemy who ran toward her.

Ian jumped out of the cab, and as he scrambled up, he saw Laura start in momentary surprise, confronted by the man who had tried to kill her. She lowered her head.

Before thought, Ian knew what she was about to do; she'd done it once to him when she had been a child, and again in the woods behind Camp Springs. Ian cut left to try to catch the man before she hurt herself. Too late. Laura yelled in fury and ran head-on into the gut of the man who threatened her. He flew backwards into the road. Ian's momentum carried him past Laura's sprawled form and past the charging forms of Lige and Ole. Ian pivoted to capture the man Laura had knocked over.

But Doc Hendricks already sat on the fellow's rear end. Lige and Ole surrounded Laura who rubbed her head where it had connected with a belt buckle. The danger was over so fast, and Doc looked so calm, holding the man's arm in a painful position behind his back, that Ian was left off balance. Laura sat, disheveled, her stocking cap askew over one eye.

She's safe, safe, his heart intoned.

His relief came out in a guffaw.

"I knew you'd do that," he gasped, "but you're too tall for it now. It's gotta be below the belt to do real damage."

He reached for her hand, feeling good about life for a moment. Her searching eyes brought him to a halt. She gazed at him as though at a mountain from which the clouds had suddenly lifted. Her dark glance roamed his face, his arms, his hands and back up to his hair.

He'd said too much. He'd been so glad to have her alive, he'd forgotten. He had to distract her, not let what she thought might congeal and become real to her.

"Yep," he said, hoping he sounded natural, "A lot of girls are prone to use that head-to-the-gut move when they're upset."

Doc, on top of the man in black, spoke around his Meerschaum. "Gut-butting works great. I've seen it cure a man of philandering for weeks."

Laura colored brightly. Ian offered his hand again. As she rose, she looked up at Ian's face, studying him, a little too intently. Her gaze seemed to look through him and into some deeper part of him.

"Shit. Let me up," shouted the man under Doc. Ian was glad for the distraction.

"Any moment my good sir," Doc assured the man. "I believe Mrs. Leszinski has brought the sheriff. He enjoyed a hot lunch at the hotel and will not take kindly to this interruption."

Ian glanced toward the hotel. There, in the wake of the good Mrs. L. was the bandy-legged sheriff of Clackamas County. He clapped jail bracelets on the man and motioned to Doc to get up.

"Let loose of my arm," the big man whined.

"Stop your twaddling," said Doc. "You offend."

Their interaction seemed to have diverted the too perceptive Laura.

Ian began to breathe more normally. The man Doc tormented was heavy, but soft, clad entirely in black. What little hair he retained had been plastered forward on his head. Ian didn't recognize the man at all, couldn't figure out what he had to do with Verheerung and Arndt. Still, at first thought, Ian was sure that Arndt lay behind this attempt on Laura.

Cooing like a mother partridge, Mrs. Leszinski folded a shaking Laura into her ample body, touching her face and arms in a search for damage. Ian watched this tender care, feeling somehow cut off.

Sheriff Garrigues grunted as he raised the captured man. "You're Payne, from down by Bend, aren't you?"

"This was purely an accident," Payne whimpered. "If you'll let me apologize to the young lady . . ."

"What brought you up here?" asked the sheriff as he checked for weapons while appearing to dust snow and gravel off the fellow's jacket.

"Embarrassed though I am to admit it," said Payne, "this piece of machinery got away from me. It was left to idle – a waste of good gas. I was merely trying to turn the thing off."

"Down there in Bend you've got a snowplow for your airfield, don't you, Payne?" the sheriff asked. "I'm sure it works kind of like this one." He took Payne by the elbow, "May we use your office, Doc?"

"And my muscle," said Doc, guiding them toward his house at the other end of the village. The sheriff looked over his shoulder at Ian and Mrs. Leszinski. "I'd like your statements a little later. Better take the young lady into the hotel. Give her some of that fine soup, Magda."

"Jah, Jah," said Mrs. Leszinski. "Inside we have also good hot chocolate, yes?"

Laura sputtered, "Is the sheriff going to believe that fellow's flimsy excuse?"

Ian maneuvered Laura from Mrs. L's motherly hug and turned her toward the hotel. "The sheriff is going to listen carefully," he whispered, "until he knows what he wants to know about why the guy tried to run you down."

Laura stood still. "You think Arndt sent him on this fool's errand?"

"No, I don't. I did at first, but Arndt wouldn't risk the man's getting caught alive."

Laura shuddered.

"But," said Ian, "if not Arndt, then who?"

CHAPTER TWENTY-TWO

FRIDAY, MARCH 13THE

Ian had been gone ever since Laura stumbled into her room after the snowplow incident. He'd drawn her a hot bath, laid out towels and a robe from Mrs. Lezinski, and told her to lock her door while he went out. At first, she'd been sure he'd gone to the sheriff's office, but as the afternoon wore on, she became convinced that he scoured the mountain, making sure everything was ready for Arndt. From her back window, she studied the threatening black of Mount Hood basalt, the vast, exposed white of its glacial fields.

She could have skied to the little cabin, confronted Richard Cameron and gotten him to tell her where Ian was. However, she wouldn't do that in broad daylight. Someone had tried to kill her – someone no doubt directed by Arndt. They would be following her movements, noting who she contacted. Laura didn't want to get Richard killed, she just wanted to make sure Ian came out of this alive. So, she sat tight.

Late in the afternoon, Sheriff Garrigues came to the hotel to talk to her, and, incidentally, to enjoy another meal, this time Mrs. Leszinski's lasagna. The sheriff claimed to have no idea where Ian might be. Laura tried to hold her growing fear for Ian in check. She toyed with chicken soup and kreplach while the sheriff informed her that Herman Payne, the heavy man from Bend, had come unglued in the jail.

It seemed that Payne was recruited by a leading German-American Bundist and given the mission to find and eliminate Laura Atweiler. Supposedly she'd become a threat to the purity of the races, although how Payne had been convinced of that, Sheriff Garrigues was at a loss to know.

"You don't look too threatening to me," Garrigues said as he stuffed another noodle in his mouth. "I tried every way from Sunday to wring the name of the Nazi racist out of Payne," Garrigues said. "I don't think he has any idea. The more fool he – doing the dirty work of a man he barely knows."

Laura sat up, pushing her soup bowl away. "Sheriff," she said, "Someone is threatened by my presence – believes I know something dangerous. The only person with reason to think so is Werner Arndt."

"Arndt?" Garrigues' wasn't much of an actor. He over-played the dumb sheriff role.

"If Arndt is near," Laura continued, "then where is Ian?"

"You don't have to worry about that boy," said Garrigues, patting her hand. "He can take care of himself. Very safe, that one."

This man who, a moment ago, feigned know-nothing stupidity had suddenly become a reassuring know it all.

"Whose side are you on, sheriff?"

"Miss," glancing around him at the empty dining room, Garrigues leaned toward her. He whispered, "We're all in this together, the whole town. If that boy were in danger, we'd all know it."

"Then think about this," she said. "Arndt is not stupid. Everyone in town keeps a watch out for him, but Arndt commands many people across the country. He can march any number of Herman Payne's around cutting us down one at a time. Arndt could take over this town while he himself remains invisible, up on the mountain, killing Ian and James."

"We are prepared, Miss Atweiler."

Laura stood, "I am going to look for Ian."

Garrigues stood, his chair falling over backwards in his haste. "Please Miss," he said, "He will be back within the hour. Please don't go out there. If anything should happen to you . . ."

"Where is he?"

Garrigues glanced around him, then whispered, "A meeting with the others. If you or I go there, the wrong people may see us."

Gone was his over-acting. He truly worried, and so Laura believed him. "All right," she said. "I'll wait one hour. Then I'll go searching."

Garrigues bowed, "He will be back. I promise you."

*   *

After Sheriff Garrigues left, Laura tried to pay Mrs. Leszinski for dinner. Mrs. Leszinski refused her money, said it was the least she could do since Laura had saved her front porch and even Mrs. Leszinski's own life from the snowplow assault by that vicious fat man. For a brief warm time, Laura reveled in Mrs. Leszinski's motherly concern. Then, two newcomers wandered into the inn, wanting to order Lager from the bar.

Laura climbed the stairs to her room. From the window, she hoped for a sign of Ian's return. She watched dark descend early in the mountain town. The tall hills to the west obscured the sun long before official sundown. Laura's mood descended with the sun. Below her, the banging of pots and pans in the kitchen annex seemed to have grown louder. Laura's head ached. She thought her stomach was having a delayed reaction to this morning's near miss with the plow.

She climbed into bed shivering, still wearing a flannel shirt and skier's long-johns. Her mind entertained a jig-saw puzzle of thoughts and memories, none of which made a clear picture. She was surprised at how frightened she was. The narrow escape from the snowplow revealed an element of random chance in life – the same a-moral luck which once had left Laura alive and her mother dead.

Using others, Arndt can murder me without any risk to him. Fearful, and angry at being afraid, Laura lay beneath the quilt, listening to the sounds of kitchen cleanup in the annex just below her window. The dull, mundane clank of pots helped blunt her awareness.

Her head ached and her eyes watered. Laura became more sick than frightened, too sick to care about anything.

She heard Vandal whine and rise up from his rug, so she reached out an arm to pet him. He seemed to feel easier when she touched him, staying directly under her hand as she drifted off to sleep.

She reached out her hand so Ian could pull her up from the street. "I knew you'd do that," he laughed, "but you're too tall for it now."

"Yep," Doc said, "Girls are prone to use that head-to-the-gut move when they're upset."

"You're too tall for it now," Ian repeated.

She saw him standing in the Aspens at the edge of the cemetery. Her father was buried in the ground behind her. Ian McKay stood, his thumb at right angles to his fingers – tense, ready to go for his gun.

"You've become a beautiful woman, Laura Atweiler," he said as he swept his short hair off his forehead. Why did he shove hair so short it needed no shoving?

The scene behind him moved, leaving Ian standing in the hall of the Battle Axe Inn, trying to convince her to let him put her skis away – his tension telegraphed by that thumb.

She saw the photo she'd carried all day, the young James, straight blond hair blown across his forehead as he turned toward the camera, one hand on his walking stick, excited, she knew, because of the tense angle of that thumb.

Laura drifted deeper into sleep, aware of the smell of smoke arising from the kitchen, vaguely glad the pots were no longer banging because her head ached fiercely, and she needed quiet to allow her thoughts to spin.

Her thoughts circled, Ian's chocolate brown eyes, his dark eyebrows just like those that were so startling in one as white-blond as James.

She'd pressed her fingers into Ian's chest, marveling at the soft, almost white hairs she found there, when his facial hair was brown – everywhere except near the knife scar.

"Arndt knifed James and then threw him down the stairwell to die," Ian said. Her father had never mentioned the knifing.

"There is one more interesting story, Laura," Ian had said. "It has to do with the mysterious death of a Corporal Myer. He was found near the Camp Springs Army Base early this morning. He'd been knifed in the face and then stabbed in the heart."

Her thoughts circled as the wood smoke circled in the night air, looking for a path to freedom. Vandal whined. He lifted a paw over her extended arm. Her hand dropped from his head toward the floor.

"I should get up and let him out," she thought.

"You've become a beautiful woman," Ian said.

Humph, she grunted. I was always at least good looking – it's when I was a girl that I looked scrawny . . .I ought to pull my arm inside. It's going to freeze.

Vandal nudged her arm again, whined and then paced toward the door. He scratched the door, then paced back to push his muzzle under her limp arm again.

I'll let you out in a minute. . . . a minute . . . You shouldn't scratch the door.

* *

Vandal grabbed her shirt with his teeth, pulling her partially out of the bed. The shirt ripped, but still his mistress didn't move. Frustrated, Vandal pawed at her back, then leapt on her with his forelegs, pulling her further out of the bed. He tried to grab her curls and pull as if she were a puppy, but her hair slipped from between his teeth. The shirt ripped further when he got a new purchase on it.

Barking loudly, he hurled himself at the door, scratched and whined then pounced again on her inert body. Distressed, he barked sharply, then threw his weight at the stubborn wooden door again.

* *

Just after sunset, Ian entered the lobby of the Battle Axe Inn. He nodded to Cameron. Cameron shook his head, indicating that Laura hadn't left the hotel since the snowplow incident. Two men leaned on the lobby bar, so Ian refrained from acknowledging Cameron. Ian recognized these men. He'd left his jacket in the grip of one of them earlier today when he raced out to warn Laura about the plow.

The grocer, Al LeGuin, had collected the jacket and given it back to Ian during this afternoon's town planning meeting. Along with the coat, LeGuin had offered a few pithy comments on the character of the strangers. The town's men kept an eye on them, but here they were, lounging in the Battle Axe Inn.

Ian leaned against the lobby mantel, pretending to need warmth from the fire, but in reality, studying the men. Something about them he recognized, but neither their faces nor body build. Something more – an air of arrogance, an attitude of superiority toward other life. Carbon copies of Werner Arndt.

Not men he wanted at his back. The tallest of the two had a face that looked vaguely familiar – dark and bristly eyebrows over sharp eyes and a long, strong face. The man moved gracefully and warily, with more self-confidence than the other. Over his beer stein, that man watched Ian. Ian was sure that the feeling of knowing was common between them. They had met. Ian believed they must have climbed together in Europe, but he couldn't remember where or when.

Cameron shifted in his chair, directing a significant glance at the men, then, without ever looking at Ian, he telegraphed his concern with the lift of his eyebrows over the thick rims of his glasses. Ian understood Richard Cameron as easily now as he had when they were together at the Stratton Home for Boys. Back then, the raised eyebrow meant "Fellow inmate looking for a fight."

Ian shifted his hips, leaning his backside toward the dining room door. Cameron read him correctly, stretched languidly, rose and sauntered into the dining room. Both he and Ian knew that Cameron could leave by the kitchen, then get help from the town. The strangers might not know the building well enough to sense that route.

The two gentlemen merely shifted against the bar, sipping their drinks as they watched Ian. For a moment, he thought he might use their presence as an excuse to avoid Laura. He could stay in the parlor, watch them until they got tired of watching him or until he placed the man with the beetly eyebrows.

A stupid idea. He had to be gone early tomorrow. All his preparations were finished. The village men were ready. The plan was in action. Laura or no Laura, he had to get to bed. Besides, he could get to his room without disturbing her at all. Without another glance in the direction of the interlopers, Ian strode across the room and up the circular log stairs.

As he reached the top stair, he heard Vandal's body thud against wood. His sharp bark followed, frantic and muffled. Ian was at Laura's door in seconds.

Locked – solid and locked.

"Sit, Vandal," he ordered and stepped back to give himself room to maneuver. Leaning heavily on his short, left leg, he raised the stronger right and dashed his boot heel against the lock. A second and third crashing blow sent sharp pain to his hip joint, but the door fell open.

Smoke roiled out into the hall, making it impossible to see into the room. Vandal limped out, then wobbled back in, whining and tugging at the rug on the floor.

Flinging his arm in front of his nose and mouth, Ian ran across the room and pushed at the window. It rose swiftly, its heavy weights clanging inside its frame. Outside, another metallic banging could be heard, but Ian paid no attention. He searched for Laura in an empty bed.

Vandal's efforts showed him where she was. Her body, lying on the rug, was being pulled into the hall by the determined but sick animal. Ian lifted her from the rug, and ran down the hall toward the stairs. The dog ran before him. At the top of the stairs, Vandal faced him, barking. Inexplicably, the dog barred the way out.

Ian's memory of the two men stopped him. They were waiting for just this turn of events – waiting for him to run downstairs encumbered, helpless to fight them off. And somehow the dog knew it.

In his arms, Laura gagged and choked. Ian ran to his own room, fumbled to unlock its heavy door and then lay Laura on the bed. Though this room was clear of smoke, he raised his own window and rushed back to the bed. Her skin shone a bright, frightening red. Frantic, Ian breathed into her as if she had been drowning, hoping to trade good air for the poison invading her system.

Within seconds, banging rattled his door. "Who. . .?"

"It's Cam. They're gone. Let me in."

Ian hurriedly opened the door and returned to Laura's body. She wrenched out shallow coughs. The dog threw up on the rug.

"I saw the pipe fall," said Cameron, holding out the wash bowl from the dresser. "When you opened her window and the smoke rolled out, I went for help. Mrs. Leszinski has gone for Doc. Ole and Joe were nearby, about to leave for Timberline. They dashed into the lobby to head off the two men. They had started up the stairs, but pushed past Joe. Vanished into the night."

Ian grabbed the bowl from Cam and held Laura over the side of the bed, soothing her forehead as she vomited her dinner. When she seemed to have gotten everything out, he wiped her face with a towel and pulled a quilt over her exhausted body. It was only when she seemed to relax into real sleep that he brought his distracted mind back to what Cameron said.

"What pipe fell?" he asked, still massaging tension from Laura's back.

"There was a pipe attached to the wood-stove chimney outside the kitchen annex," said Cameron, glancing out the front window for any sign of Doc. "It had been propped up by pine logs so it would run across the space between the two buildings. The pipe stuck through a hole cut in Laura's window."

Laura's body went ridged beneath Ian's massaging hands. He pulled back the covers and lifted her again.

"Doc's coming," said Cameron. He knelt, soothing the sick dog, who also vomited.

Laura's body, still trying to rid itself of unwanted chemicals, went into a nerve-tearing bout of the dry heaves.

Doc, clad in pajamas and a wool robe, ran into the room. It was the first time Ian had seen the man hurry. Mrs. Leszinski followed, carrying Doc's slippers. Mrs. L's breath came in quick little gasps. Laura's breathing grew deeper, more ragged.

"That's good," Doc said, "She's gulping in air, throwing up . . . All the right reactions."

"Her color," Ian said.

"Bright red . . . Happens sometimes with smoke. Move, son," Doc said. "I'll take over here."

Ian rose, reluctantly letting go of Laura. He backed two steps, hovering.

Doc glanced up. "Go figure out how they did it."

That made sense, vaguely. At Cameron's tug, Ian left the room trying to turn his mind to more practical matters than his fear for Laura Atweiler. Once down the hall at her doorway, he could see that the smoke had been confined to Laura's room. It was now a wisp of what it had been. Behind the curtain that covered the lower half of the window, he found a round cut in the window glass, fresh and sharp.

Ian ducked his head out the window to see the pipe on the ground between the hotel and the annex. "The whole apparatus must have been rigged up late today," he said. "It couldn't have been there before dinner tonight or her room would have been full of smoke when she returned from eating."

"Why are they after Laura and not you?" asked Cameron.

Ian nearly bumped his head on the window as the import of the question slammed into him. Was Arndt trying to get rid of Laura before the fifteenth? Or could it be someone else? He became convinced that the two attempts today were done by nobodies, non-professionals. The person who wanted her dead could not be Arndt. Then who directed the men in the lobby?

This second attempt had been clever, but the clumsiness of the snowplow incident made Ian sure these couldn't have been Arndt's ideas. His schemes were smooth, delicately precise – and they worked. They left no witnesses such as Herman Payne. Tonight, for instance, Arndt would have killed the dog and then suffocated Laura alone. Arndt never left anything to chance.

Ian pulled his head inside. The room supplied a picture of the dog's frantic efforts to save Laura. Her bedcovers were pulled to the floor. Pieces of her flannel shirt had been ripped away and left lying. The rug on which the dog finally dragged her to the door was tooth-torn in several places. Vandal was a persistent and loyal friend – and bloody healthy in spite of the smoke. Ian owed that dog.

"Close, wasn't it," Cameron said, reading his friend's mind.

"Too close," Ian whispered, heading toward the door. "I want to see how she is."

Cameron accompanied him to the room. Outside the door, Ian hesitated, unsure about barging in. Cameron tapped him on the shoulder.

"Nobody has more right than you. Go to her."

Ian tried to wipe the signs of worry off his face. "And you?" he asked.

"I'm going to ski up to the cabin with Ole Langendorff and Joe Patton. They think those two men from the lobby may be out there waiting to catch one man alone. Later, when they're sure no one's watching, Joe and Ole will head up to the hunter's blind and wait for you to bring them the big bear."

Ian glanced at Cameron. The man's glasses reflected the light from the hall. As usual, Cam used the glasses to hide his feelings. "You be careful, Cam." Ian said. "I'll be up before dawn. Whatever her state, I'm bringing Laura with me."

"Just don't forget to come back and take her off my hands on the sixteenth. Keeping Laura Atweiler off the mountain will be a tough job."

"Ingenuity, Cam. Use your ingenuity."

Cameron laughed. "Hah! I'll have to break her leg."

Their brief moment held affection laced with sadness. Both men knew how much rode on the next two days. They'd almost lost Laura Atweiler twice. And she wasn't safe in this building anymore. If they hadn't planned carefully enough, if they had overlooked any detail, they could lose everything, leaving Arndt with no opposition.

And clearly, they had overlooked something. A maverick had entered the game – someone they didn't know about and hadn't planned for. That wild card stalked Laura.

"I'll take care of her," Cameron promised.

"I'll be back," Ian said as he pushed open the bedroom door to see her.

CHAPTER TWENTY-THREE

Sitting beside Laura on the bed seemed intrusive, intimate – a move he couldn't afford. Nevertheless, Ian sat there. Mrs. Leszinski had dressed Laura in one of Ian's shirts and taken the torn flannel away. An hour after almost dying, Laura looked peaceful, beautiful, safe. He wanted to watch her all night – not to touch her, but to savor her existence.

Doc assured him all she needed was sleep. Doc's tone indicated that Ian might have other things in mind, but he didn't. Not tonight. Not ever. She'd gone to great lengths to separate herself from him since their arrival in town – changing rooms, hiding skis and climbing equipment.

Ian smiled to himself. This afternoon, during the town's planning meeting, Takeh Okada described how Laura hid her skis in the woodpile. And Takeh had done a great imitation of Laura muttering about some fellow named McKay being a bossy turkey. Ian grinned down at Laura's relaxed and angelic-seeming face.

At least he no longer had to worry about her skiing up onto the mountain. Takeh promised to take all her gear to some other woodpile tonight. What worried Ian most was why Laura had been avoiding him this morning. And after the near disaster in the street, she'd barely been able to look him in the eye, though he'd forced her to endure his presence long enough to get her some hot bath water and to know she'd be all right. The only time the two of them had been close in the last twenty-four hours was here, last night, when he'd taunted her sexual naiveté.

Ian drew a deep breath at the memory of her hands on his chest, her body in his arms.

By God she is sensual.

He'd been almost out of control, carrying her to his bed when he should have been escorting her downstairs to a decorous dinner.

That wouldn't happen again. If he came back . . . When he came back, he'd have to tell her the truth about James. He'd also have to tell her who set Arndt off on this rampage and forced this confrontation on the mountain.

After that, he was sure Laura Atweiler would have nothing more to do with Ian McKay or James Schoenfeld.

Slowly he made himself move away from her. Mrs. Leszinski had put an extra mattress on the floor for him – bless the mother hen. She'd known he wouldn't leave Laura alone after two attempts on her life.

That's why tomorrow worried him. Cameron was a good man, smart and instinctive. But Cameron was only one man. There would be few people left in the village able to help him if the maverick came after Laura at the cabin. Ian decided to have Sheriff Garrigues and Takeh help Cameron guard Laura while he climbed Yocum Ridge.

*   *

Smoke billowed from under the dashboard of the Packard. Her mother screamed in pain. The face of her father appeared at the window and Laura tried to roll the window down, but it wouldn't budge more than an inch.

"Open the box, Laurie. The box with the tools."

She cried for him, banging her small fists against the glass. Her mother's screams subsided to whimpering moans.

"Open the box," her father yelled. "Next to you. Give me the crowbar."

She'd cried and fumbled with the toolbox lid.

"Damn. Open it, Laurie. I can't get to you without the crowbar."

Daddy never swore. Never. Besides, he should know she wasn't strong enough to pull up the fastener.

"Laurie," he yelled at her. "You have to do it. Lay the box on its back."

She did what he said. Crying and blubbering through her mother's renewed screams, she managed to open the box and spill its contents on the seat of the car.

"Hurry. Hand me the crowbar."

Laura scrambled over the pile of tools. Through the thickening smoke, she found something with a long blade. Shoving it through the small opening, she cried, "Daddy, I can't breathe."

"That's a screw-driver. I need the crowbar. The one with the curvy handle."

She could barely see any of the tools through the smoke. Behind her, she could hear her father trying to break the window with the tool she'd given him. Her mother no longer screamed. That frightened Laura more than the piercing shrieks. Frantically she searched, all the time crying to herself.

"Laurie. The crowbar is big. It's for prying. Find it quick."

She crawled over the toolbox, feeling for any big tool. She was beyond thinking of curves. It had to be big. At last she found a very big tool – all handle and no head it seemed, but as she raised it to the window, she saw a V chopped out of the end.

"Thank God," her father said. And then all she could hear was the sound of screeching metal and the sound of her own weak voice.

"Teddy. Mommy, Teddy. Mommy." Her voice grew louder. It echoed off the roof of the burning car, off the rocks of the Flat Iron Mountains, off of the sky.

*   *

At her first scream, Ian twisted on his mattress and saw Laura sit straight up, her face filled with terror.

"Wake up, Mommy!"

Ian was up and holding her in a moment. "Laura. It's James . . . Ian. I'm here. You're safe."

"Mommy," she wailed once more, then opened her eyes. Tears hovered on her lower lid. He wiped those tears, then held her close to his chest. She coughed and sobbed, clinging to him.

"It happened again. It trapped her legs and burned . . .."

"Laura." He felt her try to control her fear, but her efforts were punctuated by wracking sobs.

"Tell me, Sweetheart." Ian massaged her head and neck, trying to help her awaken and relax. She clung to him, afraid, it seemed, of empty space and the possibility of dreaming again. He'd never seen her more vulnerable. She'd rarely admitted to fear in his presence – except fear for James's life.

"Laurie, get it out. Stop having to dream it."

She became tight and still in his arms. "Laurie?" she whispered.

"Come on, Honey. Tell me what happened."

Laura sat up, still clutching his shoulders, but looking at him with clear eyes. "Laurie." She caressed his name for her.

Ian shifted his weight to lean against the headboard and pulled her back down into his arms. "What happened that day, Laura."

After several moments, she finally said, "My mother was . . . Mother . . . she was delicate, very feminine. She knew only sewing, cooking, serving guests a fine tea – the maidenly arts, Daddy called them. He loved her helplessness. It made him feel big, protective. I became her carbon – a silly piece of organza."

To herself, Laura made a face of utter distaste, which Ian's lowered glance caught at its last curl. He bit his lip and hugged her closer.

"On that day," she said, "Dad took us for a ride in his Packard touring car to show mother a flower she might embroider on a pillow. He parked at the base of the Flat Irons – those shear dark cliffs near Camp Springs."

Her voice shook slightly, allowing Ian to feel her powerful memory of that place.

"Dad parked the car and walked into the woods to find the blossom. Mother made me lock all the doors in case any bears came along. After Dad disappeared into the trees, I heard a pop. I learned later it was the emergency brake letting go. The car rolled forward. Mother screamed, but Dad couldn't help her. Within moments we were barreling downhill toward a mountain stream.

"What about the foot brake?" Ian asked.

"Brake? Mother had no idea what stopped a car. We were two China dolls thrown about inside a tin can."

Laura lay silent, reliving those last moments just as her subconscious had forced her to do for years. Ian bent over her, trying to stop her waking nightmare with soft whispers.

Laura twisted in his arms, looking up at him. "Ian, inside there, we had everything we needed to stop the car, but we didn't know it. A toolbox sat next to me, but I didn't know anything about tools. Even after we hit the bridge abutment, I could have gotten us out in time if I'd known how to use the tools."

"Laurie, you were seven. Most little girls don't know that." Ian placated, but she interrupted.

"That's just it. Why don't they? By seven you would have known."

His voice grated, "By seven, I knew how to break into the Denver Bank."

Laura looked perplexed for a moment, then put her hand on his bare chest. His body tensed in reaction, but he heard her whisper, "Laurie? The Denver Bank?"

More audibly she said, "But we didn't. We didn't know anything. My mother died while I sat there helplessly screaming."

Ian winced.

"Dad kept yelling at me to get a crowbar and push it out. In my dream, I keep handing him the wrong tool. My mother is dying, and I push useless little tools through the window at him."

"Did you find the crowbar?"

"Yes. Too late."

Ian sat, stunned. Here she was, alive, rescued from the burning car, but always too late, because she hadn't saved her mother. Everything she had become – strong, courageous, assertive —-all of it stemmed from that powerless, guilt-ridden moment.

His turning point had been young, too. However, it had made him distrustful, even cold. Then, Werner Arndt's betrayal turned him into an emotional glacier. Only since finding Laura's photo in Arndt's cave had he felt his heart thaw. He wanted desperately to shatter his ice walls and reach through to her warmth and strength.

In his arms, he felt her crying subside. Unable to say anything helpful, Ian rocked her gently. After a long time, when he was almost sure she slept, she whispered, "Thank you."

Looking down into her earnest face, Ian tried for her sake to break through his barriers and offer comfort, but he hadn't enough practice to find the right words.

"I don't know how to take away your nightmares, Laurie."

Her fingers curved across his chest, creating warmth. "You don't have to feel responsible for my dreams of the past," she said, "only the future."

His hand covered hers, caressing between her fingers as he thought. He knew the future, too well. Tomorrow morning, he would put himself in as vulnerable a position as possible, and there, he would wait.

"Your future," she said as if reading his thoughts, "begins now, not tomorrow morning."

"The present future," he said, testing the thought.

"Make love with me, Ian," she whispered. "Begin a new future with me."

Fear iced through him.

Make love with her? When she learns the truth, she'll despise me. If I touch her that way, she'll hate herself.

Laura lifted her head so she could look him in the eye. It hurt him to see those dark, wet eyes so close, so trusting.

"I can't do that to you, Laura. What if – I mean I may not be able to come back to you."

She smiled. Those innocent looking lips seemed to be saying the most incredible thing.

"The Army issues condoms for 'What ifs'," she whispered, "I know you have the accepted brand in your pack."

"Damn!" he exploded, rolling her onto the bed beneath him – a position he thought at first would save him. "How can you know about those?"

"I live on an army base," she said, sadly.

Laura looked up at him, her face innocent, but his shirt on her body was not buttoned quite far enough. The swell of her breasts rose within the opening. His arm around her waist had pulled the shirt slightly to one side and taut across her shape. He moved one leg to disguise his reaction and found his thigh in contact with long, naked legs. Her toes explored his calf.

"Stop that," he said harshly, wrapping his leg over hers to keep her toes from tickling him. The move proved another mistake.

"What happened to your long-johns?" he rasped.

"Mrs. Leszinski took them. They smelled like smoke. My shirt too."

His eyes went back to her body in his shirt, a further error in judgement. "Damn, Laura. I can't do this. You don't know . . ."

Her hands reached up to his face, "But I do know," she said. Her finger traced his scar, holding him mesmerized as she talked. "For some reason, you believe you caused my father's death. But I also know that Arndt had to kill my father. Dad knew too much about Verheerung. He knew Arndt's contacts. Arndt was forced to go after Dad first, no matter what you did."

"But I came within a sliver of destroying Arndt before that. He would have been dead at the hands of the Nazis. If I'd kept my head, your father would still be alive."

Laura drew a long shuddering breath which reminded him that only moments before driving him to sexual distraction, she'd awakened from a nightmare. Only days before he met her, she had watched her tortured father die. What was he doing here, holding this frightened woman in his bed? She needed comfort and the safety of strong arms. He shouldn't let that make him think she needed him.

"Ian," she whispered. "I know you loved Dad, too."

She might as well have butted him in the stomach. He caved in, his head falling to her shoulder, his hard-won aloofness crumpling. His body shook with silent pain. His reaction surprised him, and he was powerless to stop it.

*   *

Laura encircled his shoulders with her arms. She said no more, merely held him as he tried to stem the rising tide of emotion. Love he had hidden even from himself. Grief he had allowed only others to feel.

Loss and guilt came first in long, terrible silence. He held back as much as he could, but Laura knew it was in there, and she knew within a breath how much her touch could bring it rushing out.

She let her lips touch the sensitive convolutions of his ear. Warm breath and ephemeral sensations made his mind loosen its grip. Finally, he let go and cried, hot tears wetting her throat and running into her hairline.

She understood that at first, his arms held her for safety. A lifetime of stiff-arming his emotions came crashing down on him. He needed her warmth and strength. She finally understood, even if he did not, who Ian McKay really was and why he'd left her before.

Only this time, she'd become an adult. This time, she knew how deeply he feared counting on the love of another human being. This time, she could be strong enough and vulnerable enough for both of them. She would make him admit the hardest thing of all – his own humanity, his need for love.

She recognized the moment his grief had spent, then the moment he regained control. A shift of his body told her when he became aware of her as the woman he loved, yet should not touch.

He lifted his head, reluctantly allowing his lips to touch her ear and then her cheek as he moved. He stopped to gaze at her, a furrow in his forehead, his eyes still wet with emotion.

"I can't explain what I just did," he said. "I don't usually . . . "

"I know you don't usually," she said, touching his face. "But you should. Don't talk, Ian. Just show me."

She lifted one hand to massage the back of his head and neck. At the same time, her leg wrapped around his hip.

He gasped. She smiled, gratified.

"Laura Atweiler," he whispered against her throat, "You will live to regret that move."

"So will you, my love," she quipped, glad to hear his old humor returning. Inwardly she prayed.

Let him live. Please, let him come back safe from the ridge.

He hesitated only a fraction of a second after her invitation. Then, his hand brushed above her breast, caressing the nap of her shirt.

"Laura," he sighed and kissed her softly. His hand descended to her breast, this time touching her fully, allowing himself to explore her erotically.

Laura moved beneath him, trying to get closer to this man who thought too much and felt too little. Her nightmare had exhausted her to the point of languid acceptance of his caresses. In moments, acceptance became pleasure. Though she knew nice girls didn't enjoy sex, she also knew she'd never be a nice girl under Ian's attention. He opened her shirt, exposing her to the cool night air. His warm hand covered her breast, one tense thumb brushing repeatedly across her nipple until it rose.

"Ian, please," she whispered, not sure of what she asked.

But he was sure, and gentle. His lips descended to suck at her aroused breast. "Yes, Laura," he murmured. His hand pushed aside the shirt, exposing more of her to his touch. His mouth and hands moved from breast to breast, molding, caressing, suckling, as if he couldn't get enough of her. His beard felt soft against her skin, causing unexpected pleasures of which even he was not aware.

Every new sensation caused her to push closer to him. Her legs wrapped his, her hands tugged at his open shirt until all the warmth and smoothness of his skin lay against hers.

He moaned. His hand moved down her side, thumb in front, fingers brushing the length of her back. She felt small, and for the first time in her life, she recognized the attraction of fragile femininity.

She let go and allowed his strength and bigness to envelop her, make her safe and cherished. For the space of their time together, she didn't need to be strong, capable, alert. She could allow him to guide her.

She smiled up at him and wrapped her arms around his back. Gazing at her, his eyes lit softly before he ducked his head. His mouth moved to the valley between her breasts and his thumb caressed her abdomen.

That thumb, often at right angles to his fingers when it should have been at rest – that thumb should have tipped her off a long time ago. And the way he flung his too short hair out of his eyes. He had all the habits of the boy she remembered, but he was not that boy. Experience and betrayal had hardened him, body and soul. The man, Ian McKay, needed her love as a woman even more than the boy had needed her family.

That thumb slipped inside her black lace underwear. She gasped. He raised up to look at her. "You wear mighty sexy underwear for a tough lady." Before she could reply, he closed her lips with his. His hand removed the black lace, returning up the inside of her thighs in a long, slow sweep. Her body shuddered at the unfamiliar intimacy.

Then, he touched her with one finger.

* *

"Oh," She gasped.

Laura's sensuous reaction slammed home to him the risk he ran for both of them. He acknowledged that she wanted his love as much as he wanted to give it. He didn't understand how she could forgive him for precipitating her father's death – perhaps because she was too afraid and too distraught to do anything else.

He knew that possibility should stop him. He should wait until they were both rational, when fear and grief wouldn't be paramount in their lives. But he also knew he might never have another chance to love her. She'd made him open up to his feelings after years of denial. It was impossible to close that floodgate so quickly.

However, he realized she had never been in this situation. He was the experienced one, the one who should exercise good sense.

Difficult though he found it, he held himself in check while bringing her body deeper sensations than she had ever known. He wanted to leave her with the memory of his love-making. He didn't want to leave her alone, pregnant and scorned.

After her pleasure crested, he pulled her close to him, feeling almost satisfied, replete in the knowledge that he could give to another human being at least a little. Lack of love and trust hadn't utterly ruined him for participation in the human race.

"Ian," she whispered sleepily. "What about you?"

"Not this time, Darling. I won't do that to you when the future is so uncertain."

"Ian," she protested, "are you never going to let me close to you?"

"Close? I feel closer to you than to anyone I have known."

"But you won't let me inside that head of yours. You don't trust me to understand."

An uneasy silence warned her. She'd come too close to the truth, too close for his comfort.

"I only want to learn how to give to you as much as you give to me," she said.

Ian held her. He was silent, but the tightening muscle in his shoulder spoke eloquently of his indecision.

"The condoms?" she asked.

His eyes closed. His jaw grew ridged. "They're not fool proof," he said. "I won't leave you wondering. When I take you, it will be because I know I can be responsible to you afterwards."

"But ..."

"No, Laura." He stopped her protest with another kiss and long, slow caresses that made her push into him, moaning softly as he brought her toward another peak of sensation.

Moments later, she sighed and hid her face against his throat.

It pleased him deeply to find he could do this for her without having to relieve his own needs. He felt cleansed, loving.

As she rested, seeming to have yielded to his self-denial. He played his fingers over her smooth shoulder and asked her, "How did you know I have the accepted brand in my pack?"

"Uhm," she moved, writhing a little so that his hand fell to her breast. "I found it when I put my extra-large sweater in the pack for you."

Smiling, he caressed her as he knew they both wanted. "I need another sweater?" he asked absently.

"Yes. And I have an extra . . ." She ran her hand over his shoulder and down his arm.

"Laura, . . ." He tensed, suddenly concerned that he'd left his alternate identification in that pack.

Laura laughed, then added, "I want to be sure you have enough clothes, in case you get bushwhacked and have to stay out there overnight. I just wanted . . ."

"Laura . . ." Ian placed a finger on her lips, stopping her. "Thank you for the sweater. How far into my pack did you dig?"

"Just far enough to see that you have everything you need in your ditty bag. First-aide kit, matches, candles, boot polish, compass . . ."

"How far?" he insisted.

"Boot polish?" she asked.

"Appearance counts," he ground out, "How far?"

"Not as far as your pin-up calendar," she said, reaching up to kiss his ear.

"I haven't got . . ."

"I hope you do," she said in her most matter of fact voice. "That would keep you warm, too."

He laughed, pulling her down and threatening her ribs with a circling finger. "I won't need girlie magazines or extra sweaters. I'm going to get you for snooping."

Trying to contain her laughter, Laura squirmed closer to his tickling finger.

"The memory of sweet revenge will heat me up for weeks to come," he taunted as his hand opened, playing over her with tenderness.

She whispered raggedly, "You won't have to go that long without a refueling, Ian McKay."

"Right," he said, "But right now, I need to sleep because tomorrow I'll have a lot of concentrating to do.

CHAPTER TWENTY-FOUR

Ian woke feeling content. The clock face showed a few minutes past midnight. Over the spill of curls in front of him, he could see out his hotel window. It was dark outside, but clear. The North Star peeked over the shoulder of Mount Hood – an omen for good, he decided.

He smiled, blew gently on her dark tresses and settled his body closer to Laura. She sighed in her sleep and moved her buttocks tight against his hips – a sweet, delicious roundness.

Ian knew he should be up and thinking. He should be going over his plans to make sure he'd missed nothing. Instead, he wrapped his arm across her waist and closed his eyes. She smelled like woman, soft cotton, fresh skin, sex and sleepiness. He set his mental alarm clock and returned to unabashed sensualism. He slept.

* *

Laura stood in the two-in-the-morning cold air, waiting for Ian to open the door to his little cabin. She'd known he would leave for the ridge this morning, but she hadn't counted on being baby-sat while he was gone. Ian had rousted her out of bed, told her to dress warmly in clothes he'd picked out. He'd already stuffed extra clothes into her pack and brought it into his room. Remembering that fact made her grow hot, even out here in the chill night.

He must have seen all that lacy underwear.

Her one concession to femininity had been to buy that black and creamy stuff and wear it under her flannel shirts and wool slacks, even when she went camping. Actually, she didn't own a stitch of practical underwear, and now she paid the price in mortification.

He hadn't said a thing about them, but he knew. She knew he knew.

He'd looked too damned smug when he woke her.

Already she missed Vandal. The dog, accepting Ian as an adequate bodyguard for Laura, had wandered down to the lobby in search of his Lady friend sometime during the night. When Vandal couldn't be located quickly, Ian had insisted that they leave without the dog. The urgency in Ian's voice had stopped Laura's protests. She figured she could find Vandal later, when she slipped away from the cabin.

In the meantime, she was sure Mrs. Leszinski would take care of the dog. Several of the men in the town seemed to have his approval as well – Takeh Okada for example appeared to be the dog's great and well-known friend. Laura wondered how often Uncle Banks and Vandal had accompanied her father to his meetings on this mountain with James. Who else had known that James might be alive? Had Colonel Johnson been keeping that secret from her as well?

Ian's voice interrupted her thoughts.

"In this place, I know you'll be safe," he said while he waited for an answer to his knock on the cabin door. "Arndt's been spotted in a cabin a mile west of town. He's keeping his cabin cold and dark, but Langendorff's been night skiing out that way all week and he noticed a new trail broken through the snow."

"I thought Ole Langendorff was going up the mountain last night."

Ian nodded, "He and the others left about one this morning. Before that, Ole left a message with Mrs. Leszinski. Don't worry. They'll be there as planned."

"I don't like it. You're just easy bait up there."

"James is the bait – the only bait Arndt will go after. I'm there to make sure James survives."

Laura started to open her mouth, then clamped it shut.

Why won't he admit the truth? After all that we shared last night, why does he keep up this pretense?"

Ian knocked softly again on the pine-log door and then a third time, each time a different series of raps which she caught as Morse Code – variations on `Open up, Bottle Eyes.' She stifled a laugh. Instead, she whispered, "What about those two men you said were in the lobby last night?"

"No sign yet. But I feel I should know the one with the thick eyebrows. He's one reason I want you here."

The heavy door opened slowly. Darkness behind the opening gave away nothing about the interior. Ian started up the steps, but seemed to realize that Laura hung back. He whispered, "Show yourself, Cam. The lady's distrustful."

Major Richard Cameron stepped into the doorway from the side of the opening, glasses reflecting the dim light of the snowy woods. He carried a rifle. That startled Laura. She'd become used to Major Cameron carrying a pencil.

"I believe you know Laura."

"Pleasure, Laura." The Major tipped a non-existent hat. Ian pulled her inside and closed the door.

"How long have you been part of this crazy scheme?" she asked the darkness.

A light flared and Laura jumped back into Ian's solid body before she realized Cameron had lit a lamp. Ian's arms closed around her.

In the bright lantern light, the Major glanced at Ian, quizzically.

Behind her, Ian answered for him. "Cam and I have known each other a long time. I trust him. You're to stay inside this cabin with him, close to the radio. In case something happens to me, you leave here with him and with no one else."

Laura trembled at the bleak prospect Ian suggested. At another level, long buried information nudged into Laura's mind. Richard Cameron was a Stratton Home Boy, too. He'd been taken under the wing of another of Dad's officers until he grew old enough to become an Army man himself. Richard had never referred to his days in the orphanage and out of deference, she'd never asked about them either. That must have been where he and Ian first met.

Ian's hands rubbed her arms as he held her against his chest. "Laura, promise me you won't leave here unless Cam believes you should."

She felt trapped. Lying wasn't her way. On the other hand, the man she loved played out one big infernal lie himself, probably because he thought it safer for both of them that she not know who he was. She could lie for equally good reasons, but it wouldn't come smoothly.

"Laura," he turned her to face him. "Promise me, please."

He was grave, tired already and worried. To ease his concern, lying was the least she could do.

"I promise, Ian." She let her gaze wander over his beloved face, the grizzled dark and white beard, the scar she hardly noticed any more, the dark eyebrows and chocolate eyes, and what should be startlingly blond hair.

He looked at her as if for the last time. She couldn't stand it. She flung her arms around him, oblivious of the wavering lamplight and the man holding it.

"Ian. Come back to me. You think and move ahead of that bastard Arndt and come back alive."

She heard him chuckle as he pulled her into his embrace. "Bastard Arndt? Laura! ..."

She held him tight, kissing his throat and reaching for his mouth. "I'll be a lady for you, then," she declared. "Just come back."

"I don't want you to be a lady," he whispered. "You're too exciting the way you are." He tilted her head back with his big hands and kissed her as if only the two of them were in the room. His tongue moved teasingly over her lower lip before opening her mouth sensuously. His hands slid to her shoulders and then down her back, pulling her shamelessly close to his body. His body told her how much he needed her and how much he intended to take from her when he did return.

She was willing to give him all he asked for, and more.

At last, he pulled back, hands on her waist. "I must go now Laura. I have to be up there before he can see me."

"Go. Swiftly. With care."

He turned to Major Cameron and shook hands with him. Cameron held onto Ian's hand, speaking quickly while he had his attention.

"Vibes Nelson radioed this afternoon," Cam said.

Ian stood still with expectation as Cameron went on, "There's been a deadly riot in New York City, whites and blacks this time. And more lynchings in the south. Californians have been harassing Japanese as they leave for the internment camps. It's getting uglier every day."

Ian's shoulders sagged. "Even if Arndt dies," he said, "what he's set off may destroy us."

Cameron gave a grim nod of agreement. Ian started for the door. Cam then hastened to add, "There is good news though. Vibes had been noticing an unusually powerful radio transmission originating out of Camp Springs."

Ian stopped, hand on the latch.

Cam went on, "About the time we took off for Oregon, he got help tracking it down. He and two other radio buffs used triangulation to narrow down the source area. One Private First Class-radio-nut finally found a building sporting a very odd lightning rod. Inside, they found Arndt's apartment."

"Wiped clean of evidence," Ian stated.

"Not at all," Cameron replied with a grin, "Wall to wall food trash, no furniture, but there was a United States map with pins marking most of the racial disturbances which occurred in the last three weeks."

"Any names? Numbers?" prompted Ian.

"A gold mine – the 'bastard'," Cam winked at Laura, "The bastard got so anxious to follow you out here, he left behind one of his notebooks with names, addresses, radio call numbers and frequencies. Evidently, the notebook was lost under some trash in the back bedroom."

Ian turned his gaze to Laura, an incredulous look on his face. Laura couldn't believe their luck either. From this lead, the COI was bound to find someone willing to sell his fellows for a little leniency.

Cam finished his good news. "Vibes and Donovan at COI are coordinating a call and pick-up operation. The first two arrests have been quiet, quick and successful."

Ian's elation came out with a sudden whoop. He whirled on Laura, taking her in his arms to whisk her around the room. "That's the best news I've heard all week," he sang out. He stopped dancing as they entered the firelight, his faced sobering slowly as he studied her bright smile.

"Laura, there's someone – someone who's been trying to kill you," Ian whispered.

"And Arndt, who will stop at nothing." Her smile faded.

They both knew he still had to draw Arndt out into the open, playing the bait to capture the bear.

Releasing her, he stepped back, smiled crookedly and all too briefly before turning to Cam. "Remember the maverick, Cam," he said.

"I'll take care of her," the Major said. He snuffed the lamp.

And then Ian opened the door and was gone into the snowy night.

It took a moment for Laura's eyes to adjust to darkness, but she pulled back the curtain and stared out the window at Ian's retreating form. He donned skis and skirted the cabin, heading up the mountain toward his rendezvous with death.

He looked too much alone, but he cast a looming shadow on the snow. The size of his hands on the ski poles was only one indication of how much he'd changed in sixteen years. His hands had always been long-fingered, but now they were also wide and strong.

She imagined he'd relied solely on his shoulders, arms and hands in those first months after he got out of the hospital. His newfound broad-shouldered body was the result of overcoming impaired legs. Now, three years later, gritty determination had those legs working well again, but for how long? Did he have the stamina in that left leg for all he planned in the next two days?

His body had changed. How much was he still like James on the inside – a gentle teacher, able to joke, unable to trust love, but excited about adventure? Had he lost that excitement and become entirely the cynic, as he described James? She didn't think so. Last night had not been spent with a cynic – a guarded man, yes. A man in need of love, but not a sneering cynic.

* *

Cameron's voice interrupted her thoughts. "I trust Ian McKay, Laura."

She smiled at Cameron in the low light from the windows. "I trust Ian McKay as well. And for the record, I recognize James Schoenfeld when I see him."

Cameron straightened as if shot. "You know?"

"Oh, he had me fooled for a long time. But that stuff he's got in the boot polish bottle isn't good hair dye – too much all one color."

Cameron chuckled. "For the record," he asked quietly, "who was that you just said good-bye to?"

Laura was glad of the darkness. A flush of warmth rushed to her cheeks as she remembered her abandoned farewell kiss. Cameron went on, "I want to know only because he claims that Ian McKay is nothing like James Schoenfeld. Were you saying good-bye to a memory or a man?"

Laura looked Cameron directly in his magnified eyes. "I kissed Ian McKay. I fell in love with Ian McKay sometime during that wretched trip from Colorado. It wasn't until last night that I realized why I recognized so many of his gestures and habits."

Cameron's mouth twitched slightly, and Laura regretted her too obvious reference to the night. To cover her embarrassment, she asked, "Why did Dad bring him to Government Camp to recuperate?"

Surprise showed in Cameron's eyes as he glanced at her. "Don't you know your Dad's connection to this town?"

She shook her head.

His smile radiated a sweet memory. "Your dad came here one winter, to ski I suppose, and met your mother. He courted her in this town, married her here before he left for the first war – the war to end wars."

"But Mother was raised in Portland, Oregon. That's farther toward the ocean."

"Yes, but she came up here to work after her parents died. She waitressed in the Battle Axe – worked for Mrs. Leszinski's mother."

Laura felt non-plussed. How had this man learned all this when her father hardly ever talked about the days before her mother's death.

Cameron seemed to sense her unease. "I'm sorry Laura. It's just that I kind of made a study of your father. Some of this James told me. It helped me to work with The General, to understand what he might think and do."

"Richard, you loved him too, didn't you."

For a moment, Cameron's mask of military rectitude slipped, and she saw profound sadness. He managed to recover quickly. "This whole town loved your father," he said. "And when he brought James, they loved him as well, because he was like your father's son."

In that last phrase, Laura saw the depths of Cameron's sorrow. He had been her father's trusted colleague, never a son to the man he admired so much – never a son to anyone.

He went on talking, trying as he must always have done, to bury his feelings. "The townspeople helped James get well – Doc especially, badgered, cajoled and cheered him into almost complete recovery." The next sentence came, slow and careful, as if he were watching her reaction. "Ian's face is changed, of course." Laura only nodded.

Cameron continued. "His body has changed a lot. Pain and hard work did that. And he doesn't laugh as much as he used to, but back then, as a boy, humor was often his mask."

"He will laugh again," she whispered as she turned back to the window. "And this time, I promise you, his laughter will be for joy."

She heard Cameron move to stand next to her. "Laura, you've always made him smile," he said quietly, as he too stared out the window at the snow. "Always. He asked about you, especially as he recovered. He wanted to know how you took his death. It worried him that it took so long for you to work your way out of depression."

"His poor little sister."

"No – never his sister. At most, a valued friend. As a boy, he was afraid to think of you as his sister. The people he loved always abandoned him, so he refused to let himself recognize that he loved you or your father in any way."

"That's why he left with Arndt, isn't it?" Laura glanced up to see Cameron watching her. She had a feeling that if she gave him the correct responses, he would tell her something more, something very important.

"Yes. He left to avoid hurt," he said slowly. "James became afraid, mistrustful of his feelings. He told me he had to get away before the General found out about his drunken mother."

"He thought Dad wouldn't love him because of his mother?"

"James had any number of excuses for escaping possible rejection. He felt humiliated by his past. Did you know he was eight when the sheriff brought him to the Stratton Home?"

Laura frowned. "I thought his mother left him when he was five."

"She did. He lived three years on the streets of Denver, hiding, stealing, fighting, working for older thugs. He was finally caught trying to cash savings bonds. They were really mock-bonds, used for advertising purposes, but he didn't know that. He'd stolen them from the bank the night before."

"Stolen advertisements! How'd he get into the bank?"

Cameron grinned, "Guess."

The picture flashed into Laura's head almost without thought, "He climbed in a window."

Cameron laughed, "Right. Third floor."

The mental image of a small, blond boy clutching the corners of a brick wall, thirty feet above a Denver sidewalk made her dizzy.

Grabbing the windowsill, Laura gasped. "He's always done it then."

"Physically fearless. Emotionally, a basket case. That's what he was when I met him."

"Werner Arndt's betrayal couldn't have helped his trust in humankind," she said.

"He admired Arndt – maybe even loved the hardness of the man. His betrayal made James bitter. Then it made him vengeful. It put us where we are today."

"Where James risks his life to draw Arndt into a trap. Why is he doing this alone?"

"He's the only man who can get Arndt out of hiding." Cameron explained, "Arndt wants to torture him."

Fear slithered up her spine. Fighting against its paralyzing effect, Laura pushed Cameron one step farther by saying, "Guilt is the real reason Ian is out there alone. Why does he believe he caused my father's death?"

Next to her, Laura felt Cameron stiffen. She put a hand on his arm. "Please, Cam. If you know, tell me. If Ian and I are ever going to have a life together, I need to relieve him of that guilt."

"I don't know if you can. He did it. There's no way to change or re-interpret what happened."

"How can I help him live with it, if I don't know what he did?"

Cameron pushed away from the window and paced the room. Laura stood very still, letting him wrestle with his conscience.

Moments later, he plopped into a wicker chair near the darkened fireplace. "You'd better sit in the rocker, Laura. This isn't going to be easy to hear."

She found the rocker by instinct more than sight, and sat down. His voice, across the small space, betrayed his tension. He seemed unsure he should be talking to her. She was afraid of what she might learn.

"About a month ago, James, or Ian. . . James discovered that Arndt had been stashing art treasures, incriminating letters and stolen jewelry in a French cave near the Swiss border. James radioed a message to a courier in Berlin, directing him to make sure Admiral Canaris learned of the stash. Canaris would then understand that

Arndt was disloyal to the Nazi cause. Fully committed Nazis don't hide vast riches near a neutral country."

"Canaris is head of the German admiralty."

"Yes, but also of its spy network," said Cameron. "The location of this cave is important to what happened. Besides Arndt, only James and Kirsten, Arndt's mistress, knew of this cave."

Laura remembered the first of James's letters to her father. "The cave above the lake at Annecy, France," she whispered.

"Yes. You read the letter?"

"Last week."

"It is you who's been in my file cabinet then. How?"

"In his files, Dad left me a message with your combination."

She could sense him trying to understand why her father would do such an unmilitary thing. "He trusted you, Cam," she said. "It's just that he wanted me to know what was going on as well."

Cam seemed to accept that. "You didn't get into my file cabinet far enough to find them, but behind the top drawer I have all your letters to James."

Laura gasped in disbelief.

"I'd never read them, Laura," Cam hurried to reassure her. "They're in there for safe-keeping." Then he added reluctantly, "I have all but the last two letters – the ones you sent to their apartment after, not yet knowing that James 'died'."

She shuddered. "Oh, God. Arndt."

"Yes," Cameron turned towards her in the darkness. She could barely make out his silhouette. "Arndt had those letters in the cave – in a box, but evidently a box he checked often."

"And my college graduation photograph?"

"Yes," he said gently. "James couldn't stand to have Arndt reading them, looking at your picture. He should have left them, but he couldn't make himself do it."

Laura finished, her heart in her throat, "And Arndt discovered them gone."

Cameron nodded. "Arndt must have returned within hours of James's discovery," he explained. "By the time James's courier in Berlin got word to Admiral Canaris, the stash had been moved. James had given away the chance to prove to the Nazis that Arndt was untrustworthy. Beyond that, he'd alerted Arndt that James was not really dead. No one but James would both know of the cave and care about those letters."

Laura's anguish made her voice unsteady. "So, Arndt came after Dad in order to find James."

Cameron reached out to offer solace. Laura leaned her head on her hands and let hot tears flow down her cheeks.

James. James. How long will you blame yourself for finally caring too much, but at the wrong moment?

CHAPTER TWENTY-FIVE

MARCH 14TH, 1942

Clanging metal woke Laura. Sitting bolt upright. She remembered last night – kitchen noises, smoke, Vandal leaping on her, then later, Doc, Mrs. Leszinski, and . . . Ian – James!

She studied her unfamiliar surroundings. Overhead, smooth beams angled down to meet a cedar wall at the head of her bed. Vague memories returned of climbing a pine ladder, of being shown into the bedroom. Cameron had left her up here to finish a night's sleep while he slept somewhere on the main floor.

Laura rubbed her temple as she surveyed the room. Its well-chinked logs gave off a warm glow, even in the white light of winter morning. The coverlet on the bed was beautiful, a quilt, each square obviously fashioned by a different artist. She had a moment to wonder where Ian had found such a treasure. Then, the clack of metal dragged her attention back to the present and the fact that this was the day she must find a way to escape Cameron's watchful eye.

Ian under-estimated Arndt, of that she felt sure. The town and Ian had prepared a trap, but Arndt wouldn't fall for it. He was too devious and too evil to be caught by a few amateur hunters, even with one of the world's top climbers as bait.

Arndt would find a way to turn the tables. He would kill Ian and then annihilate the town.

She was the only wild card they had. If she were up there, the element of surprise might help them when the crisis came. And her skis were just uphill of the cabin, right where she'd left them two nights before.

The thunk of metal once more demanded Laura's attention downstairs. She hopped from the bed and flew on freezing toes to the head of the pine ladder.

"Hi, Laura," came Cameron's voice. "Sorry to be so clumsy. I was trying to get out to the stream without waking you, but I'm not used to handling this bucket."

"You have to go outside for water?"

"Pipes are frozen," came his reply.

Laura hopped from one foot to the other. "My feet are freezing."

"Get your wools on and meet me in the kitchen. I'm not much of a cook."

"Sure thing," she said.

Now's my chance. Get dressed. Get out.

Cameron closed the heavy door. Laura ran to the bed and dragged on her socks. After donning her wool pants, she grabbed her hiking boots which were really her father's last pair from the first war. The boots were stiff with cold, but she got them laced up in record time. She thanked herself for cadging extra clothing last night. While Ian tried to hurry her from the hotel in the dark, she'd stuffed socks and gloves in pants and jacket pockets in case she had a chance like this.

Her tent was at the woodpile, back in town. She'd have to camp in a snow cave instead, but she'd done that before. She still had the matches and cigarettes and a little beef jerky with a water canteen. She'd be safe for a couple of days, barring a long storm or a siege.

She thought about going after Vandal and her tent, but discarded the idea. If she hiked down to the hotel for her equipment, she'd risk being seen by Arndt or his men. Mrs. L. and other townspeople had befriended Vandal. He'd be well taken care of.

Laura pulled on her parka and slipped her revolver into the pack before descending the ladder to the first floor. She would climb out the back window where she'd watched Ian and Cameron two nights ago.

Cameron would waste a few minutes being properly polite before he would climb the stairs looking for her. By that time, she'd be into the pines and on her way to Timberline.

She was on the third rung from the bottom when the door burst open behind her. Her back tightened. Cameron would see the pack and parka. He'd guess what she'd planned. She closed her eyes.

Heavy boots strode across the living room floor, kicked the rocker and planted themselves behind her. She plastered a big smile on her face and turned to try charm.

The body that greeted her was tall. The face, brutally angry. "Bernard!" The taste of copper pennies seeped around her tongue.

"What are you doing up here?"

"I came to get you, Laura. A man can't take his eyes off you safely, can he?"

"I left you a note and the ticket."

"You and Cameron were checking on me, weren't you? Plotting against me . . . Right under my eyes."

Laura backed up, alert to the change in Bernard's demeanor. In Colorado, most of the time, he'd been persuasively thoughtful and patient. Only once or twice had she wondered at his swift show of anger.

"Where's Cameron?" She started toward the door, but Bernard blocked her way.

"How could you string me along, Laura? How could you pretend?"

Now she was angry, "String you along? I never wanted to talk about marriage with you, Bernard. Always you had this illusion. You thought sheer persistence would make me fall for you. Where's Richard Cameron?"

"I could have saved you, but now you know too much. What Cameron hasn't told you, you've guessed."

Fear slid like cold ice down her spine. She realized what Cameron might have told her about Bernard: Bernard Johnson was Arndt's man at Camp Springs.

'Arndt … use Johnson.' That's what her father had meant. 'Used Johnson.'

"What have you done with Cameron?" She lunged toward the door, but Bernard grabbed her easily by the backpack. She tried to squirm out of the pack, but he thrust his arm around her waist and lifted her, pack and all, off the ground. Kicking and flailing had no effect on him. He was too big and too strong.

"You have to see Cameron, maybe," he said. "Then you'll understand you must be good." One arm across her stomach, he carried her in front of him out the cabin door.

There in the snow, partially hidden by the low bushes that bordered the stream, Major Cameron struggled for his life, a knife in his chest. His eyes and mouth were wide open, silently screaming out pain. The pristine snow was stained with red fading to pink as his blood seeped deep into frozen layers.

Laura pawed at Johnson's arms, desperate to reach Cameron. Johnson's grip tightened.

"He'll die before we turn our backs on him." Johnson commented. Laura died inside.

Cameron! Not Cameron – because of me. And Corporal Myer…

She kicked her boots into Johnson's legs, writhing to get free of his arms. As she watched, Cameron coughed and fought for air, but his fingers held the knife still and upright in his chest even though his instincts must have told him to pull it out. Laura realized he was even more afraid of what would happen if the knife were removed.

Cameron's fight drained from him at last. He dropped back into the snow.

Laura stared in horror.

"Why?" she moaned. "Why kill him?"

"He knew about me. That's why you ran, isn't it? He told you." Johnson continued talking as he carried her closer to Cameron's body. "You told Corporal Myer too, didn't you? He pretended ignorance, but he knew. I could see it in his eyes."

"You killed Myers?"

"I watched you feed him steak. You liked him, didn't you?"

Cameron's body raised slightly one last time, struggling for air. Laura kicked Bernard's legs and pulled at his imprisoning arms, but he pinned her against his body, hissing at her, "And last night, when the smoke began coming into your room, there was another man in there with you. You're no good Laura. A slut."

His arm tightened around her abdomen, squeezing the air out of her. "Smoke . . . in my room," she wheezed. "You put the pipe..."

He dropped her in a heap on the ground, then leaned aside to retrieve the knife from Cameron's chest. Before he could touch it, Laura scrambled away, making sure Bernard came after her. He left the knife and stepped over her. She tried to pull herself out from under his stride, but he grabbed her shoulder. Johnson, angry, was surprisingly strong.

"I have only two more people to take care of and then we can be together – alone together."

He lifted her, pushing her up the hill. "I found your skis," he said. "You thought you could hide your rendezvous in this cabin, but I recognize those skis anywhere."

He caught her about the waist again with one arm. His other hand ran down the length of her body. Even through her jacket and ski woolens, her breasts were repulsed by his touch.

"Those skis always made me imagine how you would be in bed," he said hoarsely, "so slender and well-shaped, such soft wood and smooth finish – elegant, delightful."

Laura felt rising nausea and fear. Cam was dying – perhaps already dead, but she'd get Bernard away from him before he inflicted more damage.

Swinging both elbows hard in his stomach, Laura freed herself from his grasp. She ran uphill, away from Cameron's body. Bernard's longer legs caught her easily. A shove of one hand sent her stumbling in the deep snow. Behind her, he laughed. "I've got a gun and a second knife, Laura. Start climbing the hill to your skis."

Her skis! Skiing was her element. She'd get away yet – for Ian and the villagers, she had to. Her boots were heavy, army-issue lug soles, but they kept her feet dry as she slogged ahead of Bernard up the hill.

Twenty yards behind the cabin, they arrived at the tree against which leaned her long, birch-wood skis.

Before she could grab them, Bernard reached out and ran an appreciative hand down the grain of the wood. Laura turned her face away and shuddered. When he grabbed her chin to make her face him, she saw that he'd attached a hook to each boot binding.

"I'll have you on a leash, my beauty." She closed her eyes. His hand jerked her head up. "Look at me, Laura."

She looked. He'd never displayed this face to her, tight, mean, vengeful.

"Who was the man in your room, last night?"

She stared at him.

"Bitch," he snarled. "I'll have that name before I take you." His eyes went small just before his other hand smacked into her face.

Her head exploded with pain. She was too dizzy to see as he pushed her against the tree. She slumped, holding her head in her mittened hands. Blood seeped into her mouth from somewhere back by her ear. She smelled him, sweating and working nearby, heard the soft rush of the hemp leash he pulled through the spring-loaded hooks. She tasted fear.

The pain in her head waned slightly. Then, he pulled her up. "Get them on. We've got a mile to climb."

Her small pack seemed a great weight as she leaned over to push her boots into her ski bindings. Working slowly, she gave her head time to regain its equilibrium. By the time she tightened the last binding clasp, she was able to see clearly, too clearly. She was trapped.

*   *

Oregon snow is wet and heavy. Laura had learned that the hard way during the last hour's climb. She'd also learned their destination. The flash of light she'd seen from Silcox Hut on her first night in the Battle Axe Inn should have been a warning. Any native seeing that light probably would have realized that someone was using the climbers' shelter. The light had not been the reflection of the setting sun, as she thought. It must have been his lantern shining out when he opened the door to a visitor. Bernard's bragging told her that his visitor had come to plan Laura's death.

As he pushed Laura to climb up the mountainside, Bernard jeered at her. "When that plow came down the road behind you, it was like a Felix cartoon. The look on your face when you realized you were about to be flattened – worth the trip down to town."

"I'm not road gravel yet, you sod," Laura muttered to herself, thrusting one ski doggedly in front of the other.

Bernard continued his recounting. "Then that ski bum shoved you out of the way and tackled my driver . . . That bum came to your room after Cameron, didn't he?"

"I've no idea who came to my room," Laura replied. "I was enjoying a good smoke at the time."

"You tried to run out on me, Laura. All that time playing the 'too good for you' General's daughter. Then you left with Major Cameron . . . You think I'm just going to let people treat me like that?"

She stopped, pretending to be out of breath. "People? Who else treats you wrong, Colonel?"

"Who else?" he exploded, "I'll tell you who else. Your Dad cut me out of the information chain. He thought I didn't know, but I caught on. Werner clued me in about that. And Arndt himself – another one, but I'm going to get him as soon as I take care of you."

"You're going to kill Arndt?"

"The bastard thought he could blackmail me forever – blackmail me and then set me up to die in some staged race riot. Madras, Oregon! You think I was going to let myself get shot up in some hick ranch near Madras, Oregon?"

Arndt planned the raid on Chief Labbe's home, she thought,

But she asked, "How will you find Arndt?"

"I don't have to find Arndt. I know where he'll be and I'll be waiting for him."

"Where?" she insisted.

Suddenly Bernard lifted his head. "You think you're going to get away from me, don't you?"

Laura tried to look cowed when what she felt was shaking rage.

"Don't believe it, Laura. I know exactly what I'm doing. I've planned this morning over and over again. Now turn around and stop pumping me for information. You'll never get a chance to use it anyway."

They approached Silcox Hut by following the lines for the unused ski lift. Laura had heard about this, the second lift ever constructed in the United States. It was finished in 1939, but she'd paid little attention at the time. She'd been in that deep canyon of depression following James's death.

The lift began a mile below them, at the enormous Timberline Lodge.

Above them, it ended on the downhill side of Silcox Hut. She paid particular attention to the lift, hoping to use it for escape from Johnson.

Climbing closer, she could see that an el-shaped extension of the hut formed an open barn over a large metal wheel. The wheel attached horizontally atop a high steel post. The u-shaped rim of the wheel acted as a guide. Taut steel cables stretched around the rim track so that the cable could continuously travel up, around and down the mile between lodge and hut, carrying hanging chairs, now empty and unmoving. The war had silenced the lift, shut down its motor.

As they approached it, the Silcox Hut appeared to be a massive outcrop of basalt, much like the mountain cliffs around them. Laura had an impression of looming strength, and she sensed that Bernard planned to keep her inside its thick, sound-proof walls. Even if the walls had been paper thin, there would be no one to rescue her. The only other people on the mountain were creating a trap for Werner Arndt near Yocum Ridge – miles to the west on another face of Mount Hood.

"Snowed a little last night," grunted Bernard. Laura glanced at the overhang of snow above the doorway. It was at least six feet deep on the precariously steep roof slope.

I might use that weight to bury Johnson, she thought.

"Take off your skis," ordered Bernard. She did as he ordered. "Now grab that shovel. Get this door open."

Near the heavy door stood a short-handled, narrow, but flat-nosed shovel – a weapon. As she grabbed its handle, she heard the click of a cocked revolver.

"Just shovel snow, Laura," he said, grinning.

Carefully, she placed the shovel in the snow and threw the load so that it landed well-away from Bernard, toward the ski-lift's wheel housing, constantly aware of the gun as well as the balanced snow above her. During thrust after thrust of the short shovel she hoped for Bernard to let up his vigilance, but he watched her every move. She found no chance to try anything.

When the doorsill was cleared, he motioned her to put the shovel down. She stepped aside and leaned as if to prop it against the wall. It took him several attempts to free the door from the cold-tightened frame. Laura hoped Bernard's yanking on the door would loosen the roof snow. The heavy snow didn't even shudder.

When the door stood open, he waved her inside ahead of him. Tucked against her left side, and hidden under her parka, she brought the short shovel with her. Inside, her eyes slowly adjusted to semi-darkness.

Bernard led the way into a narrow, common room. Along its walls sat benches of wrought iron and leather. A trestle table of split pine logs stood in the middle of the room. At the far-right end, on either side of a gaping, black fireplace, candles in two wall sconces had burned down to stubs.

A few feet to the left of Laura, stood the wall between the cabin and the wheelhouse. A small door seemed to offer exit toward the lift machinery. Glancing down the cabin hall, beyond that short wall she saw a longer hall where two doors were ajar. Each room contained at least one bed.

Bernard grabbed her right arm. "We'll be more comfortable down this way," he said and gestured with his gun toward the bedrooms.

Laura knew there wasn't going to be a better time. Her left arm shot out, catching his right hand with the blunt shovel. The blade cut deeply into his palm. His gun flew down the hall, landed and skittered on the stone flooring. She followed up her advantage, with a telling blow aimed at Bernard's head.

Unfortunately, her father had taught Bernard self-defense, too. He ducked and reached toward her with his longer arms. Grabbing her hand and crushing it in his, he wrenched the shovel from her grasp. He tossed the shovel into the common room and pulled her toward him with bear-like force, shoving his bloody right hand around her head. Laura could feel hair pulling out by the roots while he bent her backwards.

"That was very stupid," he grunted. He banged her head against the stone wall. Sparks of light jammed her thoughts – a light bulb flaring before it died. Pain jagged down her spine. Laura felt herself slipping down. Bernard's voice seemed to recede into the stone walls.

"I'll take you right here," he said hoarsely. "It's good enough for you." He began ripping at her jacket buttons with his good hand. His mouth descended on hers, thrusting her jaw open so his tongue could enter.

Laura gagged and bit down. Bernard's screech of pain woke her fully. He hit her in the stomach with both fists even as she spit out a chunk of his tongue. Long training and desperation made her harden her gut. With the strength left to her, she jerked her knee into his groin.

Bernard doubled over. Laura clamped both hands together and brought them down on the back of his neck, sending him to his knees.

He gagged. Laura reached behind her for the handle to the wheelhouse door. Her hand scrabbled along the wall. As Bernard began to recover, he glanced up, glaring at her, his mouth twisted with hatred.

At last she found the iron door handle. Trembling, she pushed down on the thumb lever and felt the latch rise to release the door. Not locked. But Bernard rose.

Frantic, she pushed hard on the log-framed door. It swung open with surprising ease and Laura fell sprawling on a balcony that overlooked the lift mechanism. Scrambling to her feet, she thrust at the door, trying to close it against Bernard's greater weight. In spite of his pain, he was able to keep it open long enough to come through and shove the door into Laura, knocking her against the wall. Her back struck a bank of big metal switches. Lights flickered on. Below them, a motor ground to life – the motor for the lift slowly fired up after months of silence. Pain from the switches jabbed through Laura's shoulder blade, but she saw that Bernard was momentarily distracted by the lights and noise.

She took advantage of his inattention, fleeing the length of the balcony toward the stairs that led down to the lift. She could hear his footsteps treading behind her – heavy boots, long strides, closing in, closing in.

He grabbed her small backpack just as she reached the head of the stairs. Growling, he pulled her off her feet and threw her across the floor of the balcony. His body dropped on top of hers. Pushing at her jacket, he thrust her head and shoulders over the edge of the balcony. She dangled, half on and half off the concrete floor, weighted there by Bernard's heavy body while his hands fumbled with the buckle of her wool pants.

"It's better with a fight. So much better," he panted. Blood seeped out of the side of his mouth as he leaned over her.

Beside her head, the wheel of the lift creaked against its long inertia. Below, the motor clanked and hummed, ready to push the mechanism around and around, up and down the mountainside.

Bernard yanked her jacket aside and tore at the front of her shirt. Sick with fear, Laura pounded on his head, and pushed at his hands, trying to rise from her half-hanging position. Bernard grabbed her wrists and held her arms open. He levered his body up so he could look down on her, over the edge of the balcony. "I want his name, Laura. Last night's man."

"Never," she croaked. "Rot in hell," she screamed above the screech of the motor.

He leaned farther over the edge, pushed her torn blouse aside and closed in with his mouth as if to kiss her breast.

She twisted her body away. "Bitch," he hissed, splattering blood from his mouth on her throat and shoulder.

Angry possession glittered in his eyes. He levered himself even farther up her body, pushing them both precariously near the edge. Instead of pretending to kiss her, he bit her shoulder, deep and gouging. Laura screamed in agony. Bernard laughed, let go of her hands and yanked once more at her belt. She felt the buckle give.

"His name, Laura."

"No!"

CHAPTER TWENTY-SIX

MARCH 14TH

Sprawled across the balcony, Laura fought to throw Bernard off her body. His heavy weight crushed her, lifting only as he attempted to open her wool pants. His efforts gave her enough mobility to twist and see what was behind and below her – the motor for the lift, and two long levers. Reaching down, beyond her head, Laura grasped at nothing, at anything. In the recesses of her mind flashed the information that her left arm was suddenly wet. Her shoulder dripped blood. Desperately, she flailed about for a handhold to help regain control of her life. Bernard yanked at the buttons on her wool pants. They came grudgingly open, one by one.

"About time," he grunted.

She forced herself to let his temporary success distract him from what she did. She reached behind her for a way out.

His rough hand slipped inside her clothing and grasped her waist, then began to push down on the pants cloth. "That's it," he muttered.

Fury fueled her frantic search for a hold. Circling wildly beyond her sight, her hand found a long lever.

"Lie still, bitch," Bernard hissed and leaned over the balcony for one more bite.

Laura's other hand slapped onto the lever. In an effort to slow his progress with her pants, her legs had curled tight between his legs and against Bernard's back. She held onto the lever, pulling with all her strength.

In his frenzy to conquer her, he moved his hips, his center of gravity, too far toward the edge. Suddenly thrusting her legs straight up into the air behind him, she pulled both of their bodies into empty space.

Amazement and then fear crossed Bernard's face in the blink of an eye. Grasping at her blouse, he found only shreds. His body fell away from hers, hitting something metallic beyond her line of vision. Her own body vaulted around the lever, pulling the metal handle down with her as she somersaulted.

Landing hard, she collapsed on the floor, still grabbing the lever, jerking it downward through several gears. Above her, she heard the scream of the rusty wheel roused from sleep. She couldn't open her eyes, but hung onto the lever as if her life depended on it. Bernard would grab her any minute, but she would never let go. Never.

Above her the wheel whirred into its old motion, but she didn't look.

Pain and dizziness prevented anything more than breathing.

Suddenly, a shriek of horror filled the wheelhouse. Laura ducked. No one grabbed her. The shriek broke off at high pitch. She sank to the floor of the housing, letting go of the lever to cover her ears.

The lever returned to its upright position. The motor whined to a stop.

The wheel began to grind down, sluggishly.

Laura peered around her. Blue sky shone beyond the hut walls, silhouetting the cable as it left the wheel for its return trip down the mountain. Caught between the cable and the wheel, Bernard Johnson hung. The wheel rotated one more grudging yard before coming to a halt. His body held there a moment, suspended between brilliant sky and glistening snow, and then, freed of the wheel, it dropped.

*   *

Laura sat, frozen in disbelief.

He betrayed Dad, Uncle Banks, Major Wells . . .. He murdered Cam. And now Bernard is dead.

She read the litany of Bernard Johnson's transgressions over in her mind, feeling numbed at the memory of innocent and awkward Corporal Myer. Still she felt a shard of evil had entered her heart. She'd killed men at Labbé's in order to live, and so others could live. Here, she had killed – not for justice. She did it out of fear, and revenge for Cameron and all the others.

I murdered him.

A cloud covered the sun. The day shadowed to sudden darkness. A cold wind blew up the alpine meadows and through the open wall of the wheelhouse. Laura glanced down at her naked torso and realized she was covered with blood from the bites in her shoulder and throat. She shook off her pack, wincing as she moved the arm on that side. Her torn shirt came off next. She wadded it against the gaping tear in her shoulder to staunch the flow while she rummaged in her pack for another flannel shirt and a sweater.

While she buttoned her flannel shirt, the sun came out once more, shining its full brilliance on the winking snow. Laura stood and glanced out. She saw only the mangled body of Bernard. Blood tinged the snow, just as it had near Richard Cameron. For the second time in twenty-four hours, Laura's body rid itself of everything in her stomach. She leaned against the stair rail, holding her head and her stomach as waves of agony passed through her.

Shivering and sweating, she buttoned on another sweater. Pain in her shoulder made the simple task monumental. She grabbed her parka and pack with her good hand and retreated up the stairs into the hut. She shut off the lights and the lift motor. She didn't want Arndt to hear the motor and investigate this hut.

The hut was cold. She spent only enough time in the common room to get her jacket and pack adjusted over her arms. She wore the backpack as much for its added layer of warmth as anything.

Bernard, she noticed, had stowed his own gear near the fireplace.

Beside it stood a Garand rifle, a bayonet and a box of ammunition. She'd no doubt Bernard had been at Longs Peak and used that rifle to help Arndt kill her father and his men. She touched nothing belonging to him.

In her pain-wracked exhaustion, Laura reasoned that she needed retrace her steps to Ian's cabin. She must make sure Cameron's body was taken care of. She'd get help at the village.

Laura pulled on her mittens and yanked open the heavy door. She stepped out into the blinding afternoon sun. As she blinked, a dark shade stepped between her and daylight. She looked up into the face of a huge, red-bearded man.

"Well done, Miss Atweiler," he clapped his mittened hands. "I never thought one of you would help me by killing the other."

Her body went numb with fear. "Arndt!" she spat out.

He turned to face the men who leaned against the woodpile. "You see, gentlemen, even the famous Miss Laura Atweiler has heard of me."

He turned back, grinning broadly. "I'm gratified you remember," he said. "You used to hide behind your father when I visited."

Laura shook with cold and despair.

He smiled, a disgusting twist of his lips, "You are still solemn and silent, Little One. Come out of the shadows where I may better see."

His big hand came down on her shoulder, propelling her into the full sunlight. He felt her wince from pain and stopped to survey her clothes. Red darkened the shoulder straps of her pack, her jacket front. Arndt yanked back on her pack. Laura cried out, raising her arm to protect herself, but Arndt caught her fists.

"Dieter, hold the lady's hands. She is hurt and needs care."

A small, white-faced man with thin lips stepped behind her and took her arms in a tight grip.

Deets, she realized. The man from the raid on Labbé's.

Laura's eyes closed on her pain, willing herself not to cry out again. Arndt gently opened her jacket, sweater and shirt to find the source of the blood which stained her clothes. He looked at her wound clinically, taking the ragged cloth from her shoulder with great care.

"Karl, the bottle," Arndt ordered. "We don't want Miss Atweiler to die of infection."

Someone produced a bottle of amber liquid from a pack. While Dieter held her hands behind her, Arndt pour a small amount of the liquid on her shoulder.

Fire flashed down her arm. She couldn't stop a small whimper before clamping tight her teeth. She looked up, glaring at Arndt. His gaze followed the few drops of liquid which coursed down the rise of her breast and into her shirt. A small satisfied smile touched the corners of his full lips. Slowly, he raised his gaze to meet hers. Laura held tight to herself so as not to shudder.

"I will take good care of you, Miss Atweiler." He pulled a handkerchief from his pocket, made a production of folding it and placing it on her wound. Then he closed her shirt front, allowing his fingers to linger briefly on her skin.

She jerked back into Dieter's body. Arndt smiled with his mouth, his blue eyes watching her with coldness beyond measure. For the first time in her life, Laura thought it possible that Hell could be something other than fire.

Glancing over her shoulder to the man called Dieter, Arndt said, "She must come see what happens to her James, of course."

At the callous mention of James, Laura's heart stopped.

"Arndt," Dieter's tone seemed to object, but Arndt's cold eyes settled on him, as hard as cutting diamonds. Laura felt Dieter's hands slacken their hold on her wrists.

So, Arndt controls his men with fear. Not loyalty. Not the Nazi cause.

"Miss Atweiler becomes your responsibility, Herr Haupt," Arndt hissed at Dieter. "Since you do not climb, you will thus be useful." He glanced down at Laura, "Dieter knows not to touch. You will be safe."

He turned back to the other men. "Philipe, where are the lady's skis? We need to begin our trek."

A small man wearing a brown stocking cap, disappeared around the corner and soon returned with Laura's skis. Arndt fingered the hemp before laying the skis on the ground.

"I see that Johnson was smart enough to use a leash," said Arndt. "Your reputation as a skier has traveled even to Germany." He smiled, solicitously touching her shoulder. "We expected you at the Olympic games, before the war. Was your father afraid to allow you to come?"

"My father feared nothing," she said defiantly.

A muffled snigger erupted from the group behind Arndt. Arndt whipped about to glare at a dark-haired man. The man pretended to have been coughing.

Arndt turned back to Laura, saying, more sharply, "Still we were disappointed not to have you winter with us at Garmisch-Partenkirchen."

"I was not needed. Mr. Jesse Owens and seventeen other black Americans did a very able job of representing our country in the spring," Laura said smoothly.

Arndt's lids hooded his eyes, but he chose to ignore her slight. "You were only nineteen years old, then. It would be understandable if your father felt a bit protective of you.

She spoke clearly, "The General was not protective of me. He was disgusted with your Hitler."

Arndt's eyes lit for a moment with a dark blue fire, then the ember died and he smiled. "He was so – rechtschaffen, the General – so . . ."

"Honest," Laura filled in, "He was a man of integrity, not one to snoop in desks and play false his friends."

For a moment, the fire flared again. Arndt stepped closer to her, leaning down so that their eyes were level. It took all of Laura's waning strength to stand, glaring back at him without blinking. At last he whispered, "We shall see what kind of a daughter such a man creates."

He straightened and turned to his men, speaking in German. "We shall learn more of the daughter, but not until we have killed the son – the Schoenfeld." He turned assessing eyes back toward Laura and allowed his gaze to wander slowly down her body.

"While Miss Atweiler puts on her skis," Arndt hissed at the men, "toss our friend Johnson in the gully to the east. Cover him with rocks. We don't want anyone to happen by and become upset by the great damage the little lady was able to inflict."

Laura bent to busy herself with the skis, turning her back on the make-shift funeral cortege which unceremoniously dumped Johnson's body onto a tarp and dragged it away.

Arndt watched her carefully. When she rose, he said. "You kill neatly, Miss Atweiler. However, you have a weak stomach – yes, I heard you. Before tomorrow ends, you will need to be strong, because you will see things much worse than the death of Colonel Johnson."

Shivering, even in the sunlight, Laura pondered the thin line of defense Ian McKay-James Schoenfeld had erected for himself. Arndt had trained mountain men to help him trap James. James had only his skill and the few well-meaning but ill-equipped villagers to protect him. And those villagers were the old men, the ones left behind when their sons departed for the war.

Dieter, the lady trembles," Arndt said. "Wrap her in the fur. We don't want her to die before she has seen our show."

*   *

Long, cold hours of skiing and climbing brought them to the western slopes of Mount Hood. The bearskin coat that Dieter had draped over Laura helped to return some heat to her body. A short stop for food had kept her energies at a minimal level. Her mind grew numbed by all that had happened since Johnson knifed Major Cameron this morning.

Once more, Arndt had solicitously cared for her shoulder. However, Laura was under no illusions that his concern was anything but a way to taunt her with her vulnerable position. He could do anything he wanted with her and his ministering emphasized that fact.

She withstood his touch, feeling the blood drain from her face as he looked at her. He opened her shirt only enough to get at the wound, but deliberately let his hand hover over the remaining buttons as if temptation battled with his better instincts.

Laura was not fooled. Arndt had no better instincts, only ways of drawing out anticipation and fear.

Late in the afternoon, they faced the sun as it dropped toward the horizon. Plowing through the deep snow was hard work – harder when you couldn't see. The men took turns leading, cutting a path so that the men behind moved forward more easily. They constantly scanned the field and rock outcrops for other life.

Each man was equipped with the latest in snow goggles. Laura had none. She stumbled often, annoying Dieter Haupt, behind her.

Finally, hearing Dieter's curse and Philipe's derisive laughter, Arndt came back to look at her eyes. He handled her roughly, tilting her head back so he could see what damage happened to her eyes. After he assessed the problem, he took a wool scarf from his pack, slit holes in the weft and tied it across her face, positioning the slits over her eyes. When he was finished, he grunted to Philipe, who watched him closely, "I want her to see it all tomorrow."

Arndt returned abruptly to the head of the column.

Philipe stepped in front of her, made sure she could see him and then smiled grimly while gesturing a slit throat. When Philipe reached out to touch Laura's own throat, Dieter Haupt stopped him.

"Get away, Monsieur Gerard," he said. "This one is not for you."

"Ah, but she is not for you either, Haupt," said Philipe, withdrawing his hand in a slow caress. "Only Arndt will torment this little one."

Laura bit back the bile that entered her throat. Tired and frightened, she hadn't the strength to think farther than her next footstep. Their repeated threats seemed to have robbed her of all logic.

But I must plan an escape, she told herself harshly. I can't merely accept what is happening.

Laura, march forward on the alert.

Thinking as her father would think gave her renewed strength.

Late in the afternoon, they mounted the saddle of snow between the dark ridges of basalt on their right and a tall spire of crumbly rock on their left. This rock, Laura remembered from the map as Illumination Rock.

Look ahead, Laura, she urged her exhausted self. What is ahead that can help you escape? At the very least, you have to keep them from discovering James too soon.

On the newly revealed Reid Glacier, west of the saddle, they halted. Far across Reid Glacier seemed the ominous Yocum Ridge.

Try as she might, Laura couldn't keep her eyes from staring at that jagged, knife- edge of rock. It was unbelievable that a man would even try to climb such rotten basalt. By-passing the taller serrations would be impossible. He'd have to climb each thin blade and then rappel down to the bottom of the next. Ian was up there, trusting his life to his knowledge of rock that looked as reliable as chocolate veneer.

She pulled her gaze away from the fearful sight, afraid to give away Ian's presence there.

Arndt called Dieter Haupt forward to confer with him. Waiting, the others sprawled on the snow.

Now, her mind urged her muscles. Now. Take advantage of their distraction.

Laura bent over as if to recover her breath, but she worked at the ropes attached to her ski bindings. The clipped hooks were a special design, not easily removed. She had needed a faster method. The rope had been securely tied, but not of very heavy gauge. Every time they stopped, she'd been able to work loose two thin strands on the left ski. It wasn't much. A beginning.

Arndt and Dieter returned. "Miss," said Dieter, "we go downhill. You will stay close to Dieter."

Laura stood, looking at Arndt for a clue about his plans.

Arndt chuckled, "Don't worry. The snow has covered his tracks, but I know where to find him. You go down to have a seat in the theater for tomorrow."

Arndt turned his back, signaled his men to follow, and trudged away, across Reid Glacier.

Dieter took up the ropes to Laura's skis and said. "Follow the sound of the water beneath the snow, but stay to the right of it. Further down, it becomes a very large river. We don't want you to fall in it."

There was nothing she could do but go where Dieter pointed. Dieter skied behind her holding the leash.

The behemoth Arndt led his men toward Yocum Ridge. Up on the ridge, Laura saw no sign of Ian in the darkening light. She hoped he was well hidden and aware of the column marching toward him.

Glancing over her shoulder toward the way they had come, Laura saw why the spire they'd passed was named Illumination. The light of the setting sun caught its entire height.

However, reaching back across the snow, almost touching the spire, was the threatening shadow of Arndt's burly body.

CHAPTER TWENTY-SEVEN

James Schoenfeld hunkered well above timberline on Yocum Ridge, when he saw the column of men cross the saddle between Illumination Rock and Castle Crags. Even though they were still over half a mile east and almost nine hundred feet below him, James knew Arndt's big body on sight.

With the sun setting behind him, James had no fear about using his binoculars. He scanned the group below him, able to see only indistinct, heavily-coated shapes and general demeanor. Arndt's men halted this side of Illumination Rock. Most sprawled on the snow, resting. Arndt and a much smaller man conferred.

A little apart from the others, one man, covered in a dark, sleek fur, bent over his skis, apparently working at the bindings. That one man had equipment that was distinct from the others. His skis seemed to be of a narrower design and of light-colored wood, where the others were dark- stained, and wide. He alone wore a fur coat. Something about the carefully maintained distance between that one and the others told James that they held the lone skier in awe. Or was it contempt?

Arndt and the small man retraced their steps toward the fur coated skier, then conversed briefly with him. A few moments later, Arndt and seven men began the trek again, following James's path across Reid Glacier at the nine-thousand-foot elevation. The smaller man followed the fur-coated skier on a path down the glacier west of an underground tributary to the rushing Sandy River.

So, thought James, the game begins. Those two will circle south and west. Then they'll try to cross to Sandy Glacier below the Yocum Ridge, planning to flush me out from the far side of the ridge. Joe Patton will pick them off as they climb across the waist of the ridge.

James trained his binoculars on the seven men following Arndt.

Arndt had found James's tracks at last. The men weren't having to break a path through the new snow. He'd done that for them. So, they were gaining on him.

As he'd planned.

Still, he remained wary. He'd made too many enemies in the German Third Reich not to watch his backside at every turn. It didn't pay to let down your guard. James not only watched the split group of climbers from his vantage point, he also kept an eye on the ridges above him, the Devil's Kitchen Headwall and the Sandy Glacier behind him. He was well placed, bivouacked for the night and ready to attract attention in the early morning hours. Tomorrow, he would know how well he had judged his opposition. From the master, he'd learned everything about climbing.

Had he learned as much about deceit?

*   *

Laura felt the slack on her leash. The two lines dragged in the snow. From any distance, the fact that she was hampered would be missed by an onlooker. She suspected that Dieter took her down the Reid Glacier in order to cross the Yocum below eight thousand feet at a narrow waist in the ridge. There, she knew, lay one of the traps set up by Ian, or James.

Joe Patton, builder and respected hunter, was camped in the scrub pines on the ridge, guarding the most likely path to the Sandy Glacier. Patton's trap was there to assure that the bulk of Arndt's group followed James up the mountain from the Reid Glacier side.

Unless Laura could separate herself from Dieter, and make it clear that she'd become a hostage, Patton would shoot her as well.

Their southern route added a half mile to that trip across Reid Glacier. It would be dark by the time they reached the waist. She'd have to do something soon to let Patton realize she was not one of Arndt's men. She hoped he used binoculars.

She pulled back the hood of the bearskin coat and prayed he recognized her face. As they neared the ridge, she'd try to make a break from Dieter. She had no illusions that she could get away, but it might make her status as prisoner clear to Joe. A risk. Dieter might shoot her in the back.

*   *

James watched Arndt allow another man to take the lead. It was better than he could have hoped. Arndt wasn't likely to follow James's footsteps blindly. Another man might. They were coming at a rapid pace, chased no doubt by the thought of darkness and the desire for sleep. The man in front skied well, using smooth rhythmic strides, taking advantage of every millimeter of glide, his mind on speed, not on danger.

Speed led him onto the thin bridge without noticing that James's tracks were not as deep as before, made with no human weight. Within seconds of his first step, the bridge gave way, dropping the man into the depths of a crevasse. Thick ice swallowed his scream. The man behind him nearly made the same error, but fell on his side, skis dangling over the edge. Another pulled him free of danger.

One down, James ticked off.

He rested his binoculars against his chest.

Arndt wasted no time on the fallen. He ordered his troops to skirt the crevasse and continue. He didn't even glance into the gaping maw of ice to gauge the possibility of rescue.

* *

Arndt looked over the situation as he crossed the glacier. The incident at the crevasse had frightened his men. They moved more warily, even though he led. They wouldn't get onto the ridge until morning. Arndt, therefore, needed a place to shelter during the night, close to the ridge, but protected from it. No doubt James also had firepower. And Arndt knew James was a sharp shot.

To his right, Arndt saw two steep gullies, or couloirs ascending the mountain. Between them stood a short finger of exposed rock – tall enough to protect three tents from possible rifle attack from Yocum Ridge. He turned toward the first couloir, breaking new trail for the first time since they had rounded Illumination Rock.

Arndt was reasonably sure he knew what time James Schoenfeld had arrived at Illumination Rock. The snow that covered James's path from Timberline across Palmer and Zigzag Glaciers had fallen between four and six in the morning. The cleared path from Illumination Rock to the ridge access, represented this morning's climb. The boy was on the ridge, waiting.

Arndt was also sure that James had not come up here to test any equipment for Atweiler. The telegram had come too easily into Arndt's possession. James had issued a challenge, and with the pleasure of hate, Arndt deployed his men to meet that challenge. When he caught the boy, death would come slowly.

* *

MARCH 15, 1942 MORNING

With enough morning light to work safely, James climbed the backside of the dangerous pinnacle. He'd cut it close. Arndt's men were breaking camp as James arrived atop the promontory known as the Third Gendarme – the last of three guardians of the route up Yocum Ridge. He wanted to make sure he had time to accomplish the one hundred-fifty-foot rappel off the north side of this rocky serration before the climbers were within rifle range. He didn't savor a surprise while he hung in mid- air. However, it was time for Arndt to see him – to catch the scent of the fox.

This rappel would bring him closer to Arndt and his men, but he would still be far above them on the ridge. He wanted them to see him, to believe they could catch him if they climbed up the sides of the ridge, or better yet up the steep gully of snow where this buttressing ridge met the cliffs near the summit. He wanted them to follow him into trap after trap until only Arndt was left to fight him.

Through his field glasses, James saw that Arndt, his Norwegian skis strapped to his pack, came out from the protection of the finger of rock between Leuthold Couloir and the cwm – the narrow gully which led up to Hot Rocks. Arndt had binoculars too – more powerful than James's, also heavier, and they were never used to look over the soft-shell colors of the sunrise. The glasses were trained exclusively on the slope above the climbing party – toward James's route.

What kind of a man never noticed the sunrise?

James cursed as he watched the strongly built man turn, point to the top of the rocky Gendarme, and laugh with the others. James, well aware of his vulnerability during the next few minutes, calculated the range of those rifles and he figured the time was right. Appearing atop this gendarme represented calculated risk – calculated to raise the frenzy of the chase in Arndt's mind.

James counted on what he knew of the man's arrogance. Once James had waved the red cape by rappelling off this pillar, the bull

Arndt would focus on goring. Arndt's need to protect himself from the cape and the sword would be forgotten.

James checked his ropes. Their smooth, tightly twisted strength gave him confidence. He lifted the rope coils over his head and glanced at the whipped ends to make sure the nylon held. Atweiler had first sent him nylon to test in 1940. James, though impressed with nylon, was unwilling to trust anything too far.

For the moment, he forced himself to ignore the six climbers who toiled up Mount Hood's southwestern glacier. James concentrated on driving two pitons into the rock, watching closely to be sure he didn't widen the crack which would hold them, and him.

Trust nothing to chance. Ordinarily, he climbed this ridge in dead winter, when the rocks were firmly frozen in place, but this warm weather climb had been necessitated by Arndt's timetable. The differences in day and night temperatures added to the cracking and eroding of the already unstable rocks of the Ridge.

The pitons were made of blackened metal to Atweiler's specifications – crimped, and with one reverse hook to hold in rotten rock. Tying two pitons together to distribute the weight of his rappel, James gave a quick glance at the climbers far down on the glacier below. They clambered after him, using exactly the route his appearance here dictated.

James ran the rope through the sling tying the pitons together.

Straddling the doubled rope, he drew it under his buttocks, across his left hip and up to his right shoulder. Grabbing it from behind him, he shook it out, free of his pack and skis as he stood.

For a moment, he was silhouetted against the mountain. Precisely then, Arndt turned his binoculars toward the Gendarme. James felt like a butterfly about to be pinned. He couldn't tear his own gaze away from the round eyes of the binoculars. When the man lowered the glass slowly and looked at him with the naked eye, his hood fell back.

Suddenly, James saw the man who had taught him everything he knew about ski-mountaineering – the man who had saved him on l'Aiguille, only to attempt to murder him a week later. James hesitated only a moment. Shoving aside panic and forcing himself to concentrate, he pushed off, climbing carefully with the Dulfer rappel. He leaned out just far enough for his feet to hold the wind-blown rock face. His heart skipped a beat when his leading foot met with a thin sheet of ice. The wind of the night had left a glaze on the cliff. The need for haste had to be tempered with care. As James's foot reached again for the face, he felt the prickles of awareness on his neck.

Glancing over his shoulder, he saw that the men were spread out over a fan-shaped patch of glacier. One of them was bound to find his next surprise.

Arndt was far in the lead of his men, climbing up the glacier with a determination born of hate. James remembered the extraordinary strength of the man. The pain in his leg reminded him of it constantly. The knowledge that Arndt followed made him let out more and more rope at each step until he dropped many feet at each bound. He wished he had put edge-nails in the soles of his boots to counteract the ice.

Ironically, Arndt had first shown him this rappel technique when he was sixteen. At thirty-two, James still found it the quickest method. His braking hand, behind him, controlled the speed of his descent and kept the double rope separated.

The explosion was so loud that it took even James by surprise. He looked down to see now only five men, stopped in their tracks, staring at a deep hole in the snow. A year ago, James had lost a friend to one of Arndt's mine fields. He was amazed the man hadn't suspected.

Arndt roared and charged across the field. In his lucky footsteps, the others followed more gingerly.

At about fifty feet down the pinnacle, James began to feel the heat from the rope even through the padding in the shoulder and buttocks of his wool. He had to slow down again or risk burns and torn fabric – an exposure to the elements he couldn't afford.

He stopped long enough to hear the voices of those on the glacier. Checking on Arndt's progress brought a start to his already taut nerves. A Gewehr 98 sniper rifle rested in Arndt's arms. It was the kind of rifle the two of them had used for hunting in the days before the war. Within minutes, Arndt would be within range. James's breath came in short gasps as he forced himself to concentrate before he was picked off like a mountain goat.

The climbers no longer followed James's route onto the Yocum, but were cutting uphill on the glacier, finally learning not to trust his path. James hoped they mounted the ridge by way of the Leuthold Couloir closer to the summit. That couloir, or steep gully of snow, by-passed the need to climb and rappel off the Gendarme, but James knew from experience, that it had dangers of its own. He let go the braking tension on his rope and let himself down the gendarme at a steady pace.

Without warning, James's foot splayed off the iced rock face. He hung, twisting wildly in mid-air with only his braking hand keeping him from falling the last seventy-five feet. He knew he'd caused this predicament by thinking about the past.

"Concentrate! Always and forever, Concentrate!" Werner Arndt had drilled into him. Now, it was Arndt's presence that had broken his mental control and left him hanging helplessly. Far below, he heard the one hard guffaw that Arndt had always used to express disgust with a pupil's mistake.

James steadied his mind, keeping his braking hand as tightly closed as possible. The hand was cold, and his grip would not last much longer. Breathing deeply to regain mental control, he let the rope unwind. At last it slowed, bringing him around to face the cliff.

He placed his boot soles carefully. Two deep breaths later, he let the tension off the brake hand and continued his descent.

A shout told him that Arndt's men were below and to his left on the glacier. Each man had a rifle as well as skis strapped to his back, but they were still too far away.

Step by step, the sweat crawling down his back while fear fought to climb up it, James let himself down the face of the icy cliff. They were close to rifle range now. He expected a single shot in the back at any moment. Individual German words came up to him from the group, enough for him to know they were in disagreement as to the fastest route by which to capture him.

Why don't they shoot?

James was within forty feet of the base of the gendarme. At the base, he would have access onto a notch in the ridge. From there he could climb up to the snow saddle to a maze of rock chimneys in the Devil's Kitchen Headwall. If he made it to the chimneys, there was a chance to lose them.

Twenty feet to go.

Arndt's nasal voice echoed frantically off the rock. "Nein! Nicht jehts!"

Instinctively, James let off the brakes and flew down the last of the rappel just as bullets hit the cliff where he'd been. Rock sheared off and fell on his shoulders and head as he stumbled backward across the uneven ground, pushed by the momentum of his long fall. He knocked his pack and skis against the scree slope before he caught himself and ran up the slope of the notch.

Behind him, the snow and rock at the top of the Gendarme gave a loud crack and fell straight down the cliff. A boxcar-sized portion of the Gendarme crashed down twenty feet from where he stood, bringing his pitons and rope with them.

As if in answering echo, a rumbling avalanche began somewhere on the mountain.

James jerked his attention from his near miss with the rock to the snowfields above him. A portion of the headwall west of him seemed to fold in on itself before thousands of pounds of snow ripped from the anchoring rock and plunged down the steep cliff. Another twenty minutes and he would have been beneath that load. He still had to use that route. Now that he had shown himself to Arndt, there was no other way. Suddenly, dizziness and pain in his head doubled him over. He'd been hit by the smaller rocks that preceded the main rockfall, but he was still alive, and still ahead of the men.

Arndt's angry voice rang out across the dead silence of the snow. "Damn you!" he shouted in German. "Don't shoot. I must see his face as he dies."

CHAPTER TWENTY-EIGHT

James's blood ran cold as he listened to Werner Arndt's voice, "I want to see his fear when I kill him."

The man's hate had driven him exactly where James wanted him, but James understood the fire he created. James had to move fast. Rubbing his throbbing temple with his sleeve only made the pain sharper. His sleeve came away covered with blood. He realized that one of the rocks must have given him a nasty gash.

Better rock than bullet, as long as I'm left alive, he figured.

He yanked on his rope. The pitons were caught in the pile of rock debris, burying a third of the rope. In haste, he decided to cut the rope with his ice axe and take only the two-thirds length he'd released. It would be too short, but there was no time. He coiled it as he ran toward the saddle of snow at the top of the ridge.

James's hands were still numb from the bitter wind atop the Gendarme, but he grabbed his dangling ice axe in both hands and climbed across the snow saddle, staying to the west side of the ridge, out of sight of the men who pursued him. He was sure they were headed for the couloir. Leuthold Couloir was a two hundred-foot high, extremely narrow gully connecting Reid Glacier with this snow saddle.

He maintained a quick pace until he was near the junction of the couloir with the saddle. At this point, he flopped to his belly and crawled through the snow until he had a view down the fall line onto the climbers. He could have picked them off with a rifle, but he'd chosen not to bring one, only a service revolver. Any loud report would start an avalanche like the one he'd just witnessed – unleashed power that would sweep him into its vortex.

James backed up from the edge and dropped his pack, then untied his skis. He left his skis in their wrappings to protect their edges, but lay them sideways to the gully and began plowing them toward the precipice. The snow built up quickly. What he really wanted was the loose rock underneath the snow. He'd created this mess of rock more than a week ago, as part of his preparations for Arndt's coming.

When he'd dug down to the rock, he knelt and pried under the keystone with the pick end of his ice axe. He rolled the loosened keystone toward the edge of the gully, then shoved forward on the axe handle until he felt the weight of the snow and rocks begin to fall.

Jerking back on his axe, he scrambled away from the edge. He nearly stumbled, but righted himself, grabbing the skis and pack as he backed up the slope.

As he rose higher on the saddle, he watched with fascinated horror. The avalanche he'd started took on a life of its own. The rock and snow ripped out the top of the incline, taking everything with it. He heard the panicked shouts of the men below him, the loud roar of the snow as it gathered momentum and the low moan of weighted snow compressing and cracking before it joined the falling mass. James had to remind himself that the men with Arndt were not innocent by-standers. They too meant to kill. And even with the death in the crevasse and one in the minefield, they still greatly outnumbered him.

He had no time to learn the outcome of his murderous plan. He could only hope that he had at least slowed the progress and dampened the ardor with which they followed him. His awe of Arndt's powers kept him from hoping that the avalanche had actually killed the man – his companions may have died in it, but not Arndt.

Arndt never died.

James hurried to reach the vertical chimneys of The Devil's Kitchen Headwall before Arndt could see him again. The success of James's next plan depended on his being inside the maze of chimneys by the time Arndt climbed to the top of the Leuthold Couloir.

His life depended on his knowledge of the man who followed. There was no way to disguise his tracks in the new snow. The only way to elude the man was to confuse him by making false starts up several chimneys and then returning to the one which could hide him. He would avoid the long chute that most climbers used. Too exposed for too long. He needed a place to hide.

As he approached the labyrinth of ridges which gave access to the Headwall, he darted into each potential route – in and out several times, dragging first his skis and then his pack to confuse the direction of his run as much as possible.

Far below him, halfway down the mountain, the last thunder settled on the west side of Yocum Ridge, tons of snow from the avalanche Arndt's men had set off with rifle shots. On the east side of the ridge, the avalanche he started in the couloir had stopped rumbling. James had twenty minutes at most before Arndt could see this area. Arndt wasted no time rescuing companions. He would be climbing without a thought for the dead.

James retied his skis to his pack, and slung his pack on his back before he stepped backwards over the same ground. He backed a substantial way into three of the openings between vertical ridges of rock, and climbed a few feet up the rocks in each one. The last ridge he climbed for twenty feet before he was forced to put his booted feet on the opposite wall and continue up the narrowing chute formed by two ridges.

The rock in this chute was no more trustworthy than that of the Gendarme on Yocum Ridge. An icy glaze he knew as verglas had built up inside the chute because of shadow and wind chill. The verglas made the surface nearly impossible to grip. Only direct pressure between his boots and his back gave any purchase on the opposing walls. The pressure he could maintain was reduced dangerously by the fact that his pack and his skis were between his back and the rock wall.

A simple slip here and he would tumble down the rocky maze. If he'd had more time, he could have belayed himself with rope and pitons every few yards to prevent long falls. But that made noise. He must reach the shelf seventy-five feet above the saddle before Arndt arrived atop the ridge. To have any chance at fooling Arndt, he had to change from one chimney to the next. That few minutes would be the most exposed. He had to do it soon.

At fifty feet up, he pulled his ice axe toward him using the braided leather strap that attached it to his waist harness. Keeping the pressure against his feet, he twisted to his left. The angle he needed to do the next piece of work took much of his back away from the wall and the muscles in his thighs already shivered from the work of holding him up in the chute.

James chipped foot and hand holds out of the verglas on the outside curve of the ridge behind and above him. He hammered one black piton into the dark rock and, with a C-shaped karabiner, clipped his braided axe thong to the wall. He moved his left arm very slowly up to hold onto the leather strap. Whipping his hand around twice, he wrapped it in the leather.

Even as he secured his grip on the thong, his back began slipping from the wall. Praying and cursing all at once, he swung around to face the wall that had been behind him. All his weight was now on the hand wound in the leather strap, and his back was exposed to anyone on the snowfield below.

Wildly, he reached for the handhold he had just chipped. The ice would rebuild quickly in the small crevices. He had only seconds to grab them and begin his climb around the ridge to the next chute. His right hand found the hold. His fingers clung desperately to the small ledge.

First his right foot, then his left found purchase on the rocky face. At last his position was safe enough to allow his left hand to unwrap from the strap.

For a moment, he felt sure he would never be able to control the fingers of the left hand again. In frustration, he slapped the hand against the rock face. The momentum of his action nearly loosened him from his spider's grip on the wall. He grabbed again for the axe thong and steadied himself.

"Concentrate! Always and forever, concentrate." James was almost sure it was the real voice of Werner Arndt that he heard and not his own mcmory.

Steadying his mind, he lifted the ice axe and chipped into the glassy sides of the ridge, further to his right. Inching across to his new holds, he ran out of strap length. Hesitating only a second, he wrapped the thong about his left hand, reached that hand back to the piton and opened the spring closure on the karabiner. Now his last safety net was gone. He clipped the karabiner to his harness before inching his way around the face of the ridge.

He had ten feet of cliff face to cross. His fingers and toes grew more and more numb as they held all of his weight plus that of his skis and pack. Only brashness born of fear kept him moving sideways and upwards.

At last he stood inside the next chute, clinging to the left wall, and facing the wall on his left. He lifted his foot behind him toward the opposite wall of the new chute. First one foot and then the other found solid ice against which to push. He hung, horizontal across the open chute, his knees folded toward his abdomen. In this position, facing down, he could not exert much force against the opposing walls. He needed the added strength and traction of his back.

The tips of his skis barely touched the wall near his right shoulder.

He pushed his toes against the opposite wall and was thankful to feel the rock at his shoulder shove the tips of the skis down inside their lashings, down toward his feet. He had to get them out of the way if the next maneuver was going to work.

In a move that only Arndt could have taught him, he ducked his head between his hands until his shoulders and neck were pushed against the wall. He lay crosswise to the fall, in mid-air. Only the slight scraping sound of a ski tip warned him not to do what he was about to try, but he had no more time to heed warnings.

With one quick motion, he let go of the back wall with his left foot, allowed his right foot and shoulders to pivot against the ice and ended face up, his back against the wall. The banging of his skis against the wall near his feet told him how close he'd come to failure. Another inch of length in either direction and the skis would have stopped his pivot in mid-turn, sending him plunging.

"That was stupid," he whispered to himself. Five deep breaths later, he finally believed he'd done it and not died. Arndt had always known the fastest way to change positions. He'd said that this ability was what the English really meant when they referred to "the quick and the dead."

"He who hesitates, dies," Arndt had laughed after one particularly harrowing show of gymnastic arrogance atop Mt. Blanc.

James heard the voices of his pursuers approaching the top of the couloir. Their anger echoed up the chute toward James. Those his avalanche had not killed would show no mercy. He pushed hard against the wall of the chute and climbed for all he was worth, heedless of the ice, scrambling up the last few feet to his destination. Recklessly hitching his back against one wall, alternating with his feet against the opposite wall, at last he achieved the ledge. Here the chute widened for a short space and one person could stand up without being seen from below. He pulled his ice axe up and quickly hammered one piton into the wall behind him. Gently easing out of his pack, he set it and the skis on the ledge beside him. He pulled out his rope, took the karabiner out of his pocket and slipped the rope through it in one deft motion.

He was about to replace his pack on his back when the voices below suddenly changed timbre. They had reached the top of the couloir and any motion he made now might be seen from below.

Standing on the ledge, James froze as they approached the chutes and chimneys, searching for a sign indicating which one he'd used.

"The bastard used two pitons," shouted Arndt. "As we climbed, I heard two pitons hammered into the rock. Look for them and we'll have him."

*   *

The morning was still young, but the bravado Laura already had witnessed exhausted her. She sagged against her ski pole, the weight of her binoculars merely a numbness in her hand. Dieter Haupt lowered his field glasses and let out a whistle of awe.

"Gott im Himmel," he whispered.

Yes, God, Laura's mind intoned. Only God can have helped James do it.

At the moment, there was nothing she could do for James, except to watch. He was almost four miles away, and a thousand feet above her. When he swung across the face of the headwall between one chimney and the next, she recognized the image in the photograph on her father's bedroom wall. She stood approximately where her father had been when he took the picture. Even the light was the same. In that moment long ago, The Devil's Kitchen Headwall also had been lit by a rising sun.

Now, the vibrant image was frozen into her mind.

During last night, she and the thin-lipped man beside her had crossed the waist of the ridge in darkness. Laura knew that Joe Patton had been very close to them once during that long dark climb. As they passed a tortured clump of scrub pine, Dieter had sensed the presence of another man as well. He'd spoken loudly about the gun he held at Laura's head. Joe's silence had been eloquent assent. Dieter had the upper hand.

Last night, Laura had sensed a second being, furtively slinking across the ridge behind them. The soft rub of fur on pine had notified her that they were being followed by Vandal. On the glacier, she never caught sight of even his shadow, but the wind had created high drifts out of the new snow. The half-wild dog could be crouching behind a drift, out of sight anywhere. Laura worried that Dieter might spot Vandal. She knew Dieter would shoot anything that moved. The man had grown very nervous.

But Vandal's presence gave her hope and the beginnings of an idea for escape.

Dieter had said very little to her during their night climb, but later, he talked a little. They had dug a small snow cave to protect them from the wind. Once inside, he'd tied her ankles together and then thrown their sleeping bags on top of a tarp.

"You must sleep, Miss Atweiler," he said while pulling the goose down bag over her feet. "There is nothing else you or I can do."

After he checked the bindings on her wrists, Laura huddled in her bag, gazing out at the clear sky, the mountain and the stars. The vast universe seemed to be waiting for a reckoning. Laura was sure the man next to her felt the judgement of the heavens as he lay there, staring upwards. It was obvious he didn't relish the job he'd been given. She felt sure he groped for some way out of Arndt's game.

"Do you believe in God, Mr. Haupt?" she had whispered in the dark night.

He turned sharply toward her, "After this life, nothing. In this life, the weak do for the strong."

Startled, Laura shrank into herself, but Dieter continued to look at her in the darkness. His next statement was even more surprising. "I am one of the weak, Miss Atweiler. Your father was one of the strong."

"He died."

"Yes. You were there afterwards, weren't you?" He didn't wait for her reply. "The General didn't talk until the drug. I never saw anyone so stubborn. Without the drug, Arndt would have learned nothing."

Laura sat up in her sleeping bag, intent on knowing all. A flash of silver signaled that Dieter was ready for sudden movements.

"Lie down, Miss Atweiler," he whispered, motioning with the gun. "Lie down. It will be safer not to move quickly."

She had obeyed, tense until he withdrew the gun once more. After a moment, she pursued the question upper-most in her mind.

"My father, after Arndt gave him the drug – What then?"

"He only confirmed the names we already had – spies who worked for him in Germany, Belgium, France – quite a network. But still, he told nothing new. Nothing."

"James's location?"

"Arndt already knew James would be here on Mount Hood, but your father gave away none of James's contacts in Germany."

She covered her face with her hands, breathing deeply. Her father had suffered horribly, but he need not have suffered guilt. He died believing he had given away everything, endangered all his men.

Dieter started to lie down, but Laura reached out her tethered hands, touching his shoulder to keep his attention.

"Why are you weak, Mr. Haupt?"

He sat, stiffly silent for a long moment, then lay back in the bag, sighing, "I could neither inflict the pain nor endure against it."

"But you can keep me prisoner, knowing what Arndt will do?"

"I'm his prisoner too," Dieter whispered roughly. "When Arndt no longer needs me, I'll be dead because I know too much."

Suddenly, Laura saw a glimmer of hope. "I could help you get to our intelligence agency. They'll protect you as a witness. They'll. . ."

He put a hand over her mouth. "Shut up!" he said urgently, then glanced over his shoulder at the vast emptiness that surrounded them. After a tense moment, he whispered, "No. I cannot fight him."

Laura had sagged back into her sleeping bag and waited for morning.

Morning brought this new terror – the reality of James taunting Werner Arndt and the best mountain climbers of the German Reich to follow him. She and Dieter Haupt stood on the broad expanse of the Sandy Glacier, right in the jaws of the trap set by James and the village. Laura knew there were three men on the ridge to the west and at least four more stationed in the clumps of alpine trees at timberline elevation behind her, waiting for Arndt to follow James. As long as Dieter was close to her, there wasn't a man among them who would open fire. Their trap was rendered ineffective by her captivity. She had to find some way to put her central position to use – to become the pivotal player instead of the victim.

Dieter, fiddling with his field glasses, turned his narrow white face toward Laura. "When your James rolled over in mid-air, face down to face up, I knew he would fall forever. I have never seen anything like that."

Laura bit her lip grimly. Watching James climb without safety ropes had left her exhausted. She wasn't aware of the tension in every part of her body until he climbed out of sight. Then, a wave of weariness washed over her.

When Arndt and his men arrived at the snow saddle atop the ridge, it was clear from their movements that they had no idea of James's location. Dieter, though he'd seen the whole amazing performance, was too far away to be of help. And Laura had the odd feeling that Dieter silently hoped James would escape.

CHAPTER TWENTY-NINE

MARCH 15TH, 1942

For the first time, James was glad he used American-made pitons, with blackened metals – difficult to see in the dark rocks of most uplifted mountains. One of the pitons Arndt heard him use was hidden in the wall behind him. The other was on the southern face of the ridge he'd climbed around. When Arndt saw it, he'd have no trouble guessing where to look for his prey.

James believed he heard fewer voices in the group. It was difficult to tell how many were left.

"Werner, in diesem Kamin. This chimney."

The voice was at least two chimneys west of the one where James hid. He knew Arndt wouldn't fall for his trick that easily.

"Nein," hissed Arndt, "Nicht hier." Their footsteps crunched through the crusted snow, back and forth for an eternity before James heard Arndt's voice again. "Hier."

Without further comment, Arndt began climbing exactly where James had climbed up the chute to the west. He reached the narrowed area and set his boots and back against the wall. James could hear the nails in his boots. Nails would help Arndt grip the verglas surface and rise more quickly. James let his mind relax. There was nothing he could do until Arndt either did or did not find his piton.

With a fatalism reserved for those moments before death, James let half his mind roam over his subconscious. He sought an explanation for something he'd seen last night. The other half of his mind was alert for that one moment when he might take Arndt unaware.

"Britt," Arndt called, "is there sign of Schoenfeld over there?" "I'm at thirty feet. Nothing but smooth verglas."

Britt Koenig! James had climbed with him as well. He was a mountain of a man – nothing next to Arndt, but very strong.

"I'm going to belay myself," said Britt. "This ice is treacherous." "Don't waste time. He'll get away from us above that headwall."

"He's not that fast," groused Britt.

"You don't remember what a spider he always was on the worst places," Arndt replied.

Somehow, the compliment, issued by a man who wanted to kill him, sent a warmth through James that shamed him. Arndt's least word of encouragement had always seemed to be a bone dropped for the lap dog. He thought he'd gotten over wanting those bones.

The man's here to kill me, for God's sake, thought James angrily. Why care what he thinks?

A drone interrupted the silence and the grunting of the climbers. A small aircraft approached the mountain from the south. James stiffened, pulling himself as close to the wall of the chute as possible. Then he realized that from above, no one in the airplane could tell which of them might be Arndt and which Ian McKay.

The droning sound grew louder. A shadow blinked across the chimney in which James waited. In the chute behind him, Arndt swore softly. "Gott im Himmel that man cuts it close!"

Below, a third climber called up, "That eess heem?"

A third man below us – I know that silky French voice, James thought.

"The plane," hollered Arndt, "You can see?"

"He flies down ze ridge west of us."

"Gone to circle around. We must finish Schoenfeld before our ride becomes impatient."

With only that brief interruption, Arndt resumed his scramble up the chute west of James. A moment later, James heard Arndt stop about twenty-five feet below him. Why?

"Philipe," Arndt yelled. "Look up this *kamin* to the east of me. I've found one of his pitons."

James glanced at his equipment hoping it was well back from the view straight up the chute. He took a deep and silent breath, letting it out slowly to calm his nerves.

Philipe? he thought. Philipe Gerard? Impossible! Gerard reported to British Intelligence."

"No sign of him," the man replied in soft accents of the Alsace-Lorraine area, "but it takes a sharp twist to the west after two hundred feet. We would not see him."

"We will surprise him, yet," replied Arndt.

"How so? He is ahead and must know that we follow," Philipe pointed out.

"You climb up behind him," said Arndt. "With you below and us above, we'll cork him inside."

James heard the scraping of Arndt's boots as he began climbing again. The man was fast enough to do just what he said. James's only chance was to wait for Philipe and kill him. How many others still waited below?

Within minutes, Arndt rose above him in the chute just the other side of his back. Below James, Philipe didn't bother with pitons any more than did Arndt. Their assumption of infallibility was James's best hope. There was only one place from which he could be seen – the top of the chimney. If Arndt arrived at the top before James met Philipe, Philipe would be forewarned. He willed Philipe to come at him. Boot step by boot step, he encouraged him mentally.

Rise to your fate.

James took the time now to check the piton – solid in the icy rock wall. To the piton, he silently clipped an oval karabiner tied to his climber's rope. He lifted his rucksack and slipped it on his back, scraping the wall behind him only once with the canvas fabric.

Flexing his fingers to ensure adequate circulation, he became aware of his own numbness from waiting in the strong draft that rose up the chimney. He made a fist over and over again. He had to have both hands for what he planned.

Below, Philipe grunted as he levered himself into the back and feet position needed to ascend the chimney. There was a fifty-fifty chance Philipe had chosen to put his back to James's position. Then everything would be easy. Chances were equally great that he would face James as he came up.

Just in case, James reached into his pocket for a small length of nylon rope, tied a Prussik knot attaching his body harness around his climbers' rope. The knot would not slip down the rope if tension were applied to it, but when tension let off, it could be slid either up or down a rope.

Dubious, he tested the friction of nylon against hemp several times before he was satisfied. Then, he wrapped an arm around his skis and waited.

*   *

Waiting had always been the hardest part of an operation. It left one time to remember. James didn't like memories. So few of them were satisfactory. Cold air rushing up the rock brought back the one abiding question he had about Arndt's betrayal.

James had no idea Arndt was a double agent until after they climbed l'Aiguille. Yet before they left for the climb, Arndt already suspected that James as well as Kirsten knew of his Nazi connections. He'd already arranged for Kirsten's murder. So why had he not killed James during the climb?

Why did Arndt hesitate? If killing James was Arndt's aim, a death fall off l'Aiguille would have been more sure than the fall he later engineered in the apartment stairwell.

James had never let the next thought crystallize in his mind. Its sentimental origins were foolish. He shouldn't allow his heart to credit one thin possibility – that Arndt had been reluctant to kill him.

*   *

As his thoughts circled the past, James's senses were alert to the present. He could still hear Arndt's boots receding into the chute above him. Philipe's panting indicated the speed at which he closed the gap between them. James tensed for his first sight of the man.

Sweat-slick dark hair appeared against the far wall of the chimney. So, Philipe had elected to put his face toward James's side. That meant James had to be quick and sure. The man pushed his torso up another six inches and brought up his feet. He pushed against his feet one more time, raising his torso another six inches. The next push would put his eyes on a level with James's boots and then he would know what waited for him. Philipe drew up his feet for the next push, looked up toward his route, saw James and opened his mouth to yell.

At that moment, James jammed his skis, heel first into Philipe's neck.

The only sounds which came out were a choked syllable and a gurgle. James leaned down, trusting his weight to the friction on the Prussik knot as he thrust the skis hard into Philipe. The knot held. Philipe's legs kicked out and fell, dragging his weight down. His arms reached for the skis. James leaned harder. Philipe's arms went slack, one mittened hand over the ski, the other limp at his side. The ski killed as surely as any rifle, and more silently. James leaned heavily on the skis and tried not to look at the face of the man he had murdered. His stomach lurched several times as he told himself over and over that Philipe had come to kill him. One of them had to die.

His most immediate problem was what to do with the body which hung pinned by the skis to the opposite wall of the chute. He couldn't let it fall. The man's ice axe and other tools would clatter against the sides of the chute. But Philipe was far enough below him that it would be difficult to pull him up to the ledge.

James kept his weight on the skis and reached slowly with one hand toward Philipe's neck, depending heavily on the nylon rope and his Prussik knot. Once he had a good grip on Philipe's jacket, he held the man up long enough to let the weight of the skis off his broken neck. For one long moment, the fingers in the wool cloth were all that kept the body hanging. James took the risk. Trusting the nylon, he swung his legs down, wrapping them around Philipe's chest. Now he held his skis in one hand and the body between his knees, suspended by one small Prussik knot over the seventy-five-foot fall.

He managed to lean his back against the chute wall, and with great effort bring his knees up so that he could plant his boots on the opposing wall. This brought Philipe's slack face even with his. James tore his gaze from that dead face and concentrated on what he must do. His ski wrapping was damaged when he dug in the rocks to create the avalanche. The skis were in danger of falling out of the canvas. Holding Philipe's body with his legs, James pushed the skis over his shoulder onto the ledge behind him. As soon as the body was his only encumbrance, he hitched his back up the wall. He gripped the body by Philipe's jacket as he brought his feet up the opposite wall and began the maneuver all over again. Two more times, he pushed his back up the wall until the ledge dug into his back. Reaching above him for the rope, he began to slip down the icy wall. He brought his arms down quickly. It would take the traction provided by all of his back to keep both of them up. Philipe weighed as much as he.

As he regained his nerve, James looked at the face of the man he had killed. It was Philipe Gerard, older, with the addition of a beard and some weight. When had this weasel joined forces with Arndt?

Behind James, loose rocks fell in the next chute, reminding James that he had to do something with Philipe's body before Arndt reached the top of the chimneys. He pushed up again, this time gaining only inches because more and more of his back was above the ledge. He dragged his feet and Philipe up after him. When at last he propped his elbows above the ledge, he lifted himself onto the shelf. Suddenly the angle between his torso and his knees became greater. The body began slipping away from him. He grabbed for the rope to hold himself in the shelf and pulled up on his knees with all his strength. By twisting to one side, he managed to get the weight of the body across one thigh and pulled it toward him into the ledge.

As quickly as he could, he pushed the body into the fetal position on the shelf and then got ready to leave the ledge with his gear. He tied the skis again to his pack, relieved the Prussik knot and pocketed the length of nylon rope, now satisfied that nylon was one hell of a material.

He adjusted his pack and untied the rope. Slipping it through the karabiner, he prepared to rappel as far as his shortened rope would take him. After adjusting the rope around his body, he gave one last thought to the body next to him. James reached inside the man's jacket, fishing around until he found a brown wool hat. He took off his own bright red hat and put it on Philipe's head, replaced Philipe's on his own head and began lowering himself down the chute.

In the chute to the west, he heard the continuing drop of loosened snow and rock as Arndt scrambled toward the top of the Devil's Kitchen Headwall, another two hundred feet above them.

In the solitary quiet of his own descent, the emotion he'd pushed away rushed in on him. His years with Arndt had meant nothing. After half a lifetime of shared fear and laughter, Arndt had thrown him away as easily as had his mother. And when Laura learned the whole truth of his part in her father's death, wouldn't she, with better reason, also turn her back on him?

Of course, she would – assuming he lived to see her again.

CHAPTER THIRTY

James's descent of the chute was even faster than his rappel off the Gendarme. His hands were colder, so he braked less often and less effectively. Fear propelled him. Respect for Arndt's tenacity and ingenuity was deeply ingrained in him since boyhood climbs.

His shortened rope dangled about twenty feet above the narrow snow saddle. When James neared the end, he braced his feet against the eastern wall of the chute, shucking his pack and skis. The equipment dropped into the snowdrift against the western wall of the chimney.

Their landing was muffled by dry powder blown up from the glacier hundreds of feet below him. He swallowed hard, deliberately grabbed only one of the two strands of his climber's rope and allowed himself to drop the last twenty feet, bringing the rope down with him.

His landing was not as fortuitous as the skis'. One foot punched through a thin layer of snow onto a small boulder. The other landed next to the rock. A sharp flash of heat jolted up his leg before he had a chance to tuck and roll away from the rock.

Ignoring the new pain in his right hip, James scrambled across ten feet of snow to retrieve his pack and skis. He pulled the rest of his rope out of the piton and wrapped it around his arm as he limped east of the maze of chimneys occupied by Krueger and Arndt.

Absently rubbing his legs to reduce the pain, James assessed his chances. Pain was nothing new. Ever since the fall from the sixth floor of the Berlin apartment building, he'd been dealing with weakness in that part of his body. Besides, his life now depended less on physical ability than on Arndt's nature. Would Arndt fall into his delaying trap?

James stopped where he could wait out of the wind, in the lea of the buttressing rocks. From here, he could listen to the climbers' progress toward the top of the Devil's Kitchen Headwall.

From the top, Arndt would see a crumpled man on the shelf, a man wearing James's hat. If luck were with James, Arndt would waste time climbing down to capture the man alive rather than shoot him. Arndt badly wanted to see James's face as he died.

While Arndt descended toward Philipe's body, James would be skiing toward Sandy Glacier on the western side of the mountain. This was no ordinary ski run. His route was down snow-covered cliffs – slope almost vertical.

If he made it to the bottom of the cliffs, the glacier below was another eight-hundred-foot drop – steeply inclined and so vast that James had no illusions he could escape completely across it unseen. In fact, the plan called for Arndt to see and pursue him right into the arms of the villagers.

Except for Takehiko Okada and Moses Labbé, the village men were older, left behind by their sons who were fighting the war in Europe and the Pacific. Old they might be, but they were stout and loyal. If he could get through this plunge without killing himself, James could count on them to capture Arndt and any who followed him down.

As he waited for Arndt to commit himself one way or the other, James wondered about the identities of the two men who must have died in the avalanche he'd started in the Leuthold Couloir. He knew that Arndt had wasted no time even pretending they were important enough to rescue. Were they, like Krueger and Bertholde, old climbing buddies who'd sold their soul to do Arndt's bidding?

And what of the two who split off to cross the ridge at its waist?

What had Joe done with them?

A flash of light caught James's eye. Out over the wooded and snow- covered foothills, he saw a small aeroplane heading toward the cliffs.

The plane flew low. The pilot would have to accelerate quickly to rise up over the cliffs. The noise of the engine could start another avalanche off the sheer headwall as easily as Arndt's rifles had done a half-hour ago.

James knew the risk. He moved into the shadow of the headwall and unwrapped his skis.

Arndt's voice rang out over the rock and snow. His German hissed with the wind. "Schoenfeld. Get off that bench and come up the chute. You know you're trapped, boy."

James flinched at the 'boy'. Why had he ever thought that was a term of affection? Arndt had called Kirsten 'girl' whenever he wanted her to do some menial task – whenever he wanted her in the bedroom. How blind he'd been then to the man's contempt!

"Schoenfeld. Philipe is below you. I am above you. Choose."

James watched the small aeroplane buzz over the ridge, heading for his position. He knew what he was about to do was suicidal, but he laid his skis down across the fall line. Leaning a hand on each he pushed it back and forth in the dry snow. Convinced that he had applied the best wax for the conditions, he bound first one foot and then the other to the slender boards. In a moment, they would become either the instruments of his saving or of his death.

After checking his new Hvam, quick-release bindings, James stood slowly, adjusted his dark glasses and took his bamboo ski poles in each hand. Listening to the small engine coming toward him, concentrating equally on the sound of snow melting, he heard Arndt swear in a tone no greater than a whisper. The sound of his impatience came clearly out of the chute.

"Britt, belay me. The boy is too frightened to climb to his death."

James felt elation. Arndt would go down the chute. Almost all of Britt's attention would be on the immediate job of belaying Arndt. He would also be watching the crazy pilot. They might not see James before he reached the glacier – out of shooting range, but directly in the path of any avalanche the aeroplane started.

Britt grunted as he set up the belay and then again as Arndt began to descend. James looked out over the path he would take. He would ski a little less than half a mile straight across the foot of the chimneys of the headwall. Where the western buttress gave him no choice, he'd head straight down – a drop of twelve hundred feet in less than a mile. And then the glacier, and death in the caves or crevasses if he couldn't maneuver over or around in time.

"Just sit tight, Schoenfeld. It will all be over in a few minutes." Britt's voice taunted the body on the shelf.

James pushed off. The wind hit his face and whipped at his jacket. It flapped so loudly he was sure the two climbers would hear it. He passed the first of the chimneys, quickly approaching the one he'd climbed.

There was no stopping to choose the right time to pass underneath his pursuers. Any attempt to stop would mean a plunge off this narrow shelf of snow that separated the upper headwall to his right from the steep, snow-covered cliffs falling sharply off to his left.

His dark glasses began to film up. Flakes of snow blew against them. He was afraid to rub them with his sleeve, knowing that would blur them permanently. He swiped at the glasses with an arm, managing to knock them down his nose far enough to see over them. But the glare of the snow in the mid-morning sun was blinding. The thong which tied them to his head pulled against his left ear, causing it to fold down. Sound on that side was magnified as if he cupped a hand around the ear. The aeroplane suddenly seemed to roar as it approached him.

He leaned away from the distorted sound. Trying to balance himself, he felt the skis begin to slide downhill toward his left. Repositioned over the skis, he nearly overbalanced, almost pitching himself into the void. He caught himself and thanked Atweiler for sending him these new more responsive skis.

The oncoming aeroplane, its propellers whirring, its engine whining up the glacier gave him a feeling of hopeless hurtling through space. He glanced ahead, through flakes of blown snow. The western buttress walls loomed. At the last possible moment, he planted his left pole and lifted his weight, turning the skis straight down the fall line, heading for the most important slalom race of his life. The aeroplane swooped in a near vertical climb over his head and up the headwall. Behind him, James heard the moan and crack of falling ice. He raced an avalanche.

*   *

Dieter never seemed surprised about the aeroplane. Laura was sure he'd expected it even the first time it buzzed toward them over the summit of the mountain. And now that it was on its way back, Dieter seemed to be cheered by its presence. As she worked loose a last strand of her rope leash, Laura watched the plane's low-level return from the south.

It crossed Tom, Dick and Harry Ridge, heading for Cathedral Ridge.

At least a third of the men of the village were hidden on Cathedral, waiting for Arndt to follow James into their trap.

Next to her, Dieter sucked in his breath. Laura stopped working her fingers on the loose hemp leash. She glanced up from her crouched position and watched in awe. If she hadn't been convinced before, she would know for a certainty that this was James Schoenfeld skiing under the aeroplane's path and straight downhill toward her. His cap was no longer red. That didn't disguise him. Few men on God's earth would be so courageous – foolhardy. Cold seeped through Laura.

Dieter Haupt came alert next to her, raising his binoculars. James hurtled down the steepest snowfield on the mountain. Behind him flew the sun-slivered dust of an avalanche, tons of ice and snow, falling straight down the western headwall cliffs at him. She watched, hoping the avalanche included the area on the east where Arndt climbed. It did not. The eastern cliffs were unmoved. Arndt was safe.

Laura glanced at Dieter, saw his forehead tighten as he took in the significance of that silent tableau. He sighted down his rifle barrel on the lone skier.

"The avalanche is heading for us," Laura urged, hoping to make him run.

"I fail now, and Arndt will kill me." Dieter said. "I die either way."

Laura saw there was no moving him with fear. He was more afraid of death at Arndt's hands than of burial in ice. Laura's hands were tied, but she'd loosened the tethers on her skis.

*　*

James' skis barely maintained contact with the steep descent. He fought to keep control, using his weight to force small turns in his downward flight. He had slim hope of keeping himself from falling headlong to the bottom of this near vertical course. As long as he was occupied controlling his fall, he could keep track of the possibilities: the avalanche that pursued him; the crevasses and ice caves barely covered by new snow; the rock he might not see until he jolted into it; or the patch of ice that would send him end over end down the vast distance.

James clutched his poles to his sides and used minute body movements, left, right, left, knowing that rhythm was all-important in keeping him from disaster. His weight shifted easily, too easily. In his stomach was a reeling weightlessness such as he had never experienced except in that one long fall above the Chamonix Valley.

Behind there arose the roar of ice and snow. Above him, a roar of anger. Arndt had seen him.

Hurtling toward the lower Sandy Glacier his mind picked up the protrusion on the left.

Weight shift, sharp turn right. Dark blue snow right, crevasse, shift weight, ski, listen for the tonal change. Wood over emptiness. Think ahead. Think and move. Left, right, left, left again around a lump of snow . . . concealed death.

As the fall line neared the Cathedral Ridge which divided the Sandy Glacier from Ladd Glacier, the contours of the mountain became slightly less steep – a new danger. He would be slowed, but the avalanche would be rolling faster. James skied straight down the fall line until he reached that diagonal dip in the glacier created by the beginning of the Sandy River. Sandy River Canyon might be deep enough to stop the avalanche, but climbing out of the canyon before he was buried would take great speed and greater luck.

Arndt was behind him as well. James didn't even have to look – a rapid rappel from the shelf where Philipe's body lay, and Arndt would be on his skis, every bit as crazy as James. Crazier – Arndt loved death.

Arndt would chase the avalanche just for a chance at James.

James rode at breakneck speed over a drift. His skis lifted into the air, carrying him well above a three-foot wide gap in the ice. He didn't have to look down. He knew the great depth of this ancient glacier.

Landing sent lightning agony up his left hip and his newly injured right leg. His only reaction was a sympathetic pain in his scarred cheek. The chattering of his skis over the frozen ice echoed in every fatigued muscle of his body.

His skis dipped down the slope into the narrow river canyon.

Already, boulders of ice from the avalanche plunged past him, nipping at his skis. He could smell the crystals, the decades of mold. James let go of every muscle, leaning into his skis as he searched for safe crossing over the buried river. A block of ice hit his back as he reached the bottom of the canyon. He nearly fell, but moved his arms and legs faster to keep upright. He charged across the nearest bridge of snow. It crumbled behind him. He pushed up the far side, a roar of weight and destruction following him into the canyon. His skis left narrow herringbone patterns behind him to be covered with the pursuing snow and ice.

His muscles cramped for lack of oxygen, yet he pushed on. Arndt came. Ice would bury him. LeGuin, Patton, Langendorff, Labbé, Laura – they counted on him. He couldn't stop.

The snow hurtled smaller and smaller clods past his skis. As he topped the rise out of the canyon, he realized he had actually outrun the main body of the avalanche. He had beaten one enemy. Over his shoulder, he saw two skiers plunging down the path he and the avalanche had taken. He pushed on.

He heard the return of the aeroplane. Transport for Arndt, he thought. Hess!

The motor whined up over the summit of the mountain, then dipped to follow Cathedral Ridge. James gained speed, skiing out of the Sandy Canyon followed only by the last spray of spent avalanche. Off his right shoulder, he caught sight of the aeroplane as it opened fire. A rhythmic spat of bullets sprayed into the lower bones of the Cathedral spine.

Why isn't he shooting at me?

Orange flame spurted from the front of Hess's plane. *Does he know the men are hidden there?*

Heartsick about his friends on the ridge, he watched the gun flame again toward the few trees on the ridge.

How did Arndt know about the men up there?

Had he gotten the information from someone?

The image of Laura, helpless if Arndt ever captured her, drove James. He skied more recklessly down the steep glacier. Glancing far ahead on the wide expanse, he saw a dark blur separate into two blurs for a moment before seeming again to become one. He knew there should be nothing but white and rocks ahead for another mile.

Without slowing, he shifted weight, turned slightly left to begin a steep traverse, then a shift back to the right, keeping an eye on the plane as it lifted over Tom, Dick Ridge heading south again. James swiped at his glasses, shoving them up his nose once again.

The plane had done its damage. It rose and disappeared beyond the foothills, droning toward the Willamette Valley and the city of Portland. Below James, in the middle of the lower glacier, the blur resolved into distinct figures. Two men, one in fur. At least one rifle.

How did they get past Joe? A moment later it hit him.

Joe too? Because of me?

Even while painfully aware of his responsibility for Joe, James careened toward the two men.

Still out of shooting range for a few moments.

And then he saw the distinctive dark and wild curls on the taller figure in fur.

Laura!

And Dieter Haupt!

The wind tunnel over the crevasse. Does it still exist?

Before the question was finished in his mind, his decision was made. Shifting again slightly to the west, he plowed toward the most dangerous part of the Sandy Glacier – the buttresses of Cathedral Ridge. In front of him lay a crevasse-filled ice-scape. Behind him,

Arndt and Britt crouched over heavy skis, hurtling closer with each second. Below, Haupt held Laura at gun point.

Patton could have picked off Haupt if he had no prisoner. The villagers would have taken them by now if they were just two men. And now the plane had strafed the ridge. Everything had gone wrong with the trap. It was himself and Laura in its pincers.

Is no one left alive?

James had a backup plan – one he hadn't told Laura. It was desperate.

Early spring weather may have changed the terrain and turned it into a suicide plan. He saw no other way. With resolve, and despair for the villagers, James skied toward the jumble of wind-whipped ice.

If Arndt believes I died again, I can live long enough to kill him and free Laura.

On his left, the two figures seemed more distinct as James's skis carried him down and across the glacier. His speed prevented him from noting more details, only that the man with the rifle raised it, taking aim.

* *

Laura sensed the moment when James changed tactics. He had spotted the two of them and the rifle. He turned, swiftly cutting across the fall line and heading for an enormous crevasse. Dieter saw his chance. Stepping away from Laura, he raised his Garand, sighting on the dark, moving figure.

Laura lunged. Flinging both arms up, her tied wrists hit the barrel just as the shot rang out. She fell face down. Another shot echoed off the ridge. She scrambled to her knees.

Across the vast glacier, she saw James falter. "No!" she wailed. "No."

James stumbled, skis flying up, bindings releasing under the strain of his speed and sudden fall. His arms and legs outstretched, he cartwheeled over and over, then seemed to metamorphose. James' cartwheels collapsed. He became a ball of humanity pelting down the glacier. His rolling body disappeared into a drift that rose in the snow near the yawning mouth of the crevasse.

His scream receded into the depths of the crevasse, and then silence surrounded Laura. She crumpled to the snow.

James.

Her mind could form no other thought.

Please. No.

She closed her eyes and saw the blue depths of the tomb in which he lay, broken, gray-faced in death. It was a blue grotto, a cathedral to the power of the ice and evil, demanding the sacrifice of those who dared defy.

Arndt, come now. Kill me too.

Laura became aware that Dieter crouched over her, almost protectively. A moment later, she realized he protected himself. Somehow, he'd sensed that if he didn't stay near Laura, he was a dead man. That same awareness had warned him of the presence of Joe on Yocum Ridge last night.

"Get up," he snarled. "We're hiking up there."

She lay like a lump of lead, feeling nothing but the pain of grief. In her mind came all the demons of her childhood, the forbidden fears and golems – fire, guns, the shapeless, amoral hulk of Werner Arndt. The demons had won. They had killed every human she loved. Bitter anger built inside her, making her reckless. When Dieter tugged at her bear fur covering, she turned on him.

"Hsst."

His surprised face came away with long scratches. The change in her from woman to one possessed brought terror to his eyes.

"You are doomed," she pointed at him, her two hands still tied together. "Haupt, Dieter," she recited, a steely cold implacability in her voice. "Died March 15th, 1942. No man remembers him. He was nothing."

Dieter Haupt's ears laid back against his skull. He reached out yanking frantically on her fur. She remained immobile.

"You will never leave this mountain," she said.

Dieter glanced around, furtively. Fear created a tick in his right cheek. And fear gave him strength beyond normal.

He yanked on her left arm. Her shoulder wound ripped open once again, but she didn't cry out. She merely stared at her arm. It was then she saw the bone protruding through the skin of her left wrist. She remembered the sharp crack when she'd hit it against the rifle barrel. She felt nothing, not even fear at seeing white bone or the pale skin and blood.

It is justice, she concluded in the veiled recesses of her mind. Laura Atweiler deserves at least this.

After all, she still lived. There must be some pain if you are alive when everyone else has died.

"Get up," growled Dieter.

"Leave me here," she said dully. "Go on without me."

"You know I can't do that," he said, pulling her to stand. "The moment I step away from you again, they will shoot me."

"Who will shoot you?" What she meant was 'how do you know?' but if he had only suspicions, that question would tell him he was right.

"The same ones who shot at me just now. Don't pretend with me."

"No one shot at you!" She'd deflected Dieter's first shot. He'd shot James with a second. After she fell, LeGuin, the grocer, might have had a clear shot from Cathedral Ridge, but LeGuin's position had been strafed by the aeroplane. He, too, was probably dead.

"Move," Dieter grunted as he propelled her up the glacier toward the crevasse where James had fallen. Out of the gray fog of her mind, she tried to dredge up a hope that Dieter's shot and the fall into the crevasse hadn't killed James – that if she and Dieter arrived before Arndt did, she might still rescue James. She hurried, though it was hard to move her wooden legs. Her left arm hung useless. Yet, brain and arm were still widely separate. In between slithered numbing black despair and the incongruous brilliance of sun on blinding snow.

"What happened to your arm?" Dieter reached out and lifted the rope. Agony shot up her limb, communicating clearly with her brain at last.

At her cry, he stopped. "It's broken," he said, staring dumbly at the bone. "How did that happen?"

She couldn't speak.

"Oh," he muttered, "the gun barrel."

Her legs lost their elasticity and Dieter had to grab to keep her upright. He seemed to be at a loss for a moment.

"You afraid?" she mocked, knowing that if she fell, he would be an easy target.

"James might be alive, yet," he ground out. "You climb to the crevasse or I kill him when I get there." Beyond Dieter's shoulder, Laura saw a ghost move silently across the glacier, disappearing into the whiteness. A slim hope entered her shocked mind.

"I'm going," she whispered. One ski pushed forward. "May your eyeballs shrivel in sunlight," she croaked as she shifted weight and thrust the other ski out. He backed away, frightened by the change in her. James's death had made her fearless – insane.

And that was how she kept herself moving forward, remembering all the epithets hurled at recruits by Sergeant Hospice. "May you sleep forever on glass shards," she muttered and moved another ski across the white expanse toward James's grave.

CHAPTER THIRTY-ONE

In the silence, Takehiko Okada heard the aeroplane heading toward Portland, at first, then turning abruptly north across the Columbia River into Washington State. Disaster had come swiftly on the ridge and on the glacier.

Takehiko glanced once more at his taciturn companion. Moses, The Big Labbé, had amazing control over his emotions. Both of them had seen James's body enveloped by the jaws of the deepest crevasse on the mountain. They had heard his death scream. Yet Labbé barely blinked. Impassive eyes, set jaw – nothing gave away the inner man. Only the quick pulling back of Labbé's ears told Takehiko what Labbé felt.

They said nothing for long moments. Then Labbé said, "The gods take care of him. We take care of his Laura."

A moment later, a second shriek of terror ripped across the glacier. Moses Labbé, unmoving, glanced up toward the Devil's Kitchen Headwall. Arndt's last man had tried to ski off the headwall. He followed the same track as Arndt, and before him, James. Yet, less than a third of the way down, he made a wrong move, plowing into a block of ice left in the tail of the avalanche.

"That man is dead," Takehiko whispered.

Labbé grunted assent, then pointed. "Tah-kay, Watch the dog."

Takeh pulled himself up, looking through the scrub pines. Above them, on the Sandy Glacier, Vandal inched forward on his haunches. He followed Laura Atweiler, as her captor pushed her toward the crevasse. Watching from below, it seemed as if the man would spot the dog.

However, as a farmer, Takeh was used to reading subtleties in terrain. It was clear Vandal kept high drifts between himself and Laura's captor.

"We can do that," he whispered, dropping back next to Labbé. "Have to wait until Arndt arrives at the crevasse," Labbé answered.

"From there, he will see less. Up where he skis on the glacier, he might notice our motion."

Takeh's gaze followed the progress of Arndt down the glacial field. Arndt skied back and forth, allowing his switchbacks to slow his speed so he could watch for dangerously soft drifts left by the avalanche or for crevasses in the unknown terrain. Arndt was not worried about capturing James. He'd seen Haupt shoot him. He'd heard the scream. He could afford to take his time arriving at the crevasse.

If Arndt finally did arrive, Takeh knew he would still be out of range of every man stationed around the semi-circle trap. Joe Patton had returned to Yocum Ridge after circling to the others during the night.

Joe had warned them that the figure in the bear-fur coat was Laura Atweiler, the other, her captor.

Takeh and Labbé hoped that Ole Langendorff hunkered, stationed in the trees at timberline, half a mile west. Now that James was down, LeGuin, the grocer, a crack shot, probably had left his post high on Cathedral Ridge, working his way toward the rest of them. Sheriff Garrigues also moved lower down on the same ridge, the western margin of the Sandy Glacier.

However, they also knew, Langendorff, LeGuin and Garrigues might be dead. The strafing pilot somehow had known where the trap was most vulnerable.

Labbé might be right, Takehiko decided as he looked over the situation on the glacier. They had to get closer, but they'd have to wait to make their move. So, they watched to follow the dog's lead. And while they waited, Takeh decided to bring up the inevitable.

"Labbé," he began, not looking his friend in the eye. "I'm supposed to be on that train to the internment camp in Wyoming."

Labbé frowned. "Don't worry. When this is over, we'll get you there. Then you can be a dutiful prisoner-of-war."

Takeh shook his head. "Not too dutiful." This time he looked directly at Labbé. "It's my farm. I want to sell it to you. One dollar. Sheriff Garrigues agreed to witness the sale."

Labbé's head jerked around. "Me? An apple farmer? You outa your skull?"

"I want you to have it. Otherwise it goes on the block to pay taxes. That means the Nortons get it after all."

Labbé squinted at him. "Ta-kay, how'm I going to pay the taxes?"

"Not you. Mrs. L. She'll pay taxes. You bring her apples and pears. She agreed."

"Garrigues agreed," Labbé sing-songed softly, beating on his knees as if on a skin-head drum. "Takeh agreed, Leszinski agreed. All of the people but Labbé agreed . . ." He glanced at Takeh's incredulous face, then chuckled. "Would be kinda funny to see old Norton's face. He betrays you and gets me instead."

Takeh smiled, sadly. "Yeah. I'd like to see it."

Labbé lifted his enormous hand toward Takehiko. "It's a done deal. I'll get farm books in the library and take good care of your place. And if the war effort gets bad . . . if they have to call up a one-armed Indian, I know a whole tribe that'll take care of it for you."

Takehiko's right hand disappeared in Labbé's paw.

"Now, Okada," Labbé whispered. "Arndt is arriving at the crevasse. It's time to make our move. You follow the dog's tracks. I have to find deeper drifts and gullies."

*   *

Laura stood at the downhill side of the enormous crevasse. Staring over a low roof formed of windblown ice and down into the void, her glance followed the path of James's fall. Next to her, she felt Arndt and Dieter doing the same mental calculation.

He rolled into it from the uphill side, over there, where the opening is scuffled. It's at least one hundred feet down to the first narrow neck.

Down there, on the far wall is the mark. His body hit and then slid off. The bottom . . . I can't even see the bottom.

Out of the corner of her eye, Laura saw Arndt toss something over the windblown ice roof of the crevasse, down into the vastness. It too bounced off the far wall above the narrows, then fell for endless moments before a faint splash echoed up to them.

He is dead, she thought.

"He's dead," Dieter announced.

"Did you get him with the first shot, or the second?" asked Arndt. Dieter looked surprised. "The first. The second shot was at me."

Arndt glanced at Laura, laughing, "So that's why Haupt fell on you. They can't shoot him if he's close to you." Arndt turned slowly to stare at the ridges surrounding the glacier, trying to gauge the most likely hiding places. "And that is why Hess strafed the ridge."

Then Arndt turned the ice blue of his eyes completely toward Laura. "Well, little one. The chase was a trap after all. He was very clever, your James – playing the rabbit before the hound. He used my one weakness; I don't like to lose the scent of the hunted."

"One weakness?" she dared to taunt.

He smiled, and stepped toward her, taking her shoulders in his big hands. "I have another, but it is not a weakness a mere man can use to trap me."

Laura looked up at the massive man who held her life in his hands. She was beyond fear. She could only hope he killed her soon. Beneath his wool jacket, she recognized the bulge of a gun.

I can make him shoot me. It will be faster.

He sensed his lack of control over her psyche and glanced at Dieter to see if he also noticed. Dieter scanned the ridges for the gunman.

Arndt squinted down at her. "I admit James might have succeeded, except that I had you, my dear. It was your presence as a hostage that killed him, you know."

At last she cared. Grief made her sag within his grip. He pushed the fur hood back onto her shoulders and clasped her head, pulling her toward him. "Two days in the cold air, two days of fear and pain, and you are still more beautiful than the photograph. It is such a shame."

She said nothing, merely stared at him – his hair grown out to reddish gold, narrow blue eyes dominating his granite face, a Teuton, answering to no god but himself. He smiled, grimly, moved his head down, held her body still and slanted his mouth over hers. She was ice to him.

He lifted his head, caressed her cheek with the back of one hand. She didn't even flinch. "So, that's how it will be," he whispered.

He looked up, again studying the landscape, then back at her. "Where are the men on the ridge?"

"I've no idea," she lied. When he kissed her, she had felt the gun butt pressing into her body. A plan began to form in her mind. She could kill this evil man – wipe him from the face of the earth. She would die doing it, but that hardly mattered since James had fallen in the crevasse.

Impatient for information that would help him escape the trap, Arndt pressed a thumb into her wounded shoulder and watched with pleasure as she bit her lip to keep from crying out.

"Still hurts, nein? I shall have to take care of that wound, later," he said softly, still pressing. "For now, you are to tell me the locations."

Behind him, Dieter said, "She has also a broken wrist, Herr Arndt."

Arndt stepped back and looked down. He saw the useless arm and lifted it by the shackling rope. This time, a moan did escape her. Arndt smiled broadly. He dropped the arm, causing almost as much agony as lifting it. Arndt caressed her throat, unclasped the big fur coat and yanked it down her shoulders. It caught on the protruding bone.

"Ahh." The sound escaped her before she could think. Roughly, he untied her wrists. The coat dropped to the snow, leaving her exposed to the wind that whistled up the glacier. Arndt pulled her small pack from her arms, succeeding yet again in causing agony to her wrist. She doubled over from the shock of repeated trauma, but Arndt pulled her upright.

Sweat had collected in her back where the pack under the outsized fur had made her too warm. Now the sweat seemed to freeze to her clammy skin. A shiver brought her mind back to the presence of Werner Arndt.

"Yes, little one," said Arndt with deceptive gentleness. "You are badly hurt. I can see it in your eyes." He turned to Dieter. "They always wander in the mind when the pain becomes great."

*   *

Takehiko was glad for his coat of winter rabbit fur. Labbé's mother, Christina, had made it for him years ago, a hunting coat, she'd called it. He looked like a snow mound when he held very still. Labbé had such a coat as well, and Takeh had difficulty seeing his friend even though he knew where he hid.

Breathe very shallow, thought Takeh. Do not be seen.

He was sure Arndt could kill the lady, quick. He had seen the knife in Cameron's body. Takeh watched Labbé move swiftly across the whiteness.

As smooth as a marmot, he thought with wonder. Labbé is a dancer in the hunt.

*   *

Arndt, making sure Laura always stood between him and the riflemen on the ridge, stepped behind her, holding out his climbing rope. "Dieter, tie Miss Atweiler by the waist."

Dieter Haupt glanced at Arndt apprehensively. Arndt shook the rope at him. "Now, Haupt. And no mistake. I don't want her to fall too soon."

Dieter took the rope, his hands trembling. He wrapped it about Laura, never looking her in the eye. She could not have noticed anyway. Her head hung between her shoulders, her eyes closed. She stood only because she could not fall. Arndt held the nape of her neck. The throbbing of her wrist became the only message registering in her mind.

Cold had gone. Pain had gone. Only the rhythmic pulse of inflammation kept her mind aware of life.

"Sit, Haupt." Dieter sat.

"Brace yourself. Feet out."

Dieter followed orders but nodded a question toward her skis. "No," Arndt answered, "we leave them on. Their weight will help convince her to talk."

Arndt lifted Laura from her feet. The stretching pull of his great hand against her neck sent racing messages of fear to her numbed brain. Arndt held the waist rope and lowered her over the sculpted partial roof and down into the crevasse.

Below her, the deep blue promised peace, rest. She watched her boots and skis recede into the shadows. James lay below. Her father, her mother waited for her. Sleep would come. She only regretted not having a chance to kill Arndt.

The image of James's face hovered before her. His scar shone livid red against the brown and white of his beard.

He isn't at peace, she thought. We'll be together, soon. I'll comb his hair, then he can rest.

The image of James shimmered before her, silhouetted against the whipped cream tunnel of ice. The rope at her waist cut deep into her sweater, and where her sweater folded, it knotted against her skin. Sharp pain made her whimper. The face of James mirrored her own fear. His arms reached out, ready to catch her.

He shook his head.

Arndt's voice cut through her reverie. "Where are the men stationed?" James shook his head, she thought.

"Where?" insisted Arndt.

James' head moved slowly back and forth.

"No," said Laura faintly. She gasped for air against the tight rope. Before her, the frightened face of James became scruffy, less ethereal. Real.

She blinked to clear her eyes. Her eyes widened. James was perched on a shelf of ice – the top of the glacial block that formed the downhill side of the crevasse. Above, concealing him from Arndt and Dieter, was a cornice, a partial roof of blown and frozen snow, an overhang formed by the constant wind racing up the glacier. His arms held open, ready to reach out and grab her. Ready to reveal himself in order to save her.

Arndt called. "You will tell me, or I will allow Herr Haupt to drop you twenty feet. The rope will cut deep when you stop. But you will live to feel it."

"I," Laura began. She stared at James, at the wonder of the crooked set of his mouth, the lick of sweaty hair standing straight up at the back of his head, his thumbs at right angles to his fingers as he held himself ready to grab her.

"Vass?" hissed Arndt.

"Pull me up," she said hoarsely. "I will show you where."

James nodded, still ready. It was then that she saw the crazy way his right leg was twisted under him.

Arndt laughed, a sibilant snort of triumph. "Pull, Haupt."

As Dieter pulled her to the top, Laura noticed he braced himself close to the edge of the crevasse, on top of the roof of cotton candy that hovered over James.

Arndt reached out, grabbing the rope to hurry her out of the tomb. He dangled her body above the ground, shaking the rope a little to emphasize the tormenting cut of hemp into flesh.

"You are a small terrier," he said, setting her down on her skis. "Quick to bark and quick to yelp when kicked." His enormous hands held her arms, so that she wouldn't sag to the ground.

Laura's body was as cold, as weak and as worthless as a moment before, but her mind filled with joy.

James lives.

Arndt's hands tightened on her arms and her mind cleared itself of euphoria.

Arndt is in control. I have to take control. I have to save James.

"On that ridge," said Arndt, making her face Cathedral Ridge to the west. "Where?"

Laura thought fast. No matter what, Arndt would take her with him as a hostage. She had to get him away from the crevasse, convince him to retreat to the east, where, at the narrow waist of Yocum Ridge, another trap could be set up quickly by James's friends.

Staring at Cathedral Ridge, she trembled. "Donovan," she whispered with hardly enough breath to speak.

Close behind her, Arndt took the bait. "Donovan – the COI? How many?"

She hesitated.

He wrenched her arm.

"Ahhh," she cried out.

"How many?"

Her head sank, but she managed to croak. "Ten, I saw ten."

Dieter Haupt snorted. "Ten? Impossible. I saw all persons in the town this last three days. Ten able bodied men did not exist."

It's true, she thought. There had only been the old ones.

Dieter and Arndt would automatically dismiss the young Asian man.

Dieter would have noticed only Cameron, who was dead, and a dark-haired ski bum – the one who limped.

"You lie," Arndt hissed at her.

"Donovan's men were not in town," she insisted. She grabbed at a name remembered from James's contour map. "Cloud Cap, they said. I don't know where that is."

At that moment, Dieter came unwittingly to her aide. "I saw Cloud Cap on the map. It's another climber's hut – east side of the mountain."

"So," Arndt said thoughtfully, "James brought Donovan out of Switzerland for this game." He glanced around the ridge. "Point out their locations."

"He didn't tell me locations, only the ridge and the forest below," she stopped, gasping for air.

"You know more. Tell me," he insisted.

She took a deep breath and blanched. Her chest burned from the inside. She fumbled against the rope, trying to get air.

Exasperated, Arndt twisted her body to face him. He yanked the knot loose from her waist and tossed the rope aside. "Say it," he ordered.

She tried again. "Donovan believed you would follow . . . toward the ridge . . . they'd surround you there."

Arndt's next sentence was said with such quiet, that Laura knew he became desperate. "James told you the exact locations. He would not leave you in danger, without information. Schoenfeld is stupidly soft."

"He thought I was safe," she gasped, "in the village. He didn't know about Johnson."

Arndt glared at her. "I know that Knabe," he said softly. "He told you exact locations."

Laura shook her head. She did know exact locations. They were pitifully few, but they were strategically the best. If she pointed out any other locations, Arndt would know she lied. He himself could see where the best marksmen must be. At this range, Arndt and Dieter had enough fire power to do much damage to those who had survived the strafing.

The villagers would suffer.

I have to make him think they are everywhere.

"You will tell me." Arndt's hand shot out, reaching behind him. "Haupt!" he barked. "A cigarette."

Laura's eyes seemed to tear up automatically. The memory of her sightless father's burned face swam in front of her. "They're in the woods below and strung out along the ridge," she said desperately.

Behind Arndt, she heard the flare of a lighter. "Cigarette," announced Haupt.

"We can escape back toward the Yocum Ridge . . .," Laura tried.

Arndt smiled. "You see, Dieter. The young lady knows a great deal about this mountain. He told her everything."

"No," Laura whispered.

Arndt's free arm swung back to reach for the cigarette. His coat fell open. The shoulder holster and the butt of his gun could be clearly seen. Laura steeled herself for what she would have to endure in order to get that gun. Arndt brought the cigarette around toward her, held out at arm's length. She resisted the urge to pull back.

Laughing, he gazed at the red end and then put the cigarette into his mouth. Pulling Laura toward his bulk, he watched her terror build as he drew breath. The ember flamed a deep orange. Arndt tugged the shaft out of his mouth, almost reluctantly. "Donovan will watch and do nothing for you," he said, exhaling smoke in her face. "You will die, blind, begging to tell me where they are."

"My father did not tell you," she whispered, "not until the scopolamine. You could not make him tell you anything."

"And you wish to die the same way? How foolish."

"I will die anyway. Why betray them?"

"Their silence betrays you." He raised his arm, bringing the flaming end closer to her eyes.

She flinched, waiting for him to come close enough for what she had to do next.

He grabbed her hair, held her head in a vice-grip and touched her eyelid with the cigarette. Searing pain shot across her temple.

Arndt's laughter was mere background noise to the shaft of heat that penetrated to her core. Blinding light flashed across her vision.

Her tied hands pushed aside his jacket, grabbing his gun butt. Even as she yanked it from its holster, she pulled the trigger. She had no idea if the bullets would kill him or her. It didn't matter. The agony in her head drowned out all other pain.

"Vandal!" she yelled and pulled against the cold metal. Arndt's body jerked, yanking her off-balance. Laura held the gun between two numb hands and squeezed the trigger over and over again until her finger would no longer move. Arndt screamed and dropped his grip on her hair.

"Vandal," she called again.

A snarl of anger rose from the depths of the snow.

"Ski, Laurie," James yelled. "Ski for your life."

Blindly, Laura turned. Vandal's guttural voice and Arndt's screams told their tale clearly. But where was James? And Haupt?

"Go, Laura."

He was right. Sightless, she couldn't help. If she escaped, he'd have less to worry about.

Her ski tips caught on something soft.

Arndt's body. I killed him.

She stepped backward without seeing. Her one eye seared shut – the other so wet with protective tears, she sensed only a fog of gray light. Her ski tips came free. She shifted, turned downhill, and let her weight lean forward to carry her down the fall line of the glacier. Without poles, without sight, she trusted to gravity and the benevolence of God to carry her away from danger.

Through the fog of her left eye, she saw two figures dressed in white, one a leviathan with a long dark braid swinging behind him.

The other passed closer to her — a shorter man with a steel hard determination in his jaw — the young orchard man.

Shots rang out. Laura felt the rush of air and sensed the thunk of bullets in the ice to her right. She shifted, turning left, then right again.

Behind her, she could make out the sound of fighting and of Vandal implacable, growling, twisting, wrenching at enemy flesh.

Still skiing blindly, she cringed, waiting for the inevitable shot in the back. Instead, a heart-shattering scream pierced the air and then fell away into the depths.

James. Oh God, not James.

She twisted to look back. Her skis slid from beneath her controlling weight. Her body seemed to fall forever – the skis pulled her downhill, her raised arms pulled her up until she hit the snow, flat out, skidding around and around and always down.

At last, her back slammed into a drift. Her body crumpled.

CHAPTER THIRTY-TWO

Night-dark waves greeted Laura. She rose toward the shore of conscious thought aware of anxious whispers in the hall. Her door stood ajar. Warm relief washed over her when she saw James's strong hand gripping the door, as if he were anxious to return to her side.

"His plane crashed into Mount Saint Helens?" James asked.

"And burned," whispered Doc. "They couldn't find the body – Hess, or whoever. He's beyond identifying."

James's silence seemed to reek of disbelief. After a moment, Laura heard him ask, "And our LeGuin?"

"Just a long scar. Says he'll call it his war wound. He'll flaunt in front of Langendorff and the rest of us."

James's fingers tightened on her door, "And Cam. He's talking?"

"Not yet," Doc replied, "but breathing on his own. They got the lung inflated. I've never seen the technique. Read about it. . . "

"Will he be . . .?"

"He'll enjoy your adventures from the sidelines."

James's silence seemed a prayer.

Mrs. Leszinski's whisper was urgent, "*Somebody* tried to kill Laura. We agreed your cabin was the safest place for her."

Laura tried to rise. The weight of guilt rose in her chest, obstructing air. She coughed, gasped and fell back as James flew into the room, followed by Doc.

"It's started," Doc announced. But what had started, Laura never heard for she slipped back into dark oblivion

* *

In Portland, Oregon's Emmanuel Hospital, the lanky doctor pulled the face mask over his mouth and nose before he strode into the room. He glanced out from under thick, beetling brows at the nurse and then at the guard standing next to Arndt's bed. With a dismissive wave of his hand, he got rid of the nurse. The guard stepped back, respectful.

On the bed lay a huge man, bandages swathed his chest and one arm. On his head, red-gold hairs curled up and over the edge of gauze wrap.

The doctor lifted the blanket, laying it back to expose the extremities. On the patient's left leg, the ragged edges of torn flesh had been sutured together. Each tear began as the V-shape of the mouth of a large dog.

Several bites clustered on the man's thigh, tearing toward his groin. His leg would never have its full strength.

The doctor set his bag on the bed and reached for the hem on Arndt's gown. "We need some privacy here," he said crisply, looking long at the guard. Under that steady gaze, the guard's composure wilted.

"I can wait outside the door," suggested the young man, anxious to be away from physical unpleasantness.

"Close the door as you go. He may cry out at the pain."

"Yes, sir."

As soon as the young man was out the door, the doctor removed a small steel hammer from his bag. He lay its heavy head on the patient's mangled leg. The man moaned, shuddering. The doctor watched him. He moved the hammer onto a deeper wound.

A sweat broke out on the patient's throat. His large head rolled from side to side, shoving the bandage askew off his red hair. When the doctor moved the hammer a third time, the man gasped. His great blue eyes wrenched open. Fear twisted his face.

The doctor chuckled softly. "I have watched you torture so many, Herr Arndt. Such exquisite technique. So cold. So thorough. I have learned much from you."

Arndt's huge body trembled, trying to find strength to rise. Drugs and the torpor of shock kept him at the mercy of this dreaded being. Only his throat obeyed him. At first, gurgling, inarticulate sounds rushed from Arndt's mouth. "Rudolph . . . Herr . . . nein."

"Suddenly unable to speak?" the doctor's voice was derisive. "Only hours ago, you were babbling everything you knew."

Terror cleared Arndt's mind. "Nein Herr Hess. Niemals."

"Your English was quite clear then. What has made you forget your English, my dear Arndt?" Hess reached into his black bag and withdrew a syringe.

Arndt's eyes widened, following the needle as it flashed in the light. Hess slowly pushed the plunger in, emitting a spray of blue-tinted juice. When the syringe had emptied, he retracted the plunger, filling the space with air.

"I tell them nothing," cried Arndt, desperate to jerk his exposed legs toward the far side of the bed. "They . . ."

"Don't bother with denial." Hess clapped a hand on Arndt's shoulder, throwing him into the bedcovers. "I was in the scrub room next door as you talked. They sewed. You cried and talked. See all these neat stitches?" He pressed the wound on Arndt's leg with the side of the needle.

Arndt, mesmerized, softly whimpered and watched Hess move the needle to his arm. Arndt stared in disbelief as it entered his main artery. "Nein. Nimmer."

"You taught me the principle." Hess pushed down on Arndt's sweat soaked chest with one hand. "You are no longer useful." Hess's thumb pressed the plunger. "You must go."

Arndt's eyes rolled back in pain. He clutched at his chest and hissed once. Hess withdrew the needle and flipped the blankets back over the hulking body.

"And now your young friend in the mountain, this James Schoenfeld who returns to life so mysteriously – and the beautiful daughter of Atweiler – they will die one last and very permanent death."

*   *

"You've surfaced," James whispered.

Laura turned, opening her unbandaged eye. Her plaster-covered broken arm lay on the covers of her bed in the Battle Axe.

The next thing entering her view was a walking-cast protecting James's right leg. She glanced up. The dim light from the hall shone on the side of his bearded face. He leaned over, touching her arm cast, brushing her curled fingers with the back of his hand.

"James," she whispered.

His brows knit, "James? Not 'Ian'? How did you know?"

She looked up at his unruly cowlick. "Your hair ..." her voice rasped, "this funny part . . . nowhere to go."

His eyebrows raised up into his growing mane. He shook it out of his eyes, then touched its partially black surface.

"And," she continued in an exhausted whisper, "boot-leather dye ... bad for your hair."

He chuckled, "It's actually hair dye in the boot polish bottle."

"Yech," she whispered.

James laughed and ducked his head to nuzzle her with the growing evidence of his Nordic roots.

She smiled, reaching up to touch his face, but her hand fell back to the bed. On the rug near her bed, a watchful Vandal barked softly once, then allowed his tired head to slump back onto his paws. James sat on the bed and pulled Laura's good arm close to his chest. His other arm rested on her pillow. Vandal's head moved to James's knee.

"Tell me," Laura whispered. "Others."

He answered her worries. "Dieter died of a fall. You shot Arndt three times. He's in a hospital in Portland, but he'll heal for trial as a spy."

James rocked slowly and told her the truth. "You came close to killing him. There was no other way to stop him."

"I know," she said, quaking as if she were cold. "I knew it then. I even knew it when I killed Bernard . . ."

James closed his eyes, remembering what the Chief had described to him. "The Chief and Moses Labbé followed your trail to Silcox Hut. They found Bernard's body."

Laura turned her face into James' arm on her pillow, trying to inhale the warmth of him, trying to forget the smell of death. Ian, James was alive. Alive!

Moments slipped by as he caressed her good arm and then reached to massage her neck. "The others are all right," he soothed. "Dieter shot Takeh in the shoulder, but Takeh's tough. He and Moses Labbe are on their way to Wyoming. Takeh will care for his folks at the internment camp. As for your wild aim – You hit some, missed some, and clipped my ski cap with your last shot."

Her eyes flew open. James chuckled. "It wasn't on my head at the time. In fact, it was in Arndt's pocket for various reasons, but I'm going to keep that cap forever, just to remind you to aim carefully."

She sighed and relaxed against him. James ran his hand softly over her shoulders, checking the bandages there.

"Johnson bit you?" he asked.

"Yes, but it's healing." The less he knew, the sooner those moments would leave her memory.

"Doc says you developed pneumonia – not surprising, smoke inhalation, exposure, shock."

Laura reveled in his caress. She smiled at the thought of James incapacitated by a broken leg – stuck in the Government Camp with her. That was what counted. "James," she whispered, taking his hand. "Government Camp is a good place," she said.

Puzzled, he nodded. "I like it here."

"There must be hundreds of villages like this in our country," she said.

"Well, yes."

"A Japanese orchardman, an Indian rancher, a Jewish hotel owner . . ."

Now he grasped her thought. "A Norwegian skier, a French grocer, a Mexican sheriff . . ."

She grinned, "And what's Doc?"

"A mongrel, like me."

She smiled and said, "Towns like this will save us from hatred and fear of each other."

His eyes roamed her bandaged face. "Towns like this and the courage of women like you . . ."

Laura drew a deep breath, free at last of the weight in her chest which had dragged her into sleep. She took another breath for the pure joy of it. He leaned forward, intent. She felt his hand grow hot in hers.

"Laura, I have to tell you something."

She knew what came next, but wanted to remind him of one more very good thing first. "Cameron?" she asked. "He's still improving?"

As he nodded, she saw tears glisten at the edges of his eyes. "Cam will be in the hospital for a long time, but he'll recover. Laura there's something else."

Laura touched his face. "James, I already know about my letters and the cave."

James sat stone still, visibly trying to regain his composure. "Yes, Dad died," Laura whispered. "Yes, taking the letters tipped Arndt off that you were alive. But Arndt already planned to kill Dad. He knew Dad could stop Verheerung."

James glanced at her, "Laura, you don't understand. I sped up Arndt's time-table."

Laura's voice was a mere breath. "I should have recognized Johnson as a spy. And Corporal Myers," she moaned, "Johnson had a Private call him away . . . wrong procedure, wrong chain of command. I should have kept Myers with me."

James bowed his head over their hands. "We were both guilty there."

"James," Laura whispered. "We'll have to live with our misjudgments the rest of our days. We made mistakes while trying to save other people."

James couldn't control his voice. "Laura. The General . . . I loved your . . . I loved Dad."

"I know." Laura pulled James down until his head rested on her good shoulder. "Jimmy," she whispered. "We have to skate forward. And I can't do it without you."

For the second time in a week, he cried rare, hot tears into her hair. She caressed his shoulders and head until he relaxed into her. When she pulled at him and scooted toward the wall, he practically fell into bed next to her, his cast came to rest next to her ankle. Laura pulled the comforter over them, whispering endearments and hope.

*   *

Three hundred feet down the street from the inn, at the Texaco Garage, a maroon Studebaker slid in beside the gas pump.

"You got a ration card?" the attendant asked.

"Sure do," the lanky driver said. He handed the attendant a $100-dollar bill.

"Right O." The attendant unhooked the pump.

The driver climbed out of the car, seeming to enjoy the view of snowy street and buildings as his car was being filled. He glanced over LeGuin's grocery and Langendorff's ski shop. Both had signs announcing they were "Closed until Further Notice". The man smiled. Then, his attention lingered on the Battle Axe Inn.

The attendant said, "You're all set, Mister."

The tall man barely nodded. He climbed back into his Studebaker.

The attendant returned to the warmth of his garage. He waved the big bill at his lounging visitor.

"Doc, you remember the guy at LeGuin's grocery the other day? The guy with the big eyebrows?"

CHAPTER THIRTY-THREE

"I'm down in Madras!" Doc had to shout into the phone. James could hear the east wind howling, rattling Doc's phone-booth doors. Doc hollered louder. "I think Hess headed for that airfield near Bend, but I lost him south of Madras."

"Damn you, Doc," James yelled. "Why didn't you come get me?"

Doc's voice was broken and muffled, but James made out most of the next part, "Our Laura . . .hovering . . .earth and heaven . . .wanted you with her."

James glanced toward the stairs at the mention of Laura. Doc was right. Until an hour ago Laura's breathing was labored. Now she slept soundly. Mrs. Lezinski kept the steam kettle going in their room – claimed steam was the cure. No doubt Doc would credit the sulfa drugs.

Doc put himself in danger down there in Madras and didn't have the sense to know it. James glared into the phone. "Doc, you should be watching over Laura."

"I've done all . . . reason to live. You . . . reason."

"Doc, I thought Hess died."

"Don't like when . . . don't find body . . . aeroplane crash. Makes think . . . no body to find."

James scowled. Amateurs mixed up in spy games tend to get killed. "Get out of that phone booth, Doc. It's too conspicuous. Get your tail back up here. Vite. Schnell. Fast."

"Pronto?"

"Out! I'll get Hess," James yelled.

"Great idea. Club him ... your cast."

* *

It took several calls from the inn's lobby phone to Washington, D.C.. It also took considerable persuasion, but vigilant Vivien finally spilled that her boss, Donovan of the Central Office of Intelligence, directed investigative traffic from the Portland Federal Building, only sixty miles away.

"Ian," Donovan yelled into the phone, "my secretary said James Schoenfeld called."

"Laura's found me out. I'm James again. Is the Bend aeroport under surveillance?"

"It has been since that Weasel was caught trying to plow down your Laura."

Your Laura?

James said, "Hess is capable of stealing any plane."

"All aeroplanes are locked in a guarded hangar. But Bend could be Hess's destination all right. Let me get someone on that. Just a moment."

James waited, watching Vandal pace the top of the stairs to Laura's room. The dog hardly even let Mrs. Lezinski up those stairs without a challenge.

Donovan came back online.

"We're in phone contact with security at Bend. They haven't seen him, yet. It's been six hours since Hess left the hospital."

"Hess was a patient?"

"No. He posed as a doctor and murdered Arndt."

"Murdered!" James sank to the lobby chair, trying to imagine Arndt dying. It wasn't possible.

"How?"

"Hess injected an air bubble into Arndt's blood stream. It's like having the bends. Not a pretty way to die. Arndt was dead in minutes, before the nurse checked him."

James bit his lower lip. Frustration welled up in him. "How much did you get out of Arndt before he died?"

"A lot, but not enough. We took notes as he went under the anesthetic. But we knew there was more – much more."

The sharp sting of fear straightened James's back. Hess must have heard Arndt talking.

"Arndt talked about Laura?" he asked.

"And you, James. In the operating room he kept shouting 'Schoenfeld and that woman know everything."

Fear slipped further in. He grasped at one last hope. "Are you absolutely sure the man who posed as the doctor is Hess?"

"As sure as God made eyebrows."

*   *

James called a meeting in Mrs. Lezinski's back parlor. As his friends entered, Mrs. Lezinski pulled rose and pink drapes over her windows.

The room was heavy with tapestry, dark furniture, and the clutter of sewing projects for which Mrs. Lezinski recently had no time or thought.

Ole Langendorff picked up the dressmaker's dummy and moved it next to the treadle sewing machine.

"Pardon me, Missus," Ole quipped, tipping his hat to the svelte dress form draped in dark green chiffon.

"That's Laura," Mrs. Lezinski beamed. "I make for her a dancing dress."

"Does our Laura wear dresses?" asked Garrigues, glancing at James. James felt his neck heat up.

Our Laura?

He tried for nonchalance in his shrugged answer, but couldn't keep his eyes from studying the drape of the chiffon. He changed the subject abruptly.

"We've got a problem we need to solve together," he said. "I left Vandal watching over Laura. We can't wait for Doc to get back, just cross your fingers that he's coming safely."

"And pray," said Joe Patton. He glanced around, "Prayin' sure kept me from shooting Laura when she crossed the ridge with that white-haired fellow."

"Better pray and cross," agreed Ole, crossing his fingers.

The group took up places in overstuffed chairs. As more villagers crowded in, some sat on Mrs. Lezinski's low cedar Hope Chest, others leaned against the wall. They were missing Takeh Okada and Moses Labbé who were on their way to Idaho, and LeGuin and Cameron who were recovering in the nearby Sandy Hospital. James figured they made up for the missing members by renewed determination to protect their own.

James explained his call from Doc. "I don't figure Hess to give up at killing Arndt," James said. "I think he's going to be back for revenge."

"This man Hess works from a distance," Papa Labbé said, "He shoots from the air, or lets someone else kill for him. The only time he has killed up close was at the hospital."

Mrs. Lezinski nodded, "Jah. In hospital he is not known."

"Our Laura and James know all that Arndt knew about Hess," said big Lije Coleman.

"I wish we did," said James. "Because of Arndt's ravings, Hess thinks we know everything."

"What if Hess sends others to do his dirty work for him?" asked Garrigues. "What if he waits for weeks or months and then sends someone else?"

James spoke slowly, his face shadowed by worry. "Papa Labbé is right. Hess works from afar or through others. However, he believes that Laura and I know too much. He won't trust this job to others. For the same reason, he won't wait. He wants us dead before Donovan gets up here to talk with us."

"So," said Mrs. Lezinski, "We patrol the hills until we find him."

"Not you, Magda," said Joe Patton.

Mrs. Lezinski rose out of her overstuffed chair to face Joe. "I can shoot. I have hunt partridge with Mr. Lezinski, may he rest in peace."

The others glanced at each other in uneasy silence. At that moment, Laura walked into the room, barefoot, clad in her old gray cords and red flannel shirt. "I have another idea," she said. She glanced briefly at Mrs. Lezenski's chiffon-covered sewing dummy. "We present Hess with what he wants."

* *

Laura hugged Doc for the sixth time since his midnight return from Madras. Doc wasn't complaining. She guessed he'd been scared enough to need a few hugs, especially when his car was buzzed twice by a banana yellow aeroplane as he drove over Wapinitia Pass on the way up to town. Doc was certain the pilot had to be Hess.

Now he fretted over their plan to entice Hess to Government Camp.

Laura tried to distract him from his worry with a funny story.

"Doc," Laura confided, "Before you walked in that door, we were all worried about you. Joe prayed with Garrigues – yes. Really, he did! Ole tried to pray too, but he said it had been a long time and he'd forgotten how, so he also crossed his fingers.

"By the time you barged into the Battle Axe, Ole's fingers were crossed so tightly he had trouble uncrossing them. Ole wrenched those fingers free and stared at his fists and then at you, saying, 'Would ya looka that? It works, by Gott.'"

Doc stared at her, then burst into laughter. "My Laura!"

James clumped down the stairs, smiling. "First LeGuin, and even Donovan, calls her 'Your Laura', then Garrigues 'Our Laura', now Doc claims her as 'My Laura'."

Doc glanced at James. "An affectionate 'My'. Not proprietary, my boy." Doc assessed James's outfit. He shook his head. "I see you're dressed to go through with this crazy plan."

"We've no choice." James said firmly. "The invitations to the funeral have been in the Bend, Portland, Sandy and Madras newspapers."

Doc was full of objections that he launched before James touched the bottom step. James held up a hand to stop the flow of argument. "Doc, we have to bury Hess's worries about James and Laura. We have to do it now or all of us will be watching for Hess for the rest of our lives."

Doc tried one last argument. "You can't ski on that leg yet. Permanent injury to that one will mean they'll both be too short. Then where will you be?"

"With any luck," said James, "I'll be a short man who doesn't limp."

Doc snorted in disgust, then shrugged in defeat. "Mrs. Lezenski, you might as well get that cassock ready for me. I see I'm going to have to be the priest."

* *

From the darkened back window of the Battle Axe Inn, Laura watched James limp into the Chapel of the Rivers, head bowed. He was easily recognizable in his ski cap and his red and black wool Filson jacket. Behind him, carrying a low cedar casket draped in pink and rose taffeta, marched Ole Langendorff, Joe Patton, Sheriff Garrigues and Lije Coleman. The casket they bore was adorned with evergreen boughs tied with a green chiffon ribbon.

Through the chapel windows, Laura saw the light of a hundred candles. The night's vigil had begun. Laura glanced over her shoulder into Mrs. Lezinski's parlor. Doc winked at her. She watched him straightening his cassock – a black robe of rough wool which until tonight was a blanket.

"Mrs. Lezinski has you looking more like a rabbi than a priest," Laura whispered.

"Appropriate, don't you think?" Doc said.

Mrs. Lezinski stood from her sewing machine. "All is ready." Doc turned to Laura. "I don't like this. You aren't well enough."

"In fact," said Laura, "I'm feeling better than I have for weeks. And Donovan's men found the sign of an arrow plowed into the snow on the old Summit Meadow airfield."

"Hess is coming," moaned Mrs. Lezinski. "Or he's already here," said Doc.

"Let's put on a good show for him then," Laura whispered as she hoisted her rifle. "Take care, you two. And stay clear of the target at the end of the funeral."

Mrs. Lezinski darkened the house, opened the back door, and let Laura slip out into the night.

*   *

By noon the next day, Laura knew that Hess was somewhere nearby. It was a deep-gut feeling, no proof, no sign, just too much quiet. Within her copse of mountain hemlock trees, she was well-hidden.

An hour ago, the chapel bell had tolled, calling the villagers to service. The congregation and the creaky pump organ boomed out hymns that any German might recognize as offering solace in time of death. The service opened with 'Rise My Soul and Stretch Thy Wings'. It ended with a Hebrew melody, 'The God of Abraham Praise'. Laura bet herself that Doc picked that one just to tweek Hess's Aryan nose.

Now the congregation sang 'A Mighty Fortress is Our God' as they processed to the gravesite. Doc wanted Hess to have no doubt as to the purpose of the service.

She had a perfect view of the cemetery and of the procession that slowly wound its way from the Chapel of the Hills clapboard church up Cemetery Road toward the new, shallow grave. She knew it had been difficult for Papa Labbé and Langendorff to hack that grave from the frozen, rock-filled ground above the chapel.

Laura glanced around her for the thousandth time. Any spot along this hill would give Hess a view of both cemetery and chapel. Across the highway to the south another similar ridge of hills shadowed the town.

During the night, she and her colleagues had set out from a tree shadowed side door of the Inn. They had moved one by one through the darkness to pre-planned positions north and south of the town and overlooking the cemetery. Before dawn, they were each in place, waiting for the same moment – the moment that would give away Hess's position.

The funeral procession was filled out by several families from cabins on the Still Creek Road. James had insisted they be evacuated from that area because Still Creek was between the old WPA airfield at Summit Meadow and the town. James had been afraid these families might become hostages in an escape attempt. Laura was grateful there were no tourists in the village. They would have been suspected as accomplices of Hess, or at the least could not be trusted to keep secret the identity of one of the mourners.

Luckily, today, everyone in the settlement could be counted on to understand the gravity of the situation and the necessity to play their parts well. They trudged through the snow toward the newly dug grave. Six village men carried the coffin which was draped with rose and pink tapestry cloth from Mrs. Lezinski's parlor window.

If that color doesn't tell Hess who the village mourns, Mrs. Lezinski's attitude will certainly do it, thought Laura.

Mrs. Lezinski wept openly, throwing her arms toward God, then covering her face with her hands. Behind her dramatic grief, one almost missed the three silent men. Sheriff Garrigues, on the left and LeGuin's fifteen-year-old grandson, on the right. The two supported a man in a black and red wool jacket. Young LeGuin also carried crutches that the third man was too far gone to use. The man between Garriques and LeGuin was bowed, probably drunk or drunk with grief. Above his darkly bearded face, he wore a red ski cap with one bullet hole in it.

Only an infrequent glimpse could be caught of his lower extremities, but a few times Laura noticed the white of a plaster cast on the man's right leg as he awkwardly thrust it forward.

Laura's left arm ached just from watching the man's progress up the road. Her cramped position within the hemlock trees didn't give her much chance to stretch her legs or her arms. She glanced over the hillside, searching for the flash of a rifle barrel or a telescopic sight – anything to suggest Hess's location.

The rifle barrel on Laura's weapon had long ago been painted with a dull brown. Last night, James brought her the Springfield International Match rifle from his cabin above the Battle Axe Inn. She'd recognized her father's initials where he'd carved them into the stock.

She sighted along the barrel toward each potential hiding place on the ridge. The site showed her no shadow, no motion, no clue. Still, the snowbirds who had become used to Laura's presence during the night, who had chirped and fluttered throughout the sunrise were now too quiet. They'd been holed up in their nests since ten o'clock this morning.

Hess was here, somewhere.

The funeral procession stopped at the gravesite. Villagers arranged themselves around the wet mud of the grave. Mrs. Lezinski turned to hug the grief-stricken man. She cried, "James, she is gone. Gone." She leaned heavily on James, weighing him down with her grief. His arms wrapped around Mrs. Leszinski, then dropped at his side as she moved away. He stood bowed and broken at the foot of the grave. Young LeGuin helped James arrange his crutches so that he supported himself.

The pallbearers set the casket on the ground. They removed the rose and pink tapestry, folding it reverently. The priest spoke softly for a few moments. It occurred to her that he might be eulogizing her. She was suddenly curious about what he might have to say concerning the short life of Laura Atweiler.

When Doc finished speaking, the pallbearers grasped the ropes, lowering the casket into the hole. When it rested at the bottom, the priest raised his arms and intoned a loud crisp prayer for the soul of 'our daughter Laura'. He asked loudly for support of 'our brother James in his sorrow and pain' Mrs. Lezinski fell to weeping and had to be held back from throwing herself into the grave.

Once Mrs. Lezinski was safely calmed, the first of the villagers tossed a handful of mud into the grave. Sheriff Garrigues picked up a clod of dirt and helped the stricken James toss it onto the coffin. Then Garrigues and LeGuin's grandson helped the priest fill the shallow hole.

Garrigues then ushered the villagers toward the road and toward life.

When Garrigues leaned over James, urging him to come away, James merely stooped lower over the newly turned dirt, saying nothing, making no gestures, gazing woodenly at the grave.

Garrigues and LeGuin both spoke to him, urging him to return to the village. At last, the priest encouraged both men to leave James alone in his grief. The others left James and reluctantly followed the rest of the people. All of them entered the Battle Axe Inn to prepare for the wake.

When the last man came into in the inn, the heavy door shut. Laura mentally tensed, counting seconds. At fifteen, one shot rang out. Laura saw the flash from off to her left. James toppled backwards, splashing in the muddy road, his white cast sticking stiffly out, his other leg folded under him. His arms came to rest on the ground above his head. The black and red jacket fell open, revealing blood red over his throat and chest.

Laura jerked. Fear welled up in her throat, stopped her breath and shot bitter bile into her mouth. The birds chattered and fluttered, but never left their protective shrubs. Laura regained control and trained her father's rifle on the spot from which she'd seen the flash. The birds hushed, commenting in mutters, but not venturing into the air.

She would get one chance. Hess would wait to make sure James didn't move, and that no one watched the scene. Then most likely, he would retreat off to the east, away from her, heading for the highway and down to the airfield. That was the only time Laura might see him.

Two minutes went by. Laura's broken wrist became stiff in its cast. Her whole body tensed for the moment of Hess's move. She kept her rifle ready, her eyes scanning the circumference of the group of pines where Hess hid. At last she saw the dark shade of motion. The branch on the downhill side bent slightly. A tall man emerged, skiing toward her across the fall line. He was coming. Not going.

Laura breathed out through her nose, squeezed the trigger and reworked the speed firing mechanism. Hess faltered, then tucked his poles and bent toward his skis, picking up speed. Laura stood and sited down her barrel once more, but saw Papa Labbé just beyond the man, raising his own rifle. Laura pulled up, afraid of hitting Labbé.

Papa pulled up as well. Hess skied at Laura, his breath steaming gasps, blood spreading over his jacket from her first shot. From under his thick, stiff brows Hess glared at her. She raised her rifle and through the site, saw Labbé dive for the trees.

"Heraus, knabe," Hess shouted. "Out of my way, boy."

In his eyes, she recognized icy hate, worse than Arndt's. Hess's eyes bulged with zealous righteousness. Hess raised his ski pole. She pulled the trigger as he thrust the pole toward her side. Her shot smacked into his arm. He doubled over with pain, but then, he pushed his pole into her chest, pushing her back, in spite of the bullet-proof vest that Donovan had given her.

Hess turned on his skis, letting ice and shaped wood do their work. At great speed, he diverged from Laura's position, heading toward the timber at the edge of town. She rose to her knee, fired once more, and saw Hess jerk from the impact just before he disappeared into the trees.

Labbé hollered. "You hit him." He skied after the trail of blood, following Hess toward the highway.

Labbé shot at him once more, but the man was fast, crossed the highway and darted down into the woods near Still Creek.

Laura skied out of the hemlocks toward the cemetery and the town as the village men poured out of the Battle Axe, rifles at the ready. Her shots had signaled the closing of the net around Hess. Each man knew his position and his role in the snaring of this murderer. Hess would not stand a chance. He would be hounded into the arms of Donovan's men.

Before she gave in to the pain in her broken arm, Laura stopped at the grave, pulling back the coat of the fallen man, amazed at herself for having to check, to make sure that the man who died at the grave of Laura Atweiler really was nothing more than Mrs. Lezinski's dressmaker's dummy.

James awaited Hess and his aeroplane at the old runway near Summit Meadow.

* *

From his position behind the boulder marking a pioneer gravesite, James shot the right front tire of the Studebaker. The car whomped into the ditch at the side of the Still Creek Road and rolled heavily onto its side. Smoke arose from the engine house. There was no motion from within the cab.

Fine, thought James, Blow up.

He scrunched down into his brown leather jacket, scratched at the top of his leg cast and leaned against the boulder's covering of pungent moss. He waited for the smoke to scare Hess from his tipsy fortress. A minute passed. The door on the driver's side squalled open. Two raised arms showed.

"Throw out your guns. Both of you climb out," James yelled.

A luger flew out. "I alone am," shouted a German voice. "Out."

One man, not tall, not Hess, crawled from the car.

"Get Hess," James ordered the man. Joe Patton had seen Hess jump into the Studebaker just before it turned down this back road to the old airfield. Joe's pell mell run down the hill to warn James was about to pay off.

"Kein Hess hier," the man straightened. His hands were held carefully away from his body. "Hess left the car." He jerked his thumb over his shoulder in the direction from which they'd come. "A kilometer. Up the hill."

"Aw shit," said Langendorff from the next tree.

"Cover me," James said, as he skied into the road. Inside the smoking Studebaker he found no bodies, no Hess and no skis. Hess had his skis on. He could have gotten a long way in either direction while the car crept along over a kilometer of steep, icy road.

Or Hess could be right behind them. "Joe, Ole. Hess is loose."

Both men hunkered down in the woods, checking behind them. James motioned the man at the car to put his hands behind his back. Taking what was left of his climbing rope from his jacket pocket, James tied the man to the axle of the Studebaker.

"Gott im . . . "the man complained.

"It would have blown by now if it planned to," said James. "Think Hess will rescue you?" he taunted.

At that moment, James heard the engine of a small aeroplane. Its drone, echoing off the underbelly of the car, came from somewhere south of the meadow. Heedless of his cast, and of Hess's possible hiding place, James raced his skis toward the southern end of the meadow, toward the camp where the WPA workers had lived while they built Timberline Lodge. At the end of that cleared area, James and Ole had spent the night felling trees. Their logs obstructed the runway of the landing strip. James counted on Hess being somewhere in the field or at its edge, waiting for the plane.

Come out, James mentally urged Hess. Show your desperate self, you Devil.

As he skied through the cover of trees, James saw the bright yellow plane nose up over the foothills south of the airfield. It dipped as if aiming at the runway. Its engine faltered as its pilot must have seen the logs. Then the engine buzzed hard to regain altitude. The yellow craft lifted and flew north over the town and on toward the summit of the mountain.

Hess was nowhere in sight. Now that the plane was gone, the vast meadow lay silent. James heard only the slow gurgle of a creek under the snow. James took greater heed for his safety. He faded farther into the woods at the edge of the old WPA camp. He listened and watched. He couldn't see Patton and Langendorff, but he trusted them to be watching out for Hess in the woods near the road.

Far to the north, the yellow plane banked over Timberline Lodge, and then it turned east.

Off to James's left, a white-coated rabbit skittered across a small empty space. Startled, James watched the animal thump toward a melt-hole where the creek was near the surface. The rabbit thrust his nervous nose into the water. A shadow darkened his patch of sunlight. The rabbit thupped a rapid tattoo on the ground and wheeled to dive into his thicket. James glanced up. A hawk soared lazily across the meadow and on west toward Tom, Dick and Harry Ridge.

To his right, James heard the drone of the yellow plane, again from the south.

Does he think the logs have moved from the runway?

James kept his eye on the meadow and the edge of its surrounding woods. He hoped Hess would show himself as the aeroplane was forced once more to scratch its landing. James caught yellow out of the corner of his vision. He realized immediately that something was different.

Glancing toward the plane, he saw a black net unfurl from the open cockpit. The net opened, trailing behind the wing, well out of the way of the propellers. It brushed the tops of the two pine trees at the end of the meadow.

In the center of the meadow, three hundred yards away, a figure rose, covered with snow. For a moment, James didn't believe what he saw.

The plane swooped low into the meadow. James aimed at the snow- covered man, pulled the trigger and watched his bullet make a trail in the dead meadow grasses, ten yards short. The man in the meadow stretched out his arms and let the net envelope him. James ran toward the plane.

The plane buzzed up over the nearest Engleman Spruce. The man clung to the net. James raised his rifle, shooting at the fuselage. He saw a stream of fuel bleed back over the net and the man. Far out of range, the plane rose, barely clearing the trees and the ridge at the north end of the meadow. The last James saw of it, the man climbed the net toward the cockpit. The engine stuttered, caught and hummed solidly.

Stunned, James listened to that drone until it was beyond hearing. He believed he would hear that sound for the rest of his life. And every time he heard it, it would mock him. He had lost Rudolph Hess.

CHAPTER THIRTY-FOUR

Laura leaned her back to the ladder in James's cabin. Once she'd entered the front room, she found she couldn't move. James hadn't noticed. His back to her, he pushed another log into the wood stove.

"There," he said, "that'll get the kettle boiling soon. Mrs. Lezinski wouldn't want you to be without steam for your lungs." He strode stiff- legged in his cast, carrying the rest of the wood to the fireplace.

The room was cool, yet sweat ran down Laura's back as she remembered facing Bernard Johnson from this very spot.

James glanced up. He must have seen that something was wrong. "Laura," he said quietly. "Laura, it's over."

"It was Bernard. Bernard killed Corporal Myers."

James dropped the wood into the hearth basket. He limped toward her. The air around him stirred with the odor of freshly cut pine. Pine and hemlock.

Laura knew she smelled of death. James gripped her shoulders, made her look up at him. "Laura, is this where you were when he came in?"

"He killed Corporal Myers because I fed Myers a steak," her voice broke. "Steak and potatoes. That boy would be alive if I hadn't. . ."

"Laura, Bernard Johnson would have killed him no matter what you fed him. He wanted you to think it was your fault. Johnson was crazy, vicious. And that night, he followed Arndt's orders."

Laura gazed at the wood stove. "I shot Arndt."

"Thank God you did."

"And then Hess."

"A square hit on the man who thought he'd just killed me."

"I shot him three times. How could he still climb that net?" she asked.

James raised an eyebrow. "Rudolph Hess is a cat. But he used three lives while we had him in our sites. Donovan's people are convinced Hess had to put that leaking plane down somewhere near the Canadian border."

She gazed at James, "Did it work? Does Hess believe we're both dead."

"You betcha he does. That funeral was brilliant, Laura. Brilliant."

"Why didn't he kill me when I shot him? Twice, then he ran right past me and I shot him again."

"I found his rifle in the snow, along with a trail of blood. You made him lose it before he got to you. And now we have his finger- prints."

She tipped her head back, as if she could make the tears return to her eyes. James's arms surrounded her. He pulled her head against his chest and whispered into her hair, "It's over. Bernard won't hurt you anymore. Arndt is dead. Hess is gone."

They stood in each other's arms, giving and taking warmth from the quiet and from the solid beating of their hearts. Laura tried to pull the tension from James's neck, then remembered how heavy and rough her plaster cast would feel, and let her broken wrist merely rest on his shoulder.

On the wood stove, the teakettle began to burble. Outside, they heard the *thwick, chink* of shovels as Doc and Sheriff Garrigues rescued Mrs. Lezinski's cedar Hope Chest from the "grave" behind The Chapel of the Rivers.

James chuckled at the sound, "I guess I have to believe in the resurrection, don't I?"

"You came back to life," whispered Laura. She was afraid to let go, to relax, afraid to trust the joy she knew was within her arms. So much had happened. So much was still to accomplish before they could all be safe.

"After the war," James murmured into her ear, "will you marry me, Laura?"

She stopped breathing.

He plunged on. "I haven't much. And . . . I'll have to go back to Europe when my leg is better. But you can live here in your mother's cabin until I come home."

"My mother's cabin?"

"Yes," he pulled back to watch her reaction. "Didn't you know?" Laura shook her head.

"This cabin belonged to your mother's parents," he said. "After they died, your mother was living here when your father met her. She worked for Mrs. Lezinski's mother."

Laura stepped back from James. "Dad told you this?" She could hardly believe James knew details she'd never heard.

James touched her face with the backs of his fingers. "Sweetheart, your dad had to talk those first weeks, just to make me want to live."

"He hardly ever talked about mother after she died."

"He didn't like reminding you, or himself either. But when he brought me here, he opened up about all kinds of things. After Werner Arndt threw me . . . after I nearly died, I was just a breathing body, lying still for hours on end. So, your dad talked to me. After days and days, he began to talk about things he never told anyone else."

"Why didn't I know about this cabin?" Laura, in her sudden hurt, had to have a reason for her father's secrecy.

"This was a safe house as long as no one knew about it," James said. "No one."

She glanced around with new eyes. The furniture was arranged with very wide paths from the kitchen through the living area to the bedroom on the main floor – wheelchair paths, she realized. "You were in great pain here," she whispered.

He swallowed and glanced away, his jaw tight. "Some pain. For a while," he said. "But worse than pain was remembering Werner's face as he stabbed me. I'd worshipped him since boyhood, lived with him until I was an adult, and worked with him for thirteen years. And he cared nothing about me. Nothing."

Laura's heart broke for him. She touched his faced, massaging the tight scar near his eye. "You had love," she said, "and a family, once, but you were afraid to trust it."

"That was a wonderful year," he said, holding her gaze with his. "I cherish every moment of it."

"Even when I got angry and butted you with my head?" she asked, remembering the snowplow driver.

"Especially then," James laughed. "You were such a determined little girl, and a resourceful fighter." He pulled her closer into his body. "Laura, I remember that year, but I am different. You are different. I am not that boy."

"I love you as you are now," she whispered. "And I loved you long before I realized you were James."

"Truly?" he leaned back, looking down at her with a teasing gleam in his eyes. "And might I hope for an answer to my previous question?"

She chuckled. "I've always wanted to know a bank robber . . ."

"Cam told you that!" he ducked his head, but she saw the color rise in his face. He was still embarrassed by that long-ago incident.

"James . . ." she said, but felt him stiffen as if to ward off a hurtful blow.

"You don't need to answer me now, Laura," he said. "I . . . I can give you time to consider."

"James . . ."

Behind him, the teakettle rattled with its boiling energy. He started toward it, but she pulled him back to her. He glanced at her, unsure, she saw, of how to back off gracefully, to give her a way out.

"James Schoenfeld," she said firmly, "will you marry me?"

His pent-up anxiety whooshed out of him in a shout. He grinned and pulled her back into his arms. "You better believe it, Sweetheart." His hand rose to cup her head. His eyes focused on her lips. But she interrupted his intended kiss.

"Marry me now?" she asked.

"Now?" he backed up to glance at her, "You know I'll have to leave for Switzerland as soon as my leg heals."

Swallowing hard, Laura wanted to speak, but kissed him instead. She started by kissing him softly, but he cradled her head in one hand and let his other hand caress her throat. Heat raced all the way to her foot.

James deepened her feathery kiss until she wrapped her good arm around his back again and relaxed into him.

He moaned. "Oh, Laura."

He backed her into the ladder. She arched her back and kissed him with her whole body – touching him with every inch of herself.

His hand slid down from her throat to cover her breast. "This damned flannel shirt has been driving me," he said.

"It was yours once," she whispered pulling him onto the sofa with her. "You want it back?"

"Anything to get it off you." As he leaned over her, his hand slipped down to the button between her breasts. "You've been wearing these for fifteen years?"

She shook her head. "Boxed them up. Hoped you'd come back and wear them again, yourself. Then you died."

James rose slightly, "I'm sorry you had to deal with my death. We thought it better for you and safer for me, if you really believed it."

"I know, James. I understand now. But God, it was hard to lose that dream of having a big brother."

"Is that. . .?"

"No. You were Ian when I first trusted you – in that stupid tumbleweed field where my driving nearly killed us both. You were Ian when I realized I loved you as you helped those poor soldiers and the Japanese families in the railroad station. I'm asking Ian McKay who happens to be James Schoenfeld to marry me now."

"Now?"

"Now," she answered, "in spite of the fact that I also have war work to do."

"What?" James straightened.

"Donovan –Wild Bill I guess they're calling him now."

"He offered you a job?" James's eyes flared with disbelief.

"Don't be so surprised," Laura bridled. "Bill thinks I have an eye for details. And, he says I have 'chutzpah'."

"Mrs. Lezinski taught him that word. Where the hell – the heck – what in hell's name does he want you to do?"

"He wants me in Lucerne, to act as a clearing house for information."

James stood suddenly, pacing the room. "Lucerne? Do you know what kind of a hot bed of intrigue Switzerland is right now? A neutral country they call it. That means everybody comes there to find out what everybody else is up to. There's not a safe street corner in the place, if you're a spy."

"That's what he said, too. He wants us to find Dad's missing agents. He hopes they went underground and need help getting out. We could make a big difference, see to it that information got to the right hands, and stayed out of the wrong ones."

"Us?"

"You and me."

James shook his head, strode past the wood stove, knocked into the teakettle, grabbed at it and ended up blowing on his palm while steaming water spread over the floor.

"On the window," Laura said, rising from the sofa to help him.

"What?"

"Put your hand on the window. The cold will stop the burning." He stopped pacing, stared at her. She gestured at the frosted pane.

"Schiest," he sputtered and slapped his hand on the window. Relief from the pain hit him in the stomach. He closed his eyes and took a deep breath.

When he spoke again, his voice radiated iron control. "You can't go to Switzerland. How can I do my work and always be looking out for your safety at the same time?"

Laura gazed pointedly at his hand on the window, "And here I was, wondering how I could work while worrying about you. You take a lot of chances – break a lot of parts. Donovan says they have a good hospital in Lucerne."

In two strides, James backed her into the sofa again until she lay down. Tapping on her arm cast, he said, "I break parts? I break ...?"

"You're sputtering ..." she gazed up at him and then slowly leaned back on the pillows.

He stopped, standing with most of his weight on the uncast but shorter leg, arms akimbo, thumbs at right angles to his fingers. Moments of tense silence were broken at last by a rush of released breath. He sat down heavily, taking her good hand in his undamaged one, he gazed at her and then bent his head over their entwined fingers.

From her prone position, she could see only the whorls of blond and blackened hair that fell softly about his head. She smiled.

His muffled voiced sounded resigned. "This reminds me of a long and exasperating automobile ride I recently took." He glanced at her.

"If the rest of our days are going to be like this, with you taunting me and worrying the hell out of me, we might as well get married now."

"Why?"

"At least we'll enjoy the nights," he said thickly.

Her eye brightened with mischief as she reached for him.

Assured of her acceptance, James fell softly into her embrace. He thought she whispered something like, "Even in war time, secret agents aren't always working."

"That's right," he answered in her ear.

"Yes," she continued, "Have patience. I may be home occasionally."

James moved his mouth over hers and unbuttoned the first of several buttons. The maneuver proved effective. It silenced her for a delightful, long time.

ACKNOWLEDGEMENTS

Especial thanks go to my mother, Wilhalmena Williams, who taught me to look behind the headlines and understand those who grab for power. She taught me to understand the human suffering it causes.

My thanks to many friends and family who, as I grew up, shared their memories of this time in our history. And also, thanks to the archivists of the many newspapers across the country who saved the history of attempted sabotage, and of the race riots in many cities during the early war years.

Frozen Trust is based on events of 1942 when Nazi spies were arrested for industrial and military sabotage, and for fomenting race riots in cities across the United States. Sabotage was important to Nazi plans.

However, the greatest enemy within our borders turned out to be our well-fed fears, and hatred of our own diversity.

Thank you to Dr. Peter Reagan who talked to me about climbs on Mount Hood, especially his harrowing experiences on Yocum Ridge. And Thank you to Scott Light who kept me informed about the skills of mountain and rock climbing from my very first novel to this one.

Thank you to my early readers, especially to Margaret Arwain Price whose comments kept me rewriting to improve and let me know that the stories in *Frozen Trust* were important to tell.

Thank you to Woody Richen who traveled with me to the final Colorado training camp for the Tenth Division Ski-Mountaineers. As always, Woody encourages, edits and cheers – a very inspiring set of skills.

There is a wonderful exhibit of the history of this important division at the Mountaineering Museum in Golden Colorado and a newer museum of their work in Fort Drum, New York.

ABOUT THE AUTHOR

Rae Richen's stories and novels, articles and interviews bring focus to the themes that drive our human race. Rae's fictional characters face a confusing world of hypocrisy and courageous honesty. Their humor and friendships help them forge new solutions to age-old problems.

Rae has worked in many capacities that show up in her writing: historical researcher, musician and landscape designer. She teaches writing to adults, young adults, and the reluctant reader.

Discover her humorous stories and thoughtful essays at www.raerichen.com/blog.

You can reach Rae at www.raerichen.com, or at www.lloydcourtpress.com .

Other Books by Rae Richen

You can find these stories at many print and online outlets. Discover them at www.raerichen.com/books There, you can read first chapters of each novel and get access to occasional free offers.

HISTORICAL NOVELS OF ACTION AND ADVENTURE

Uncharted Territory

Scapegoat: The Price of Freedom

Scapegoat: The Hounded

NOVELS OF SUSPENSE, ESPIONAGE AND ROMANCE

In Concert

Frozen Trust

Sentinels of Solitude

A Fool's Gold

MYSTERIES AND THRILLERS

Those Who Curse You

Without Trace